# *NONCOMBATANTS UNDER FIRE*

Julia couldn't venture out because of the Confederate sharpshooters. She was watching when several Union cavalrymen came riding up—shots rang out, and the horses leapt into swift motion. Then she had an idea. She stood in the front door, out of sight of the sharpshooters—but visible to the advancing Union troops. She became a living danger signal. No one got shot while she was there.

But the Confederate snipers at the intersection less than four blocks away knew someone was warning the passing Yankees. They couldn't hear a voice, but at times they could see a thin white arm waving from the doorway. "Must be a girl or a woman," groused one of the rebel soldiers.

"Don't make no difference," roared his sergeant. "Throw some lead into that doorway!"

# DAYS OF DARKNESS

# THE GETTYSBURG CIVILIANS

## An Historical Novel

## By
## William G. Williams

**B**

BERKLEY BOOKS, NEW YORK

This Berkley book contains the complete text of the original hardcover edition. It has been completely reset in a typeface designed for easy reading and was printed from new film.

DAYS OF DARKNESS:
THE GETTYSBURG CIVILIANS

A Berkley Book / published by arrangement with
White Mane Publishing Company, Inc.

PRINTING HISTORY
White Mane edition published 1986
Berkley edition / November 1990

The Putnam Berkley World Wide Web site address is
http://www.berkley.com

ISBN: 0-425-12353-7

BERKLEY®
Berkley Books are published by
The Berkley Publishing Group, a member of Penguin Putnam Inc.,
200 Madison Avenue, New York, New York 10016.
BERKLEY and the "B" design are trademarks
belonging to Berkley Publishing Corporation.

PRINTED IN THE UNITED STATES OF AMERICA

15   14   13   12   11   10   9   8   7

# CONTENTS

# LIST OF ILLUSTRATIONS

# INTRODUCTION
## *by William C. Davis*

I have never forgotten a question I asked a distinguished Civil War historian friend of mine several years ago. "What first got you interested in 'the war'?" I inquired.

His answer was a model of brevity.

"*GWTW*," he said.

He let me stew in my puzzlement for a few moments before he expanded the acronym and said, *Gone With the Wind*. That made it all quite plain.

And in my experience, he is not alone. Thousands were first lured to an interest in our Civil War through that single, moving novel, just as thousands more have been attracted to this ever-compelling field by other fictional works by such as Stephen Crane, Winston Churchill, and the host of more popular authors.

It is largely in this spirit that *Days of Darkness: The Gettysburg Civilians* offers such promise, for through the eyes of the people of this small Pennsylvania town, as depicted in fact and fiction by author William G. Williams, the same drama and pathos that has captured so many in the past may take new prisoners in the interest of Civil War history.

This kind of "docudrama" approach sacrifices nothing of authenticity in its effort to breathe life into the simple folk who populated Gettysburg in 1863. Especially moving is the depiction of their plight as, in the aftermath of the battle, the "population" of Gettysburg increased ten-fold thanks to thousands of wounded men in blue and gray. Never in American history have the people of a single town been so inundated with the flotsam of battle. Through the reconstructed experiences of the real-life people of Gettysburg, all readers can be brought closer to the all-too-real trauma and tragedy of all civilians in all wars.

\*\*\*\*\*\*

(Mr. Davis is a distinguished historian and author of eighteen books, including: *Breckinridge: Statesman, Soldier, Symbol, The Battle of New Market, Duel Between the First Ironclads,* and *The Battle of Bull Run.* He is a former president of the National Historical Society and was editor-in-chief and editor of that organization's monumental six-volume series, *Shadows of the Storm.* He is also the editorial director of Historical Times, Inc., which publishes *Civil War Times Illustrated* and seven other national magazines.)

*Dedicated to*

*my father, William David Williams (1904–1963),*
*who taught me the importance of history,*

*and*

*my mother, Norah Lavinia Evans Williams (1902–1986),*
*who showed me the importance of people*

# A REASON

The works written about the great Battle of Gettysburg are legion. Millions of words have poured out in books, poems, songs, speeches and the tales of those who fought there, those who lived there and those, who over the past century plus, have guided countless millions of visitors over its hallowed ground.

But all that I have read about this turning point in America's history has dwelled, primarily, on the soldier. What of the civilian—the man whose farm became a campground for the dead; the woman who, without training, became doctor and nurse under the most trying conditions; and the child whose growing experience was surrounded by the gore of human sacrifice.

Their stories are there too, buried by time on the upper shelves of little used libraries in the veiled collections of odds and ends about our past. Bits and pieces of those stories appeared as parts of newspaper articles late in the 19th and early in the 20th centuries. Some were written in diary form and left for friends, relatives and a few interested outsiders.

But, in the whole, they've been ignored.

Long after the armies of Robert E. Lee and George Gordon Meade left Gettysburg, the townsfolk continued to nurse and feed and bury the tattered remnants of those great armies.

I have tried to tell their stories as they told them, at times guessing at what they said by what they did and, conversely, guessing at what they did by what they said. I hope I'm forgiven for filling in the blank spots in their stories by those means. My excuse for that is simply that this book was not meant to be a documentation of that event for historians but rather a living picture of common people caught up suddenly in a shattering experience.

I have not invented any characters. The people are real; they lived. I have not created situations beyond those aptly described in their writings or hinted to so broadly as to make them plausible.

And I have not changed matters of historical record, although I find there is disagreement even among historians, particularly on exact figures.

Finally, this tribute to those whose stories lie within would not have been possible without the guidance of several people, including: Dr. Richard J. Sommers, author of the widely acclaimed *Richmond Redeemed, The Siege at Petersburg* and archivist-historian of the United States Army Military History Institute, Carlisle Barracks, Carlisle, Pennsylvania; Colonel Jacob Sheads, a retired teacher and soldier of Gettysburg who lives his historical background daily; Thomas J. Harrison, chief park historian, and members of his staff from the National Park Service at Gettysburg; Dr. Charles H. Gladfelter, director of the Adams County Historical Society and the volunteers who man that repository of wonderful words, pictures and memories; James Cole of the Gettysburg Travel Council, whose roots in that community go back to the Civil War and beyond.

And to those who directed me to, found or provided photographs, including: Mike Winey at the U.S. Army Military History Institute; Ross Ramer, a Gettysburg photographer who owned a house which figured prominently in the battle; Sister John Mary, archivist for the Daughters of Charity, Saint Joseph's Provincial House, in Emmitsburg, Maryland; and Bill Frassinito, whose book, *Gettysburg: A Journey in Time*, is a classic.

To the people of Gettysburg who offered information and friendship . . . Mr. and Mrs. Ray Culp, who invited this stranger into their home for a look at family relics and anecdotes . . . the gentleman who came off his front porch when he saw me examining a historic church, told me what he knew of the church's history and then gave me his perfectly delightful calling card, which said, simply, "George T. Raffensperger—Retired".

Finally to dozens of friends who offered encouragement through three years of work.

And, most importantly, to my wife, Mary Jane, who gave of her time so that this might be written.

—*William G. Williams*

# DAYS OF DARKNESS

## THE GETTYSBURG CIVILIANS

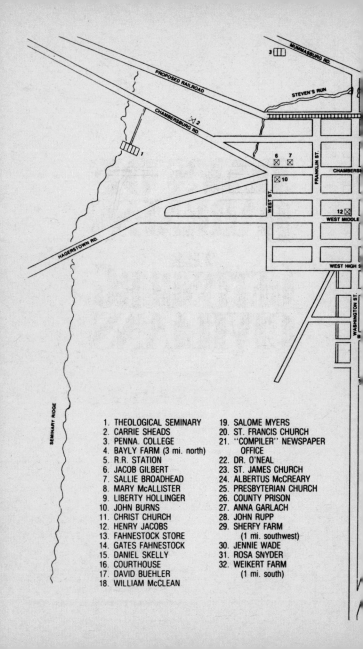

1. THEOLOGICAL SEMINARY
2. CARRIE SHEADS
3. PENNA. COLLEGE
4. BAYLY FARM (3 mi. north)
5. R.R. STATION
6. JACOB GILBERT
7. SALLIE BROADHEAD
8. MARY McALLISTER
9. LIBERTY HOLLINGER
10. JOHN BURNS
11. CHRIST CHURCH
12. HENRY JACOBS
13. FAHNESTOCK STORE
14. GATES FAHNESTOCK
15. DANIEL SKELLY
16. COURTHOUSE
17. DAVID BUEHLER
18. WILLIAM McCLEAN

19. SALOME MYERS
20. ST. FRANCIS CHURCH
21. "COMPILER" NEWSPAPER
    OFFICE
22. DR. O'NEAL
23. ST. JAMES CHURCH
24. ALBERTUS McCREARY
25. PRESBYTERIAN CHURCH
26. COUNTY PRISON
27. ANNA GARLACH
28. JOHN RUPP
29. SHERFY FARM
    (1 mi. southwest)
30. JENNIE WADE
31. ROSA SNYDER
32. WEIKERT FARM
    (1 mi. south)

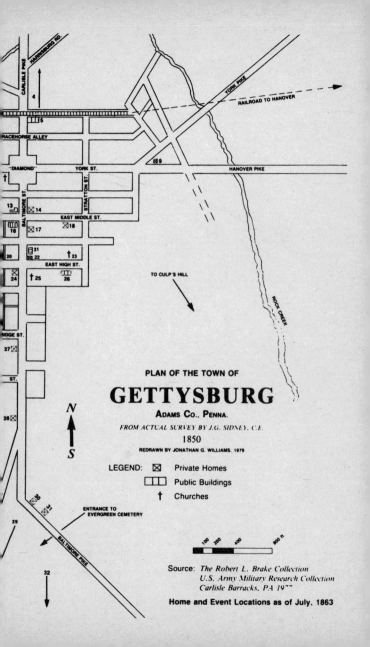

HARRISBURG RD.

CARLISLE PIKE

4

YORK PIKE

RAILROAD TO HANOVER

5

RACEHORSE ALLEY

"DIAMOND"   YORK ST.   9

STRATTON ST.

HANOVER PIKE

BALTIMORE ST.

13   14

EAST MIDDLE ST.

16   17   18

20   21   22   23

EAST HIGH ST.

24   25   26

TO CULP'S HILL

ROCK CREEK

RIDGE ST.

27

ST.

28

**N**

**S**

## PLAN OF THE TOWN OF

# GETTYSBURG

### ADAMS CO., PENNA.

*FROM ACTUAL SURVEY BY J.G. SIDNEY, C.E.*

1850

REDRAWN BY JONATHAN G. WILLIAMS, 1979

LEGEND:   ⊠   Private Homes

▭   Public Buildings

†   Churches

30   31

ENTRANCE TO
EVERGREEN CEMETERY

29

BALTIMORE PIKE

32

100   200   400   600 ft

Source: *The Robert L. Brake Collection*
*U.S. Army Military Research Collection*
*Carlisle Barracks, PA 19⎯*

**Home and Event Locations as of July, 1863**

# FOREWORD

It was raining softly on Saturday, the Fourth of July, 1863. The tough fighting of the Battle of Gettysburg had ended. At least 6,000 Union and Confederate soldiers were lying dead on that field of battle which covered the village itself and the ground around it, particularly a bloody valley from the southern tip of town through what had been abundant farms.

Robert E. Lee was making plans to retreat to Virginia. A wagon train seventeen miles long would carry more than 5,000 of his wounded men, some of whom would not survive that arduous trip.

But left on the field, from both sides, were 22,000 wounded—some, already in makeshift hospitals, disfigured and dismembered for life; some still lying where they had fallen victim to an enemy's bullet or shell. For every man, woman and child living in Gettysburg, there were almost ten wounded soldiers.

The rain grew heavier that Fourth of July, so heavy that some wounded men, lying in gullies and too badly hurt to move themselves, drowned.

It wasn't until Sunday, July 5, that Union Commander George Gordon Meade knew for sure that Lee was retreating. When Meade's troops pulled out too, few soldiers and doctors were left by either army to care for the wounded and bury the dead.

Burials began immediately but the task was enormous. On July 14, a week and a half after the battle had ended, a journalist visiting the field wrote:

"The grass which once grew there was almost ground to a jelly. Hundreds of dead horses, still unburied, lay on the field. Many of the men were still unburied.

"There is something impressive about a dead man on a battlefield. To see him lying there with his hands clenched, his limbs drawn up with ramrod or musket firmly held, lying just as he was standing when the fatal bullet struck him, teaches a sad lesson. To see scores of them is more impressive than that . . . To feel that that tree whose bark is stripped off showing red stains on the wood has received the gushing blood of some poor soldier, is by far the best teacher of war's equals . . .

"And when all is over, men still lie on the damp ground, undisturbed as they fell, with hawks and crows and buzzards sailing lazily over them, their countenances bearing an expression of horror as the bleary, bloodshot eyes, the blackened face and the contorted features turn up towards you.

"When all this is seen and the fact that thousands like them have lain there before is pressed upon the mind, a remembrance is left which cannot be erased . . . Sermons may be exhaustive and vain but the lessons taught by a dead man slain in battle, lying in his gore, is worth 10,000 holiday exortations."

And when, finally, those men were buried the work was hurried. Some graves were so shallow that bits of uniform or a limb were above ground. Some were trenches holding up to 200 bodies. Dead horses were left to rot. Piles of amputated arms and legs were massed around buildings used by the surgeons.

By Monday, July 6, the summer sun beating down on that brutal scene added the horror of smell, a stomach-churning odor which hung like a wet blanket.

Faced with those surroundings, Gettysburg's 2,400 citizens began the months-long task of caring for the 22,000 wounded. Many more died, but most survived, thanks in part to the men, women and children who sacrificed their time, their food, their homes, even their own health for soldiers who had almost shot their town from the face of the earth.

This story, then, is that of the civilians.

# CHAPTER
# 1

# First Light

Sallie Broadhead glanced up Chambersburg Street for signs of Joseph. The blast of the train whistle meant he would soon be home from work.

Mary peeked out the door, looking for her father too. Her tiny hands, by habit, traced the etchings in the worn red brick, then moved automatically to her white dress to wipe away the dust.

"Ah, Mary, child, your dress is getting so dirty. And daddy will be home soon. Inside with you, quickly, shoosh, in!" Sallie waved her fingers and the small form scurried back into the dim hallway.

Mother was smiling so tiny Mary smiled too.

Sallie loved children. That's why she had become a school-teacher. She had loved her own teachers back home in Pleasantville, New Jersey. Now here in the crossroads village of Gettysburg she was loved too.

1

It was a pleasant town—a combination of farming and small business folk. Set between two ridges, anchored by a grove near a cemetery, and two institutions of higher learning, Gettysburg offered gentle hills, small streams, stone for buildings and trees for firewood. But most of all it offered people—good people—living contently in a neat village 12 blocks long and scarcely half that in width.

Sallie was just past 30 and had been a mother for three years. Joseph enjoyed being an engineer. He liked the run to Hanover because he got home every night.

"Hey, love," Joseph's voice carried through the house as he gently closed the front door.

Sallie smiled at that. Joseph had never forgotten his childhood days in England, a quarter of a century earlier. He called everyone "love," everyone he was fond of, but not men, or boys; my, no.

She embraced him tightly, wiped the soot from his chin and kissed him lightly, glad that his job had spared him from going to war. She tried to push away; there was supper to put on the table. But Joseph held on.

"Heard some news today, love. Rebels were crossing the Potomac in heavy forces . . . moving north. Governor Curtin sent a telegram telling everybody to move their stores as quickly as possible."

Sallie turned her head, to look excitedly for Mary. The tiny girl was sprawled on the kitchen floor, tracing the lines her father had drawn on a homemade calendar. The figures jumped out at Sallie.

1863. JUNE. Monday, the 15th.

"We could be in some danger?" she questioned.

"We'll see; we'll see," said Joseph, brushing his hand through her long hair.

Sallie slept well that night until shortly after midnight when Mary cried out.

"Mama, drink. Mama."

Sallie struggled up, still groggy, to get the water. A noise in the street shook off her sleepiness.

"Joseph, get up. Look out here. There's a fire."

"What are those people hallooing about?" he asked as he

leaned his head out the narrow window. The fire, he saw, was not in town. It was miles to the south, in Maryland perhaps. Biggest bunch of buildings that way would be Emmittsburg.

"Hello, what's going on?" he shouted down to some men in the street.

"The Rebels are comin' and burnin' as they go," one shouted back.

Word spread quickly the next day. The fire, indeed, had been in Emmitsburg, seven miles south, just across the Maryland border.

"Some damn fool livin' there set 'er off," the station master told Joseph when he reported for work. "Twenty-seven houses, thirty-five families out on the street. You imagine that? Weren't Rebs at all."

"And, looky this, Joseph, come down on the telegraph last night. Governor Curtin issuin' orders for the Pennsylvania Militia. Presidential proclamation callin' for 50,000 volunteers to fight for the Union. Whewy, 50,000 soldiers. Whewy, we'll never see that many troops at one time."

Joseph examined the telegram, shaking his head as he read. Yep, that's a lot of men alright, he thought. Not concerned about that as much as these damn stories floating around, true or not.

"The wife was talking to Salome Myers, you know, the second assistant to the school principal. She said the darkies made such a racket up and down by her house last night that they couldn't sleep. Poor folks must really fear those Rebs. Afraid of being caught and made slaves, I guess," Joseph said.

"Those black folks mostly live down southwest of town, you know, not far from Salome's father's house on West High Street."

"Aw, ain't that many of them, are there?" the station master asked.

"A goodly number. There's about 20 of them holding down fulltime jobs so with families and all might be 50 or 60. A bunch of their women wash clothes and several nurse. Then there's a shopkeeper, that one shoemaker and a bunch of laborers."

"They ain't got much to worry about. Rebs ain't gonna come this far north again," the station master said.

"Probably not, probably not, but these stories are sure scaring bloody hell out of womenfolk here," Joseph yelled back as he moved down the track to his engine.

A day later, as Joseph strolled down Chambersburg Street, he passed Salome Myers and asked her about the black people of Gettysburg.

"Oh, the population of colored people, I should imagine, is between 300 and 400," she replied. "Did you hear we got another report today to the effect that the Rebels are coming. It turned out to be another false report. I'm getting very tired of all the fuss."

Joseph respected the opinion of school teachers, like his wife and Miss Myers.

"Well, being only seven miles from Mason and Dixon's Line, I reckon we can expect such reports," he said.

"Well, it's bad enough on most people but think of the coloreds," Salome said. "I know not how much cause they have for their fears, but it's a terrible reality to them. Some of them got away today. Those who are obliged to stay at home are at the shortest notice suddenly transformed into limping, halting and apparently worthless specimens of humanity."

"Yes m'm. It's a real shame," Joseph said, shaking his head in agreement. "My regards to your parents, Jefferson and your sisters, mam."

He tipped his soot-covered cap while Salome nodded in return.

"Thank you, Mr. Broadhead. I trust your Sallie and sweet little Mary are well."

Salome Myers hurried along, not wanting to be late again for supper. But school was out and it was her vacation time. Her mother and four younger sisters were quite capable of cooking for the family, now reduced to those six plus Papa since Jefferson had married a month earlier.

She scurried past the Catholic Church, just six doors away from her home on West High Street, and noticed a young man in uniform entering the sanctuary. The uniform reminded her of the one Papa wore while he was with the 87th Pennsylvania Volunteers and Jefferson's when he was with the First Pennsylvania Reserve.

Both were home for good from the war. Both had disabilities because of this stupid war, Salome thought to herself. Now, Papa, a justice of the peace, and Jefferson, a printer, both at least safe. Away from the war.

Susie, Jennie, Belle and Grace were already at the table as Salome swept into the dining room.

"Any news, girl?" asked her father as he walked from the kitchen drying his hands for the evening meal.

"The Rebels are still coming, another report. It has set this town in a perfect uproar. The excitement was intense for awhile but it gradually subsided when it was found that the report was false. I am getting very tired of all the fuss consequent upon border life, though the reports do not alarm me. On the contrary I am sometimes quite amused by seeing the extremes to which people will go. They seem perfectly bewildered."

"Ah, mother, listen to your educated daughter. Pretty speech she makes, eh? Not alarmed, she says."

"Please, Papa, do not make fun of me," Salome pleaded.

Mr. Myers stroked his daughter's long hair.

"Not in jest, my Salome, not in jest. But we have to keep our spirits light. The news from the war is always bad."

Salome was staying close to home these days. She still wasn't alarmed but she was uneasy.

On Friday, she burst excitedly into the house and confronted her mother.

"Some of our boys from the 87th just got home. They were in a battle in Winchester, Virginia, last Sunday. Uncle William Culp and cousin David Myers are among them," she shouted happily.

Then her head dropped.

"But they know nothing about our other uncles and cousins," she murmured as her mother reached out with both arms to hold her.

"The boys retreated," Salome continued. "Their ammunition gave out and they made for home. Poor fellows. They have been on the road since Monday evening. Dear me! What times!"

Talk of the 87th filtered into the Broadhead house too.

When Joseph got home that night, Sallie blurted out what she had heard:

"Oh, Joseph, they say the 87th Pennsylvania got a terrible beating at Winchester a few days ago. Some were saying that a captain, two lieutenants and a lot of other men were killed or captured.

"At 10 o'clock this morning, it was rumored that some of the men were coming in on the Chambersburg Pike, and not long after about a dozen of those who lived in town came in, and their report and presence relieved some and agonized others, and . . ."

Joseph put his hand over her mouth and whispered, "Slow down, love, slowly, calm down."

Sallie took a deep breath in an effort to compose herself. Then she was off and running again.

"Those whose friends were not of the party were in a heart-rending plight, for those returned ones could not tell of the others. Some would say, 'This one was killed or taken prisoner,' and others, 'We saw him at such a place and the Rebels may have taken him,' and so they were kept in suspense.

"Oh, Joseph, where will it end? Where?"

His arms encircled her and she nestled comfortably into his chest. When she opened her eyes to reality she caught sight of the dirt on Joseph's shirt.

"Oh, darn, now I've got that soot in my hair and on my face. Oh, Joseph, sometimes I wish you were a banker, or a baker, anything other than a railroad man."

"Yes, love, bloody soot all over and you're still beautiful."

"Off with you, and with that dirt. Dinner's ready."

# CHAPTER
# 2

# All Talk

Saturday, June 20, and the rumors continued.

Sallie Broadhead told Joseph, when he came home from work that night, that there was great excitement in town all day.

"The report was that the Rebels are at Chambersburg, Joseph, Chambersburg. That's getting close. A day's march, perhaps?"

"Yes, I reckon a day."

"Refugees were coming in today. Did you hear?"

"Yes, love, coming from the west, perhaps Chambersburg, they tell me at the station. I haven't talked to any."

Sallie puffed up her chest: "I have. Some of them say the Rebels number from twenty to thirty thousand. My goodness, Joseph. That's a terrible number. I can't imagine a bunch of soldiers that large. Some others say that Lee's whole army is advancing this way."

• • •

Six blocks away, Salome Myers was bringing her father up to date.

"Some cavalry from Philadelphia, who armed and equipped themselves, came in tonight. They are entirely and altogether volunteers."

"And tell me, Elizabeth Salome Myers, how you know all that?" her father asked.

"I talked to a few of them, Papa."

"Salome, Salome, please be careful. Strangers, in the army, away from home. You know what I mean."

"Papa, I'm not naive. And I am very careful."

It was after midnight as Fannie Buehler stood outside her house talking to other residents of Baltimore Street. She had heard the talk too and didn't know what to believe.

She had convinced David to hide outside town along with his assistant postmaster that day. If Rebel troops came, they'd sure arrest any federal officials. David was 42 now, five years older than his wife, and much older than the men signing up for military duty. But his postmaster's position, his background as a lawyer and his reputation as a staunch Republican would make him a prize catch for Confederate troops.

Now Fannie, knowing him safe, began to think about the rest of her family. Her mother had been visiting most of the year and two of her sister's daughters were here from Elizabeth, New Jersey.

"Rumors, stories, refugees, soldiers!" she said exasperated. "We're in a condition to believe anything, good or bad."

She glanced at the Adams County Courthouse, just across the street. People who normally would be sleeping were rushing in and out in futile attempts to run down the truth of the situation.

She went back into her house. Mrs. Guyon was still up too.

"Mother, they say that many citizens of Gettysburg are preparing to leave on the early morning train. I want you to go to Elizabeth with the girls and take my Martha, Myra and Henry with you. I'm going to stay here with Kate and Allie."

"What? Frances, are you daft, girl?"

Fannie stopped her short: "Mother, Kate is 12 now and can help me immensely and little Allie at four is too young for you to cart all the way to New Jersey. The others are old enough to travel and take care of themselves but too young for me to handle all of them here should trouble come."

As Mrs. Guyon and the children boarded later that morning, the church bells were pealing in time with the train's bell.

"Last time you'll hear that train clanger for awhile," said a voice behind Mrs. Buehler. It was Joseph Broadhead.

"Oh, morning, Mr. Broadhead," she said, half startled. "What, ah, what do you mean by that?"

Joseph doffed his cap.

"We're moving all the rolling stock east, over to Hanover and York. Don't want the Rebs to get any engines or cars, if they come this way, and we can't afford to lose any equipment. They would most certainly bust up and burn anything they couldn't use."

Fannie Buehler didn't like talk like that but she was wise enough to realize that the railroad was taking a very practical step.

Joseph didn't ask why Mrs. Buehler was at the train station. So many people were leaving town these days. The villagers were jittery and taking no chances. But he knew he had some good news for her.

"I saw Mr. Buehler riding in on Blacks Turnpike a while ago as I was walking to the station," Joseph told her. "Didn't you pass him on the way up Baltimore Street?"

Mrs. Buehler beamed. "No, I didn't. He may have ridden down Washington. Thank you."

David was looking for something to eat when his wife and two children got home.

"Ah, Fannie, how glad I am to see you," he half shouted as he grabbed her by the waist and kissed her tenderly. "We've been up at Joe Bayly's farm but the rumors seemed to quiet down so I thought it was safe to come back."

Fannie told him about her mother and the other children, got his nod of approval and then busied herself to fix him some breakfast.

It was Sunday. A day of peace.

Salome Myers had gone to early church but was back home within minutes.

"Don't rush, Papa, unless you're going up the street to Mass. Our church isn't operating today."

Mr. Myers' face drew into a tight question mark, his bushy eyebrows curving at the top, his thin nose tapering down to the rounded dimple on his chin.

"Had no preaching. Reverend Isenberg has skedaddled. And the town is pretty clear of darkies," she explained before he asked.

"What happened?" he blurted out.

"Well, the excitement today is worse than ever and I think it is about as great as can be. For the first time in two years I have been excited and alarmed. The Rebels, Papa, the Rebels have taken possession of Fairfield."

Mr. Myers' eyes opened wide with fear. "Good heavens, eight miles away and more to the west than south. You say the darkies are gone. Where to?"

Salome hunched her shoulders: "Who knows? They have nearly all left. I pity the poor creatures. Darkies of both sexes are skedaddling and some white folks of the male sex. I am glad I am neither a man nor a darky, though girls are not so much better off. Oh dear, I wish the excitement was over."

Six blocks away, Sallie Broadhead was making a notation in her diary:

"Great excitement prevails and there is no reliable intelligence from abroad. One report declares that the enemy are at Waynesboro, 20 miles off; another that Harrisburg is the point; and so we are in great suspense."

Later that day she added to her note:

"The report now is that a large force is in the mountains about eighteen miles away, and a call is made for a party of men to go out and cut down trees to obstruct the passage of the mountains. About fifty, among them my husband, started."

And later still, when Joseph and the others had returned, she made a further notation:

"I was very uneasy lest they might be captured, but, they had not gone half way when the discovery was made that it was too late; that the Rebels were on this side of the mountain, and coming this way. Our men turned back, uninjured, though their advance, composed of a few men, was fired upon. About seventy of the Rebels came within eight miles and then returned by another road to their main force. They stole all the horses and cattle they could find, and drove them back to their encampment. We did not know but that the whole body would be down upon us until 11 o'clock when a man came in and said that he had seen them and that they had recrossed. I shall now retire, and sleep much better than I had expected an hour since."

Sunday, a day of rest, had ended peacefully.

And so it remained for days.

"Where've you been, girl?" Mr. Myers asked Salome as she closed the front door late on Monday afternoon.

"Went to the store, but there is very little to be bought, Papa. The store looks quite desolate."

"Merchants have been hiding their goods, or moving them out of town," her father said. "They don't want the Rebs to take everything they own."

"Papa, do you really think we'll see Rebels here? I mean, we've been hearing talk and rumors, rumors and talk for a week."

"Who knows. I was reading the *Compiler* here, out today. Look at the headline:

"TO ARMS.

"In accordance with the presidential proclamation for 50,000 volunteers, troops are pouring into Harrisburg from all quarters," Mr. Myers read from the Gettysburg weekly. "A company of 60, students and citizens of Gettysburg under Captain Frederick Klinefelter, left here Wednesday morning. Captain Bell's cavalry, ready to leave Thursday morning, didn't leave because of being assigned special duty in Adams County. The emergency will not admit of delay."

He adjusted his glasses, glanced further down the page, and added: "Ah, another item here, girl. Headline is: INVASION OF PENNSYLVANIA.

He went on reading the subheadlines: "EXAGGERATED RUMORS. ONLY 2,000 CONFEDERATES AT CHAMBERS-BURG."

Myers murmured along, "invading force of Rebels dwindled down from 40,000 to 2,000 . . . ah, let's see, extent of excursion to Chambersburg . . . messages say the Rebels conducted themselves civilly and paid for all the supplies they obtained.

"Ah, the editor says here: 'How reports so exaggerated and false as those which gave rise to the late panic could have organized is a mystery which we hope can be speedily solved, that means may be adopted to prevent similar impositions hereafter. The anxiety and inconvenience and expense occasioned by these false reports are too serious to be encountered without earnest resentment."

"Amen," piped in Salome.

On Tuesday, June 23, another report from the west: "Rebels are coming certainly," a neighbor told Salome.

And that night she told Papa: "Nearly everybody looked for them, but they disappointed us." She smiled weakly.

"Yes," her father said calmly. "I imagine you're disappointed. I think you'd as soon get this whole mess over and done with."

By Wednesday, the rumors were flowing like nearby Rock Creek, from the north and, of course, from the west.

When Joseph Broadhead got home that evening, his wife was full of news.

"The Rebels have, several times," she said rapidly, "been within two or three miles, but they have not yet reached here."

"Obviously," Joseph replied.

"Two of our cavalry companies are on scouting duty here, but they can be of little use, as they have never seen service. Deserters came in every little while today and reported the enemy near in large forces. This morning early, the postmaster got a message saying that a regiment of infantry was coming from Harrisburg."

Joseph broke in with news of his own.

"Well, raw militia they are. The train bringing them came within ten miles when it ran over a cow, which threw the cars off the track. No one was hurt and they are now encamped near the place of the accident."

Sallie was drinking it all in. She waited briefly to make sure Joseph had no more and then she continued as if he had never uttered a sound.

"The town is a little quieter than yesterday. I believe we are getting used to excitement, and many think the enemy, having been so long in the vicinity without visiting us, will not favor us with their presence.

"Some folks who came in from the west, Chambersburg area, I guess, said the Rebels had carried off many horses. Some who had taken their stock away returned, supposing the Rebels had left the neighborhood, and lost their teams.

"Joseph, I don't want to leave here even if they come. I'm sure they wouldn't harm Mary and I. But I fear for you. I think that if I leave they'll tear through our house proper, taking what they want."

Joseph knew she was right. The stories he had heard of Confederate troops in northern towns confirmed that. Those who stayed to protect their properties usually were able to do just that, except for horses, of course, and some food.

By Thursday, the village's dwindling population was ajitter with talk.

"There is a good deal of excitement. The Rebels are near, they say," Salome Myers blurted to her father.

"We're getting so used to the cry, 'the Rebels are coming,' that when they do come they'll take us unawares," Mrs. Buehler said to ten-year-old Gates Fahnestock, who lived at the next corner, at Baltimore and Middle Streets. Gates' father and two uncles owned Fahnestock Brothers, the general merchandise store across the street.

Gates had been telling her that his father and uncles had chartered a railroad car.

"Three times, at least, it's been filled with goods from the store and sent on to Philadelphia, and held there out of reach of General Early's army," the boy told her, obviously proud to be aware of what was going on in the family business.

And Sallie Broadhead complained to Joseph: "Everyone is asking—where is our army that they let the enemy scour the country and do as they please? They say that Lee's whole army is on this side of the Potomac and marching on Harrisburg; and that a large force is coming on here to destroy the railroad between here and Baltimore. Even the militia didn't come to town today, but stayed out where they camped yesterday."

Sallie was running again and Joseph had to take her in his brawny arms to calm and soothe and reassure her.

"A lot of talk, love, but no action. Don't you worry."

# CHAPTER
# 3

# They're Here

It was 10 a.m. Friday when Sallie Broadhead heard horses coming down Chambersburg Street from the Diamond. She and Mary stood in the doorway as the militia passed through town, headed west. Hundreds of men, many on horseback, and wagons moved quietly down the dusty street heading out past the Seminary where students—what was left of them—were trying hard to keep their minds on theology.

Sallie went back to her kitchen and the bread she had started to bake. She felt safer with the militia between her and Confederate soldiers.

But she was unaware that the militia stopped three miles to the west and before they could unpack their baggage were hit by Rebel cavalry.

The sound of shooting carried back to the kitchen, floating along with a breeze, much like the fragrance of her ovened bread. But shooting was nothing new. She had heard such noise before. Only this time, she thought, it seems louder, and closer, and more guns, perhaps.

Her complacency was short-lived when she heard galloping and yelling.

Snatching up tiny Mary, Sallie rushed to her front window. Militiamen were all over, running, sometimes walking backwards, those on horseback leading the way.

She could hear them yelling to other residents about the Rebs.

"Whole blasted army out there," shouted one excited youth.

"They captured about 200," she heard a young officer on horseback tell a bearded superior who was standing in the street trying to slow the runners.

"We've got a rear guard posted. By gawd, stop this running! Form up there! Assemble at the Square!" the bearded officer shouted, swinging his sword wildly through the air.

As the streets cleared and the noise died down, Sallie rushed to the kitchen. Her bread was burning.

"Oh, Mary, hurry, Momma has to get the bread out. Oh, dear, Joseph will be so disappointed if that bread is burned!"

Her kitchen problems took her mind away from what had happened in the street. For several hours, there was an uneasy quiet. But at 2 o'clock Mrs. Gilbert from two doors away pounded on the Broadhead door and then opened it just an inch or so.

"Sallie, Sallie, Rebels, only two miles from town now. Oh, Sallie, what will we do?"

Sallie was in the hall, comforting her and saying, "How many times have we been told they're just coming and failed to appear. I pay little attention to these rumors," she said, knowing full well what a whopping lie she had told her neighbor.

And no sooner had she done that then they heard wagons coming, dozens of them, hellbent eastward, thundering up the wide dirt street as the women watched from Sallie's doorway.

They knew instinctively that the rear guard had been pushed back and the wagons were rushing to stay out of the way.

No more than a half hour had passed when Sallie and Mrs. Gilbert saw them coming. Mostly gray-clad; some in butternut;

others in various colors. A late-running militiaman was giving the warning: "It's Jenkins Cavalry! Rebel cavalry coming in! Take shelter!"

Mrs. Gilbert slid into the hallway but Sallie stood her ground and described the scene for her quivering friend.

"Listen to those horrid yells. Enough to frighten us all to death."

She couldn't see far enough to know but Jenkins' men were moving into Gettysburg on three roads. They soon were swirling around the five-house row where the Broadheads, Gilberts and three other families lived.

Sallie stayed in the doorway while the cavalry passed. But when she saw foot soldiers coming she closed the door.

"They might run into the house and carry off everything we have," she explained to Mrs. Gilbert, leading her upstairs so that they could watch the oft-rumored Rebs moving cautiously through the western end of town.

"They seem very orderly, don't they?" she said as she opened one window.

"How many Yank soldiers in this here place?" barked one grimy, bearded sergeant.

Sallie shuddered to hear a Southern voice, in her town. Then she felt a smattering of compassion for the man. He had no shoes, just strips of an old gray blanket tied around his feet. She could see where blood had dripped through the filthy coverings. She almost felt like searching out a pair of Joseph's old boots.

"I don't know how many soldiers are here."

"You are a funny woman. If I lived in a town I would know that much," shouted patchfoot as he trudged on toward the Diamond, three blocks to the east.

The last of the troops stacked their arms on both sides of the street in front of Sallie's home and sat there talking amongst themselves for an hour.

Sallie whispered to her neighbor: "What a miserable-looking set. They have all kinds of hats and caps, even to heavy fur ones, and some are completely barefoot. Listen, you hear? Sounds like a Rebel band playing up at the Square." (She always called the crossroads in the center of town the Square, not the Diamond, as many others did.) "Southern tunes, I suspect. Oh, Mrs. Gilbert, I cannot tell you how bad I feel to hear them and to see that traitors' flag floating by.

"Oh, oh, come here, look at this. My humiliation is complete."

Mrs. Gilbert peeked out in time to see the captured militia being marched by guards into the very town they were sent to defend. Last in line was an officer and behind him a black man on as fine a horse as Sallie had ever seen.

One of the soldiers who had been sitting in the street glanced up and saw Sallie admiring the horse.

"We captured this horse from General Milroy, and do you see the wagons up there? We captured them too. How we did whip the Yankees and we intend to do it again soon."

Sallie's eyes moistened. She wished Joseph were there. Then she decided he was better off over at Hanover Junction, where he had taken a train that morning, completely unaware that there was any possibility the town would be raided.

Please, God, keep him safe, was the only thought that raced through her mind.

Mr. and Mrs. Buehler, along with Kate and Allie, had had a simple lunch and he had gone back to sorting letters in the Post Office, which was really just a room in their house. Fannie had gone upstairs to her sewing machine "to finish off a piece of work."

She was busy for no more than a half hour when Kate came bounding up the steps.

"Oh, Momma, the Rebels are here sure enough."

Fannie looked up, thought of all the past rumors, and went back to work with simply, "I guess not."

"Yes, indeed, they are, hurry down!"

But Fannie didn't hurry. She finished her sewing, closed up the machine and went leisurely down the stairs. She told her husband the latest news and they were both still chuckling when a neighbor stuck his head in the front door and shouted:

"Postmaster. The Rebels are marching into town. Hurry up or you'll be caught."

"Possibly you had better go and see how things look," Fannie told her husband.

Buehler went two blocks, to the Diamond, where a friend, Dr. Stoever, hailed him from across the street.

"David, flee for your life! It's Early's Division, they say, infantry, coming up the Chambersburg Road."

Fannie was still watching from in front of the house as David came running back. Then she knew—the Rebels indeed had arrived.

David had been preparing for this day. He knew that as U.S. postmaster, the Confederates would arrest him for being a federal official. So he had purchased a satchel for his valuables, his personal and official papers and a few necessary articles he might need. The satchel sat waiting, never unpacked but with room left for stamps and other government property.

Now Fannie was running to the post office room, for the satchel and an umbrella; it had begun to rain. She met him at the door.

"My God, woman, forget the umbrella. I'd rather be wet than dead. But what of you?"

"David, hurry! Don't think of me. We'll be fine."

And with that and a quick kiss, he was off again. When Fannie last saw him he was turning the corner on Middle Street on a dead run.

Then she saw Rebel cavalry, darting across the Diamond, heading east on York Street, the very direction David was heading and only two blocks between them.

Then came infantry, through the Diamond and then a right turn to move south on Baltimore Street. They would pass by soon so Fannie rushed inside, closed the shutters, took down the Post Office sign, locked the doors and hid the keys in her bosom.

That done, she and the children returned to the front door just in time to see Confederate troops file past and move on up toward Cemetery Hill.

"Long looked for and you are certainly here at last," she whispered to herself. Realizing the children had heard that she continued the conversation:

"I never saw a more unsightly set of men. Look at their

dirty, torn garments, no hats, no shoes and footsore. I pity them from the depth of my heart."

She thought to herself: How strange! They excited my sympathy, and not fear, as one would suppose. She wondered what their coming meant; what they were going to do; and how long they were going to stay.

Fannie and Kate sat on the stoop and watched as the last of the soldiers disappeared over the hill. Allie and his dog, Bruno, sat in the dirt, both unimpressed with the spectacle.

Before long, other soldiers, mostly officers, were gathering across the street near the Court House. Fannie learned that Generals Early and Gordon were among them, negotiating terms with the burgess and the town council.

She could hear them demanding supplies and the town fathers explaining that provisions were low, that many goods had been shipped, along with money, to Philadelphia.

The generals, she thought, seemed to be accepting the fact that the town's businessmen had prepared for their arrival wisely.

By midafternoon, word had spread that no demands would be made on the citizens of Gettysburg by the troops. But Fannie also heard later that some horses had been stolen and some cellars were broken into by hungry soldiers.

"But so far as can be done, the officers seem to be controlling their men and the soldiers are behaving well," she wrote on the back of an envelope for what she thought would be a diary for David.

"I learned later that the soldiers were referred to as the 'Louisiana Tigers'."

Not all of the soldiers had marched past the Buehler's home. Hundreds had cut through Washington and Franklin Streets, and across Middle and High.

"Such a mean set of men I never saw in all my life," said Salome Myers to her father. "High Street doesn't look the same with them prancing around out there.

"Why, Papa, they're flying around looking for stray horses. It's very provoking to see them riding around and doing as they pleased."

Mr. Myers had not ventured out. Men of the town had been warned by militia to avoid contact with the enemy. So he listened to his daughter's description.

"Must have been several hundred cavalrymen who came in first and then followed by several thousand infantry with their old red flags flying and them yelling like fiends.

"I wasn't afraid of them. I didn't even think of them as Rebels until two of them rode by furiously brandishing their sabers and pointing pistols. At last we have seen the Rebels."

Mr. Myers sighed, "Yes, at long last."

Young Gates Fahnestock was most impressed by the fierce-looking men atop huge, sweaty horses.

"Look at 'em ride. Wild, huh?" Gates said to Charles, Sam and James, his brothers, as they watched Rebel cavalrymen move down Baltimore Street from the slatted shutters on the second floor.

But the yelling and a few fired pistols were too much for little James, then only 3. He ran downstairs to his mother.

His father, also James, was trying with other businessmen and town officials to bargain with the raiders. "We need flour, meat, groceries, shoes, hats and, ah, at least ten barrels of whiskey, or five thousand Yankee dollars," an officer said cooly. Money and supplies were scarce so the Confederates settled for shopping tours through the village stores, where they found very little that a soldier could use. Fahnestock overheard some of the officers talking about leaving the next day, some of the men going east to Hanover and York and others north to Carlisle, site of a century-old U.S. Army post.

"Probably be damn little of any value there either," one of the officers muttered.

Tillie Pierce was in school that afternoon, at the Young Ladies Seminary, when the word was passed from lip to lip: "The Rebels are coming."

The call came during the regular Friday literary exercises. The girls and Mrs. Eyster rushed to the front portico. To the west, past the Theological Seminary, was a dark, dense mass moving toward them.

"Children, run home as quickly as you can," Mrs. Eyster shouted.

A 15-year-old girl didn't have to be told twice. Tillie made tracks and was still on York Street when she heard horses behind her. At the Diamond she swung right and ran five blocks down Baltimore Street to her house. She scrambled inside, slammed the door shut and ran to the sitting room, where she could peep out between the shutters.

"Human beings? Yech," she whispered to her mother, who had joined her instantly. "Look at their rags and the dust. Wild riders. All that shouting and yelling and cursing. And why are they firing those pistols?"

"Trying to scare us, Tillie," her mother's voice quivered.

"And doing a job of it too," the daughter replied.

Tillie learned later that some houses—though not hers— were searched. Some, they say, were even ransacked.


Anna Garlach was helping her mother tend to little Frank, born earlier that year. At 18, she acted more like a second mother than a sister.

Just before the Rebel cavalrymen came down Baltimore Street, Anna had seen dozens of Gettysburg residents running their horses south out of town. One was a mail carrier who dropped a pouch in front of the Garlach house as he rushed to get away. Mrs. Garlach picked it up. She would return it to Mr. Buehler, who lived a few short blocks up the street, back toward the Diamond.

Anna was horrified when she saw through the window Grandmother Little talking to some of the soldiers.

When the old lady came inside, Anna demanded to know what the talk was all about.

"They asked me what I thought Rebels were like and whether I thought they had horns. And I said I was a little frightened at first but then found them like our own men. And they smiled and went away. You think I'm a dang fool, chile? I've been around long enough to know you gotta be nice to a man with a gun."

And with that, Grandmother Little pranced back the hallway to the kitchen.

Anna's father wasn't so nice when he returned home from dickering with the Confederate officers over the town's ransom.

"They brought in the body of George Sandoe from the Baltimore Pike," he told his family. Anna said she recognized the name but couldn't place the man.

"He was home guard, member of Bell's Cavalry. After his unit pulled back from out past the seminary seems Sandoe was near his home, about a mile south of the cemetery. Rebs surrounded him down in a thicket and he refused to surrender. They shot him."

Anna bowed her head.

"So the first one dies, almost in his front yard. How many more will go like that?"

Mr. Garlach tried to soothe her, saying, "But remember, Anna, Sandoe was in uniform, a soldier and armed. If we do not resist we will survive."

Anna wasn't the only concerned 18-year-old. A few blocks away, at the northwest corner of Middle and Washington Streets, in a large double house lived Henry E. Jacobs, just graduated from the Pennsylvania College at Gettysburg, where his father, Michael, was professor of mathematics and natural philosophy.

Henry was occupied with special reading that Friday, for he was preparing to study the law, a profession which appealed to him greatly. He had told his father that he really couldn't comprehend what an invasion of their soil could mean.

On this day, he found out.

"They seem very firm and businesslike," he told his mother after he and Professor Jacobs returned from a meeting of town leaders and Confederate officers. "They wanted supplies, like flour and shoes, but found we really had little of anything left. They were considerate enough."

Henry, like Anna Garlach, had seen dozens of men riding and herding horses through town just before the Confederates arrived.

• • •

One whom Henry recognized was Joseph Bayly, a farmer who lived three miles north of Gettysburg on the Table Rock Road. And with him, riding just as hard, was his oldest son, 13-year-old Billy.

"Your Pa and Billy are taking the horses to Hanover or York for safe keeping," Harriet Bayly answered when eight-year-old Jane inquired. The Baylys had six children and it was all that Harriet could do to keep the young ones hushed when they heard a mass of guns popping down toward Gettysburg.

"Maybe they got Pa and Bill," Joseph Junior piped up.

Harriet Bayly bit her lip and just looked southward, watching a dust cloud moving across the horizon.

Billy Bayly and his dad looked back and saw the dust too. And knew what it was. The real thing, this time. Running to save animals was nothing new for him.

He thought back to the summer of '62 and this summer too when there was a steady stream of skedaddlers from Maryland to Pennsylvania every time the enemy was reported crossing the Potomac.

Unfortunately, the alarms usually came at night. Billy hated getting up but once up he thought the world of riding like the wind through the darkness with what he imagined to be Johnny Rebs nipping at his heels.

Town boys didn't have such experiences.

As he rode, Billy thought back to the last days of this school term when studies were boring and teachers were tired and let students tell tales to amuse the class.

"On one occasion," Billy told the class one day, "the rumors of the near approach of the enemy became so alarming and convincing that my father, with some of our neighbors, joined a procession of hundreds of skedaddlers en route for Harrisburg.

"After having worked on the farm all day I rode one horse and led another through that night, reaching the state Capitol, 35 miles distance, next morning. Once across the Susquehanna, we felt comparatively safe and, having taken up our quarters with a Dauphin County farmer, our party of six men and two boys turned in and helped our farmer friend harvest his wheat crop.

"No enemy appearing we returned home several days later and found our wheat cut and stacked by a party of skedaddlers from Maryland who had spent some days on our farm in our absence."

The students "oohed" and "ahhed" and Billy just grinned and felt good, because he knew every word was true.

Joe Bayly was 54 that summer, too old for military duty and needed to run the farm. But he still had problems trying to explain those skedaddling trips.

He got tired of telling town folks that it was to protect his livestock, not for his personal safety.

"Without horses, the farm's dead," he said over and over.

Billy had been working in the fields this day too when a noon rain drove him and his father to the shelter of the house.

"Word's out again, Joe. They say the Rebs have crossed the foothills. Maybe you and Billy ought to get started," Mrs. Bayly told her husband.

Joe decided to wait a while to make sure it wasn't another false alarm. Rain was moving slowly south. If rebs are out west of town heavy rain might stop 'em for a while, he reasoned.

They ate lunch and Billy found a cool spot in a darkened room in the house and promptly fell asleep. He thought he was dreaming when his mother shook him violently:

"Billy, Billy, Rebs comin'! Pa wants you out to the barn. Right now!"

Billy was shoeless and coatless as he raced to the barn. Father had already saddled up and as Billy ran in he found himself being tossed on the back of Nellie, a beautiful chestnut mare.

As he passed the house, Billy reached out and grabbed a bag his mother held in outstretched arms. He knew it probably had bread, maybe some dried beef and most certainly his shoes and coat.

Along the woods-bordered ridge which constituted the west boundary of the farm Billy saw soldiers moving rapidly eastward, the same general direction they were riding.

The rain had brought heavy clouds and darkness, making it

impossible to see the color of the uniforms or flags. Joe took no chances, and signaled Billy to whip it to Nellie.

One of Billy's uncles and several other neighbors had stopped by the Bayly farm to sound the alarm and then had ridden off. But at the rate Joe and his son were riding it took little time to catch that band.

Four days later, when he returned home, Billy told his excited mother the whole story:

"Our first purpose was to go toward Harrisburg again, but fearing that the enemy had cut us off in that direction, we turned toward Hanover. On crossing one of the roads radiating from Gettysburg I noticed a horseman coming over the hill toward us and being anxious for information about the enemy I hung back and let the party go on, having every confidence in the fleetness of Nellie."

His mother smiled and thought: What a story teller!

"The horseman, covered with a rubber poncho splashed with mud, rode up to where my horse was standing, and I recognized him as a recruit in Bell's Cavalry whom I knew, so I said, 'Hello, Bill, what's up?'

"If you don't get out of here pretty quick you'll find out what's up. The Rebel cavalry chased me out of town about fifteen minutes ago and must now be close on my heels."

"But where is the rest of your company?"

"Oh, hell—that's what he said, Ma—oh, ah, well he said, 'I don't know; they ran long before I did. But you git or you'll be got.'

"Then away he rode toward Harrisburg and I went galloping after Pa. Anyways, we found out later that the soldiers we saw along the ridge near home were members of a regiment of emergency men, signed up for a hundred days. Mostly they were students at the college. They had gone out from Gettysburg and ran smack into the Reb cavalry coming in from Chambersburg. When we saw them they were taking short cuts to freedom, not wanting to be guests at Libby Prison."

Mrs. Bayly interrupted. "Some of those soldiers were farmers from here abouts, not as swift of foot as those young, narrow-framed students and a good many of them were taken prisoner that day. We suspect that they've been marched down South."

Billy listened intently and just as intently returned to his story.

"To get back to our riding party. We continued for about fifteen miles and darkness approaching, concluded that the Rebels would not overtake us that night so we put up with a farmer who fed us abundantly.

"We rode away in the morning and had stopped at another farm. We never thought that cavalry moved so fast but we got our first shock and surprise by the sudden appearance of four Confederate cavalrymen.

"To say that we were rats in a trap caught by our own stupidity about describes the situation. The barn on this place was unusually large. There were about twenty horses stabled in it, including ours, and we all thought what a fine haul they would be.

"While some of the men got into a heated argument with the soldiers over the war, Papa, two others and I worked our way quietly to the barn, the farmhouse shielding us from view. We figured to get our horses, which we did, mounted in hot haste and jumped them over a fence into the meadow and cut out for the timber a quarter mile away. After a run of several miles we stopped in a heavily wooded section in York County where we concealed our horses and were given shelter in a farmhouse.

"Hay and corn and water were carried to the horses for two days while Confederate cavalry was passing by on the main roads on their way to York and the Susquehanna River. That's when we decided it was safe to come home."

Mrs. Bayly smiled: "That's quite a story, Billy. You're such a young man now, handling a man's job."

"And what happened here while we were gone, Mama?"

"Well, the Rebs did come on Friday last. They did no damage, maybe because I served some of them a good meal. The poor men were starving and I didn't have the heart to turn them away, if, indeed, I could have. After that meal, an officer placed a guard at the house and the barn to keep his own men on their good behavior."

• • •

Yes, Friday, June 26, was a long day, thought Salome Myers as she prepared for bed. Her brain teemed with the events:

How exasperating the thought that, tonight, we are under the control of armed traitors. Two of them at the door for two hours. Imagine! Talking to Papa about the war and their Southern rights and Papa telling them we were for the Union unconditionally. Papa really stood up to them. Ah, but I must say, they were reasonable and their conversation was interesting.

After supper, Fannie Buehler and her children went back out to the front steps. The rain had passed away and the sun had set. Clouds now and then blotted out the moon but the temperatures were pleasant, normal, Fannie thought, for late June.

Neighbors gathered to chat and watch the soldiers across the street cooking a late supper with camp kettles set up inside the Court House fireplaces.

It was 9 o'clock when two of the soldiers, seeing Fannie and the children, crossed the street and asked permission to sit down.

"You're here. Sit," Fannie said brusquely. She noticed they were not as dirty and ragged as the men she had seen earlier. And they seemed more civil; at least they were well behaved.

The talk was long and pleasant with no bitterness.

"We never been north before, mam. Surprised to see what good shape things is in here," said the younger of the two soldiers. (Hardly more than a boy, Fannie thought.)

"Yes'm, t'was high time we left Virginia to find a land of plenty. It's strange to find a town so full of men and boys and good things to eat. Back home, it's just the women folk and no food. But how come y'all got all these idle men? Our men and boys are all in the army; why aren't these?"

"Oh, we have all the men in the army who are needed, and thousands standing ready to fill up the ranks as they are thinned out. We have all the men and all the money we need, and while I feel very sorry for you, the sooner the South realizes this fact the better it will be for you."

The soldiers looked at her and then at each other, wondering how much of that to believe.

"Well, we haven't as many men left in the South as you have and not as much money, for look at these ragged clothes, but we will get better ones after we have been North awhile," the older soldier said.

"Oh, how long are you going to stay?"

"Well, mam, all summer, of course," the younger one replied.

Fannie was startled. All summer? What would she do? David could not return and she couldn't leave.

Soon one of the men asked her what time she and the children went to bed.

"Anytime before ten o'clock," Fannie told them.

"Then we'd better not keep you out here," the older one said as he rose. The younger one followed. "Nite, mam."

Fannie made sure the house was locked up tight. She put Kate and Allie to bed and took Bruno to her room, where he normally wasn't allowed. She finally realized that she was alone—except for two young children and a dog—in a large house surrounded by enemy troops.

# CHAPTER
# 4

# They're Gone

Despite her fears, Fannie slept quite soundly and was up at dawn, her normal rising hour. She opened her eyes and wondered whether it had all been a dream.

But when she peered out through the curtains she saw troops in the street, all astir, preparing breakfast. The Court House wasn't burned down; everything seemed normal.

Fannie went about her routine: breakfast for Kate and little Allie, who were up early this Saturday; let Bruno out the back door; bring in some wood for a cooked meal at noon; and haul a bucket of water for washing.

That done, Fannie went to the front door. The young soldier she had talked to the night before was on the street, packing a rusty frying pan into his blanket roll and wrapping the roll around his back like a knapsack.

"Leaving?" Fannie asked timidly.

"Movin' on to York, mam," he said quickly, and just as

quickly looked around to see if anyone else had heard. He grinned sheepishly and Fannie knew he wasn't supposed to tell her that.

By nine o'clock, the village was clear of troops and the streets were full of town folk, trading stories so fast it made Fannie's head spin to try to listen.

"Bastards ran all the railroad cars that were around—fifteen or twenty of 'em—out to the east. Burned the Rock Creek Bridge and the cars and tore up the track," said one gnarled, bewhiskered old man.

Fannie pulled her children away from that conversation and continued walking toward the Diamond. Eden Norris was riding into the broad opening in the town's center and spotted Fannie.

"Mrs. Buehler, Mrs. Buehler," he called.

"Good news, Mrs. Buehler. Your husband escaped," he shouted, dismounting before his horse had even stopped. He yanked back on the reins and the saddle horn to make the bay wheel.

Fannie smiled, pulled the children close to her side and pleaded, "Oh, tell me all that you know, Mr. Norris."

"Well, David said that after he turned to run up Middle Street a driver with an empty wagon came rushing past, slowed and yelled for him to jump in. They turned up Stratton Street and reached the corner of York—you know, where St. James Church is—and just as they turned east on York, here come the Rebel cavalry behind 'em dashing down the street from the Diamond.

"They were chasing a slew of 'em and some got caught. David said they were shooting at the wagon so he jumped out and made for the woods. Then he came down the Bonaugh-town Road to my farm. I had sent all my horses to York for safekeeping," Norris said, looking quickly at the fine horse standing beside him. "This one I borrowed from a neighbor this morning after we found out the Rebs were leaving.

"At any rate, David just couldn't walk anymore and the only thing I had left was a raw-boned nag that nobody would want, 'cept your husband. Off he went for Hanover. I'm sure he's okay."

And with that Mr. Norris mounted up, tipped his hat and trotted off.

Fannie felt relieved.

Unlike Fannie, Sallie Broadhead had not slept well the night before. She was up before dawn, peeking very carefully around the curtain in her bedroom window and thinking to herself:

Here I am, wondering if Joseph got his train to Hanover Junction last night, and him not thinking the Rebels were so near, or that there was much danger of their coming to town, and me left alone, surrounded by thousands of ugly, rude, hostile soldiers, from whom violence might be expected.

Sallie sobbed, quietly, but not for long. She stayed in her room until little Mary woke up and came looking for breakfast. By that time, Sallie heard a great deal of movement outside. Everyone was moving toward the Diamond, eastward. They were leaving; the Rebels were leaving.

Sallie waited another hour before she opened the front door. Then she and Mary walked to the train station. Perhaps Joseph was back.

"No, we walked back through the woods," one grimy railroad hand told her. "But your Joseph got captured and paroled right away. He went on to Harrisburg; at least that's what we were told.

"He'll be back soon; don't you fret. He probably thought the railroad could use him there since the Rebs were down here."

"Thank you," Sallie whispered and turned away. At least Joseph was alive, and free, and apparently well.

While the village was clear, the surrounding country was not. Up Table Rock Road, at the Bayly farm, Harriet was pestered all day Saturday by bands of roving Confederates.

Jane was skeptical.

"Are they really Rebs, Momma?"

"Well, child their dress indicates that that is the fact and I suppose it's true because they're all in search of something to eat."

• • •

A dozen miles due south, other troops were moving about that Saturday too. Night had fallen and Sister Mary Louise was preparing for bed. The huge Gothic building was ghostly quiet as candles flickered out and the nuns settled down for the night.

Sister Mary Louise was secretary of this Emmitsburg community of the Sisters of Charity so her position called for sleeping quarters near those of Mother Ann Simeon. In fact, their room was one, divided only by folding doors.

Mother Superior was in bed, though not yet sleeping. Sister Mary Louise was still up. She thought she heard unaccustomed sounds; she listened; they became clearer. She moved to the window and looked out; lights were flickering on the hill toward the tollgate and the sounds became more distinct—yes, horses, horses neighing.

Mother Ann was up now too and both women dressed hurriedly.

"Soldiers," the other woman said sharply.

"Whose?" asked Sister Mary Louise.

They crossed the lawn to the Academy building before Mother Ann answered: "We're in Maryland. Who knows!"

The black-clad nuns slipped across the porches and fairly ran up the exterior staircase that led to the Children's Infirmary. Ever so quietly, they stole up to the observatory over the music rooms and were soon joined by other sisters who had heard noises too.

From that high point, they stood looking through the dark at the lights of what seemed to be a vast army encamped in the fields around St. Lazare's, where the priests lived.

Within minutes, Mr. Brawner, the overseer, who lived with his wife in a small house between St. Joseph's and the tollgate, came calling for Mother Ann.

"It's okay, Mother Ann. The soldiers asked whose farm this was and I told them it belonged to the Sisters of Charity. They wanted to turn their horses loose in the clover fields. I couldn't very well refuse them."

"And whose solders be they?" the old woman asked.

"Why, Yankee blue, mam. Heading north to stay between Robert E. Lee and the White House."

• • •

Daniel Skelly was in that miserable period of life being old enough to work but too young to go to war. He was employed by the Fahnestock Brothers and had been in New York with older Fahnestock workers—well, really buyers they were—since early June.

Daniel, Thaddeus Slentz and Edward Craver left New York City on Friday morning, June 26 and reached Hanover late that afternoon, where they expected to change trains for the ride into Gettysburg.

It was five o'clock when a train bulging with people pulled in from Gettysburg.

"Last train out; Gettysburg is being raided," a woman herding four children replied when Daniel asked what was happening.

"Well, doesn't that beat all," Slentz fumed, slamming down his carpet bag. "Guess we'd best hole up here tonight."

Daniel was up early on Saturday, shaking his older companions and urging: "Let's get going. No Reb's gonna scare me out of getting home."

The three were in the express office, making sure the goods they'd bought were headed in the right direction.

"Don't quite understand why the Fahnestocks are moving stock to Philadelphia for safekeeping whilest we're bringing more goods in," Daniel remarked.

"Well, boy, stuff we bought they need to sell right away. Things they shipped to Philadelphia were long-term stock. Didn't need all that right away so there's no sense in leaving it sit around for the Rebs," said Craver.

They were still in the express office when Confederate cavalry rode into Hanover.

A tall, bearded sergeant and two other lanky soldiers hitched up outside and strode into the express office. They looked briefly at the three Gettysburg men but didn't say a word.

Daniel watched as they sifted through packages, opening some and throwing others. One of those opened contained men's gloves. The label read: FAHNESTOCK BROS., GETTYSBURG, PENN.

"We'll appropriate these items," the sergeant announced as they carried gloves and several other packages out of the office. "In case anyone asks, just say they were picked up by White's Cavalry."

The Gettysburg men waited until the Rebel troops rode out. Then they hightailed it for the railroad, found a handcar on a siding and started pumping for home.

They were rounding a bend near New Oxford when Daniel spotted the bridge over Conewago Creek.

"Whoa," he yelled. "Rebs must have burned this one out."

"Right, gents, only a nice ten-mile walk from here. We'll be home by five," shouted Slentz, jumping down from the car.

And at five, as they plodded into town, they learned for the first time that they were probably trapped. Confederate cavalry east in the Hanover area; troops north advancing perhaps at this very minute toward the state capital; and what could be the rest of Lee's army to the west, nestled in the protective bosom of the Allegheny Mountains.

"They could march in here any minute," Daniel said to his father. "And where's the Army of the Potomac? They're supposed to be fighting Lee."

Old Mr. Skelly shrugged his shoulders.

The sisters of Charity could have told Daniel Skelly.

As Sunday, the 28th of June, dawned over Emmitsburg, Maryland, Mr. Brawner and his wife fed soldiers coming in throngs to the little house near St. Joseph's.

The Brawners weren't worried. A Union officer had posted guards around the house, and over the ground.

"Fagged out with fatigue and hungry as wolves," Sister Mary Louise murmured to an aide as they passed among the troops with long loaves of freshly baked bread.

"Would you like something to eat?"

"Glad to get it, mam, but couldn't take it unless the captain of the guard gives permission."

It didn't take long to get permission nor much longer for the ragged troops to scare up some hot coffee to wash down large swatches of warm bread.

• • •

The nuns and priests were busy that day with services for their parish, the children at the academy and thousands of men and boys in blue.

In Gettysburg that morning, Harriet Bayly used a mule to pull her family in a wagon to Sunday services.

On the way home, she stopped with neighbors to have Sunday school lessons in the country school house.

"Might as well take 'em home, Mrs. Bayly. Kids are too keyed up with this Rebel business to learn much," the superintendent told her.

Sallie Broadhead left church in time to see hundreds of Union cavalrymen pass through town.

"Seems like this long line will never get through," she remarked to another churchgoer as they waited to cross the road. "I hope they catch the Rebels and give them a sound thrashing."

Salome Myers saw them too and rushed home to tell her folks.

"Must be thousands of cavalry which just passed through. Said they're a division in Hooker's Army. They stopped east of town and sent out pickets. And they said that advance pickets of Hooker's Army moved in earlier, but I didn't see them.

"But I was glad to see our noble-looking Union troops; quite a contrast to the dirty mean-looking Rebels who call themselves 'southern chivalry.'"

It was raining fiercely when Salome arose on Monday. She thought first of the coming Fourth of July holiday. Holidays were always fun. Good fun; good food; good friends.

The feeling lasted until she got downstairs.

"They say the Rebels are near again, Salome, and our cavalry has gone to meet them," her mother announced.

"God be with them," Salome said solemnly.

By evening, Salome could see the glow of campfires in the mountains to the west again. She told her father about the lights.

"I'm told that our men in great numbers are advancing from Frederick and we may expect a battle both near and soon. God help us, for surely our cause is one of justice and humanity," Salome said.

"Aye, daughter, and the Rebs say the same," Mr. Myers remarked as he picked up the June 29th edition of the *Compiler*.

"Look at this. A body would think nothing was happening around us. George Eckenrode has his political announcement on the front page. Listen to this political talk: 'At the solicitation of numerous friends I offer myself as a candidate for sheriff at the ensuing election subject to the decision of the Democratic county convention. Should I be so fortunate as to be nominated and elected I pledge myself to discharge the duties of the office to the best of my ability.'

"Wonder if he could arrest all the Rebs for raising a ruckus?"

Mr. Myers laughed at his own humor but Salome found nothing funny in it at all.

"Well, my girl, perhaps this suits your mood better. It says here: 'Gettysburg Marble Yard, Meals and Brother, East York Street. We are prepared to do all kinds of work, such as monuments, tombs, headstones, etc., at the shortest notice, and as cheap as the cheapest.'"

"Father, that's downright morbid."

Mr. Myers turned the page without a comment.

"Ah, it says here that Colonel Staley of the 87th Regiment, Pennsylvania Volunteers, arrived here yesterday to recruit men. I didn't notice any recruiting hereabouts."

Mr. Myers mumbled aloud as he skimmed down through the page two war news:

"City troop of Philadelphia arrived yesterday a week ago . . . fine body of mounted men . . . furnished own uniforms . . . yes, yes.

"Now then, here are the true facts. Rebs captured 40 men of the 26th Pennsylvania Volunteers last Friday . . . 150 troopers from White's Cavalry . . . Georgia brigade of between 2,500 and 4,000 . . . several hundred more cavalry and a battery of artillery that evening . . . Rock Creek bridge burned . . . 17 railroad cars burned. Hmmm, hadn't heard this before. One of those railroad cars had stores for Colonel

Jennings' regiment and another had a lot of muskets. They didn't take the guns; just burned the car. Guess they didn't have ammunition to fit those muskets.

"And look, they burned Thaddeus Stevens' iron works at Caledonia last Friday. Oh, and it says that of the 40 men captured, 36 were paroled."

Salome was listening intently, drinking in every word as her father dug scraps of information from the columns of the newspaper.

"Did you hear," he continued, "that a Reb was captured on York Street at noon Saturday by one Sergeant George Glynn of Hunter's Cavalry. Listen to this:

" 'The Reb was dressed in a blue coat with gray pants and was riding leisurely along when Sgt. Glynn gave chase. Glynn fired. It was a Rebel chaplain. Soon after, another Reb was captured; he was a dispatch bearer.'

"Let's see, what else. Ah, it says there was a large body of Rebs at Mummasburg Friday night, probably at least 10,000, and General Ewell was reported with a force at Shippensburg that same night.

"Well, lots of news, eh, Salome," he said, handing the newspaper to his daughter.

She continued reading, but only those things which did not smack of war.

"Here's an advertisement from Strickhouser and Wisotzkey. 'Receiving from the city twice a week suited to wants. Fresh and salt fish, hams, shoulders, sides, hominy beans, salt, apples, potatoes, oranges, lemons, confections, tobacco, segars. Baltimore Street. Wanted, butter, eggs, lard and other country produce.'

"Here, Papa, you can go shopping. It says here: 'Do you want a nice Joe Hooker hat? Call at McIllhennys'.' "

"Yes, Salome, just what I need. A Joe Hooker hat. Probably well-designed but poorly made."

Sallie Broadhead braved the rain to walk to the station to see if there was further word of Joe. She left Mary at Mrs. Gilbert's.

"Our cavalry came up with the Rebels at Hanover and had

quite a spirited fight," Sallie told her neighbor when she returned. "Some men at the station say their infantry had reached York and had taken possession, as they did here, and demanded goods, stores and money, threatening, if the demand was not complied with, to burn the town. Dunce-like, the people paid them twenty-eight thousand dollars, which they pocketed and moved to Wrightsville.

"A company of our militia, guarding the Columbia bridge over the Susquehanna, retreated and fired the bridge, which was entirely consumed, preventing the enemy from setting foot on the east bank.

"But I can't help wonder, Mrs. Gilbert, how long we'll be able to hold off these threats before they kill us all."

That night, Billy Bayly and his father rode back to their farm.

"Rebel cavalry passed us while we were hidden in some timber and bushes," Joseph told his wife. "I had to return now; I was quite anxious about your welfare with so many soldiers around."

Harriet smiled against her husband's massive chest as she welcomed him back.

"Look there," Joseph said pointing west. "Look at those camp fires in the mountains. That's just eight miles away. Looks like more, much more than last week. Looks like they're up there in force."

To the south, at Emmitsburg, the Army of the Potomac was concentrating thickly in the neighborhood, thought Sister Mary Louise.

There were encampments everywhere, including a large force in the woods next to the nuns' garden.

"General Meade has made the Fathers' house his headquarters," Mr. Brawner informed Sister Mary Louise.

"Meade? Who is Meade? I thought this was part of Hooker's Army of the Potomac," she replied.

"T'is the Army of the Potomac, mam. Only thing is Hooker was relieved of command yesterday. George Gordon Meade is the boss now."

The nun continued on her walk to see what she could do for this never-ending blue streak of humanity. Soldiers flooded the land, but they were polite. The place being under martial law, how could they be otherwise, she thought.

She noticed that many took advantage of the opportunity and went to confession. Father Gandolfo heard them in the Stranger's Chapel and Father Burlando in his room.

"Poor fellows," she heard Burlando say later. "It may be the last chance for many of them."

But Sister Mary Louise wasn't involved in confessions. Her task was to serve. That service on this day was extensive and she told Mother Superior about it that evening.

"Sister Stokes does a marvelous job as head of the farm. Why today, as squad after squad of soldiers succeeded each other, and all going away liberally supplied, she knew that the ordinary quantity of bread baked for the community could not suffice for such a disbursement. So she went to the bakehouse to see if anything was left for the sisters' breakfast. To her great surprise the baking of the day was yet untouched. They had been feeding this vast concourse out of the ordinary portion prepared for themselves."

"Perhaps a little miracle of our own, Sister?"

# CHAPTER
# 5

# Storm Clouds

Sallie Broadhead turned and tossed that fearful Monday night. It was one a.m. Tuesday, June 30, when she heard the tapping on the front door. Sallie froze.

Is there a gun in the house? What if there were? I couldn't shoot anyone, she thought.

She squirmed out of the high bed as if the floor were made of egg shells and almost crept to the window.

"Sallie, Sallie, love," she could hear a voice faintly calling.

"Joseph?" She was opening the window, not knowing whether to smile or cry. "Joseph?"

"Aye, love, t'is me, home again."

She fairly flew down the stairs to unbolt the heavy door. It took two minutes, no, more like four, maybe five before she would let go of Joseph and let him speak.

"How? What?" She didn't know what to ask first.

"Settle down, girl, and I'll tell you. Rebs caught me but

treated me well for several hours. Then they got a chance to get one of their own back but didn't have any Union troops to bargain with. So they gave up two of us civilians for their man. Well, they paroled me; made me promise I wouldn't come back to fight them. With all the Rebs in the area I figured I'd better head north to stay away from them. Thought if I got nabbed again I might not be so lucky.

"So I hitched rides to Harrisburg, thinking I could get word there on when this area was cleared out so that I could get back to you. We got word there early yesterday so I started walking from the city at 9 o'clock Monday morning. And do you think I could get a ride? Saw no wagons on the road and the occasional horseman who came past was heading north. I did hear some horses heading south after dark but didn't know but that they might be Rebs so I hid in the brush till they passed."

Sallie squeezed him again and whispered in his ear, "You'll never now what good spirits you've put me in but the idea now is get you to bed—to sleep. You look so fatigued."

Joseph couldn't argue. He wasn't accustomed to thirty-six mile hikes.

The Broadheads arose late on Tuesday morning. The sun was well up and blanketing the rising ground in and around the village.

Joseph stuck his head out the second floor window. He glanced to the left; few people were on the streets for a Tuesday. Then he looked to the west and knew why. On the hill overlooking his house he could see the bright sun glancing off muskets and horses and gray uniforms.

Sallie looked too, but reluctantly.

"Every moment I expect to hear the booming of cannon. I can't help but think they'll shell the town," she said.

"They're only reconnoitering the town, love. They'll make an advance if there's no force to oppose. But as I was walking in last night I heard talk up on the Diamond that there was a heavy force of our troops within five miles, cavalry, they said. That'll scare the Rebs off for a while."

Sallie was not convinced.

"It begins to look as though we will have a battle soon, and

I am in great fear about that," she said in a deadly serious tone.

"And, oh, Joseph, I read in the *Compiler* yesterday that General Hooker had been relieved. The change of commanders in the Army of the Potomac, I fear, may give great advantage to the enemy. Our army may be repulsed."

Joe could only hold his wife then, for he had no more answers that might calm her fears.

The cavalry Joe Broadhead had heard about showed up in Gettysburg at noon that Tuesday.

Salome Myers thought there were several thousand as they trooped enthusiastically through town. She was one of those who sang for the gallant troopers and the horsemen cheered in return.

But the movement of such a large group of Union regulars— not militia—also meant that trouble could be expected . . . serious trouble. When Salome got home, she scribbled her thoughts into her brimming diary:

"We feel utterly defenseless . . . Children and women went about wringing their hands, alternately bemoaning our impending fate and praying for deliverance. Many of the remaining men and darkies left today. Jefferson has gone to Harrisburg and father hunted up an old gun, loaded it and left it in the house and then went out to hear what could be heard. Mother said, 'There is this gun ready loaded for the Rebels to shoot us.'

"In the midst of our terror we laughed, for not one of us knew how to handle a gun."

Mrs. Myers and her daughter weren't alone in their uncertainty.

Harriet Bayly didn't have close neighbors on the farm but word did travel along Table Rock Road.

"The whole air seems charged with conditions which go before a storm," she suggested to her husband. "Everybody is anxious; everyone is asking what is going to happen and what will we do if the worst should happen?"

Joe Bayly had no answers either.

• • •

Three days had now passed since the Union army's forward units arrived in Emmitsburg. Father Burlando still was doubtful of soldiers, any soldiers. He spent every night outside the convent, scarcely resting. At the least sound, he appeared.

Mother Superior felt his concern too. Each night she posted two sisters to patrol the house—inside.

"Keep all dark after the usual hour for retiring so that our guards outside might not know there are guards within too," she told those going on night duty.

The captain of the guard had posted a soldier at the foot of the steps leading down from the kitchen to the pantry and another at the corner of the infirmary.

Sister Mary Louise wondered who was protecting whom from what.

On this Tuesday evening, Father Burlando learned that the Sisters of Charity had been given a requisition from a colonel to have a large amount of bread baked within a certain time.

Mother Superior was furious.

"Even if we sat up all night and baked, we could never prepare such a quantity of bread as was called for," she complained to the priest.

Burlando walked into Emmitsburg immediately and asked to see General Meade.

"The general is asleep and cannot be disturbed. What's your business?" Meade's secretary said gruffly.

When Burlando told him it concerned the baking of bread, the secretary became even gruffer.

"The general will have nothing to do with that. He would not act in the matter even if he were awake," he half shouted even as he was reading the requisition Burlando presented.

Then in a calmer voice, the secretary advised:

"Looks like this was made without proper authorization. Take it down the street, to the commissary, Scofield."

Burlando got the matter cleared up when Scofield, indignant at the sight of the paper, told him the requisition was illegal.

"Don't give those soldiers anything; they're amply supplied with stores."

And with that, the priest started back to the convent with the good news.

Henry Jacobs had heard about the Rebs being out to the west of town again. He climbed up into the dusty attic, forced open the garret window and got a clear view up the Chambersburg Road leading to the mountains.

With him he carried a small telescope his father had borrowed from the astronomical department at the college. His father, finished now with college classes for the summer, joined him.

Henry peered through the powerful glass.

"Ahh, I can see on the top of the hill a considerable force of Confederates. Looks like they're coming down from the mountains.

"Wait, what's this? On the summit, father, it looks like a group of officers. They seem to be sweeping their horizon with their field glasses. Would be funny to think one of them is looking at me as I look at him."

"Anything else?" Professor Jacobs asked.

"Ahh, yes, back of the officers, but largely hidden by the shoulder of the hill, I can distinguish both infantry troops and some artillery.

"But nothing else appears . . . whoa, hold on. Those officers on the crest of the hill are turning and riding back."

At that moment a roar of shouting arose from the street below. Henry and his father ran down to the second floor front bedroom, threw open the window and looked into the street.

"Union cavalry, en masse," Henry yelled and turned from the window hitting the steps three at a time. He flung open the front door and was talking to a trooper who had stopped nearby when Professor Jacobs caught up.

"It's General John Buford's divison," Henry shouted to his father, "coming up the Taneytown Road."

"We got two brigades here to give the Rebs hell," the trooper who had stopped told the father and son.

An officer came riding up and demanded street names and the best road to the Confederate position. When he got the

information he shouted orders to other officers who had
followed him.

"First brigade keeps going up this street—Washington
Street—till they get out of town; then hold them there until I
find out what the hell Buford wants to do. Second brigade goes
up another block or so to West York Street, then left till they
clear town.

"Move it, dammit, move it!"

The junior officers whipped their horses and began, almost
simultaneously, to yell out orders.

The trooper remained at the intersection outside the Jacobs'
house. Henry learned that his job was to keep rear units moving
in the right direction and not right or left onto Middle Street.

"You seen the Rebs out to the west?" he asked.

Henry nodded his head up and down.

"General Pettigrew's men, South Carolina men. Poor bug-
gers, most of them, we's told, are shoeless. That's why they're
headed this way; they heard there was a warehouse full of
shoes here. Takin' the shoes off'n a foot soldier is liken to
takin' the horse away from me," the trooper said, with a smug
look on his bearded face which showed obvious pleasure in
knowing what was going on.

With Union cavalry moving out the Chambersburg Pike,
Henry felt safe in getting a closer look. He walked the half mile
from home to the end of town and then up the rise to the
Lutheran Theological Seminary on Seminary Hill. He climbed
the stairs to the third floor of the large brick building and then
up to the narrow stairs which led to the cupola on the roof.

With his telescope the whole horizon could be brought into
view. Henry began an examination of the mountains to the
west.

Wherever he saw a clearing, he also saw smoke curling up.
And around the campfires he could plainly see men walking,
attending to camp chores, cooking—all the activities of an
army held in leash.

They show as clearly as though they're not more than a
couple of hundred yards away, Henry thought. And below him,
on Seminary Hill, were Buford's men, hundreds upon hundreds strung out in a wide arc from the seminary to the north.

Henry felt like the captain on the bridge of a great ship of war with his men clustered at his feet.

As Henry Jacobs kept his vigil, Daniel Skelly was busy delivering an order from the Fahnestock store on West York Street. It was 4 p.m.

In front of him, in the middle of the intersection of Washington and Chambersburg Streets, sat an impressive-looking officer on horseback, entirely alone, facing west and obviously deep in thought.

Daniel asked a soldier standing next to him if he knew the officer.

"Yep, that's John Buford, General John Buford, best damn general in this here army."

Daniel was doubly impressed. What calmness; what a soldierly appearance, he thought.

The only thing that bothered him was the general's coat. He had never seen a soldier dressed like that. It's like a hunting coat, he thought.

"What's he doing?" Daniel inquired.

"Deciding where to place Gamble's brigade and Devin's brigade," the soldier answered. "That man is a professional; knows what he's doin'."

Daniel felt he would sleep more easily that night.

"Looks like you boys got this one well in hand. Expect we won't be seeing much more of those Rebs."

The soldier didn't answer.

"It was a novel and grand sight, wasn't it, Daniel?"

He turned around sharply to see Tillie Pierce coming up the street.

"What was?"

"The cavalry coming up Washington Street earlier. I've never seen so many soldiers at one time. They say there are 6,000 of them. But they're Union soldiers and that's enough for me, for I know now that we have protection. I feel they're our dearest friends."

Daniel just shook his head. Young girls are impressed so easily.

Tillie continued:

"Some of us girls were standing down at High Street when they passed by. We wanted to encourage them so my sister started singing the old war song, "Our Union Forever". We didn't all know it so we just kept singing the chorus.

"And it helped to cheer our brave men. We felt amply repaid when their faces brightened and they cheered and thanked us."

"That was nice of you, Tillie," Daniel said matter-of-factly. "Good day." And off he marched.

The movement of such a large body of Union troops had stirred the patriotic blood of the civilians.

Anna Garlach and her parents invited some of the troopers in and fed them until the pantry was virtually empty.

"Come back tomorrow and we'll have a good dinner for you," Mr. Garlach told the last few, who hadn't gotten as much to eat as the earlier arrivals.

Young Gates Fahnestock was much too excited that day to eat at home. Along with several other boys, Gates walked out to Buford's camp on Seminary Ridge.

"Let's go back out tomorrow morning, real early," Gates suggested as they walked back home. The boys smiled and nodded.

Carrie Sheads saw the boys walking past her school on the Chambersburg Pike. As an educator—principal of the Oakridge Seminary—she knew the children of Gettysburg were caught up in the excitement; she prayed fervently that they would survive but she knew that the armies included boys not much older than Gates and his friends.

Carrie Sheads had dismissed anxiety as report after report of an invasion drifted through town that summer. In fact, she had become indifferent to the idle rumors.

But I feel differently about this situation, she thought, looking a scant two hundred yards to the west as Buford's cavalrymen spread north and south along a line of battle.

Miss Carrie had established the boarding and day school for young ladies in the brick house her father, Elias, built just for that purpose. Elias was that kind of father to his three daughters and four sons.

Most of her students had come from the southern states, so

the war had cut deeply into her work, though that didn't hold a candle to the tragedies that had befallen the Sheads family.

David, the oldest son, had contracted tuberculosis in the army and came home to die. Elias had both feet shot off in battle and died in an ambulance. Robert had been seriously wounded in the neck, was discharged and now lingered on in poor health at home.

But Carrie's parents had been hurt worst of all when Jacob, the youngest son, ran away to join the army after his father refused him permission to enlist. Jacob caught the mumps and died in camp.

Carrie and her sisters and brothers were great-grandchildren of John Troxell, one of Gettysburg's first settlers. She cherished that heritage and wanted no one to take it away from her by destroying the physical property that was her hometown.

It angered her that Rebels might be on the verge of doing that very thing. But she still had a glimmer of hope and an undaunted spirit for the good of the Union.

"That will be all for today," she told the few remaining students. "Tomorrow we'll observe as a holiday to enable you to visit the camp and contribute to the comfort of the weary and hungry soldiers."

The girls beamed, stood, nodded, said in unison, "Good afternoon, Miss Sheads" and quietly filed out. They were obedient until they got to the road. Carrie listened to their squealing and laughter and jumbled words. She was only a few years older than them and she understood how they felt.

Mary McAllister closed early that day too. A spinster of 41, she had operated a general store for years. She enjoyed that because she was one of the few females anyone thereabouts had ever heard of as being the owner of a business.

Mary felt concerned with all of those cavalrymen riding through town. Besides, few people were shopping and she had little left to sell.

So she hurried back to the brick house at 41 Chambersburg Street where she lived with her sister and brother-in-law, Martha and John Scott. She enjoyed living there. It was just a half block west of the Diamond and right across the street from Christ Lutheran Church.

Yes, Mary felt very happy with her existence here. But on this day, this last day of June, she felt threatened.

Dr. John W. C. O'Neal had gotten a message that morning that his services were needed out at Shrivers farm on the Mummasburg Road for a sick man. The sick man turned out to be a downed Confederate.

"What's he doing here, Shriver?" the doctor asked.

"They said he couldn't keep up with the march and asked if he could rest in my barn. Well, the poor fella looked like death warmed over and I couldn't turn him away, doc. He's in the barn yet."

The doctor walked carefully into the smelly barn. The man lay in an empty horse stall, an old blanket pulled over his frailty.

"What's the trouble?" O'Neal asked very physician-like, as if treating a fellow townsman in his office.

"Over marched, I reckon," the man drawled slowly, his eyes rolling as he tried to focus in on the figure hovering over him. "Jest plumb tuckered out. Can't go on. Feels like I walked all the way from home—in New Orleans."

O'Neal was shocked when he pulled the blanket aside for an examination. The emaciated figure; the body sores; the swollen, blood-encrusted feet.

"Where's your shoes, man? Where are your supplies?" O'Neal asked, wondering how the Rebel soldier even got this far.

"No shoes. Socks fell apart back—in Virginny. No hat, no coat—just ma blanket and those," he said, pointing to a rusty canteen and a clean but old musket lying in the corner, half hidden by straw.

O'Neal pulled the blanket back over the gaunt figure, briefly looked at the sun-scorched face and balding head and said no more.

Outside, he told Shriver, "Do what you can for him. Food, water, rest are what he needs. But I'm afraid he's about done for. To put it simply, he's just worn out. I'm on my way to

Bream's mill to see William Myers. He's been sick and while I'm out here I might as well check on him."

"Watch out for Rebs, doc. They're crawling all over the place," Shriver warned.

O'Neal hauled himself atop his old horse, nodded to Shriver and rode off. He hadn't ridden far before he encountered a string of men marching in line, almost like they were advancing in battle.

They won't interrupt me, O'Neal thought. Old gray suit, old gray horse. Guess I look harmless enough.

He was right. They looked and then turned away. But the doctor felt that even as they seemed to ignore him there were other eyes watching him.

As he neared the old Herr tavern, O'Neal encountered a body of Confederate troops coming from the direction of Cashtown.

A sergeant stopped the doctor and then conferred with a young officer who rode off back along the column. Within minutes the young officer came galloping back and motioned O'Neal to follow him.

"General Pettigrew wants to talk to you," he told O'Neal.

"Name, age, address, profession and your business out here today, sir," another officer inquired as the man O'Neal assumed to be Pettigrew stared at him.

"I'm Doctor John O'Neal, 42. I live in Gettysburg and I'm making rounds to check some patients, including, I might say, one of your soldiers who was left in a barn."

As he talked, the young officer dismounted and was looking into O'Neal's saddlebags.

"Looks like a medicine case, bandages, a few surgical instruments and a list of names with ailments noted beside them," the young officer said aloud as he peered into the saddlebags.

Pettigrew nodded and, maintaining his gaze at O'Neal, said firmly: "Very well, my good doctor. You may go and attend to your patients."

And with that, Pettigrew and his entourage rode off and the column of infantry began moving past O'Neal.

He had ridden only two hundred yards when he heard

hoofbeats behind him. It was the sergeant again, yelling, "stop, stop!"

"In these·days, when you're told to stop, you stop," O'Neal murmured to his old horse as he pulled back on the reins.

"Pardon, sir, but the general has more questions for you."

As they rode up to the head of the column again, O'Neal saw Pettigrew standing by the edge of the road, tracing something in the dirt with a stick for the benefit of his staff officers.

"Ah, doctor, my apologies for delaying you," Pettigrew said as he kicked away whatever he had been drawing in the dirt.

"Were there any Yankee troops in Gettysburg?"

O'Neal looked him in the eye and answered: "I have no information of any Union forces being in the town."

"When did you leave town?"

"Just a few hours ago."

"Do you have any area newspapers with you?"

"No, general, I don't," O'Neal said. Then he added: "General, if I did have any matter of information I couldn't give it to you for I'm a medical practitioner and not an informant."

Pettigrew smiled.

"Very well, doctor. You may go, but only back the way we've come, not forward through the lines."

O'Neal looked back along the empty road, wondering what he would run into next and whether he was really safe out here. Having been, he thought, fully examined and given comparative liberty, he felt comparatively safe.

These men are moving toward Gettysburg, toward home, he pondered. If I leave them the next bunch I run into might not ask questions but take me prisoner.

"Can I stay with your unit, general?" he asked.

"As you wish, doctor," Pettigrew said as he swung himself back into the saddle and motioned a forward movement once again.

They moved east along the Chambersburg Pike and were passing through the gate of the tollhouse kept by the Johns girls when the advance halted. Pettigrew and his staff rode forward to where the sergeant had thrown up the halt sign. O'Neal rode up behind them, slowly.

In the distance he could see a half dozen mounted men, all in Union blue.

Pettigrew turned, his mouth screwed into a look of anger.

"Doctor, I understood you to say there were no Yankees in town. There are mounted men," he shouted, pointed ahead along the road, "and they are evidently from the town."

"I'm confused, general. I can give you no reasonable account. There were no forces of any kind in town when I left early this morning. What's there now I don't know."

Pettigrew, seemingly satisfied, turned to another officer.

"Colonel, we'll fall back. I want no encounter at this point. Move the column back to that tavern."

O'Neal was ushered back along the road, away from Gettysburg again, away from his family. They reached Herr tavern and Pettigrew ordered a further withdrawal, this time to Marsh Creek.

At Marsh Creek, O'Neal was told to dismount and his horse was led away.

"Good morning, doctor," a voice called out.

O'Neal turned. The voice, and the face, seemed familiar. But the uniform wasn't. Who did he know in the Rebel army?

"Montgomery. Doctor or major now. You and I worked together years ago at the Baltimore Hospital," the man informed him.

O'Neal never did know his first name, not even at the Baltimore Hospital. It was just Doctor Montgomery. But now, amidst the enemy, he felt he had at least one friend.

"Come, doctor, the general says I can take you back to Cashtown. You can meet our divisional surgeon, Doctor Spence."

Along the road, O'Neal thought the line of advancing Rebels would never cease. Must be thousands of them, he thought.

O'Neal spent that afternoon getting a guided tour of the division's hospital facilities and, in company with Spence and Montgomery, enjoyed a long and pleasant dinner at a nearby farm.

Toward evening, he took the Rebel doctors to the nearby home of an old friend, Doctor Stem, and was surprised to find that Rebels were camped all over Stem's property. So he suggested that they go see another physician, Dr. John A. Swope about two miles from Cashtown.

"Sorry, doctor, but we'd best return," Spence said. "However, I can get you a pass to visit your friends. It will protect you and your horse from the regulars but beware of the hangers-on. Those misfits who follow the army will steal you blind."

O'Neal thanked Spence and Montgomery for their help, waved a kind goodbye and rode off again.

Dr. Swope wasn't at home but his tenants, Mr. and Mrs. Codori, told O'Neal he could stay the night in the house.

O'Neal slept fitfully, getting up frequently to make sure his horse was still tied to an apple tree in the front yard. But the Codoris didn't sleep.

Soldiers, late in the evening, had brought flour to Mrs. Codori. They paid her in Confederate money to bake bread and biscuits.

"And that's what she did, all night long," Mr. Codori complained to O'Neal at dawn on July 1.

# CHAPTER

# 6

# The First Day

After breakfast, O'Neal left the Codoris and started back to Cashtown. In the distance, toward home, he could hear the scattered firing of muskets.

He had been told, the night before, to report to General Heth's headquarters on this first day of July. When he reached the place only an orderly was in sight and he seemed to be packing for a move.

"Good morning," O'Neal approached the soldier. "I am here to report according to a promise after permission was given me to move about last night. And to whom shall I report?"

The soldier looked up briefly and returned to his chore.

"I don't care to whom. I'm here making ready to move these things and so far as I'm concerned you can go to the devil."

O'Neal didn't argue and just sat down to watch a detachment of the Rebel army flow past.

Wah-whoom! O'Neal heard the cannon in the east.

"There goes Archer's gun," shouted one of the men marching past.

No one seemed interested in this country doctor on such a busy summer morning so O'Neal climbed into the saddle and rode slowly along the road eastward, toward Gettysburg, with the gray army.

He soon caught up to two other men on horseback, one a general.

"Good morning, general," O'Neal said, tipping his hat as he pulled alongside the pair. He quickly explained who he was and what had happened.

"And now you're trying to get home. Well, doctor, I wish you well," the general said.

O'Neal learned that the man's name was Stuart—but was much too old to be the famed Confederate cavalry chieftain. This Stuart, the doctor was told, had been in command of Maryland militia before the war. He and his orderly were en route to Baltimore.

As they got to the church above McKnightstown, just six miles from Gettysburg, Stuart turned to his orderly, said he was tired and needed rest.

"There's a Mr. Mickley, who lives just across the road in that brick house. I'm sure he'd allow you to rest there," O'Neal suggested.

And when the doctor explained that having a southern general in your house was a sure-fire method of keeping southern troops out of your front yard, Mickley quickly agreed to the arrangement.

O'Neal bid the old man farewell and kept along his route, reaching Seven Stars—just four miles from home—before finding his path blocked.

At the Marsh Creek bridge just east of Seven Stars, O'Neal found the firing to his front from both artillery and infantry just a bit too hot.

Guess I could ride around this army, he thought. And so he started, following lanes and back roads, moving north, then east, then north on angles again. By the time he got to Hamilton's blacksmith shop on Keckler's Hill, due north of

Gettysburg and within sight of the Harrisburg Pike, it was noon. Confederate infantry was moving down Table Rock Road behind him to the west and down the Pike to the east.

For minutes he just sat astride the old horse and watched, occasionally glimpsing Rebel cavalrymen moving southward, over the hills, stopping to browse now and again, as if waiting for someone or something to clear out obstacles ahead of the line of advance. O'Neal began moving south too.

He could see the Bayly farm and Meadow Valley Farm and then Boyd's school house, and soldiers, all around, in packs, in droves, pressing forward, their movement silenced by the roar of musketry to the south.

It was late afternoon when O'Neal reached the outskirts of town. He was in the thick of scattered fighting. Three cannons were in position on Baltimore Street, at the north end of the village.

Since the guns were pointing away from him, O'Neal at first didn't worry. Then he reined up his horse and thought: If these guns are pointing that way then there's a good chance that Union guns are pointing this way. He turned the tired horse to the left and got off Baltimore Street. One block east he began riding down quiet Stratton Street. At Stevens' Run he rode down under the wings of the bridge to escape what seemed to be closeby firing. When that quieted down, he continued to Middle Street. Home was a short distance away when O'Neal heard a voice call out strongly:

"Halt! You can't go through here."

O'Neal looked around into the barrel of a six-shooter held steadily by a burly Rebel sergeant.

"But I just live down there and I want to go to my family."

"I can't let you through," the burly sergeant answered.

"The man who can get me home will be rewarded with a bottle of good whiskey."

The sergeant holstered the gun.

"Let me see if I can get you permission," he told O'Neal.

The sergeant turned the corner but the doctor didn't dare move. Other Rebs had appeared at the end of the block and were watching him closely. In less than a minute the sergeant reappeared around the corner.

"I'll get you home if I'm certain you'll give me that whiskey."

The sergeant patiently waited while O'Neal's wife and their children hugged the doctor and cried and asked all kinds of questions. When the doctor glanced around he saw the sergeant nervously fidgeting with the flap on his holster.

"Whiskey. Ah, yes, it's right here."

One of the people gathered at Hamilton's blacksmith shop earlier that day had been Harriet Bayly. She wondered aloud what Dr. O'Neal was up to and he explained; then he asked her too.

"Well, doctor, I hurried through with my morning work and went to a point on the farm from which the mountains for many miles are visible and which also overlooks the valley above town. Then I came over here to see what news had traveled.

"And I can see, from the neighbors gathered here, that they're as anxious to see what was going on. We didn't see no soldiers earlier and, for a while there, it got rather quiet.

"Joseph went to a neighbor's on business very early this morning and my oldest boy, Billy, went to town with some of the neighbor boys."

With that, Harriet's Uncle Robert stepped in and said to her: "Suppose we walk out the ridge road a little ways and see if we can find out what's goin' on."

They started walking, to the southwest, generally toward the Chambersburg Pike.

"Careful out there," O'Neal shouted after them, "there's a lot of fighting going on."

About a mile away, Harriet and Uncle Robert came across a dozen mounted Union soldiers standing by the roadside. The horses looked as worn out, dirty and tired as the men they carried.

"Why don't you get them some grass from that field?" Harriet spoke up to the surprised troopers.

"Dare not, mam, 'gainst orders. We been ridin' all night but we's been told to stay away from farm fields, barns and houses. Get shot if'n you get caught."

Another trooper, older and perhaps in charge, spoke out with authority: "We been anticipating an attack in this area. You seen any Rebels abouts?"

Harriet was about to say no when a cannon shot to the south caused her to drop to the ground. It sounded like it had whistled over her head.

The troopers hadn't moved.

"Quarter mile away, mam," said the man in charge, "but it answers my question."

Then, as if by magic, thousands of men rose from the earth in the direction Harriet and Uncle Robert had been going. They had been lying in the fields to the right and left, apparently waiting for that cannon as a signal.

"Better get home," the man in charge shouted at them as he wheeled about and led his band a hasty retreat.

The roar of battle was now pounding in their ears as Harriet and the old man hurried along the ridge road.

Suddenly, from a dusty cross trail, a large group of Rebel cavalry darted out and blocked their route.

"You're under arrest," a young officer shouted, pointing his long, curved, gleaming sword at Uncle Robert.

"You hurry home as fast as possible. I'm old; they won't keep me long," Uncle Robert whispered.

It sounded like the sage advice Uncle Robert was famous for, so Harriet moved through the clustered horses without so much as a challenge.

One trooper bent down from his saddle and asked: "Any Yankees out there?"

"You go on and you will soon find out; I didn't stop to count them," Harriet shot back, her eyes narrowed to a hateful gaze.

"Madam."

Harriet wheeled about to the new voice. It was an officer, clean shaven and neatly uniformed.

"Madam, you are in a very dangerous position. I suggest you move to the rear."

"Exactly where is that?"

"Due north, madam, out that way," the officer said, pointing a gloved hand.

By the time she got back to the blacksmith's shop, Harriet figured she had passed through several thousand troopers. But they had all been on the road, between the fences, and not spread all over the fields.

"Maybe it just seemed like thousands," she told the blacksmith, who by this time had been pressed into service by walking troopers with limping horses.

At the shop, Harriet left the road and took a short cut across the fields for home. There had been a large flag pole near the shop where a flag had been flown since early in the war. Harriet noticed that the pole had been chopped down. She had to step over it on a path in the field. The flag at the end was torn and dirtied. Harriet paused and looked north, then south. All she saw were uniforms, gray, dirty, tattered uniforms, all pressing forward, toward Gettysburg.

To the south, Harriet could see only smoke and dust and masses of gray moving like waves through the green fields. And beyond, a roar, a noise soldiers who had come home from other battles had described: the roar of battle, of death and dying.

At one point, a young infantryman told her she was under arrest. But a grizzled sergeant came along, released her and kicked the youngster in the butt to move him along, southward.

Harriet's family was greatly relieved when she finally got back home. They treated her like an erring child, rather than a woman with "Where've you been?" and "Don't you know we were worried half to death over you?"

Confederates were about the farm too, some demanding food; others eyeing the stock.

A cavalry officer looking for horses asked about the unbroken colts in a meadow.

"You can have them if you can catch them," Harriet told him. Then she sat out on the porch to watch what turned out to be a short, unsuccessful chase.

Foragers had already killed most of the chickens, and even had the gall to bring the dead birds into the house to have them cooked.

One officer tried to apologize for the chicken thieves.

"Chickens! Chickens! That's the least of my worries. Look, out there," she cried, pointing a thin finger. "Out of a flock of a hundred sheep nothing remains but a few carcasses left on the hillside fields, where they had been shot and left to die."

Some of the cows had been driven into the barn and Confederate officers had done their duty in keeping hungry troops out of buildings. But the best of the Bayly beef herd was gone, including several steers just ready for market.

So between trying to hold together the remains of her farm, Harriet spent the rest of that day and part of that evening baking and cooking for her uninvited guests, and doing that begrudingly so they wouldn't tear the place apart board by board.

"Tell me, captain," she said to one officer who had been doing his damndest to protect the farm, "why is it that you southerners are marching in from the north? I heard tell that you came up from Virginia and Maryland. Did the whole army get lost?"

The young captain smiled, then laughed.

"No, mam. We'd gone up through Carlisle and were heading for Harrisburg when we got orders to converge on this area. Does seem kind of strange though. Your army is moving up from the south and here we are, coming down from the north."

Harriet watched, fascinated by the units which had moved through. And now, late in the day, the stragglers were trying to catch up or were being threatened by officers on horseback with huge, whirling swords, admonishing the slow movers to "hurry along or, by gawd, I'll cut off your legs at the knees and you'll have to crawl home."

"There's been scarcely an hour during daylight that large bodies of Confederate troops haven't moved along the public road or across the farm from the Carlisle to the Newville road," she told Billy. He'd noticed too.

Even stragglers were in fair humor. They could see the prospect for victory ahead and perhaps a few days of rest living off this rich farm country.

One bearded veteran, his rifle slung across both shoulders and his arms entwined around the stock and barrel, called out as he strode past:

"We're sure to win this one, lady. The seat of this war is gonna be transferred from the south to the north."

As he chuckled at his prediction, Harriet wasted no time in shouting back:

"Oh, yes, you boys are well fed. You have been living off the fat of the land for several days and feel very hopeful, no doubt. But why are you not in line of battle fighting to make your prophesy sure?"

"There are enough to lick the Yanks without us," the veteran shouted back, still laughing.

And a man walking beside him offered another excuse: "We have to stay back here. We belong to the hospital corps."

That night, when many of the soldiers came begging for supper, Harriet noticed a great many of them had also asked for a handout that afternoon.

"A lot of your men are shirking their duty," she whispered to the captain. "They're not moving south at all. They're just loafing in my yard."

"I'll look into it immediately. Thank you, Mrs. Bayly."

And as he walked off the porch into the gathering darkness, Harriet clenched her fists and said to herself: Oh darn, now why did I tell him that? He'll get those men moving and that'll put more of their soldiers into the fight. Darn.

With the captain outside, Harriet felt relatively safe. Still, she wished her husband had come home. She did not tell the children but she assumed that Joe had been captured. Sitting up through the night could not bring him home so she locked the doors securely and got the children to bed, all but Billy.

It was then that she learned of his adventures that day.

"Guess I better tell you, Ma, before you hear it someplace else," the teenage boy began.

"After Pa left on his errand and you went off this morning, several friends and I walked to Gettysburg. Must have been nine o'clock when we pattered up the main street and found the Army of the Potomac had got there afore us."

Harriet's weariness was melting away. She couldn't smile at this boyish restlessness because she didn't know how the story would come out. And she didn't dare scold, for the same reason, at least not yet. So she just sat at the edge of Billy's bed and listened.

"We didn't stay long, excitin' and glorious as it was to see troops swing into town, send out guards, or whatever they call 'em and then rest on their muskets for orders.

"Somebody told us we'd best go home. We could hear the guns poppin' and weren't sure which way was the best way to git out of there. But we didn't sit around trying to figure out that either. We just skedaddled.

"We even passed some of the Union guards and they'd yell at us and tell us to go this way or that way. They didn't know themselves so we figured we just had to go the way we thought best.

"Well, we got on top of the ridge, you know, up this ways from the Seminary, on the Newville Road, and we stopped for a breather and to look over the situation. Not far away we saw a couple of farms that we know but no troops in sight, just one Union guard—on picket, that's what they called them soldiers out in front of the army—pickets.

"So, we figured this was too dull after what we had just left in town. And one of the other kids said, 'What's the use of goin' home, boys? Let's go back along the ridge and pick berries. There's lots of ripe raspberries.'

"Two of the boys decided to keep headin' home but the other two and I went back along the ridge picking berries. And, I'm tellin' you, Ma, those berries tasted so good that we plumb soon forgot all about the war and the soldiers when all of a sudden—BAM!"

With that Billy threw his arms out, sat straight up in bed and bounced. Harriet almost ended up on the floor.

"For land sakes, boy, do you have to shout that loudly?"

"But, Ma, it was a cannon and the old cannonball came sailing over our heads. It lit in some bushes right near us. And then more guns, bam, boom, whiz, va-boom. We took off like three scairt jackrabbits.

"And as scairt as we were, it was truly glorious. I'd been dreaming about this day, Ma. Member last summer when I tramped fifteen miles with that regiment of new recruits from Philadelphia expecting to see a battle and all I got was sore feet from walking and a sore bottom from Pa?

"But here, today, here was a battle right at home and a bang-up show at that. Well, anyhow, we realized those cannon balls weren't comin' our way so Joey and another boy and I . . ."

Harriet cut him off quickly: "Joey? You mean to tell me that one of the so-called friends you had with you was your nine-year-old brother? William! What . . ."

Billy smiled and said, "Oh, Ma, he insisted on comin' along and how was I to know we'd get in the thick of things.

"Anyway, we perched ourselves on the top rail of a fence along the Ridge Road. We was just down the road from the blacksmith shop, but it looked all but deserted. So we were watching when all of a sudden, we see this big bunch of Rebs and clouds of dust comin' down on us from up in this direction.

"It was all we could see—soldiers and muskets and horses and dust. They had spread from the road out through the fields. Musta been thousands of 'em, wave after wave. The wheat and the corn and everything else in those fields was disappearing under their feet, like a swarm of locusts eatin' up everything in their path.

"That's when we took off again, for home, to get out of their way. We had to cross the fields in front of 'em, but I don't think they saw us or, if they did, figured we were just kids who couldn't hurt 'em. Boy, if'n I'd had a gun . . ."

"If you had a gun, you'd a better still be hightailing it home, young man," Harriet warned.

"Well, when we got home, the aunts and cousins and some neighbors thought we'd all been captured—you, Pa and me. So, they was all runnin' around here and not doin' nothin' worthwhile. So I saw to it that the rest of the horses and some of the cows were driven into the barn. But I couldn't get to the sheep before the Rebs were down on the farm too.

"They wanted me to help them catch chickens. That's when I developed a limp and they told me I didn't amount to a good hurrah as a chicken catcher."

Harriet smiled: "Smart lad, you are."

"Yes, but they hoisted me up into the cherry trees and made me break off whole branches of cherries for them. That's where all them cherries came from that you made into pies. Pa's goin' be whoppin' mad about that too. Some of them trees got so many branches broken off they won't get no fruit next year."

If Billy Bayly was one of the youngest folks to get caught up in the excitement of the day then John Burns must have been one of the oldest.

He was 73 but was still active as the town's constable and on this first day of July he felt compelled to do his duty as an officer of the law, and as a patriot.

Major Thomas Chamberlin was in the thick of the fight with his 150th Pennsylvania Volunteers on the ridge west of town, trying along with John Buford's dismounted cavalrymen and other units to hold back the flowing Confederate tide from the west and north.

It was almost mid-day when Chamberlin observed the bony-framed old man trudging up the hill, moving with a deliberate step and carrying in his right hand a rifle at trail arms.

"Look at the way that old fella is dressed," Chamberlin said to an aide. "A waist coat, swallow-tail coat with brass buttons and a, ah, ah, my gawd, look at that high silk hat. Looks like something out of the past, doesn't he?"

Chamberlin watched as John Burns moved up behind the left battalion, where the major was standing.

"My name is John Burns. Can I fight with your regiment?"

"I guess so, Mr. Burns, but perhaps we'd best check with our colonel. He's just over there, Colonel H. S. Huidekoper."

Chamberlin introduced them.

"Well, old man, what do you want?" Huidekoper demanded.

"I want a chance to fight with your regiment."

"Can you shoot?"

"Oh, yes," Burns smiled. "I was in the War of 1812. Fought with Scott at Lunday's Lane," he said, holding up his musket, which Huidekoper thought looked like it might be a relic of that war a half century before.

"Yes, I noticed your gun. But where is your ammunition?"

Burns slapped his left hand on his trouser pockets, which were bulging with cartridges.

"Certainly, you can fight with us, and I wish there were many more like you. But I want you to move over there, into the woods for shelter, not out here in the open. Over there, with our Iron Brigade, that's where I need you, Mr. Burns."

With apparent reluctance, the old man began to shuffle off toward the trees, fumbling in his pockets for a cartridge as he moved.

Sallie Broadhead, who lived almost directly across Chambersburg Street from John Burns and his wife, had been up early that morning to get her baking done before any shooting started. She had just put her bread into the pans when the cannons opened up.

"Joseph!" she screamed. "What shall we do? Where can we go? People are running here and there outside, screaming that the town will be shelled. No one seems to know what to do."

Joseph hauled his wife into his arms and brushed her hair softly.

"We'll stay right where we are. We're safer inside than outside, but I'm not sure that this house, or any house on this end of town is too safe. We should go to a house on the east side of town.

"You take Mary now, quickly. I'll stay here; I don't want the soldiers to steal what little we have."

It was 10 o'clock when Sallie and Mary scooted up the street. Sallie thought the shells were flying around quite thickly, although she saw none land. But, for the first time, she saw another horror of war; wounded men were moving up Chambersburg Street, into town, away from the fighting.

Bloodied shirts and pants . . . filthy bandages . . . limbs hanging limp . . . over there, a man whose eyes were covered with a red-stained rag carrying another man whose eyes were strong but who would never walk again on two legs . . . moans . . . screams when pain became too severe to go on further.

Sallie hurried on, wanting to stop and help but knowing that she must first get Mary to safety.

For the first time, really and truly, these pitiful remnants of men began to make her realize her fearful situation and forced her to ask one bandaged soldier: "Will our army be whipped?"

The soldier looked up, glanced down at Mary and smiled,

then looked at Sallie again: "See them Reb prisoners being brought up the street?"

Sallie looked down past her house. The street seemed to be full of gray-coated troops, their arms empty of guns, trudging along and surrounded by trigger-ready Yankee guards.

"Yah never seen such a dirty, filthy set in all your days? Naw, lady, we ain't gonna get whipped. Not today, leastwise," the soldier said as he moved away.

Sallie stopped for a moment to look back at the approaching prisoners. All kinds of clothing; most of it ill-fitting. Many were barefoot. A few were wounded.

Sallie's first reaction was pity. These men, though Rebels, were suffering. Dirty, exhausted, hungry, wounded, captured—hopeless.

Mary and her mother soon arrived at the home of a friend a few blocks away and the girl was safely tucked away inside. But Sallie couldn't stay in, not after what she had seen.

She took a bucket of water and some clean rags and sat out at the doorstep. And she got so wrapped up in cleansing the wounds of passing men that she soon forgot her fears, even as artillery units and fresh infantry troops rushed down the street, moving west, to reinforce the Union line.

Such bustle and confusion, Sallie thought, but she worked on.

She had lost track of time when she suddenly noticed that the men moving into town from the west were coming now not at a slow walk but on the run. And they weren't wounded, at least not most of them.

A man in civilian clothes whom Sallie recognized as a local resident came riding up the street on a lathered horse, shouting to all outside: "Retreat! It's a retreat! For God's sake, get into your houses! Rebs are at the other end of town! We'll all be killed!"

The chalk white color of the man's face, the beads of perspiration on his forehead, the wide eyes and screaming voice as he stopped in front of Sallie did as much to frighten her as his words.

She ran inside the friend's house and they quickly moved everyone to the cellar. Outside they could hear the running troops, the galloping horses, the caissons hauling guns back through town. Through it all cannons and muskets were firing and that firing was getting closer and closer.

There was a brief pause in the running noises and Sallie peered out between the iron grates in the tiny basement window. Except for a straggler or two and bodies strewn about the street, it looked like the place was empty of Union troops. But then came more running and shouting and Sallie saw, this time, gray uniforms rushing past, sometimes stopping to reload and fire, and then run again.

Hours passes; no one knew how many exactly. Then the firing died down and seemed to be coming more from the south of town than the west.

Finally, Sallie could wait no longer.

"I must try to find Joseph," she told her friend. They crept upstairs and Sallie opened the front door ever so carefully. A Rebel corporal was sitting where she had sat earlier; he was bathing his dirt-caked feet in the bucket she had used to clean wounds.

"It's okay, lady."

"Can we come out?" Sallie whispered nervously, still peeking around an inch of open doorway.

"Certainly," the corporal answered. "We won't hurt you."

Sallie opened the door slowly and stuck her head around the corner. The street was covered with blankets, knapsacks, cartridge boxes, a few rifles, some dead horses and the bodies of some men, but not as many bodies as she imagined there would be.

Sallie asked the corporal if she and Mary could return home.

"It's just a few blocks that way," she pointed.

"Lady, soon's I get these strips bound around my feet again I'll personally escort you and the little 'un there."

Sallie knew she shouldn't be helping the enemy but when she got home and found Joseph safe and her house intact and her soldier-escort not demanding anything she convinced Joseph to give the corporal a pair of his boots.

The boots were too big when the Confederate took off the rags he had wrapped around his feet. So he stuffed the cloth into the toes of the black leather and pushed some more down behind his heels.

Joseph and Sallie and little Mary watched as he clomped back and forth in front of the house proudly showing off his new possession.

"Ain't had no shoes on for two, three months now. Gotta write home to ma missus and my young un, little girl not much older than yours there, and tell 'em how kind you folks been to me. Thank you kindly," he said softly. Sallie saw the tears welling in his eyes as he turned and marched away.

"Well, love, all is fairly quiet now," Joseph soothed her as they closed the front door.

"Yes, but oh how I dread tomorrow. We don't really know what will happen," she answered.

Mary McAllister didn't plan to open her general store on this first day of July. The Rebels, she knew, were too close.

But Mary and her sister, Martha Scott, were up early this Wednesday morning. They were baking bread for, well, for anything that might come. People had to eat.

Noises outside sent Mary running to the front window.

"Martha, come see. Union infantry running at the double quick."

They could hear the soldiers calling out for water. The sisters ran to fill buckets in the backyard well and dashed back to the street. They held up dippers filled with the cool water. Soldiers snatched them, swallowed the little bit of water they didn't spill, threw the dippers back toward the women and kept running.

They had forgotten about their baking and by the time they got back to the kitchen all of the biscuits had burned.

It wasn't long after the last troops poured through the street that Mary noticed people who lived farther west along Chambersburg Street rushing past. She particularly noticed Sallie Broadhead and pretty little Mary. And close behind came the wounded.

The first wounded soldier Mary McAllister saw was being helped up the street by John McLean. John was too old to fight but he was a responsible and civic-minded Gettysburg resident and here, on this day of days for his town he was doing what he could to help.

The soldier was on a white horse and old John was holding the man by the leg. Blood was running out of a wound and down over the pure white flanks of the animal.

Mary's brother-in-law, John, had been sick and in bed, too weak to move. But he struggled to get downstairs and got to the front door. When he saw the wounded man, he fainted in the doorway.

Belle King, a neighbor, came out and helped them carry the man into Scott's house, stepping over John Scott in the doorway as they did. The horse ran off but no one seemed to care.

"Bring him in here and put him on the lounge," Mary directed. "I don't know what in the world to do, but we'll think of something. I'm sure of that."

They had no sooner gotten the man, now unconscious from loss of blood, onto the lounge when Mrs. Weikert, another neighbor, poked her head into the hallway and yelled: "They're bringing the wounded into the church. We can be of use there."

Mary told her sister to take care of the wounded man on the lounge and ran to the linen closet. She tore up several white sheets for bandages, filled a wooden bucket with water and hurried across the street to Christ Lutheran Church with Mrs. Weikert.

An officer was shouting orders: "Take those cushions off the pews and put them in the aisles."

The sanctuary was filling rapidly as stretcher bearers and those who had helped or carried wounded comrades from the field delivered their loads and stepped over those already lying down to get back outside.

Mary watched as a badly wounded officer was carried in, his blue jacket drenched in red and his eyes rolling as he stared up at the high ceiling.

The surgeon grabbed Mary by the arm, squeezed it until it hurt and shouted: "Go get some wine or whisky or some other stimulant."

Mary thought of Mr. Guyer, who lived next door. He drank. He should have spirits in abundance.

She banged on the door and then let herself in. There stood Guyer in the hall. Behind him, in a dining room, she could see a small stand with several bottles and a wine rack.

"Mr. Guyer, can you give me some wine? It's for the wounded."

"The Rebels will be in here if you carry that out!"

"I must have it. Give me some," Mary shouted as she grabbed a bottle from the rack and stuck it under her apron. Guyer did not try to stop her.

In the church, the surgeon poured a little wine into the young officer's cracked lips. The officer choked and the wine ran out of the corners of his mouth and he died. Just like that, he died.

Mary stood, as though she'd been frozen into a block of ice. She had never seen anyone die like that. She didn't even know his name, or where he was from, or anything! Dead. She had watched as his blood drained away, taking his life with it.

The surgeon moved Mary away from the corpse and told her to wet cloths and put them on the wounds of other men.

"You must keep busy, madam, for our sake and yours," the surgeon said softly.

Later, Mary told the whole story to her sister but was careful that her weakened brother-in-law did not hear.

"Well, I went to doing what they told me to do. Every pew was full by now. Some were sitting; some were lying; some were leaning on others. Some soldiers who were bringing in the wounded had torn down all the doors in the church and put them across pews as operating tables.

"The the surgeons went to work. They cut off legs and arms and threw them out the windows. Oh, Martha, the screams of those poor men who were still conscious I shall never forget."

"I heard them too," Martha said softly.

Mary continued:

"One who came was only a boy with seven of his fingers nearly off. And he said, 'lady, would you do something for me.' A surgeon came along and said, 'what is the use doing anything for them?' and he took a knife and cut off the fingers and they fell to the floor.

"I felt I could take no more and had sat in a pew to regain

my senses. Then a shell struck the roof and everyone got
scared. Someone yelled, 'they are going to shell the church.'

"That was all, Martha. I got up and left, just walked away
from all that suffering because I thought we would all surely
die if we stayed inside. Those high stone steps out front were
just covered with more wounded. I could just barely get past.
And the streets were full of soldiers, some running, some
barely dragging themselves to safety.

"An officer begged me not to try to cross the street. He was
afraid I would get trampled by the stampede. 'Oh, I just want
to go home,' I told him. But I had to walk up as far as
Buehler's drug store before I got across the street and back
home.

"Then I saw our front step covered with blood and thought,
'Oh, all are dead.' I couldn't believe the number of soldiers in
the dining room and I could see that not all were wounded. I
heard one coming through the hall behind me yelling that the
Rebels were firing grapeshot up the street and everyone had to
get off the street or be killed."

As Mary spilled out the story to her sister they both
continued to run water to wash wounds and tear sheets for
bandages.

A tall man with blood on his face interrupted Mary:

"Colonel Morrow, 24th Michigan," he said, putting his
fingers to his cap in salute.

On his forehead Mary could see a small cut and dried blood.

"Can I do anything for you, sir?" she asked.

"Yes, if you would just wash this handkerchief out."

Mary rushed to get water; she rinsed out the soiled cloth and
placed it against the colonel's sweaty forehead. Then she
asked: "What happened?"

"Just grazed, mam. Bullet just grazed me."

Next she tended to a young Irishman, name of Dennis Burke
Dailey, from the 2nd Wisconsin. Dailey was fit to be tied
because he thought they had been led into a trap. He peeked out
a kitchen window.

"Rebs out in the alley," he whispered. "No escape there."

Mary opened the kitchen door a crack. Rebels were tearing
down the fence at the back of the yard.

"I am not going to be taken prisoner, colonel," Dailey said firmly. "Where can I hide?"

Mary looked toward the stairs and quickly said, "up there."

"No, no," Dailey replied. "But I can fit in your kitchen fireplace and partway up the chimney."

Morrow stepped toward Dailey, put a hand on his arm and said: "You will not. You must not endanger this family."

Dailey's anger could be seen through his clenched teeth but he did not speak out against Morrow.

Through all this Dailey had been carrying a sword, in addition to the one strapped to his waist.

"Here, take this sword," he said to Mary, thrusting the extra weapon toward her. "Keep it at all hazards. This is General Archer's sword. He surrendered it to me. I will come back for it."

Mary held out two hands and Dailey gently laid the sword in her upturned palms. She turned to the wood box next to the fireplace, moved some sticks, buried the sword and replaced the wood.

Dailey kept up the explanation as she hid the prized weapon from view.

"You see, our Iron Brigade captured Archer this morning. Archer wouldn't give his sword to the first man to reach him because he was only a private. I was the first officer there so Archer consented to give up his sword to me."

Colonel Morrow then reached inside his jacket and pulled out a small black book with a torn leather cover.

"Here, take my diary. I don't want them to get it," he told Mary.

She didn't know where to put it so the Rebels wouldn't find it and she didn't want to disturb the woodpile again because she could now plainly hear Rebels in the back yard. So she turned her back to the men and slipped the small book into her bosom.

Morrow was not fooled. As Mary turned around, he said bluntly: "That's the place; they will not get it there."

In the meantime, Martha had been collecting the names and addresses of all the wounded men in the Scott house and had gone upstairs to fetch an old coat of her husband's.

"Here, Colonel, this can replace that tattered uniform jacket," she said as she returned.

"Thank you for the thought, mam, but I cannot do that. I cannot attempt to disguise myself. And you men," he shouted, looking around the room, "you'll act like gentlemen and give the Confederates your correct names."

A pounding, loudly on the door.

"You must open the door, mam," he said to Mary. "They know we are in here and they'll break it down."

Mary obeyed immediately.

"Oh, here is a bird," said a crusty-looking Rebel sergeant as he confronted Morrow at the kitchen door. He said nothing more as a young lieutenant pushed in beside him, looking at the colonel and demanding: "Your sword, sir."

Morrow unbuckled and complied.

The Rebel lieutenant motioned Morrow and Dailey, the only Union officers there, toward the door. Dailey refused to move until he was pushed by the crusty sergeant.

Then Dailey turned to Mary and pleaded: "Give me a piece of bread."

"I have just one piece and it isn't very good," she replied.

"That doesn't make any difference. I haven't had anything to eat for twenty-four hours and no telling when these Rebs will feed us, if ever."

Mary turned to the table, picked up a hardened piece of bread and thrust it into Dailey's outstretched hand. It was the last she saw of him.

Morrow thanked her for her hospitality, saluted and walked out the doorway.

The young lieutenant remained and looked around the room.

"You men listen and pass this to the others in this house. Those that are not able to walk we will not take; we will parole them. But if you do recover we expect you'll never fight again."

Some snickers greeted that remark.

A dozen walking wounded were marched out of the house. Then Mary and Martha rushed to get the remaining half dozen into beds.

"Get them pillows. Make them as comfortable as possible," Mary commanded.

Mary had to go downstairs to answer a knock at the front
door. Several Confederate Officers introduced themselves as
surgeons and one said:

"Our men tell us you have wounded here. Now if you had
anything like a red flag, it would be a great protection to your
house, because it would be considered a hospital. Our men
would respect it."

Martha had overheard and was already digging out a red
shawl when Mary returned upstairs.

"Mary, get a broom. We can attach this old shawl and fly our
flag."

They had tied the shawl to the broom and were getting ready
to fasten it from the upstairs window.

The pounding of horses' hooves, the yelling and then the
pistol shots made them freeze. Were they doing something
wrong?

The sisters looked down the street. Seven Rebels were riding
along like drunken farmhands in town for some fun. The
horsemen had stopped near the church across the street and had
yelled to some of the wounded Union troops who sat or laid at
the top of the church steps.

Then the shot rang out and Mary saw a Union officer, who
had come out of the church, topple down the stone steps to the
ground.

Someone on the steps was yelling: "Shame, shame, he was
a chaplain."

One of the horsemen shouted: "He was going to shoot!"

"With what, that ceremonial sword around his waist? That's
all the arms he had!" the wounded man yelled back.

Mary could see the horsemen were looking closely at the
officer. One checked the body and told the others: "He's
dead."

He said no more, climbed back on his horse and the seven
rode away.

Mary bowed her head in the window opening and cried. This
day had sapped her strength. She wondered how many more
she could endure. Then she and Martha went back to work
caring for their wounded.

• • •

The girls at Oakridge Seminary, the few who remained there, were abruptly awakened this first day of July. The school which Carrie Sheads tried so desperately to keep open was less than a good stone's throw from the crest of Seminary Ridge. It was, in fact, closer to the Seminary than it was to the Broadhead and Burns houses, near the western extremity of the village.

First came the heavy boom of artillery, soon followed by the sharp volleys of carbine and musket shots. So suddenly and without warning had the war thrown its bloody mantle about them that there was no time to withdraw to a safer spot. They could actually see men under fire atop the ridge.

Within minutes, Carrie Sheads found herself as head nurse, superintendent and chief cook of an army hospital. The wounded told her how John Buford, with a handful of cavalrymen, had held off the Confederate advance until John Reynolds, leading the Union First Corps on the run, moved to the line of defense. They told sadly how Reynolds had fallen from his horse, struck by a sharpshooter's bullet, and died. And they told how General Howard had taken command and had pulled his line back from Seminary Ridge, through town and out the other side to Cemetary Ridge.

Most of what Carrie and her girls learned came from the last men to withdraw, the men of the 97th New York under Lieutenant Colonel Charles Wheelock.

The 97th rearguard action dwindled into hand-to-hand fighting as Wheelock attempted to lead his regiment through a fast-closing hole as the Confederates maneuvered around him.

The escape route was through the grounds of Carrie Sheads' school. But the route closed and with cold steel bayonets pressing in from all sides and shells flying from front and back, Wheelock jumped up on the front steps of the small building and waved a white handkerchief.

The Confederates, in the confusion, apparently didn't see the surrender flag. The onslaught continued. Wheelock opened the door of the building and yelled:

"Someone, anyone in here, get me a large white cloth."

Carrie Sheads ripped a tablecloth from the dining room and

plunked it into Wheelock's outstretched hand. It did the trick. The firing stopped. Wheelock, by then exhausted, moved through the house, opened the basement door and went down into the coolness to rest. Several other officers followed him.

A detail of Confederates broke through the outside cellar door and a young officer, noticing his catch of officers, shouted at them:

"Stand still, Yankees. No one moves or I'll show y'all what they mean by southern grit. Y'all drop your sidearm belts."

Wheelock had been somewhat shielded by his officers and was trying to snap his sword in half when the lieutenant spotted him:

"Damn it, I said to drop sidearms. That means pistols and swords. Now, I'll take that sword, colonel."

"I'll never surrender my sword to a traitor as long as I live," Wheelock said, his head lifted up and his sword held tightly in both hands.

The lieutenant drew his pistol and said, calmly:

"I told y'all to hand it over, colonel. Now y'all do it now or I'll blow a damn hole clean through that pretty blue uniform."

Wheelock stood at attention, let go of his sword with one hand and tore open the top button of his jacket. Then he ripped open the white shirt underneath.

"Shoot, Rebel. I'd rather die than hand this sword over to you."

Carrie's father, who had rushed to the school when the shooting started, had climbed down the basement steps too. He stepped between the Confederate brandishing a pistol and the Yankee protecting his sword.

"Please, gentlemen, don't be rash," Sheads said calmly. Two Confederates pulled him away.

Then Carrie stepped in.

"Why would you want to kill a man so completely in your power?" she pleaded with the lieutenant. "There's already been enough bloodshed. Why add another defenseless victim to the list?"

Then she turned to the colonel and pleaded with him:

"Why be so rash? Surrender your sword and save your life.

By refusing to do so, you'll lose both and the government will lose a valuable officer."

Wheelock remained at attention and stared coldly at the young Confederate. Then his glare softened as he looked at Carrie and explained:

"This sword was given me by my friends for meritorious service, and I promised to guard it sacredly, and never surrender or disgrace it. And I never will while I live."

While he was talking, other prisoners had been marched into the basement and the young lieutenant turned to see what other spoils this battle had brought.

Carrie, seizing the opportunity, took Wheelock's sword from his loosened grip and hid it in the folds of her dress. When the lieutenant turned back to confront Wheelock again, the colonel smiled: "I am ready to surrender, lieutenant, but I'm afraid one of your men has taken my sword. He went up the stairs."

The lieutenant glanced toward the stairs, stared at Wheelock momentarily and hastily looked around the cellar.

"Fine. Now fall in with the other prisoners, colonel."

As they started to leave, Carrie touched the lieutenant on the arm and said softly:

"I beg your pardon, but my girls have counted seventy-two wounded men in this house. Can't you leave some of your prisoners to help care for them?"

"I've already left three," he replied.

"But three are not sufficient."

"Then keep five and select those you want,—except commissioned officers."

So Carrie selected five who seemed the worst for wear, the ones she felt would have the worst of it as prisoners. Then she and her girls got on with the business of nursing.

Young Gates Fahnestock had been up early this July 1. With some friends he had walked out Chambersburg Street, only to be chased home by a Union cavalry officer.

"Get home, all of you. This is not a picnic. You'll get hurt. Home. Now!" he shouted, turning the head of his horse toward them as if he'd run them down.

So Gates and his friends went to the Fahnestock house on

Baltimore Street, climbed to the attic, went through the small window and sat on the roof. It was a perfect view of Seminary Ridge.

"Geez," one boy exclaimed as a shell whistled high over their heads. The others looked up quickly, trying to see the projectile. Two of them almost rolled off the roof from twisting around too quickly.

"Hey, come down off there," a voice yelled at them from the backyard. It was Uncle Henry, who also lived in the house. "You kids loco? Get down. Right now!"

The rest of the morning and most of the afternoon was a frustrating time for young Gates. His friends had to go home and he had to stay inside.

It was almost 4 o'clock and the fighting had been raging in the streets for hours when someone began banging on the front door. Mrs. Fahnestock opened it immediately and a dozen Union soldiers poured in.

"Sorry, mam. Rebs are pushin'. Gotta hide for awhile."

"Go wherever you wish," she said nervously.

Gates watched as some went to closets; a few dashed upstairs and some went down to the basement. Gates could barely keep up. First he went to the cellar and thought it funny that one soldier was kneeling in the potato bin and trying to cover himself with potatoes.

Dashing upstairs he could see men under beds and behind boxes in the attic. It looked to him like a game of hide and seek in which no one, not even the dumbest kid, would have trouble finding those hidden.

And it wasn't long before the seekers came. Mrs. Fahnestock asked that a Rebel officer be present while the house was being searched to prevent damage and theft. The request was granted.

One by one the prisoners were marched out from the closets, from under the beds, from behind the boxes and, amidst a roar of laughter from three Rebels in the cellar, from the potato bin.

"Damn, Yank, I'da eaten them potatoes, not gotten under 'em," one shouted as he rolled with laughter.

The only one they didn't find was a captain from Ohio.

When the house was quiet, he came out from behind a long front room drape.

"Who's left?" he said to a startled Gates.

"Why, ah, none sir, cept you, of course."

Hearing the voices, his mother ran into the room.

"Mam, I'd appreciate you call in a Reb officer. Don't want to leave my men, so I'll surrender."

Mrs. Fahnestock was shocked: "No, save yourself. We'll hide you. Please."

"No. I'll be fine. Got taken prisoner once before down in Virginia and got exchanged. I'll be fine. They'll treat me okay. But my men have never been prisoners. I can keep their spirits and hopes up."

Gates was sent to the door to peer out and call to the first Rebel officer who passed by. It didn't take long. The Confederates were already setting up camp on the sidewalk just outside.

Gates learned that they were called the Louisiana Tigers, part of General Early's command.

"Got any hay, boy?" a grizzled old sergeant asked.

"Out in the barn, out back," Gates stuttered.

The sergeant sent several men around to get the hay. They came back with arms full and spread it on the brick sidewalk and then laid down.

Gates watched that evening from the second floor window as the wounded, from both sides, were hauled into the Court House. His mother had been cooking all day and sending bread and cakes across the street to that makeshift hospital.

One of the Tigers outside, watching the steady stream of fresh baking, asked if they could have some.

"Not until all those wounded men are fed, Union as well as Confederate," she said.

"Yes, mam."

Mother finally told Gates he would have to help run the bread and cakes over to the Court House. So with each trip Gates lingered a little longer, amazed but unafraid of the massive suffering in that building. He was fine until he witnessed his first amputation. A blue-coated soldier, fully awake but almost drowned in whisky, was screaming as a surgeon cut through the bone of his mangled arm.

Gates felt flushed. His head was light. The man's screams had blocked out every other sound. Then, mercifully, he passed out as the surgeon packed the bloody stump with old rags.

Gates ran outside and gulped fresh air. Then a remarkable feeling of self-control swept over him and he stepped back into the Court House. He was fascinated by the way the doctors and those assisting could hold their sympathy in control and allow their ability to help the wounded.

Gates felt he too wanted to do something to help these men so he tried to ignore the horror to do a man's job. It worked fine. He ran short errands, got bandages, hauled water. Then mother came to take him home.

Gates was exhausted as he left the building.

"Good night, sir," he said to a Confederate surgeon who had sent him on several errands. "My mother insists that I go home now."

The surgeon looked up, put his right hand to his head in salute and smiled: "Ah, yes, good night, my good man. Fine job you did."

Gates smiled back. Rebs ain't too bad; least some of them, he thought.

Anna Garlach watched that morning as a neighbor, Jacob Benner bundled his son, Major Daniel Benner, into a wagon. The major had been home for several weeks recovering from wounds and was, even now, too ill to move by himself.

"Got to get Dan away. Damn Rebs'll take him if'n they find out he's an officer," Mr. Benner was explaining to Anna's mother. Anna's uncle, Robert Little, and his wife decided to go too.

"Maybe you'd better come too, Mrs. Garlach, along with the young 'uns."

"No, Mr. Garlach walked up to the cemetery this morning to see what he could see from there. I must wait until he comes back," she told the old man. "But I am sending little Katie down the Baltimore Pike to a friend's farm with John Norbeck and some others."

Mrs. Garlach waited all day for her husband to return. She and Anna kept 12-year-old Will and baby Frank inside. Neighbors began to drift in too, at first to keep the manless family company and then because there seemed to be safety in numbers. By evening there were eleven, including Mrs. Hannah Bream and her daughter, several members of the Sullivan family and the McIlroy family.

There was little to do but talk and Anna told them of her day.

"I was sitting in the yard stringing beans for dinner when I heard the first shot this morning. I was frightened but I finished the beans and mother cooked them with a bit of ham. But none of the soldiers who were here last night came back for dinner. I guess they got caught up in the retreat.

"One did come back wounded. I don't know his name but he was a sergeant in a New York cavalry regiment. Before the retreat was in full swing he rode up out front, hobbled in and showed us where he'd been wounded in the calf. Mother was bandaging his leg when he noticed Union troops fairly flying by outside.

"Ye gods, we're skedaddlin'. They ain't capturin' me. Thank ya kindly, ladies," he shouted as he jumped up and pulled his trouser leg down over the dangling bandage. Hobbling back out to his horse, he pulled himself into the saddle and galloped away.

"There were more people in that street today than I've ever seen before. In front of the house the crowd was so great at one point that I believe I could have walked across the street on the heads of the soldiers."

There was water from a rainstorm in the Garlach basement and Rebel troops who had searched for Union soldiers kept telling the family to seek shelter in a cellar.

So finally, the Garlachs and the others went to the next house up Baltimore Street and immediately went to the cellar. Anna felt safer but Mrs. Garlach began to worry.

"What if your father gets home and doesn't find us? We must go home, Anna."

After dark, Anna picked up the baby and her mother led Will

by the hand back to their house. They made up beds on the floor in order to be lower than the windows and tried to go to sleep. Will and the baby finally dozed off and Anna nodded, but Mrs. Garlach couldn't help wonder what had happened to Henry.

With her family safely bedded down, Mrs. Garlach stepped out the back door with a bucket of scraps for the pigs in the stable. Along the path, at the woodshed, she heard a voice in the dark.

"Madam, here, over here. Please do not be afraid."

Mrs. Garlach knew the voice was coming from inside the woodshed but she could see no one in the darkness. A piece of wood moved.

"I am General Alexander Schimmelfennig of the Union Army, Commander of the First Brigade in General Schurz' Third Division of General Hovard's Eleventh Corps."

"What?" Mrs. Garlach couldn't follow all that explanation, particularly from a man whispering in a German accent. "Oh, never mind. What are you doing?"

"I rode into a dead-end alley this afternoon. Climbed over your fence and have been hiding in here since then. I need help to get avay."

"I'm afraid you're stuck here. There are Rebels all around us. But you are welcome to come into the house."

"Danke. No, thank you. I cannot be captured. If I stay here can you bring some food and vater?"

"I will do what I can, General," Mrs. Garlach said and continued on to feed the pigs.

Later, under the pretense of going out to the pigs again and not knowing if she was being watched, she carried some biscuits wrapped in cloth and a bottle of water in the bottom of her bucket.

Schimmelfennig, crouched behind a barrel and a stack of wood, ate slowly that night.


Tillie Pierce had just finished her noon meal when Mrs. Schriver, a neighbor, rapped firmly on the front door.

"I'm getting out of town," Mrs. Schriver told Tillie's mother. "Going down the Taneytown Road to my father's house on the east slope of Round Top. Away from this horrible fighting. Thought you might want me to take Tillie."

Mrs. Pierce quickly agreed that would be best. They packed a small bag with clothes and by one o'clock Mrs. Schriver and Tillie were walking down Baltimore Street.

"We'll go through Evergreen Cemetery. That's the easiest route," Mrs. Schriver said.

"Mrs. Schriver, I don't believe I even know who your father is," Tillie said as they marched up the hill to the cemetery.

"I was a Weikert. Jacob Weikert is my father."

"Oh yes," Tillie smiled. "I know him. Bless me, I never connected the two of you."

It was then that both saw soldiers among the gravestones in the cemetery. Union troops they were, setting up cannons in this field of the dead.

"Better hurry," one of the men shouted. "Rebs may start shelling us up here soon as they see our cannon. Go south."

Tillie glanced back toward town and across it to Seminary Ridge. She could see patches of blue and gray and butternut and sometimes the colors, amidst the white smoke, were mixed together. And she could hear the shooting.

Hand in hand, the two fairly ran down the opposite hill of the town cemetery to the Taneytown Road. A mile away they reached the Weikert farm on the plain north and east of the hills known as the Round Tops. No sooner were they inside then they heard horses and wagons. It was Union artillery. Drivers were shipping their caisson teams along the muddy road, heading north. Tillie watched from a window, her mouth open in wide amazement. Then came the infantry, wave after wave at a slow run along the firmer edges of the dirt road and some dashing through the tall grass on either side.

Tillie noticed the infantrymen, when they spied the Weikert spring, breaking ranks for a quick gulp of the cool water. She ran outside, grabbed a bucket from the porch and began carrying water from the spring to the road. Back and forth she went, countless times, to satisfy the dry throats of these battle-bound men.

Others in the family were carrying water for the same purpose from the deep well.

When night fell, the water brigade slowed and then stopped. No more men were coming from the south, but a few were beginning to wander back from the north.

The first wounded soldier Tillie saw had a thumb tied up.

"That's dreadful," Tillie cried out to him.

"This?" he answered, holding up the bandaged hand. "Oh, this is nothing. You'll see worse than this before long."

"Oh, I hope not," she said.

Tillie, in a few short minutes, found he was right. The wounded began to arrive by the dozens. The teenage girl finally ran into the house to tell someone.

"It's terrible, Mrs. Schriver. These wounded men are all over. Some are limping. Some have their heads and arms in bandages. Some are being carried. And some are even crawling. Can you imagine? Crawling!"

"I know, child. Now listen, we must help. You and my younger sister, Beckie, go out to the barn to help father."

Beckie, who was just a few years older than Tillie, led the way through the barn doors to a scene that neither expected to see.

The barn, aglow with lanterns, was full of wounded, most of them lying where they had been placed, unable to move. The groaning and crying, the struggling to move into a more comfortable position, the pleading for doctors or attendants to help them was too much for the two girls.

They ran back to the house, crying bitterly. In the kitchen stood an officer with a Bible in his hands. He said he was an Army chaplain.

"Girls, do all you can for the poor soldiers and the Lord will reward you," he told them softly.

Tillie looked up at him and his solemnity and calmness in the face of this great tragedy made her burst, unexpectedly, into a laugh.

"Oh, sir, I beg your pardon," she said immediately as the shame of her laughter swept through her inner self.

"Well, it is much better for you and the soldiers to be in a cheerful mood," he responded as he put one hand on top of her head as though he were blessing her for some good deed.

• • •

Daniel Skelly was to meet an old friend, Sam Anderson, at 8 o'clock this Wednesday morning. They had rekindled their boyhood friendship the day before when Sam and his wife came back to Gettysburg to visit Mrs. Anderson's father.

"So you enjoy living in Kentucky, do you, Sam?" Dan tried to start a conversation as they started out for the Mummasburg Road to the north.

"It's great, Dan. It's not Pennsylvania or Adams County or Gettysburg, but it really is nice."

They chattered away as they walked to a point just beyond the college building. Union troops were all over but here, in one field, was the unit in which Dan had several acquaintances.

"It's Colonel Deven's brigade of Buford's Division. Good cavalry outfit," Dan explained proudly. "Remember the unit we saw riding in yesterday? That was Gamble's brigade, same division. I understand they're out to the west."

It was while they were standing nearby that Colonel Deven got an order from Buford telling him to move west of town to help stop Confederates advancing along the Chambersburg Road.

Dan and Sam scurried across the fields to Seminary Ridge, more commonly known as the Railroad Woods because of the railroad right-of-way being cut through there.

"I'm going up to the Seminary. Maybe I can get up to the cupola. That should be quite a view." Sam announced.

"I'll stay here," said Dan, who noticed quite a few men and boys from the town gathered near the spot where railroad workers had been cutting through the ridge.

One of the men called to Dan: "Hey, Skelly, stay around. Should see a few Rebs take a good lickin'. Safe enough watchin' from here."

Dan nodded as he ran to a good-sized oak. He climbed up into a sturdy limb for a good seat for the first real, honest-to-god fighting he'd ever seen. Course he had seen Rebs before, recalling just three days earlier when he had the run-in with Reb cavalry in the Hanover express office.

He figured the shooting he could hear was out around Marsh Creek; that was three miles west.

"Damn, hope they get closer than that," he shouted to no one in particular.

One thing he could see were some Union skirmishers falling back. And on a ridge about a half mile in front of him, Dan could see some of Buford's cavalrymen dismounting and taking cover on a line which blocked the Chambersburg Pike.

He could clearly see the military bearing of Buford's men. No confusion. Everyone moving smoothly. Each fourth man taking the reins of four horses and leading them back away from the line. Troopers checking weapons and building small barricades—a few stones or old logs or pieces of fence.

The fighting was moving rapidly toward him, Dan thought as more skirmishers came into view. Suddenly, almost a solid line of mixed uniforms—some gray, some butternut, some apparently great mixtures of other colors liberally sprinkled with dirt.

"Buford's men on the ridge are engaged," Dan yelled to those below him.

Before the last word left his mouth it was drowned out by a shot and shell overhead. The artillery had opened up. One shell crashed through the top of Dan's oak. That's when he started a rapid descent.

Dan saw that he wasn't the only one running. There was a general stampede of unarmed men and boys and a great number of Union soldiers.

He started for town along the railroad cut but after a few hundred feet he slanted southeast through a field. He was nearing the Chambersburg Pike just east of Carrie Sheads' school when a thud shook the ground around him. He glanced sideways to see a cannonball twenty feet away. His pace quickened.

Dan had just gotten to the pike when several officers on horseback almost ran him down. They were rushing to the action on Seminary Ridge. A soldier sitting by the side of the road tending to a minor arm wound recognized the riders and shouted:

"It's General Reynolds. Infantry must be comin' up. Gawd, about time."

Dan kept moving toward town and could hear the courthouse bell ringing nine o'clock. The pike was now full of soldiers, many running as fast as possible away from the fight; others pretending they were fighting a desperate rear guard action by stopping now and again and pointing a rifle toward the rear. But they didn't fire and soon they'd turn and run some more.

Dan headed for the Fahnestock store. He knew the observatory on the roof would make a good vantage spot. He wondered what had happened to Sam.

He raced up the steps to the trap door in the roof and out to the spot where the Fahnestocks had built a railing and set up some benches.

Others had thought of this spot too. Mrs. E. G. Fahnestock, wife of Colonel Fahnestock, Isaac Johns and Augustus Bentley were leaning against the railing, drinking in the huge stage to the west and the play unfolding before them.

More than two hours had passed on the roof when Dan heard noise in the street below, outside the courthouse. A general and several officers had entered the building and had come back out. They were yelling that they couldn't find an entrance to the belfry atop the courthouse.

"Sir," Dan yelled, "There's a good observation point up here. Wait, I'll come and guide you up."

When Dan got down to the street, a gloved hand was shoved out and the general announced: "I'm Oliver Howard, Eleventh Corps, and I thank you for your assistance."

They bounded back up to the roof with two of Howard's aides right behind.

Howard made a careful survey with his field glass, first checking the fields and ridges to the west and northwest. Then he began to count and study the roads which poked out from the Diamond like spokes in a wheel.

"General Howard, General Howard!" a voice yelled from the street.

Howard peered over the railing at a scout on horseback. Dan recognized the man as George Guinn, a member of Cole's Maryland Cavalry and, before the war, a resident of Adams County, just a few miles south of town.

"Sir," Guinn shouted. "General Reynolds has been killed and you're to report to the field."

Dan followed Howard and his two staff officers down the

stairs. Howard stopped on the third floor to give orders. He told one aide to ride back and meet the corps, which was marching north from Emmitsburg.

"Speed 'em up. Tell General Steinwehr to occupy that hill back there, where that cemetery is. Tell him to fortify it."

He told the other aide to wait for the corps and take charge of moving it into position through the town.

"And when they get here, get them bands up at the head of the columns. I want them playing and playing lively airs."

Then Howard, outwardly calm, walked down the rest of the stairs. On the first floor he almost bumped into a very agitated Mrs. Samuel Fahnestock, the oldest member of the family.

"I can see fire in your eyes, madam, but I assure you that my men will not touch your property and will do all that is heavenly possible to keep Lee's army from touching it too."

Then Howard walked out of the store, mounted and rode up Baltimore Street.

Dan returned to the roof and found that the fighting had moved closer to town and that the streets were crowded with men, horses, wagons and some civilians.

At one point he glanced down onto Middle Street as guards marched a column of captured Confederates to Baltimore Street and then turned them southward. One of the prisoners was on horseback, which seemed strange to Dan, although he could see the stars on the man's shoulders and knew that he was a general.

"Who's that?" Dan yelled down to one of the guards.

"That's General Archer. Iron Brigade caught him and several hundred of his brigade."

By noon, Dan and the others on the roof could see shells whistling overhead. They decided to seek a safer vantage point. When he got to the first floor, a bearded captain asked that he take him to the observation deck.

"I am Frederick Otto Baron Van Fritche, Eleventh Corps, at your service," the captain informed Dan, saluting and clicking his heels simultaneously.

The trip to the roof was brief. Von Fritche looked around briefly, saluted, clicked his heels again and left. Dan was impressed.

Once outside, Dan decided to go to the Diamond.

There, one of the first people he saw was his mother scurrying across the street with two buckets of water, looking for thirsty wounded.

"Mother, this is a dangerous place for you to be!" Dan said as he took the buckets away from her.

"Nonsense, no fighting here, just wounded. You forget that two of your brothers were taken prisoner in Winchester and I pray that right now, if they are thirsty, that some civilian is giving them water too."

"Okay, mother, then we'll go down here to the McCurdy warehouse. I hear they're using that as a hospital."

Mrs. Skelly was shocked as they crossed the railroad tracks near the warehouse. Wounded soldiers were everywhere, it seemed.

"Worst ones are inside. They need the water," a doctor in bloodsplashed frock shouted as he saw the buckets. "First Corps got shot up badly this morning."

Inside, the Skellys stared in disbelief. The floor of the large warehouse was covered with humanity—the dead and dying, the prayerful and the scared; some boys too young to be away from home; some men too old to be anywhere but home.

Virtually nothing was being done for them. Wounds were not being tended to; the dying were left to die in loneliness and despair; those who might survive but didn't know for sure were left to cry, or scream or stare wide-eyed at oozing wounds.

The Skellys carried water, bucket after bucket, and did as the few doctors available bade them do to make the suffering seem less horrible.

It was one o'clock when Dan and his mother, on their way home, reached the corner of Chambersburg and Washington Streets. They couldn't cross over; the street was full of infantry marching "quick time" toward the front.

Dan asked one of the soldiers hurrying past who they were.

"Eleventh Corps, Schimmelfennig's division," came the answer.

The weather had turned hot and sultry and Dan pitied these men in their warm uniforms, carrying guns, blankets and canteens.

He could see people along Washington Street, standing with buckets of water and dippers. Soldiers were stopping, filling their mouths with water and then rushing to get back to their place in line.

Dan did what he could to help the wounded still on the streets into buildings. Scarcely an hour had passed when he noticed some of the men who had quicktimed past him at one o'clock now hobbling back into town wounded.

By midafternoon, the churches and warehouses on Chambersburg, Carlisle and York Streets were full of wounded men. Then the courthouse, the Catholic, Presbyterian and Reformed Churches and the school house on High Street were filled. Finally, the people of Gettysburg began helping, dragging or carrying the battered and shocked troops into their homes.

Dan began carrying water into the courthouse where a neighbor, Julia Culp, was helping to care for the men. Dan knew that Julia had a brother in the Confederate Army who had moved south years before the war and a brother in the Union Army.

"Best stay away from the badly wounded, Miss Culp. T'aint a pretty sight," he suggested.

It was close to four o'clock when an officer quietly circulated through the courthouse whispering to civilians that they best get home and hide in the cellars.

"Rebs are breaking through. Looks like they'll take the town," he told Dan. "Appreciate your help here but it looks like we'll have to leave our badly wounded here and pull back."

Dan saw to it that Miss Culp got home safely. Then he started toward his house further down West Middle Street.

It's all lost, he thought, as he ran along the sidewalk. God, how terrible.

At Washington Street, outside the home of Professor Jacobs, a part of the Iron Brigade was falling back. Dan saw the regimental flag; looked like the 19th Indiana.

The shooting was sporadic but Dan figured that Rebs must have been up Washington Street. A young lieutenant, one of the last men to turn the corner, felt a bullet rip into his foot.

He hobbled up the street until he got to where Dan was

standing outside the Skelly house. Dan helped him into the yard between his house and the Bowen house. The cellar door was standing open at Bowen's.

Without uttering a sound, the officer took off his sword, sword belt and pistol. He hobbled down into the cellar and hid the belt and pistol. But as he came back for the sword, Confederate soldiers ran into the yard and grabbed him.

Mrs. Skelly had been watching the whole scene from her kitchen door.

"Can't you see the man is wounded?" she yelled at the Confederates. "Let him come in and I'll tend to that wound. The poor man will bleed to death if you lead him away."

The Confederates were dumbfounded. Orders from a woman?

A sergeant who seemed to be in charge stared momentarily, motioned to Dan to help the lieutenant into the house and said firmly: "We'll be back for him, mam."

With that he ran his men out of the yard and continued pursuit of the 19th Indiana.

Dan stayed inside helping his mother care for the lieutenant and watched events from the window.

It was seven o'clock when he ventured out into the yard and peered up and down Middle Street. It had become a line of battle with Confederate troops strung out both ways as far as he could see.

Some of the troops asked if they might sleep in the yard; others asked Dan if his mother would permit them to cook some food over her stove.

"Since we seem to be in your hands now would you mind telling me where you're from," Dan asked one private who was cooking in the house.

"Well, sir, we're from lots of places but we're now in Rodes Division, Ewell's Corps."

Later that night, Mrs. Skelly was preparing for bed and said to Dan: "These Rebs act like gentlemen. I don't think we have anything to worry about tonight. Listen to how quiet they are outside."

Dan just nodded. He never even thought he'd make it

through the day in one piece. Now here he was, ready to crawl into his own bed, not hungry, not scared, just tired.

That first of July had started off normally for the Skelly's neighbor down Middle Street, Professor Jacobs and family.

The professor heard a few rifles cracking that morning as he rode out to the college for his eight o'clock class. The first hour had come to a close when a rap on the classroom door interrupted.

The Union officer in the hallway identified himself as Lieutenant Bonaparte, U.S. Signal Corps. Jacobs thought the name was appropriate for a military career.

"Sir, if you please, can you take me to the roof? I'm trying to find key locations in the area. We have reason to believe now that we may have a key engagement here today."

Jacobs, mainly a mathematician, was also a practical botanist and geologist. He knew the Gettysburg area better than most.

"I would suggest, lieutenant, that whatever else you do, you make sure to secure that hill directly across town from where we are, over there to the southeast."

Bonaparte looked through his field glass.

"You mean that hill with the stones? Oh, they're tombstones. You mean the cemetery?"

"Precisely," Jacobs said.

Back home, the professor's son, Henry, and the rest of the family were preparing to follow orders reportedly from General Reynolds that all civilians should abandon their homes and flee eastward.

Before anyone could leave, countermanding orders came.

Despite the booming guns to the west, Henry felt the second order meant that Union troops were winning the day.

It was half-past ten when he walked up the two short blocks to Chambersburg Street. Troops were moving in all directions. Fresh ones going west out the Chambersburg Pike; wounded ones straggling back into town.

Henry noticed two generals on horseback pause in front of the Eagle Hotel; they seemed to be talking quickly and coolly.

"Look, Buford and Reynolds!" he overheard a nearby soldier exclaim to the man marching next to him.

Henry thought the noise of the battle seemed to be getting closer and when he saw Reynolds and Buford turn and start galloping out toward the fighting he figured it was time to get home. His father was putting up his horse in the shed out back when Henry ran into the yard.

"Let's go up to the garret, son. Let's see what's becoming of Gettysburg."

From the garret window they could see south along the Taneytown Road. A ribbon of blue was moving toward them on the road.

As they got closer to town and the end of Washington Street the troops suddenly began to swing a half turn to the west, moving through the fields to bypass the town and heading directly for the spot where Buford's cavalry had made its stand.

"Must be Reynolds' corps, from what Lieutenant Napolean told me this morning," Professor Jacobs said. "Look, Henry, they're throwing out pioneers ahead of them."

The term was new to Henry. "Pioneers? In the army?"

"Well, about the same as civilians moving west. They're soldiers who move ahead of the main body to tear down fences and other obstructions so that the infantry can move quicker."

Henry figured that Reynolds' men must have numbered in the thousands. They were, he estimated, about a third of a mile from the house, close enough to see faces with his field glass. They were nearing the rise of Seminary Hill and spreading out.

"They're forming a line of battle," his father explained.

Henry watched the faces. Most were solemn. Some looked frightened. Many were apparently shouting. He could see heads turn as shells sailed overhead, puffed into white smoke and detonated with a bang.

From the other garret window, Henry could see to the north and by leaning out the open window to the west and east. The whole town and all its environs seemed to be crowded with happenings, all disjointed, yet all having some obvious relation to the immense panorama of strife which seemed to be unrolling.

From Willoughby Run, where he had heard the Confederate

General Archer and his whole brigade were captured, he could see the wounded moving back the mile and a half from the front to the middle of town. Before the morning ended, Henry had learned that General Reynolds had been killed, that General Howard had swung into and passed through town on Baltimore Street and that the Rebels were pushing in the Union line along the Carlisle and Harrisburg Roads.

Howard's corps moved right up Washington Street, right under Henry's window.

He marveled at how they kept the pace without breaking rank, flowing through and out into the battlefield beyond, a human tide at millrace speed.

Far down the road, behind the passing regiments, Henry could hear a roar of cheers. It rolled forward, faster than the running of the men who made it, like some high surge sweeping across the surface of a flowing sea. The roar got nearer until Henry saw a group of officers coming at a brisk trot with the cheer always at their horses' heels. Among them rode one man in a colonel's uniform who held his head high and smiled. Henry learned later that the colonel had been a Confederate prisoner, had recently been freed and was going back into battle with his men.

The Eleventh Corps moved up Washington Street to the Carlisle Pike and swung out past the college, its fierce head ramming into the battleground while its roaring tail still swished through the streets of Gettysburg.

Through the afternoon they watched from the garret.

It was almost four o'clock when Henry noticed that same Eleventh Corps, which had swept up his street at noon, now being overwhelmed, beaten and completely routed. They were fleeing back through town, in wild disorder. He could see hundreds and hundreds being surrounded by Rebel troops, others stopping their flight and raising their hands in surrender and many finding themselves trapped in alleys and highfenced backyards.

"We'd best take cover too," Professor Jacobs said softly.

The young man and his father carefully closed the garret windows, more out of custom than need, and then ushered the family into the cellar.

From a window at sidewalk level, Henry could see the legs of men rushing by. He pressed his face against the glass and peered up Washington Street as far as possible. No one was running nearby but across the street and twenty yards up he could see a Union soldier running, his chest heaving for breath. He was in full flight, not turning nor even thinking of resisting but neither was he surrendering.

Then Henry heard shouts of "Shoot him! Shoot him!"

Close behind the lone Yank were several Confederates, on the run too. A rifle cracked and the Union soldier, now directly across the street from Henry's window, flew forward and then down. He didn't move.

It was the first of several such chase-and-kill scenes Henry saw through the tiny window that afternoon. There seemed to be mass confusion. Confederates would run by and within minutes one or two Yankees would dash down the street.

Henry imagined that what he had seen from the garret was still going on—that retreating Union soldiers were getting lost in the narrow streets and alleys and the maze of backyards and fences and trying to run their way out of town in between groups of Rebels.

More than a half hour had passed when Henry noticed a lull in the stream of runners and their hunters.

All seemed quiet for a few minutes until the gathered family was collectively shaken by a thunderous pounding on the front door. Henry and his father bounded up the stairs and opened the door. Five Union soldiers fell into the hallway, slamming the door behind them.

"We're with the Bucktail Regiment, upstate Pennsylvania!" a sergeant blurted out. He stopped to catch his breath. "Burlingame here got hit in the leg." He pointed to a pale, youthful soldier whose right pantleg was drenched in blood.

"We need shelter, please; Rebs get him and they'll march him to the rear and he'll bleed to death!"

Professor Jacobs was nodding his head up and down all the time the sergeant spoke.

"Me and Scotty here'll stay with Burlingame till we can get em back. You two skedaddle while ya still can," the sergeant ordered two other men.

Professor Jacobs directed the sergeant and Scotty, with the limp Burlingame between them, to his study. Someone had pinned a piece of paper to the man's shirt. On it was scrawled: "Cpl. H. L. Burlingame, Co. C, 150 PA."

"Did that in case we lost him," the sergeant explained when he saw Jacobs examining the paper.

"Here, we'll pull this sofa away from the wall a few inches. Lay him on this blanket against the wall," he instructed them.

The high-backed, black horsehair sofa was large enough to conceal a man from obvious view, provided no one was really searching for him. They bound up the wound, stopped the bleeding and gave Burlingame some water. In his exhaustion he soon fell asleep.

While that was going on, Henry was keeping watch at the front door. When he saw Rebel troops coming down the street and stopping at each house he shouted a warning.

Professor Jacobs took the sergeant and Scotty to the cellar where he hid them behind a pile of wooden crates normally used for storing vegetables.

By five o'clock the searchers were banging on the Jacobs' door.

"Beg your pardon, sir," a Confederate lieutenant said, saluting Professor Jacobs, "but we know that Yankee troops entered many houses. We'll have to search."

The professor knew that resistance would be fruitless. He opened the door widely, saying only "of course."

It only took minutes to find Burlingame and not much longer to flush out his companions, who put up no fight for fear of harm coming to the family.

"Please, sir," Professor Jacobs addressed the lieutenant. "The wounded man would be an encumbrance to you. With that leg wound, you would have to provide him with medical care which could go instead to one of your own. Why not leave him here? As you can see, he can't go anywhere on his own."

The lieutenant stared at the foggy-eyed Burlingame and nodded.

"Take these two," he ordered.

The sergeant and Scotty shook hands with Professor Jacobs,

thanking him for his kindness to their companion, and marched out to the street.

Henry went to the door too. He glanced up and down Middle Street and knew immediately that his town was firmly in the enemy's possession, at least this part of town.

Troops outside were already setting up cooking fires and tearing down fences. Henry didn't know if they needed the wood for fires or were just being ornery.

"Y'all look mighty peeved at them fences acomin' down," a voice said.

Henry turned to see a smiling Confederate soldier in his late teens, or maybe early 20s, at least close to Henry's age.

"Makes it easier for infantry to move sted aclimbin' over fences. And we know that nobody is hidin' in the next yard, awaitin' to pick us off," the Confederate said.

"Oh," Henry answered, trying to pretend that he really didn't mind seeing the fence he and his father built being torn apart.

"Where are you from?" Henry asked.

"Dole's Brigade, Rodes' Division, Ewell's Corps," the young soldier sang out.

"No, I mean where do, er, did you live?"

"Jo-ja."

"Where?"

"Jo-ja, 'lanta."

"Georgia, oh yes," Henry stammered, finally understanding.

That night, after darkness fell, Professor Jacobs remarked to his wife: "You know, they are of course the enemy, but they're still gentlemen. They even apologized for having to tear down the fence."

Henry nodded in agreement and added: "After they had eaten dinner this evening I saw a whole row of them reading from their pocket testaments. They breathed fire and fury at their foes, and they were full of what they were going to do to the hated north, but they don't forget that they're Christian."

It got very quiet after dark, an almost merciful hush. The Jacobs family prepared for bed.

Henry opened the window in his bedroom to get what little

breeze was blowing away the heat of the day. But the open window also brought in the smells of war—gunpowder, lathered horses and men and a potpourri of who-knows-what cooking over open fires.

Henry laid down to sleep amid that still world, when from the brooding silence, out where the battle had raged, he heard a forsaken soldier crying in a soft southern voice:

"Wahta, wahta."

The plaintive cry went on and on, interrupted by long periods of silence.

The solitary cry, its anguish uplifted in the pitiless truce of the night, racked Henry's heart. He got up, pulled on his trousers and crept downstairs. Outside he found the Georgia boy sitting against the side of the house.

"Don't you hear that? Sounds like someone from your state!" Henry begged.

"Ah hear. Y'all know where that voice is acomin' from? Out there. That's no-man's land," the Georgian protested as he pointed toward the Union lines. "Ah hear, and how y'all think ah feel. Sergeant says nobody goes out. Might be Yank sharpshooter waitin' to see a shadow move and then 'bam.'

"Yeah, ah hear. Now leave me be, Yank," he said, pulling his cap down over his eyes.

Henry fell asleep with the frightful voice ringing in his ears: "Wahta, wahta."


Salome Myers had a difficult time getting to sleep that night too.

What a change in one day's time, she thought as she stared through the open bedroom window at the bright, twinkling stars.

Just that morning she had stood at the corner near her house as the Union Army's First Corps passed by on the rush. Some of the troops were cutting across the fields just south of the Myers' home on West High Street; others were moving up Washington Street and they were the fortunate ones. Salome and some girls from that neighborhood were handing out all kinds of food to the men as they swept by.

Salome thought about how the girls, herself included, sat on the doorsteps after the troops had moved through, their heads swimming with bright flashes of how the First Corps was probably, at this very moment, pushing the Rebs back into the mountains.

We just weren't prepared, Salome thought. First, the horse, blood running from its head, being led down Washington Street by a young black boy. Then that man, that soldier, held up by two other soldiers, his head bleeding too, but bandaged. A horse, then a man. Salome didn't like to think about how her stomach twisted when she saw the man. She had turned her head away and it felt like it was spinning clear off her body.

Then the wagons began moving back through town. Some had wounded men draped over them. The girls couldn't understand why the wagons would be returning. Wouldn't they be needed to help drive the Rebels away?

Soon the streets seemed full of soldiers, most of them wounded; some of them helping the wounded. Salome suggested that the girls go home and she went into her house. It was about four o'clock when a man rode through on horseback: "Women and children to the cellars; the Rebels will shell the town."

He repeated his warning over and over as he rode along, threading his horse between the horde of humanity now in the streets.

For two hours, the Myers family, joined by some neighbors, kept to the cellar.

Now lying peacefully in her own bed, Salome heard the sounds of that late afternoon concert—the rattling of musketry, the screeching of shells, the unearthly yells of charging troops and wounded men and the cries of her frightened younger sisters cowering in that dark cellar.

At one point, she recalled with a smile, some of the Union prisoners were forced to sit on the sidewalk quite close to the cellar window.

"Psst, pardon, mam," a voice hissed from the street.

Salome looked up through the cellar window to see a young Union soldier peering in the open window.

"Yes," she whispered back.

"If'n we give you our names and addresses would you write home and tell our people that we been captured here?"

Salome nodded quickly and ran to get pencil and paper.

"Wilbur Jones, 10 Market Street," the soldier began. All told, Salome took down 13 names and that very night she wrote a letter to each address.

And she helped her mother cook after Doctor James Fulton, a surgeon for the 143rd Pennsylvania Volunteers, said food was urgently needed for the wounded in the Roman Catholic Church just up the street and the United Presbyterian Church at East High and Baltimore Streets.

It had been a long day, Salome thought, so long and tiresome that she thought she could hear a voice in the distance calling for "water, water." But the voice had a southern twang.

Must be hearing things now, Salome thought as she pulled her head into the big fluffy pillow and drifted off.

Fannie Buehler had pushed aside the suggestions of friends that she flee town with her family on the morning of July 1.

"Where is safety?" she asked them. "You'd think that to go north would be safe, but Confederates are coming from that direction too."

So Fannie stayed, keeping her children inside, out of the way of some other civilians who seemed to be running every which way and officers on horseback ordering everyone to their cellars.

No, she thought, best stay here. At least we have a cellar. Much better than being on the road.

Three of her sisters-in-law from Chambersburg Street had arrived just ahead of the wounded, seeking to move away from the west end of town.

As the wounded began to pour into town, Fannie watched one of the town fathers struggling with the courthouse door. From the shouts and profanity she heard it seemed that no one could find the key.

Wounded men, wondering why such attention was being paid to a mere door when people were dying, began to look for other open doors.

"Why'ncha just bust a damn window or kick the damn door

in," shouted one bearded infantry man as he dragged his bleeding right leg toward the next building. "Them bastard Rebs'll probably tear the door off anyhows for firewood."

No one was paying him any attention.

Others, noticeably weak from loss of blood, or shock, fatigue, lack of food, or water—maybe a little of each—began banging on doors and asking for help.

Fannie had her door open before anyone could knock.

The four women forgot about the danger promptly as they started tearing up sheets for bandages.

"To the cellars, to the cellars! Rebs are going to shell the town!" Fannie heard the cry from the street. She had heard it before and had moved the children down but stayed upstairs herself. However, this time, with others in the house, she felt compelled to obey. The women helped the wounded men down the narrow steps into the cellar where light from two sidewalk windows provided just enough illumination to see the layout of the room. The men could see doorways cut into the walls on either side of the room, each of which led to another room beneath the large house. A window in the back of each room, looking into the back yard, provided cross-ventilation when open so the three rooms, though merely dirt-floored, were dry.

Fannie never did like being in the cellar. 'Like a mole, underground,' she had told David. So after getting the wounded men settled and leaving a sister-in-law in charge of each of the three rooms, Fannie went back upstairs.

Some of the excitement had passed away, she noted, though the streets were still full of people and the wounded were still being brought in. She walked through the dining room and kitchen and peered out through the back window. An alleyway led between the Buehler home and the house next door and Fannie could see Union troops lying on the bricks which covered the three-foot wide alley.

They looked dead, but they still grasped their guns. Fannie watched for a few seconds and realized that they were not dead, but were utterly exhausted and gasping for breath.

One by one, they crawled to the walled-in back porch where Fannie had often served summer evening suppers. They pushed themselves up against the walls, out of sight of even anyone passing by the back yard.

Fannie startled them as she opened the door, but all were too tired to move very far. She had a bucket of water in one hand and a long-handled dipper in the other.

"Bless me soul, an angel," murmured a red-haired sergeant who looked to be twice the age of the very young men around him. He let the others drink first while he answered Fannie's unasked but expected questions.

"Eleventh Corps, mam. We was fightin' in the woods t'other side of town. Rebs kept pouring in. Musta been thousands. Pushed us through the street across from your place," the sergeant said, pointing back toward Middle Street, between the courthouse and Fahnestock's store. "Just hadda get these boys in out of the shootin' for a breather."

Fannie's heart went out to the boys, a few apparently young enough to be her own children, if she had married at seventeen.

"You're welcome to stay here or inside. We have wounded in the cellar so it's somewhat crowded."

"Can we help with the wounded?" the sergeant offered.

Fannie shook her head, saying: "No, nothing serious there, only flesh wounds. Painful, but I think they can manage."

"Well, we'll cart our own on outa here," he said.

It was then that Fannie noticed not all the men in the alley had crawled onto the porch. She looked around the corner; at least a half dozen were still lying on the pavement.

The sergeant and his boys, now breathing easier, began to stir. They crept back into the alley, picked up their wounded comrades and disappeared again out through the back yard heading southeast, toward the cemetery.

It still seemed fairly quiet so Fannie told the wounded men to come back upstairs. It would be easier to feed them and care for their wounds upstairs, and they'd have the benefit of the sun on the back porch.

Preparations began for a meal for all. And two men, both with very minor wounds, offered their help. One was a German and the other an Irishman, Fannie learned.

The German, a man named Frey, was a Pennsylvanian, from Berks County, less than a hundred miles east. He was about 40, of a genial disposition, very fatherly in his ways and fond of children, she observed.

Little Allie, too young to understand what was going on, still required the care that a child of three demands.

"I'd like the privilege of taking care of the boy," Frey told Fannie.

"You may be biting off more than you can chew with that little tyke, but you're welcome to try," Fannie said.

Fannie never did catch the Irishman's last name but his Christian name was John and that was enough for communicative purposes.

John made himself busy building a kitchen fire, bringing in coal and wood, keeping water boiling for any purpose, paring vegetables, washing dishes and offering enough funny lines to keep everyone's spirits up.

"Mam, I don't know how you kin afford to feed these men, what with your own to feed," John said during a serious and private moment.

"There's no worry. My thoughtful husband made sure we were well stocked. There's at least two full barrels of flour, a summer supply of hams and lard, butter, eggs, coffee, sugar, tea, apple butter, and, in the garden, onions, some peas, beans, new potatoes and some old ones.

"We have no bread and I don't see how we'll have time to bake much, but we do have biscuits and, from what I'm told, that beats that hard tack you boys have been eating."

Frey and John, at Fannie's direction, moved her extension table from the dining room to the back porch and drew it out the full length. And from it, late that afternoon, the Buehler "patients" enjoyed the first square meal they'd had in weeks.

Fannie also got out a large wash boiler and John began making corn meal gruel to be carried to the wounded in the courthouse.

The meal had almost ended when someone began pounding fiercely on the front door.

Fannie hesitated, visibly shaken by the noise.

One of the wounded men turned slowly from the table and suggested, "If I were you I would answer the door at once. If you don't you may fare worse."

Fannie moved quickly through the kitchen and down the hall. At the door she was confronted by four Confederate soldiers, including one who introduced himself as Harry Gilmore.

Fannie had read about him in the *Compiler*. He was known as the Brigand Chief and was distinguishable by his cocked hat and feather. The paper said he was from Baltimore.

"Madame, you have Union soldiers concealed in your house, and I have come to search for them," Gilmore said abruptly.

"You are mistaken, sir," Fannie replied, holding her head up and barring the door with one arm. "There are Union soldiers in my house, but none of them are concealed. They are all lying around on this first floor; step in and see them."

Gilmore looked baffled but he stepped inside when Fannie dropped her arm.

"Land ah goshes," said one young Confederate as he looked around the wounded in the front room. "These here's the Yankee boys who was opposite us this mornin' on picket before we got pulled back into the line."

"Hey, Yank, member us?" shouted another.

The Confederates were smiling as they checked each wounded man in the house and on the back porch. They seemed relieved that at least none of these Yanks, whom they had faced in the early hours before the heavy fighting began, were seriously wounded.

"Geez, Reb, where ya been? You sure moved slow gettin' this far. Ain't gonna win no war movin' that slow."

The speaker was a burly private, probably no more than twenty. A bullet had passed clean through the fleshy part of his thigh.

The Confederate laughed and the whole household broke out into smiling faces. Fannie was flabbergasted.

The bantering went on for nearly half an hour before Gilmore put a stop to it.

"Alright, enough. We got a job too. I suspect you're not hiding anyone, madam, but we have to search anyway," he said with a hint of apology.

Fannie led the way upstairs. The two soldiers who followed

looked in each room, under every bed and inside each closet. Then they followed her to the cellar.

When she got to the foot of the stairs, Fannie's heart sank. She remembered that her main stock of provisions was there and she feared that the Confederates would just help themselves.

Hams were hanging just over their heads, between the beams. On shelves, disguised only by a thick layer of dust, were jar after jar of lard, butter, potatoes and other food.

Fannie supposed the soldiers saw all of it, but they said nothing. Perhaps, she reasoned, they know that I have wounded men to feed.

Back upstairs, Gilmore and his soldiers prepared to leave.

"Well, Yanks, didn't find no more of you hidden about, so I guess we'll just go capture the rest of Mr. Meade's army," one laughed.

"In a pig's ear," shouted back the burly Union private.

They all laughed.

"We'll be back for you boys later," Gilmore shouted as the four Confederates moved through the front door.

Fannie, amazed that they hadn't taken any food, was even further astonished when she looked into the back yard. There, neatly stacked since the Union troops had first arrived, were their muskets, still untouched. She wondered if Gilmore or his men had even noticed them.

War! How strange, she thought, staring through the kitchen window at the stacked guns. You shoot a man; then you laugh with him. You pursue your enemy but you don't take his food; you don't even remove his weapon. Surely, it is a game, this so-called art of war.

When the Union army struck its tents that morning in Emmitsburg, it took only minutes for the fields of troops to collect their baggage and pound dust on the road north. By 4:30 they were moving and before dawn the valley of St. Joseph's had lapsed into quietness again.

Father Gandolfo, later that morning, was on his way to say Mass and was unaware of the army's departure. He still saw soldiers, in strange uniforms to be sure. But these days one hardly knew which army he was looking at just from uniforms.

"Halt, where are you going, Father?" a musket-carrying soldier said as he blocked the priest's path.

"I am going to say Mass at St. Joseph's. It's quite alright. We have General Meade staying at our house in town."

"Oh, General Meade, is it? My humble apologies, Father, but Mister Meade holds no position of importance in Marse Robert's army."

Father Gandolfo then realized he was talking to a Confederate soldier and that the few other troops he saw were not from the Union forces which had camped there the night before. He glanced around, rubbing his eyes in the morning sun.

"Yes, yes, I see. General Meade has moved on. Well, now, that puts a new light on matters, doesn't it, my son?"

The soldier laughed and lowered his gun: "We could have much worse enemies, Father. Sorry to have detained you, but if I were you I'd be awfully careful about moving about."

The priest, now fully aware of what had happened, could see that the few infantrymen and a few dozen cavalrymen were moving from the west, apparently keeping track of Meade's northernbound army.

Gathering his trailing skirt in his hands, Father Gandolfo hurried on toward the church, saying to himself and anyone who might hear the gurgle in his throat: "Lord, give me the brains to remember which army I'm talking to or the wisdom to keep my big mouth shut."


The first of those troops who pulled out of Emmitsburg before dawn were rushing up Gettysburg's Washington Street with Albertus McCreary and his friends cheering them on.

The boys sat on a fence on High Street, next door to the home of Salome Myers.

"There are enough soldiers here to whip all the Rebs in the South," Albertus yelled to his friends. "Yahoo, go get 'em."

It seemed like hours before all the troops had passed. The boys jumped off the fence and fell in at the rear, rushing up Washington Street and then out the Chambersburg Pike.

"Maybe we shouldn't go out there. Might be dangerous," one of the boys cautioned.

"Ah, won't be any fighting. Them Rebs'll run soons they get a sight of our boys," another shouted back.

They were close to Seminary Ridge when the shooting, til then just a few rifle pops, got going.

Albertus watched as shells began hitting the troops along a line on the ridge. One shell came flying over the line, hit the ground and exploded too close for comfort. The boys turned, as if by order, and headed back into town.

Taking short cuts through the alleys, Albertus got back to his home at High and Baltimore Streets in short order. His father was waiting at the door.

"Where you been, boy?"

"Just down the street, pa, watching the soldiers go through."

His father said no more but pulled him inside and closed the door. The rest of the family was gathered in the front room.

"Now, mother, I'll tell you again," Mr. McCreary addressed his wife, a conversation which Albertus had apparently disrupted when his father heard him running down the brick walk.

"We can't get out of town. We're probably surrounded by soldiers by now and I don't care which side they're on, it's neither healthy nor wise to be moving around when they're out there armed to the teeth and raring to fight.

"The safest place we can be right now is here, in our home."

Mrs. McCreary, tears glistening, nodded and turned toward the kitchen.

At noon, the family sat down to dinner and were nearly done when a racket in the streets took them all to the windows.

There were Union soldiers everywhere, running and pushing each other, sweaty and black from dust and probably gun powder. Most were yelling for water as they ran.

"Buckets. Get buckets of water, and dippers too," Mr. McCreary ordered. From the porch on the side of the house, the whole family got involved in giving drinks to hundreds of retreating troops.

Albertus couldn't believe one figure running toward him. It was a boy. Couldn't have been more than 12, about Albertus' age. But he was in a Union uniform and carrying a drum.

Seeing someone his size, the drummerboy stopped at the porch, accepted a drink and handed his drum to Albertus.

"Here, keep this for me," the drummerboy shouted. Tears had streaked his dirt-stained face and he tried to brush them away as Mrs. McCreary begged him to come inside.

"No thank you, mam, gotta stay with my unit," he shouted back as he ran off.

Albertus watched until the boy was out of sight. Then he took the drum to the cellar and hid it under a pile of shavings.

The carrying of buckets went on and the grateful soldiers stopped long enough for a long swallow before moving on.

"Great goodness," Mr. McCreary yelled, "Look up the street."

The family stopped and stared. They could see soldiers just a block away, fighting hand-to-hand with pistols, gun butts, bayonets and swords.

An officer in blue came galloping by and shouted to the family:

"All you good people, go down in your cellars or you'll be killed!"

The warning sent a chill through young Albertus. He had never thought of being killed. That just happened to soldiers in far away places. Didn't it?

Neighbors who were also outside but lived in wooden houses with no cellars rushed to McCreary and asked for shelter.

"My, yes, hurry!" he told them.

McCreary positioned everyone along the front walls of the cellar, under the windows so that stray shots coming in would do no harm.

He was still getting everyone in position when the sound of gunfire and husky shouting could be heard just outside. There were thuds on the side porch and the sound of boots running over the cellar doors in the pavement.

Everyone listened intently. They heard one loud voice plainly ring out: "Shoot that fellow going over the fence!" A shot rang out and a man cried out.

The cellar was dark, except for the light the small windows cast on the back wall. And in that light they could see shadows of human forms racing back and forth.

Albertus shivered. Kill us?

Soon, the individual guns became like one and the noise was

continuous. Then came a loud boom and the house shook. Albertus popped up, stepped in a hole in the wall and peered through a corner of one window.

"Cannon," he announced before his father dragged him down. "They got a cannon out there, right in the middle of the street."

No one kept track of the time but the noise began to grow dimmer and farther away. Still they didn't move.

Suddenly, without warning, the cellar doors on the pavement were yanked up and sunlight flooded half the cellar. Five Confederate soldiers jumped in amongst them.

Albertus covered his eyes. Yes, he thought, we are gonna be killed.

The women began to cry and gathered their children around them. The men stood, not sure of what to do.

Mr. McCreary stepped forward.

"Gentlemen, this is my house. I beg you not to harm these unarmed people. We are civilians and we all live here, in this village."

A form moved toward him and the light from a window caught a red face, covered with freckles, and very red hair, dirty, sweaty, a gun raised in defense.

"We're looking for Union soldiers," said the freckled Confederate.

"There are none here," said McCreary.

"Gotta look anyway," said the soldier as he motioned his men to herd everyone upstairs.

No one in the house had heard them enter, what with all the racket outside, but the Confederates found 13 Union soldiers hiding, most of them on the second floor. They assembled the prisoners in the dining room and began taking down names.

McCreary, not knowing how to explain his statement that no one was hiding in his house, did not try. Instead, he looked at the soldiers, from both sides, and announced: "Gentlemen, won't you have something to eat?"

Since they had never finished the noon meal, the table was still set with the remains of dinner. Mrs. McCreary brought out more food and prisoners and guards sat together.

Albertus knew what he could do to help. Taking pencil and

paper he went to each Union soldier and asked for his name and home address.

"I'll write to your families," he told them.

"Better write to young Samuel's family too, cause young Samuel don't know how to write," a Confederate corporal laughed. A private sitting across the table blushed and lowered his head; then he laughed too. Soon they were all chuckling— Yankees too.

It's more like a big family dinner than a sit-down meal between enemies, Albertus thought.

The McCrearys didn't have to go back to the cellar that day. By nine o'clock, the Union prisoners had been marched away and the Confederates left moved outside to set up camp in the street.

No one in the house undressed for bed. But they all laid down, exhausted and uncertain about the next day.

Catherine Snyder, as was her habit, was up at four o'clock that morning to start her baking in the big outdoor oven. She had moved into town from the farm after Conrad died in 1860. He had been a good husband but never wealthy. And with eight children to support, Catherine found she had to work almost continuously.

The small house she had bought at the southern end of town, just where Baltimore Street became the Baltimore Pike, was comfortable. It was within a few hundred feet of the cemetery where Conrad was buried and the next-door neighbors, particularly 16-year-old Jennie, now about 20 years old, were a blessing when she needed help with the children.

Her own Lucinda was 16 and Mary was 18; so they helped. The four middle children pretty much took care of themselves. One of them, John, 13, was working and staying at a farm east of town. But someone had to be responsible for five-year-old Lobranson, and Rosa, who was four, and, of course, Erzmanthus, born the year his daddy died.

Catherine set the dough for that day's baking, for her family and for the sales too. Then, as the first light of day crept into the valley, she went to the garden to pull weeds. Finally, the sun's warm rays gave her sufficient light to cross the road into the woods and the blackberry patch.

Little Rosa just loves these for breakfast, she thought as she moved through the patch.

What was that? A rustling! Movement! Someone in the timber?

"Hello, good morning," she called to the direction of the noise.

"Lady, best get home," a voice came back, followed by the form of a blue-coated soldier emerging from the woods. Catherine could see other men moving behind him. There were a dozen. No. Several dozen, perhaps. Great heaven, the woods are full of them, she thought, frozen at the berry patch.

"Bad place to be, lady. Best get home," the blue-coated soldier said again, now only ten paces away from her.

She didn't need to be told again. Off she scooted, gathering up sons and daughters in the garden as she moved for the house.

But the work couldn't stop. There was butter to churn and bread to bake.

Catherine heard the shooting begin. It seemed to be all around her so she decided to keep her brood intact at home.

When the first wounded Union soldiers and some Confederate prisoners began moving back down the Baltimore Pike, Catherine and her children fed them fresh bread spread with newly-churned butter.

Little Rosa hung on the front gate, swinging back and forth and wondering what all these soldiers were doing in her street. And what are soldiers? And why did some get hurt?

One man, clutching his arm, stumbled near the gate. Lucinda ran to help.

"Grapeshot through the arm," the man explained as Lucinda asked his problem. "Can't go no further, gal. Losing too much blood."

He pulled his hand away. Lucinda winced at the sight of the redstained sleeve and the tattered jacket. Rosa knew that when she fell and scraped her knee and it got red she hurt; this man must hurt too, so she asked her mother for a piece of bread and butter for the man with the hurt.

Catherine looked and decided he needed more than that.

"Take him in the house," she ordered two other soldiers. "There's a spare room to the left; put him on the bed."

"No, too dirty. I'll get your bed dirty. Just lay me on the floor," the man begged.

"Heavens no," Catherine protested. "I said put him on the bed."

Right behind them an army surgeon tramped into the room and quickly examined the wound. He turned to the men who had borne their wounded comrade in and whispered, "Have to amputate that arm, right now."

Catherine heard the decision too and decided that home was no place for the younger children.

"Mary, pack some things for you and the three youngest. I want you to get them out of here. Take them out to Aunt Susie Benner's. No Rebels out that direction."

Mary was ready to go in minutes. She picked up Erz but told Rosa and Lob that they'd have to walk.

They were headed northeast to get around Culp's Hill, then east over Rock Creek. Just outside town Mary heard something hissing and thought it was a snake. Something flew overhead, hit the brush ahead of them and rolled to a stop.

"Stay away from that," she yelled to Rosa and Lob. "Let's go this way."

"What is that?" Rosa asked impatiently.

"It's a cannonball, and I hope it came this way by mistake," Mary answered quickly as she rushed the children away. She wondered why it hadn't exploded. Weren't they supposed to? Mary wasn't sure but she didn't wait to find out.

It took two hours to make the short trip, what with carrying Erz and continuously coaxing the other two to stop playing along the way. But the walk made them hungry—it was lunchtime when they arrived at Aunt Susie's—and tired. Mary felt relieved now that the little ones were safely away from the battle.

Attorney William McClean heard the firing start that morning from his home on East Middle Street. It was from the west and he wondered about his father on the farm up the Mummasburg Road.

"Fannie, you and the girls will be safe until I get back. I want to make sure my father is alright."

"We'll be fine, Will. You go ahead."

McClean turned up Baltimore Street, went through the Diamond and a few blocks north turned a half-left onto the Mummasburg Road. Halfway up the ridge with the shooting getting louder McClean was stopped cold. A shell dropped close by and exploded.

"That utterly removed all of my curiosity," he told his tearful wife after running back home.

McClean ventured out once more, but stayed in town. He saw General Reynolds ride out from the Diamond to the front and, as McClean learned later, to his death. And he saw Archer's Brigade, disheartened and humiliated by their capture, being marched through town on their way to the Union rear.

Then came the wounded, some in wagons, some on stretchers, some walking.

He went home again, filled a bucket with cool water, grabbed a tin cup and stood out on his street, offering refreshment to the walking wounded. And he kept a bottle of wine hidden by the door. When he saw a soldier who seemed weak from loss of blood out came the wine.

"It's a constant, moving panorama," McClean whispered to his wife when she brought him a slice of bread, some cheese and a cup of hot tea for his own lunch. She also had a plate piled high with chunks of fresh white bread, crackers and bits of cheese and a bowl of sticky molasses.

The steady train of humanity continued to move through town. Some stopped for help; some stumbled and could go no further; some continued on, moving south, their eyes never curious about where they were being led, just moving away from the death and destruction that had rained down upon them.

A New York soldier, whose right thumb had been shot off, stopped when Mrs. McClean offered to help. She had washed the stump and was applying ointment and a clean bandage when he saw Union troops running down the street, climbing fences and rushing into houses.

"Gotta go. Thank you good people, but I gotta go," he shouted despite her attempts to make him stand still until she could tie the bandage on. And off he ran.

He was followed by a wagon full of wounded who were shrieking and groaning as the driver whipped his horses into a run over the rutted streets. McClean imagined the cries to be the most tortured sounds he had ever heard.

Then came a moment of quiet, a lull. The streets seemed temporarily deserted. McClean rushed his family inside. His wife, their three little girls, a domestic servant named Ann Leonard and McClean crowded onto a platform behind the door at the top of the cellar steps and waited.

Then they heard a voice shouting, "Don't touch that water; they've poisoned it."

McClean assumed they were talking about the bucket he had left outside. He also assumed the Rebels had arrived.

There was no shooting, at least not close by and no one was banging down doors. McClean ventured out of his hiding place.

He watched from the curtained front window. Tired Confederates were sitting along the curb, opening knapsacks thrown aside by the fleeing Yankees and getting a chuckle from reading letters they found.

McClean felt it safe to open his door. A few soldiers shouted greetings and some had gotten up and were walking toward the house when they turned to see a large man, an officer, come galloping up.

"It's General Monaghan," someone shouted. "Hurrah for the state of Georgia!"

"Men, I salute your devotion to your duty here today. I am right proud of the way you drove back the foe. You are to be commended," Monaghan shouted. Then he rode away.

McClean looked at his pocket watch. It was almost four o'clock. He didn't notice six-year-old Mary, his oldest daughter, raise the front window. But he did hear her begin to sing, "Hang Jeff Davis on a Sour Apple Tree."

The soldiers stopped their rummaging and turned to listen to the child. A few were smiling but most didn't look too pleased.

"Mary, that's enough, child," her father warned.

"Should teach your young'uns better songs, mister," a tattered and dirty soldier sitting closest to the window said matter-of-factly.

"Yes, well, children hear these things, you know. Come Mary, close the window."

The McCleans, father and daughter, disappeared back into the house.

Jacob and Elizabeth Gilbert walked away from their row-house home that Wednesday morning when they realized the fight had started on their end of town. They suggested that Sallie Broadhead and her daughter, who lived two doors away, leave too but Sallie refused.

The Gilberts walked the three blocks to the square and then turned down Baltimore Street and stopped at the house of an old friend, Henry J. Stahle, editor of *The Compiler*.

The newspaper's printing office was located in a portion of the Stahle home.

Wounded troops were already pouring in and army stretcher bearers were combing the neighborhood for bandages and lint. Elizabeth got busy cutting strips of cloth and Jacob began carrying what supplies he could find to the courthouse nearby.

It was late afternoon when someone carried the wounded colonel into the alley alongside the *Compiler* office and then into the Stahle's dining room. The wound in his leg seemed severe, Elizabeth thought, as she watched him being carefully lain on a couch.

Within minutes, Confederate troops were in the house, looking for hidden Union troops.

"He's too bad off to be moved. You folks best keep him here," a Confederate sergeant told Elizabeth after he looked at the colonel.

She was asked to care for the man personally so she bathed and dressed the wound. Jacob brought him some soup and cool water.

"I'm W. W. Dudley, colonel, Army of the Potomac," he told them. "I certainly appreciate what you're doing for me, but I think I need a doctor to look at this wound too. Can you get one?"

"Well, colonel, it appears that the Confederates are in charge now and I assume that only their surgeons are available," Mr. Stahle responded. "I'll see if I can get one to stop by."

Stahle noticed that as he talked to a Confederate surgeon outside the courthouse a number of townspeople were watching from a distance. The doctor agreed to come to his house with him.

"I'm afraid this man is going to die. That leg needs to come off but so do the arms and legs of a hundred other men. I don't know if we can get to him in time," the doctor said after examining Dudley.

"Listen," he continued, "I'll give you a pass to get him through the lines. Put him in a wagon and move him immediately. Perhaps the Yankees have better hospital facilities and can save him."

Within hours, Dudley was lying in the back of the wagon heading south through Union-held territory to the village of Littlestown.

It was then that the Gilberts decided to return home.

A half block from the house, a Confederate officer on horseback stopped them to ask where they were going. Satisfied with the answer he advised them to stay in their home.

"Your house will be safe if you stay inside. If you leave it again I cannot guarantee that it won't be ransacked. If you hear shooting go to your cellar," he told them.

"Yes, thank you, we'll do that," Jacob responded.

They were glad to be home. It had been a long day. Sleep came easily.

Liberty Augusta Hollinger had turned 16 this summer, the eldest of four girls and one boy. Her parents owned the big house at the eastern end of town on a large plot where the York Pike and the Hanover Road split off from East York Street.

Mr. Hollinger was at the warehouse on Stratton Street near the railroad, just three blocks from home, when the cannon began booming. He wasn't surprised. He had heard troops moving through town all morning. But the grain and produce business didn't wait for battles, so he stayed at the warehouse.

Liberty was outside the house watching some of the neighbors piling a few precious possessions into wagons and scurrying off toward Hanover.

Two riders were approaching from town. Liberty could see they were Union officers but it wasn't until they were at the front gate that she noticed both were wounded.

The younger one—she thought he was a lieutenant—called to her:

"Miss! We need some help! Captain here has a bullet in his neck and I've got one in my wrist."

Liberty got water and some cloth to wrap their wounds.

"I'd suggest you get to the cellar. Rebs may be coming this way," the lieutenant said.

Mrs. Hollinger heard the warning and fainted.

"Any men here?" the lieutenant asked.

"No, father is at his warehouse," Liberty replied. "It's just us, and my little brother and sisters."

"Let's take that rocker from the porch to the cellar," the captain suggested.

Liberty was amazed to hear him speak. She didn't know where the bullet had lodged but she could see the wound on the side of his neck and a bulge just behind it. He was obviously in pain, but he seemed to know what he was doing.

"Imagine your cellar, like most, is a bit damp. Can't put your mother on that damp floor so we'll sit her in this rocker. Your sisters can steady her til she comes around," he said.

The captain held his head to one side, apparently taking pressure off the imbedded bullet, and the lieutenant stuck his wounded hand between two of the buttons in his jacket. They picked up the rocker and carried it to the basement through an outside door.

Carrying the unconscious Mrs. Hollinger down was a strain but the two men managed.

"Now you keep all those kids and yourself down here," the captain said. "We're gonna keep movin' so the Rebs don't take us prisoner."

And with that they walked unsteadily back up the six steps leading to the yard, dropped the wooden cellar door and rode off.

Liberty was trying to revive her mother. Then she thought: I didn't even thank them or say goodbye.

It wasn't long before Liberty heard rifle fire getting closer. She peered through a cellar window which faced to the northwest.

There were Union troops in the fields, in the streets, in the yards, and all of them were running—some faster than others—to the south toward Culp's Hill and the cemetery.

Some were running through her yard, tearing through carefully-tended flower gardens and trampling the vegetable patch out back. Close behind were a different set of men— Confederates. The sun glistened on their bayonets and Liberty's chest shuddered.

The roar of the fire became deafening and it aroused Mrs. Hollinger. And somehow, during that mad pell-mell retreat, Mr. Hollinger had locked his warehouse and scooted home.

He was there in time to comfort his awakening wife.

When the ruckus settled down, Mr. Hollinger went upstairs and was peering out the front window when a band of Confederates rode into the front yard and called his name:

"Hollinger. Mr. Hollinger. We'd like to speak to you, sir," a captain shouted to him.

As he stepped out onto the porch, the officer rode up to the steps and addressed him:

"Mr. Hollinger. We're told that you own that warehouse back by the tracks. We need food and I'm forced to confiscate that warehouse. The keys, please."

"I cannot do that, captain."

"Well, sir, I had wished to avoid damaging your building but we can get in."

"Well, if you do I cannot prevent it, but I am not inviting you by giving you my keys."

"That's your choice, sir. Now then, we'd also like to use your house and have your womenfolk bake for us," the captain said.

"No sir, I won't allow that either."

Just then, Julia, two years younger than Liberty, stepped out onto the porch. Julia was the family beauty with dark brown eyes and long brown curls. She had a beauty that was midway between that of a child and a young woman.

For a moment, the Confederates seemed to just stare into that soft, lovely face.

The captain tipped his hat but said nothing. He motioned his band away and they rode down York Street toward the warehouse.

Before dark, the same band returned twice.

First, they wanted a horse and cow which were in a fenced yard beside the barn. Mr. Hollinger said the animals were too old to be of any use. The Confederates rode away.

Next, they were back asking if they could graze their own horses in a corn patch out back. Mr. Hollinger said they couldn't. They rode away again.

Liberty was astounded. She thought that Rebels would take what they needed; these soldiers were gentlemen.

Must be father's silvery head that awakened their respect, she thought to herself. Her father was not yet 43 years old but his hair and beard had turned gray early and were now as white as snow, making him look quite venerable.

Indeed, that night, the Hollinger family, except for mother, who was still nervous about the entire situation, settled down to sleep as if this had been just another July 1st.


H. S. Huidekoper hurried along West York Street, cradling his shattered right arm in his tense left fist. Some blood was still trickling down through his fingers but he was sure that the cord tied above the elbow had finally stemmed the flow.

It seemed like such a long walk from McPherson's barn, as he heard it referred to and where he tried to hold together his part of the 150th Pennsylvania Volunteers against the Confederate onslaught.

They said there was a hospital in a church on this street. Yes, there it is, just up the street; looks like a Catholic church.

Huidekoper looked around as he walked. These poor, frightened civilians, he thought. They're bewildered. They're trying to help us and probably wondering whether they should flee or stay and protect their homes. Gads, war is sometimes tougher on them than the soldier.

Those walking near him were mostly privates and corporals. And they stared at him: an officer, a colonel at that, walking to the hospital. That's probably what they were thinking. Or perhaps they were wondering how one so young could be a colonel. At 21, he was one of the youngest colonels in the army.

Huidekoper took a drink from a tin cup held out by a woman, nodded his thanks and moved on. She reminded him of a woman who lived next door to his parents back home in Meadville, Pennsylvania, some 200 miles from this spot.

Would he ever see home again? It had been three years since he left his studies at Harvard to recruit a company of men in Meadville.

Now, here he was, at half past five on this Wednesday and what was the date? Ah, yes, the first of July, just three days from the glorious Fourth. And would he survive to see that grand patriotic day?

He turned into the church, between the massive pillars and through one of the three front doors. Just inside he passed an operating table—a door ripped off its hinges and placed over two small tables.

A doctor glanced at him and immediately began fingering the injured arm.

"Looks like whatever hit you has crushed the bones in the elbow area, colonel," the doctor said.

"Minie ball caught me," Huidekoper answered.

"Find a seat over there and we'll get to you," the doctor said, motioning him to the left of the crowded sanctuary.

Huidekoper glanced around. There were wounded everywhere: some unconscious; some with eyes aglare with fright and silent screams in their mouths; and some in the excruciating agonies of pain and dying. The moans and cries and shouts of those who could no longer stifle the roar of nerves stretched beyond the breaking point made Huidekoper wish he were still outside.

This is not a church or a hospital, he thought. It is a death house operated by the devil himself.

At the fourth pew on the left, he found room to sit. He unbuckled the belt which held his sword scabbard and revolver; they fell clanging to the floor. Then he tried to sit comfortably.

"Say, fellows, be good enough to tear this pewdoor off its hinges and place it crosswise on the back and front of the pews," the colonel said to two orderlies passing up the aisle.

"Yes, sir," one answered. It took little effort to rip out the flimsy hinges and put the small door across the pews.

Huidekoper lifted his swollen arm to the door. It helped some.

"I appreciate that. And if you have some whiskey to help me kill this cursed pain, I'd be quite grateful," he said to the orderlies.

"Yes, sir, plenty of whiskey in this town. I'll fetch it."

It was the biggest swallow of whiskey Huidekoper ever had.

He heard a nearby bell ringing the hour of six o'clock when a surgeon in a blood-stained apron came and said it was his time.

Huidekoper held his right arm carefully as he arose and followed the surgeon back to the operating area. He climbed onto the door-table and laid down. A surgeon pressed a cloth over his nose and mouth and Huidekoper whiffed the familiar odor of chloroform.

It wasn't enough. He could feel the doctors probing.

"Oh, God, don't saw the bone until I've had more chloroform!" he pleaded. Then his head fell to one side and his eyes rolled.

When he awoke, he was still on the table.

"You took my arm off, didn't you, doctor?" he said to a man he recognized, Doctor Quinan, the surgeon of his regiment.

"I thought you were only going to examine and dress it! Well, next time we march through Maryland I'll have to salute with my left hand."

He felt giddy but there was no pain, just a mild throbbing in the stump which hung strangely from his right shoulder. The chloroform and whiskey had left a throb too but he wasn't dizzy.

Huidekoper swung his legs over the side of the table and the surgeons helped him sit up.

"Find a place to lie down and stay there. You'll need rest," one of them advised.

He stepped carefully over soldiers in the aisles and moved back to the left. Someone had taken his pew so he kept moving. Climbing the steps to the pulpit and still stepping over the cluttered remnants of humanity he looked around. Back at the other end of the church, above the operating area, was a gallery.

Working his way along the aisle, Huidekoper found the stairs to the empty gallery. He climbed up the narrow stairway, his head just inches away from the organ and closed his eyes. He could hear music. Someone playing the organ? There was no one there. He closed his eyes again. Ah, blessed sleep.

# CHAPTER
# 7

# The Second Day

Doctor John W. C. O'Neal arose on Thursday, July 2, with no fear of what would happen that day. After his ride behind the enemy lines he felt prepared for anything.

"But promise me you won't make any calls outside town," his wife insisted after he said he could not just sit idly by while the battle went on.

O'Neal's regular patients included the people in the Adams County almshouse. He decided that he would attend to their needs if the fighting prevented him from going elsewhere.

He stepped out the front door, walking briskly past the *Compiler* office next door, and headed north along Baltimore Street.

A Confederate captain in the street saw O'Neal's medical bag.

"Doctor!" he called.

"Yes, captain," O'Neal answered immediately and stopped walking.

"Making rounds, doctor?"

"Yes, going up to the almshouse to check on patients."

"Alright, but I suggest you wrap a white cloth around your left arm so that our men don't molest you."

O'Neal drew out a clean, white linen handkerchief. He folded it in half and then in half again and wrapped it around his upper arm.

"Here, let me tie that for you," the captain said, moving toward the doctor.

"Thank you, captain."

"My pleasure. Good day, sir."

"Good day, captain," O'Neal answered and moved on his way.

I wonder, he thought, if these Southern troops detect a trace of my Virginia accent. He had been in the north for years but others had told him they could detect the accent.

Funny that these Confederates, if they do hear that accent, do not ask me where I'm from, he mused. Ah well, best let those thoughts wither. I love Virginia but we must preserve the Union.

Harriet Bayly had given up waiting for her husband to come home Wednesday night. She had been sleeping for hours when a tapping sound at the front door, just under her bedroom window, awakened her.

It must be Joseph, she thought.

She was heading down the stairs when she heard Billy behind her.

"Ma, what's that?" he whispered.

"Knock at the door. Might be your pa," she whispered back.

Harriet unlatched and opened the door a crack.

"Mam, please mam, kin ah come in," said a tiny voice on the porch.

Harriet opened the door wider. In the moonlight she could see the uniform of a Confederate soldier but the body inside was that of a mere boy.

She motioned him inside and quickly closed the door.

The boy stood there as Harriet and Billy eyed him up and down.

He had neither hat nor shoes, no gun and no pack.

Harriet drew the curtains and lit a candle. She saw that what remained of the boy's uniform was filthy.

"Name's Henry Fowley," he said suddenly, as if he knew the questions would start. "Was in a North Carolina regiment and got caught up in that fight yesterday. Regiment got broken up and scattered. Ah been wanderin' around all night, tryin' to stay away from pickets. Yours is the first house ah come to."

"It's a wonder them guards outside didn't see you," Billy said.

"Only saw one on his feet and he was in your back yard, headin' for the barn," Henry explained.

"How old are you, son?" Harriet said calmly to the still shaken, skinny boy in gray.

"Almost seventeen, mam."

"And you want us to help you find your regiment?"

"No, mam. Ah don't intend to do any more fightin' for that Confederacy. Kin ah stay here?"

Harriet took a deep breath, glanced around the room as if to find someone listening to the conversation and finally turned to Billy:

"Go get some of your clothes for Henry. You got a new brother, looks like. And then let's get some sleep," she said, looking at the clock on the mantle. It was two a.m.; Thursday had started early.

She didn't sleep much more and soon the first rays of dawn were dancing down the hallway and into her bedroom. Harriet got up and dressed quickly. She got her market basket from a closet and began to pack.

Some old linens would be helpful. Old sheets were quickly torn into strips for bandages. Pins too went into the basket. Downstairs, she packed day-old bread and, from the cellar, she picked several bottles of homemade wine.

Billy heard her shuffling around and came to investigate.

"There must be wounded all over the countryside. I'm going to see what I can do for them. You make sure Henry stays well hidden."

"Yes, ma," Billy said.

Harriet headed through the fields to the southwest, where Wednesday's fighting seemed to be the heaviest. Troops were already on the move, heading south.

An officer on horseback stood in her path not far from the farmhouse.

"Madam, I must know where you're going," he said with a tip of his cap.

"I imagine there are wounded who need help. I'm going to help," Harriet said without hesitation.

"Fine, but I insist that you tie a white cloth around your arm to signify your medical duties," the horseman said.

Harriet put down her basket and whipped out a bandage. She turned it around her arm and neatly tucked the ends in. Then she picked up her basket as the officer backed his horse out of her path.

"That way," the horseman pointed. "There are plenty of wounded still in the fields down there."

Harriet nodded and plodded on.

She crossed two rises before coming on the panorama of destruction. As far as she could see were men, living and dead, and fallen horses, broken gun carriages, disabled cannon barrels and confusion.

The sun was well up and broiling. The first group of men she walked into were mostly Union troops.

"Gawd, lady!" one soldier cried out from beneath a zig-zag fence where he was trying to escape the bright sun. "We been here for a whole day, since yesterday morning. No food, no water. Damn Rebs won't help. Please lady, help us."

Harriet saw the dried blood along the side of his head. He didn't look badly wounded, more like a man gone crazy from a minor wound that affected his mind more than his body.

He didn't pursue the conversation after Harriet offered him a hunk of bread and poured him a small cup of wine.

She moved from man to man for half an hour, giving food to the hungry and wine to the faint.

Many were unconscious, or dead.

The first wound she tended to was in a young soldier's back. Harriet cut open his coat up to the wound. Someone had stuffed a bandage into the opening but it was so clotted with blood that she couldn't remove it for fear of starting the bleeding again.

"Is there water nearby? I must wet this bandage to get it loose," she asked to anyone who was listening.

A man lying nearby shook his head from side to side and then said: "There is a little bit of tea in my canteen that I'd been saving. Maybe you can loosen it with that."

Harriet poured the tea over the clotted bandage. It was enough to soak and loosen the hardened cloth. She dabbed away some dirt near the bullet wound. The man moaned. Then she covered the hole with a clean bandage and tied a strip around his waist to hold it in place.

As she continued to patch and mend as best she could she tried to shut out the constant, pitiful cries of "water, water."

Confederate troops were moving through the field too. Some were checking the dead and emptying their pockets, or questioning the living about their wounds. But they seemed to be doing little else.

"Is it possible that none of you will bring water to these poor men?" Harriet shouted out, rising from the ground and wheeling around as she yelled.

Nearby, an officer on horseback turned to see who was yelling and rode over.

"These men have no water, madam?"

"That's what I said! No water! And you have men just walking around, stealing from these poor souls," Harriet said, her voice still loudly revealing her anger.

"Sergeant, have five men mount up and collect some water," the officer ordered.

"Wells nearby are all pumped out. Both sides been pumpin' 'em since yesterday morning."

"Damn it, sergeant. I—beg your pardon, mam—sergeant, I didn't ask for excuses. I said to get some water."

Harriet rose an arm and pointed to the north.

"Over there, about a half mile, there's a good spring. Should be plenty there," she said.

The sergeant and his men, laden with canteens, were back in quick order.

Harriet was helping pour the water into parched throats when a short stocky man in a white frock and a Confederate officer's cap walked up with a bearded, middle-aged soldier.

"Excuse me, but this is one of our doctors," the man said in a thick accent. "He's German, like me, but he does not speak English. He's been assigned to look after the Yankee wounded."

Harriet smiled weakly. A doctor who can't communicate with his patients?

"He wants you to show him what you've done for the wounded," the soldier said.

As he examined each man and looked at Harriet's nursing skill, the doctor murmured, "goot, goot."

He's as gentle as a woman in his touch, she thought. Guess I can go home now.

On the way, in another field, Harriet saw hundreds of Union soldiers. A few were standing but most were sitting. None appeared wounded. But Rebel guards around the field told her the men were prisoners.

As she passed, several called out, asking her to take the addresses of their families.

"Rebs tell us we'll be movin' south in about an hour," a teenage soldier told her as he scribbled his mother's name and address on a page he had torn from his pocket Bible.

The guards told her to move on.

As she neared home, she could see Joseph and Billy running down the lane to her. Joseph grabbed her and hugged her tightly.

"Lord, woman, we were worried! Where you been?" her husband asked.

Harriet blurted out her story quickly and then asked where he'd been.

"I got caught up in what looked like the whole Confederate cavalry. They'd raided York and they wouldn't let me turn around and come back. They said to just keep headin' east and stay out of the way.

"I thought it was decent of them not to give me any trouble and to be concerned about my safety.

"Well, anyhow, after a while I turned around and took some back roads and got into town about the time the Confeds were comin' through too. I hid in a cellar and by the time things had settled down enough for me to come out somebody had unhitched the horse and stole it.

"Didn't feel it was too safe to be walkin' home as it was gettin' dark so I stayed in that cellar and started walkin' back this morning.

"I was just gettin' ready to come lookin' for you."

Harriet smiled. She was glad he was home. Then the smile faded as she remembered the wounded back in the field. She asked Joseph if she could pack more bandages and bread and go back.

"No, Harriet. Our boys are gettin' ready to attack, from what I hear. And when they do, they'll probably be pushing the Rebs right through that field. No, too dangerous. Besides, you said that German doctor was tendin' to 'em.

"And the kids need tendin' too. Poor Billy here tells me he's been pickin' cherries for these soldiers all day. That right, son?"

Billy turned his palms up to show the stains. His lips were stained the same color.

"Troops been passin' by all day, ma. Big units, small ones. And all of them wantin' cherries. Henry helped," Billy sputtered.

"Henry? You let Henry out of the house?" Harriet was gasping.

"No he didn't," said Joseph. "I did. When Billy told me about the Reb I told the boy he'd have to take his chances workin' around like everyone else. I don't want the Rebs findin' a deserter being hidden by us. They'd probably burn our place down if they did.

"No, Harriet, I told the boy to pretend he was just one of the family, but to keep his mouth shut. He's been up in the cherry trees, breaking off branches and tossin' 'em down to his late comrades-in-arms, though they didn't suspect nothing."

"Rebs ran off some steers, ma," Billy butted in excitedly.

"Oh no, Joe," she murmured.

"Fraid so, Harriet. Them eight, big, stall-fed steers were driven off and ever since I been smellin' steak roastin' just over that hill," he said, pointing to a thin trail of smoke rising from behind the hill.

"All the hogs are gone too."

"What else have they taken? I thought we were being treated well," she exclaimed.

"Well, Harriet, I think what's been passin' through today is bottom-of-the-barrel Rebs . . . those hangers-on who linger behind to grab what they can and avoid the fightin'.

"One of 'em got some money too."

Harriet's jaw dropped. But before she could utter a sound, Billy was explaining.

"Member you told me yesterday that some woman friend of yours had asked for your chop pickle recipe and you asked me to write it down from your book? Well, I got around to doing that this morning.

"Went to the desk for a scrap of paper and a pencil, hardly noticing a young loafer slouched in a corner of the front room. I thought he was sleepin'. When I rolled up the desk top I saw a twenty dollar greenback there in a jar.

"Well, I got the paper and your recipe book and took it out to the kitchen table where there was better light. Left the desk top up. Later when I took the recipe book back I could see that the loafer was gone and so was the greenback.

"I'm really sorry, ma. I shoulda been more careful."

Harriet put her arms around her son, drew his head into her bosom and patted his back.

"Don't worry, Billy. We all make mistakes. I hate to lose all that money—it was money I was saving for new clothes for everyone. But we can make clothes.

"It's more important that we're all safe. But maybe, Joe, we should keep these soldiers out of the house from now on."

Joe shook his head in doubt and replied: "That might be easier said than done. Course it's strange they don't mind walkin' into the house but, far as I know, they haven't been in the barn. Got three horses hidden in there that they haven't found.

"And you know, it's funny that . . . well, let me start at the beginnin'. Just before you came home, Billy and I went to the barn cause those two-year-old colts were raisin' a ruckus and I was afraid the Rebs would go in and find the other horses. So we led the three colts out into the pasture.

"You should have seen those soldiers tryin' to catch those colts. You know we hadn't broke them yet so they're pretty frisky.

"Well, it was a case watchin' them run around tryin' to get them ponies. They finally got ropes and then the show really began. They were trippin' over those ropes and over each other til they finally gave up and let the horses alone.

"Billy and I were watchin' from behind the barn."

"Yeah, and Pa and I were laughin' so hard we were afraid those Rebs would catch us," Billy chimed in.

"I guess we need some laughs. I'm glad you two had the chance," Harriet said.

Supper was a happy occasion for the family that night. All had come through dangerous experiences these last two days without harm. And after the meal, they all went about their chores as if nothing extraordinary had happened.

Just before nightfall, when his chores were all done, Billy climbed up on the roof over the front porch. It was his favorite place for being alone but tonight it had an added attraction.

He had been hearing cannon firing all evening and now, as darkness began to sweep across the hills he could see flashes of the battle to the south, perhaps right in Gettysburg.

It was a thunder of guns, a shrieking, a whistling, a moaning of shells before they burst, sometimes like rockets in the air.

As he sat alone, wrapped in shadows that late twilight casts over field and meadow, Billy could see neither a soldier nor anyone from his family. No results of the battle were visible. No shifting of scenes or movement of actors in the great struggle could be seen.

It was simple noise, flash and roar, like the roar of a continuous thunderstorm and the sharp, angry crashes of the thunderbolt. From what he had heard during the day the nearest guns must be at least two miles away. But he could feel the shock, or maybe he was just reacting to the noise.

No, by golly, when several cannons went off at the same time, the windows shook. In fact, the house itself shuddered.

Then, as darkness cloaked even the nearest trees in eerie

hiding, the sound began to subside. The firing had stopped. The quiet, after such a concert of booms and crashes, was deafening too. Not even a cricket chirped and Billy could hear the beating of his own heart.

He was back inside the house, seated at the kitchen table under the lights of candles and discussing further the events of the day with his parents when a knock came to the front door.

Joseph answered it and was greeted by three Confederate officers.

"Good evening, sir, if you have the space we'd like to rent beds for the night. It's been so long since we've had a decent night's sleep and tomorrow promises to be a busy day."

The speaker was a captain, tall and lanky with the look of a horseman in swashbuckling plumed hat, boots which covered his knees and long gloves worn through the fingertips by countless hours of holding reins. With him were two lieutenants, cavalrymen too but not as imposing as their leader.

"Yes, we have a guest room with two beds. You're welcome as long as you respect the honor of my house," Joe said.

The captain held out two dollar bills, good stuff, not the Confederate money.

Joe thought the offer was extremely generous, just for the use of a room overnight. But he remembered the stolen twenty dollars and took the bills without a word.

There was no conversation as the officers entered the house. They were introduced to Harriet and Billy as they passed through the kitchen to reach the stairs. No names were exchanged, just a simple "this is my wife and my son" from Joe.

The officers saluted feebly, having already removed their hats as they entered the house, and murmured "good evening."

Harriet could see the exhaustion in their faces as they turned to climb the stairs.

A half hour later, on his way to bed, Billy passed the spare room. The door was closed but the light of his candle picked up a strange sight in the hallway. There, on the pegs where the family normally hung coats and hats, were swords in their scabbards and pistol holsters, but no pistols.

Strange that a soldier would leave his sword exposed in the

house of the enemy, Billy thought. Boy, would I like to have that stuff. Wonder what would happen if I hid it away tonight? Or maybe I could use these swords to capture them? And what would I do with them after I captured them?

Billy fingered the swords with care, not wanting to knock the heavy belts from the pegs. Then he went to bed.

His father noticed the strange trappings too on his way to bed.

"Looks like a compromise to me," he told Harriet after they had passed through the hallway and were safely in their own bedroom.

"Looks like those fellows are sayin', let's trust each other but let's not be foolish. We'll leave our swords out to show honor for your house but we want you to know that we're sleepin' on our pistols."

"I certainly don't plan to endanger that trust," Harriet replied as she untied the ribbon that had held her long hair in a bun all day.

"Nor I," said Joe. "Nor I."

The first thing Sallie Broadhead learned that Thursday morning was that Confederate troops had robbed a house across the street the night before. The owners had fled during the day, apparently leaving the house unlocked.

In the confusion, neither Sallie nor Joseph had noticed the four-horse wagon parked outside the house. There had been wagons by all day and she had stayed inside after dark.

"They went from the garret to the cellar, they did," a neighbor told Sallie. "They loaded that wagon full of furniture and clothes and food and just drove off. Just plain highway robbery! That's what it was."

Sallie and Joseph and little Mary had just finished some morning chores when the cannonading began. It was ten o'clock and they went right to the cellar.

It was lunchtime when it subsided and they came up again into the sunlight.

"I'm going to pick beans. We must keep food on the table," Joseph announced. The cannons had drowned out lesser sounds but as he knelt in the garden, Joseph could hear bullets whizzing overhead. He felt safe enough, with four-foot fences on either side that could probably stop low bullets. But he was careful not to stand up.

"Goodness, Joseph, so many beans!" Sallie exclaimed as he carried a bucket full of green beans into the kitchen.

"I picked every one, love. I'm not going to leave them for Rebs to pick."

Sallie snapped the beans and prepared enough for their lunch. She had also baked a pan of shortcake and boiled a piece of ham, the last ham they had in the house.

It was the first quiet meal they'd had in two days. Sallie enjoyed it immensely, Joseph could tell from the way she chewed purposely and smiled between bites.

The solitude did not last long. By four o'clock the storm broke with terrific violence. Sallie thought it sounded as though heaven and earth were being rolled together.

Since their home was at the end of a five-house row, Joseph felt they'd be safer in the basement of the middle house, the one occupied by the Gilberts. It was soon after they'd settled themselves comfortably when it struck.

It sounded like the house was coming down about their heads when the shell drove into the top two feet of the basement wall.

"Oh, God," Sallie screamed, clutching Mary and burying her own head under Joseph's arm.

Bricks and dust were flying. No one moved. Joseph thought there would be an explosion. But there was nothing, except the continuous noise outside of guns and men and horses.

As the dust settled, they could see a conical-shaped hunk of metal sticking through the inside of the wall. A half-dozen bricks were dislodged where the missile had punched into the basement.

"It's a shell," Joseph almost whispered as the dust filtered down to the floor. "Don't anyone move. I suspect that if it hasn't exploded by now, that it won't  . . .  but I'm not sure."

For almost two hours they sat, moving very little but staring less and less at the shell pointed their way.

At six o'clock, the cannonading slackened and then stopped almost completely.

"The fighting for today must be almost over," said Gilbert.

They moved upstairs and peered through the front window into a scene of bloody carnage. Bodies of men littered the street and the screams and cries of wounded filled the air.

Musket fire. Bullets whizzing outside and thumping into stone and brick. Then the artillery again.

"Back to the cellar!" shouted Joseph. And down they went to stare at the cursed shell again. "Don't touch it. Just leave it be."

The hours passed slowly now. Little Mary had fallen asleep and one by one the others dozed too.

By ten o'clock the firing ceased. Joseph picked up Mary and nudged Sallie.

"I think it's safe to go home, love," he whispered.

Outside, Confederate troops were lounging in the street. They had carted off the living and the dead but the odor of rotting horseflesh, some of it two days old, hung thickly in the hot summer night.

"You folks best figure on movin' out tomorrow," said a thin, red-bearded sergeant boiling coffee over a small fire in the street. "Spect this here town might get shelled."

"Thank you for the warning," Joseph replied as he slipped Mary and Sallie two doors up the street to their house.

"If we have to leave I'd better wash out some clothes for Mary," Sallie said as her husband carried the limp child up to her bed.

She was afraid to light a candle so Sallie washed a dress and stockings by moonlight in the kitchen.

Then she tried to rest but sleep would not come.

"It's out of the question to either sleep or eat under such terrible excitement and suspense," she whispered to Joseph as she snuggled up to him in bed.

"Uh, huh," he answered, his eyes already shut and his breathing becoming somewhat heavy.

Mary McAllister had trouble sleeping Wednesday night. But she was up early Thursday. How could anyone sleep in such an atmosphere?

She found out first thing that the chaplain who was gunned

down on the steps of the church across the street was the Reverend Horatio S. Howell of the 90th Pennsylvania Infantry.

A Confederate surgeon had knocked on the front door.

"I had to apologize for what our men did yesterday. We regret terribly about the chaplain. I instructed that he be buried earlier this morning in the church yard," he said to Mary.

"Sorry to have disturbed you, but I felt I had to apologize to someone from your town."

Mary nodded as if accepting the apology. The surgeon turned quickly and walked back toward the church.

Martha Scott, Mary's sister, was up early too and suggested that perhaps they should begin cooking food and baking bread for the wounded.

"You can hear those wounded men in the street just begging for bread," Mary said. "We just have to feed them!"

Mary had her first batch of bread in, then went upstairs to check on the officers.

"Liquor. Can you get us some good liquor, mam?" asked one, shoving an empty canteen toward her.

"I'll try."

Alex Buehler, the druggist, told Mary he would fill the canteen for fifty cents.

Back home, Mary gave the canteen to Lieutenant Colonel James Thomson and Captain Jacob Gish of the 107th Pennsylvania. Before long they were singing.

"That's the last time I get them hard liquor," Mary told Martha in the kitchen as they listened to the fractured melody drifting down the stairs.

Mary began checking the men in the living room, changing bandages, offering words of encouragement.

She had removed the soiled bandage from the side of a young Union infantryman and saw, in the brightness of daylight, that the bullet which had downed him was just under the skin in the middle of his back.

Mary ran over to Belle King's and pleaded with the Confederate surgeons for one to tend to her patient.

"You can take the bullet out. I can even see it!" she begged.

They ignored her.

"Either you come or I'll report you to your superior officers," she shouted.

"Woman, we have more than we can do right here. Go home. Leave us be," said a bald man who seemed to be the oldest and perhaps the senior man at King's.

Mary huffed, "I'll get Doctor Robert Horner, one of Gettysburg's fine physicians," and out the door she pranced.

With only a small surgical knife and an instrument which looked like tweezers, Horner operated on the Scott's living room rug. He made an inch-long incision next the the lump in the soldier's back, locked onto the bullet with the tweezers and applied a slight amount of pressure with his left thumb. The bullet popped out.

The soldier had not made a sound, only tensed his muscles with each movement the doctor made.

Horner stuffed a clean piece of cloth which had been soaking in boiled water into the hole left by the bullet's exit.

"Ahhh!" the soldier screamed. "You're burnin' me."

But the heat had overpowered the pain of the operation. The soldier settled as the bandage began to cool.

"Here, take that and put it in your knapsack for a keepsake," Horner said as he pressed the bullet into the soldier's upturned hand.

"I feel better already," the soldier whispered as he squeezed the flattened shell.

Mary put warm, wet cloths over the wounds and smiled down.

The soldier smiled back. Then he closed his eyes and fell asleep.

The Rebels had found the meats and bacon Mary had hidden in a corner of the basement. And the barrels of molasses too. They filled crocks full of gooey molasses and carried it out but they only took a small portion of the meat.

From Boyer's store on the corner the soldiers brought back cod fish and begged Martha and Mary to cook for them. And then they ate, slowly, tasting each bite, as if it was their last meal.

They used all of the tea they could find, but they didn't find the small supply of tea and coffee Mary had hidden away.

Five surgeons had moved into the house and told Martha she would have to cook for them. Mary shared some of the meat from the basement and baked cake with some shortening on a griddle on top of the stove. As fast as she baked the little cakes, they were gobbled up by the hungry doctors.

It was after dinner and the surgeons had gone back to their gruesome tasks when Mary answered a knock at the back door. A Confederate soldier saluted and announced: "I'm here to guard your house, mam."

He boldly stepped inside as Mary stepped aside. Then, from around the corner, came another soldier, this one scruffy and dirty. He slammed the door behind him.

"Get me somethin' to eat," ordered the scruffy one.

"I beg your pardon," Mary answered.

"Ya heard me, woman, git it now, afor I get mean."

"Get out!" Mary pointed toward the door, her finger shaking uncontrollably. "Get out, now!"

"Hell, woman, ya ain't big enuf ta throw me out."

Mary turned quickly, marched down the hallway and opened the front door. It didn't take long to spot an officer in the street.

He was a tall man, with a fiery red beard, middle-aged, and a captain . . . or was that the mark of a major? Mary dismissed the question. He was an officer.

"Sir, sir . . . yes, you, would you mind coming in here for a moment?"

The officer got to the door just as the two soldiers appeared in the hallway.

"These are two of your men and I want you to get them out," Mary told him.

"Hi, hold on. You ask us to leave and yet you got wounded Yanks in there and treating them fine too," said the man who had told Mary he would guard her.

"She ordered us out and got a little lippy," added the scruffy one.

"I wish we were all out of here," the officer shouted. "Now you men leave this house immediately and don't let me see you near it again!"

The soldiers grunted, lifted their fingers to the brims of their hats and shuffled off.

"Now," the officer said to Mary, "in return for that favor, perhaps you could feed me. I haven't had anything substantial for a few days."

She spread bacon and bread and molasses before him. He ate a little bread and a bit of meat.

"May I have a clean plate, please," he said as Mary put half an apple pie on the table. He cut a small slice, and ate it with delight. When he finished, he nodded his head at Mary, smiled but said nothing, and walked out of the house.

Soldiers have strange behavior, she thought.

The night had passed too slowly for Gates Fahnestock. As soon as he was up, he headed for the roof. But shells whistling through the air sent him back to the second floor.

By early afternoon, Gates knew that another attack was under way. He could hear the growing artillery fire, and the whine of heavy shells over the town made him realize he was in the very middle of the fight.

The Fahnestocks soon retreated to the cellar, fearful that one of the whizzing shells might fall short.

Gates became fidgety. He couldn't see anything outside.

"Gates, get that shovel and dig a deep hole here near this wall," his father told him suddenly.

Gates stared at him for a few seconds. Why in the world do we need a hole? Oh well, at least that's more fun than just sitting here.

The ground was hard and dry for the first few inches. Then the digging became easier.

His father carried over a box which had been sitting in a corner. Gates recognized the container. It was lined with tin and had often been used for the storage of important papers.

"Your mother and I have put the silverware and other valuables in here," his father explained.

"Would the Rebs steal those things?" Gates inquired.

"Well, maybe so, but we're more concerned about the house catching fire from the shelling," his father answered.

He put the box in the hole and Gates shoveled the dirt back in. By the time the job was finished, the noise outside had settled. They could hear troops ambling back up the street.

Upstairs, Mr. Fahnestock looked outside and then yelled down to his family that it was safe to come up.

Gates opened the front door a crack. The Louisiana Tigers were back. But there didn't seem to be as many now and they didn't seem too happy.

They looked exhausted and discouraged.

"Damn Germans in Howard's army! Can't talk English but they fight like they was protectin' the fatherland," Gates heard one soldier tell the man sitting against the front of the house.

Gates thought it wise to stay indoors. His father agreed.

"They may be in an ugly mood. Doesn't sound like they did too well today," Mr. Fahnestock told his son.


Anna Garlach, her mother and brother Will were up early Thursday.

"Anna, you take care of the baby while Will and I do something to cover the water in the cellar. We can't stay down there in all that water," her mother said.

So as Anna watched, with little Katie in her lap, Will and Mrs. Garlach rolled logs from the back yard into the wide outside steps to the cellar. Mr. Garlach had gathered the wood to make rungs for chairs. The logs were short and fat and all of the same length so Will stood them on end in the water and laid planks across.

The cellar was in three layers, with banks of dirt floor on either side and a dirt valley between. The valley had never drained from the last rainstorm and now the water there was a foot deep.

Mrs. Garlach covered the high banks with planks to avoid contact with the damp earth.

Now there was room for everyone to sit or lie comfortably, on either of the high banks or over the water on top of the log and plank covering.

At the foot of the inside steps Mrs. Garlach placed a sharp axe.

"Do you expect to cut firewood down here, mother?" Will inquired seriously.

"No, son, but if the house is shelled or fired and we become trapped down here at least we'll be able to chop our way out."

Makes, sense, thought Anna.

"Now, we'll stay in the kitchen most of the time, but when you hear firing I want everyone to get into the basement," Mrs. Garlach instructed.

"I suppose, now and then, you'll have to peek out of the doors or windows, but I don't want anyone to go outside again. There are Rebs in the house behind us and our boys just up the street and we're here in the middle. I suppose both sides will just shoot at anything that moves.

"Except, I will go out, with my white bonnet and white shawl, on the pretense of feeding the hogs, to take some bread and water to our General Schimmelfennig out in the wood pile."

Anna took advantage of her mother's allowance to peek out. Through the front window she had a good view of the Winebrenner Tannery building along the alley just across Baltimore Street.

She watched as Confederate infantrymen—most probably sharpshooters, she thought—built a barricade from the alley out into Baltimore Street.

No one hid behind the brick and board wall but after it was done she noticed the soldiers put hats on the tops of sticks and held them at the top of the wall.

"Ping."

Anna would hear the shot just as the hat flew off the stick. The soldier would fish his hat back up with the stick and hold it up again.

"Ping."

They're playing games, Anna thought. Then she noticed that for every shot which hit a hat there was a corresponding shot from one of the houses behind her.

It didn't take long to realize what was going on. The Rebs in the alley were setting up decoys. Every time a Union sharp-shooter saw a hat go up and fired, a Confederate sharpshooter concealed in one of the houses behind the Garlach's house would fire at the flash of the Union rifle.

She couldn't see the riflemen, from either side, but she did notice the firing was slackening off. The decoys, she realized with a sickening feeling in the pit of her stomach, must have worked.

As the day wore on, refugees from nearby houses who no longer felt safe at home filtered into the Garlach's fenced-in backyard and then into the house. There was Hannah Bream and her daughter, Anamathea, the McIlroy family and several members of the Sullivan family—eleven more people.

Mrs. Garlach assigned spaces to all on the boarded cellar floor, and just in time too. Towards evening, they heard heavy firing from the vicinity of Culp's Hill, just a few hundred yards to the east, outside town.

"Everyone, get to the cellar at once! We'll eat supper when it's over," Mrs. Garlach commanded.

It was a late, cold supper they ate that Thursday.


Sleep had been almost impossible for Tillie Pierce. It was the strange bed at the Weikert farm, the confusion in the house all night with soldiers coming and going, doctors operating under lantern light on screaming men and her own curiosity as to what might happen next.

When the Thursday dawn came, she still felt exhausted. But she did what she could to help the wounded that morning.

It was almost noon when she stopped for a breather and that's when she noticed dozens of rough boxes placed along the road just outside the garden fence. She shuttered at the sight of the six-foot long boxes, narrow at one end and wide at the other.

Tillie picked up her skirts and ran around to the back of the house to escape the sight. What she saw out back was worse than the boxes. Spread in a line behind a low stone wall were the bodies of blue-clad soldiers, their guns still in hand or lying nearby.

"Picked off by Red sharpshooters from up there on that big hill. Fell right where they are now."

Tillie wheeled around. The words had flowed from a tall, sunburned soldier with thick, graying hair and both arms wrapped in bandages.

The girl needed no further explanation. She ran again,

straight into the kitchen where Mrs. Weikert and her daughters were baking bread.

"What's the matter, child?" asked Mrs. Weikert.

"I don't think I can stand the smell of food. I can't get rid of the smell of death!"

The old woman smiled and wrapped a flour-stained arm around her house guest.

"Tillie, we must go on. Forget what you have seen and just do what must be done. Now, we need your help here.

"Look here, as soon as one ovenful of bread is baked it's replaced by a new load. These worn-out men are gobbling up every bite we can prepare."

It was the medicine a teen-age girl needed. Soon she was up to her elbows in dough, not quite forgetting the sights outside but at least keeping them from dominating her.

The work went on into the night, through the noise of nearby battle and the groans of the wounded who continued to pour into the tiny farm.

Tillie spent the evening carrying pieces of fresh bread to the soldiers in the house, on the porch and out on the grass.

One soldier, sitting near a doorway in the house, beckoned Tillie to him. The man was holding a lighted candle in his hand and was watching over a wounded soldier who laid on the floor next to him.

"Can you get me a piece of bread, girl? I'm famished, but I don't want to leave my friend."

Tillie nodded a quick yes and was back in seconds with a huge chunk of dark, warm bread.

"Oh, my, that's delicious," the man drooled as he chewed.

Tillie stayed until he had finished.

"One more favor. Would you mind holding this candle and staying with my friend for a while? I'll be back shortly."

Tillie said nothing but took the candle and squatted on the floor.

The wounded man, stirred by the talk and movement, opened his eyes and began a conversation with Tillie as though they were oldtime cousins, though he was old enough to be her father.

Tillie finally mustered up the courage to ask: "Are you injured badly?"

"Yes, pretty badly."

"Do you suffer much?"

"Yes, I do now, but I hope in the morning I will be better."

The other man returned and sat beside his friend.

"If there is anything I can do for you I would be glad to do it, if you would only tell me what," Tillie said as she rose.

The wounded man looked up at her, his eyes reflecting the pain and loneliness Tillie felt was inside him.

"Will you promise me to come back in the morning to see me?"

"Yes, indeed," Tillie answered with a half smile. "Yes, I will."

Dan Skelly was up early on Thursday. It was a bright, clear morning and would have been a wonderful time for a brisk walk up to the cemetery or up the hill to the Seminary. But no one was moving about, not even in town, let alone out to those prominent points now bristling with cannon and infantry.

"Oh, you can move about a little," suggested a sergeant sitting on the Skelly stoop with a cup of hot coffee in his hand. "But be careful, snipers, you know."

It was a relatively quiet morning, save for the occasional exchange of shots between pickets or sharpshooters.

The first rays of the sun drifted over the buildings and down Middle Street. Feels like it's going to be one of those hot, sultry days, Dan thought.

"Hey, Yank," the sergeant called out. "You ever seen General Lee?"

"No, sure haven't, but he's a pretty famous man."

"Well, you're in for a treat. Here he comes up the street."

Dan was flabbergasted as Lee rode by unattended and without any apparent recognition from the soldiers along the street. The horse, Traveler, which Dan had also heard about, shuffled past, carrying the commander of the Army of Northern Virginia past Daniel Alexander Skelly, a merchant's helper of Gettysburg.

Dan watched the general ride to the corner, then turn south

along Baltimore Street. He wondered aloud where Lee might be going, to whom he would be talking.

"Old Massa Robert sometimes neglects to inform as to his plans," the sergeant smirked.

Dan spent a good part of the day in the fenced yard behind the Fahnestock store. At four o'clock he heard heavy cannonading to the southeast. Best get home, he thought.

"We're going to stay in Harvey Wattles' cellar for awhile, Dan. It's good and dry and large enough for many people," his mother said as he arrived home.

Settled in at Wattles, Dan told his mother about a Confederate major he had met in the back yard at the store.

"Said he was originally from Pittsburgh, but went south years before the war. I didn't get his name," Dan said.

"We talked about the war and the causes leading up to it and the result thus far on both sides. He was a fair-minded man and reasonable in his opinions."

"Did you learn anything about what's going on here?" his mother asked.

"No, it's just like it's been. Cut off from all communication with the outside world, we know nothing about our army. Everyone I've talked to is completely in the dark as to how our army is located and how much of it has arrived.

"These Confederates keep that clam-like silence on anything concerning the battle."

Hours passed before anyone felt it was safe to go home.

One of the women who had been sitting in the Wattles' living room before the cannonade began had placed a hat box on the chair where she sat before going to the cellar. When she retrieved the box that evening, Dan pointed to a small hole through each side.

"Was that there before?" asked Dan.

"No, and I can't imagine where it came from," the woman said.

"A bullet passed through there," Dan said, pointing to a shattered pane in the window behind the chair. He eyed the trajectory and glanced at the opposite wall.

"See, there it is, a bullet lodged in that wall. Good thing you got out of that chair," said Dan.

"Oh, my, my, yes! That bullet would have hit me in the—well, it would have hit me."

It was almost dusk when Dan and Will McCreary, out on an errand for the Fahnestocks on Chambersburg Street, were stopped by two soldiers who where escorting a woman on horseback.

"Hey, you two, hold up!" one Confederate ordered, his rifle pointed their way but slightly skyward. "This here lady is the wife of General Barlow from your army. He was badly wounded yesterday and our General Gordon is letting her behind the lines to nurse her husband.

"Someone told her that her husband was taken to a McCreary house on Chambersburg Street. Where might that be?"

Dan looked at Will: "Can't be your place, of course."

"Naw," Will answered. "Only McCreary on this street is Smith McCreary."

They guided the soldiers and Mrs. Barlow to the house. But it was in vain; Mrs. Barlow was disappointed to learn her husband hadn't been there.

"No, sorry, mam. Someone else had come here asking about him yesterday. I inquired too and learned today that your husband supposedly was taken to the Joseph Benner farm on the Harrisburg Road."

Smith McCreary gave them directions and the soldiers and Mrs. Barlow left.

When Dan and Will got back to the store, Mr. Fahnestock asked both if they'd mind sleeping on the second floor of the store that night.

"I'm afraid that any empty store is a temptation to these troops who have so little. Having someone inside might make them think twice about looting us," he explained.

Fahnestock had also asked several other young men and boys who worked for him to stay overnight. But first he ordered each to go home and tell his family.

A window from the second floor room was open. The overnighters, bunched near the window in the dark room, tried to hear what troops lying beneath them on the sidewalk of Middle Street were saying.

"Damn Rebs. Between the way they whisper and these

funny accents I can't understand a word they're sayin'," one of
the boys nudged Dan. "I'm goin' to bed."

That sounded like a good idea to Dan too. It had been a long
day.

The dreadful sounds of what he supposed were wounded
men crying out for water the night before were the first
thoughts Henry Jacobs had on Thursday morning.

There was a great bustling about outside on Middle Street
and Henry lost no time in getting dressed to see what was going
on.

"It seems to be a time of general preparation among the
troops," Professor Jacobs, who had been outside watching,
told his sleepy-eyed son. "And, that in turn, had seemingly
brought about a paralysis of action on the part of our neighbors.
No one is moving about."

Rodes' division, posted along Middle Street, had finished
the stone wall started the previous afternoon opposite the
Jacobs' home.

"A spectacle of ruin and a promise of destruction," Henry's
father termed the wall.

Henry spent the day, as his father suggested, reading and
helping his mother carry water, prepare meals and clean the
house.

It was half-past four by the hall clock when Henry heard the
beginning of considerable artillery firing and then a tremendous roar of musketry. He fancied it to be coming from south
of town, perhaps a half mile away.

But the firing also brought scattered shots further north and
bullets began whizzing around the Jacobs house, forcing the
family to the cellar.

At eight o'clock, when it seemed the nearby shooting had
died down, Professor Jacobs suggested that he and Henry
sneak into the backyard to see what was happening.

They were just a few feet from the door when they realized
that bullets were still whizzing overhead.

"The firing has decreased appreciably, son, but it only takes
one to kill. Run!" the professor shouted.

No sooner were they safely back inside the cellar then they

heard a loud moan and the thump of a body on the sloping outside cellar door.

Henry peered through one of the small windows on either side of the door.

"I think he's dead. He's not moving," he announced.

As the time dragged on and the firing south of town seemed to quiet, they could hear new muskets barking, this time more to the east and southeast, perhaps near the cemetery or maybe Culp's Hill, the next prominent rise to the east.

The noise was almost deafening, even in the cellar.

With darkness came an end to the thundering sounds. Henry and his family went upstairs.

Henry noticed something different outside. It was the voices. They didn't sound like the courteous, considerate Geogians.

"They been moved," a young private answered Henry's query. "We's from North Carolina and those fellows just down the street are the Louisiana Tigas."

Henry moved back inside, his feelings mixed.

"I hope the Rebs didn't win today, but somehow I also hope those Georgia boys didn't get hurt," he told his father.

Professor Jacobs nodded with a smile.

Doctor Fulton, the Union surgeon now trapped behind enemy lines, was at the Myers' front door early Thursday morning.

"The Rebs must trust you to let you walk around like this," said Mrs. Myers as she and Salome let him in.

"That's no problem. With so many wounded from both sides we have to work together with faith. But I've got more important business now and no time for chatting.

"We must get girls and women up to the churches. Our boys are suffering for want of attention."

Salome cringed at the thought. I can't do anything unless I'm out of sight of the wounded, she thought. But the idea of someone suffering for lack of attention was too strong. The humanitarian beckoning was too great.

Salome went with the doctor to the Roman Catholic Church.

She stopped inside the outer door. There in the vestibule the surgeons were at work, cutting away the disease of war.

She pushed on into the sanctuary, the eerie darkness of that poorly-lighted room suddenly enveloping her. Even in broad daylight, it was necessary to burn candles or lanterns for light.

Men were scattered all over, some lying in pews and some on the bare floor. The groans of the dying penetrated Salome like a chill wind of winter.

She steeled her resolve to stay and do what must be done.

"What can I do for you?" she asked the first man inside the door, kneeling beside him as she asked.

The mournful, fearless eyes looked up and a weak voice responded: "Nothing. I am going to die."

The resolve melted and Salome stood up, pushed back out through the vestibule, sat down on the church steps and cried. No one came to her to say, "here, stop that! There's enough trouble." But no one came to comfort either.

Salome sat for a few minutes and once again girded herself for the challenge. She got up, passed through the doors once again and knelt beside the same man.

"He was wounded in the lungs and spine. There's not the slightest hope," the surgeon whispered in her ear. "But you can do him a world of good in his final hours."

The words came haltingly from the wounded man's pale lips and Salome wondered if he should be talking at all.

He was Sergeant Alexander Stewart, Company D, 149th Pennsylvania Volunteers, and he told Salome of his home, of his aged father and mother, his wife and his younger and only brother who had enlisted with him.

"My brother got wounded several months ago. He's home now but unable to walk," Sergeant Stewart whispered, tears glistening in his eyes.

"Perhaps you should be quiet for awhile," Salome suggested. "Save your strength. I have a Bible. Would you like me to read something to you?"

Stewart's mouth widened in a forced smile.

"Oh, would you? Just before I left home, my father and I kneeled in prayer and he read me the 14th Chapter of John. Could you read that for me?"

Salome opened the worn book, quickly finding the chosen spot and began:

"Let not your heart be troubled; ye believe in God, believe also in me.

"In my Father's house are many mansions; if it were not so, I would have told you. I go to prepare a place for you.

"And if I go and prepare a place for you, I will come again, and receive you unto myself; that where I am, there ye may be also . . ."

As Salome read on, she noticed that Stewart was staring at the high ceiling of the church, the smile still upon his sunburned face.

When she had finished, he thanked her and asked one last favor: "Would you take the address of my family and send them my dying message of love?"

Salome nodded and tried to hide the tears rolling down her cheeks.

When Stewart fell asleep, Salome moved on to comfort other wounded men, both Confederate and Union. It was late in the day when Doctor Fulton approached.

"You've done a marvelous job, my girl. But I'm afraid it doesn't end with the setting of the sun. Your friend, Sergeant Stewart, doesn't want to die here. He asked if he might be moved to your house so that you might read to him. I've already asked your mother and she approves if it's alright with you."

Salome's smile told the doctor that it was alright. Within minutes, two stretcher-bearers were carrying Stewart to the Myers' home. Walking slowly alongside, holding the sergeant's limp hand in hers, was the girl who thought she couldn't stand to be near the wounded.

They placed Stewart on a couch in the living room where he could be watched easily.

That night, as shots built into a thunderous roar from the vicinity of Culp's Hill, the Myers family rushed to the cellar. Except Salome.

"We can't move Sergeant Stewart and I can't leave him up here alone," she told her mother.

With doors and windows shut to keep out the dust raised by

horses and wagons in the street, the Myers living room became stifling. Salome fanned Sergeant Stewart with a newspaper.

To be safe, she had lain down on the floor. Balancing herself on one elbow while fanning got very tiring, so she got up, walked around to the side of the backless couch and began fanning with the other hand.

It seemed like only seconds since she had moved when a cannon ball came crashing through the roof, the second floor ceiling and down onto the spot Salome had just vacated.

Plaster pelted both, despite Salome's attempt to shelter her patient with her arms, head and upper body. And the shock left both of them trembling.

"You must . . . go down . . . with others," Stewart coaxed, still trying to catch his breath. "Nothing . . . can save . . . my life . . . but you must . . . not risk . . . yours."

Salome, brushing the plaster dust from his face, shook her head no.

The cannon ball, its energy spent after busting through the roof and upper floor, had bounced and rolled across the room. Salome stared at it, wondering if it would explode, and knew something must be done.

She opened the front door, called to a young officer nearby and explained what had happened. The officer said he'd have his men remove it. When it was gone, Salome resumed her fanning and Stewart, exhausted, fell off to sleep.


Fannie Buehler stayed indoors all through Thursday. Late that night with little else to do, she brought her diary up to date.

"Thursday, July 2, 1863:" she wrote, then paused for thought.

"The fight went on, with the dreadful slaughter of human life, the roar of the artillery and of musketry, with the groans of the wounded and dying, baffles all description.

"At one time it was all so near to us that we closed our ears crouched into a corner, not knowing how to endure it. The ground trembled, on which our house stood, and the awful continuous roar of the cannon was far worse than the heaviest thunder from heaven's artillery.

"That was when the artillery got possession of Culp's Hill (so a soldier had told her) and fought back of the Reformed Church."

(Days later, in a footnote to the fight for Culp's Hill, she would add: "To me, that was the most awful time of the awful battle.")

Fannie patted little Allie, asleep on the bed beside her, and wished that her husband were home.

Albertus McCreary, with boyish curiosity, wanted dearly to stick his head out the front door quickly and then draw it in to see how many Union sharpshooters would mistake him for a Reb.

"Don't even joke about it, boy," his mother scolded. "You stay away from the windows too in the parlor. It's not safe. You can go out on the side porch."

Albertus didn't really enjoy talking to the soldiers waiting in reserve along High Street, next to the side porch. He didn't know how much malarky they were feeding him.

"Union Army is on the run, boy," one had said. "We done took Harrisburg, Philadelphia and Baltimore already, and we're near ready to take Washington. It's all over for you folks."

But anything was better than confinement in the cellar whenever cannonading began. It wasn't only the noise that bothered him; it was the vibration too. How much of that can a house take?

He was astounded by the deaf and dumb man who had taken refuge in their cellar when he and his wife were caught outdoors during a period of heavy shelling.

"He can't hear the shells but he can feel the vibration, probably better than we can," his wife explained.

The man made strange motions with his fingers and hands. His wife nodded her head toward him and then turned to Albertus:

"He said that was a heavy one."

Albertus was amazed. Not only could this man distinguish between light and heavy shelling but he could also talk with his hands.

During a lull in the battle, Albertus sat on the porch and just watched the southern troops.

How poor they look, he thought. Ragged. Dirty. Hungry.

He watched one man with a loaf of moldy bread and a canteen of watery molasses. The man broke off a piece of bread and poured molasses over it. He seemed to be thoroughly enjoying the meal.

"Is that all you have to eat?" Albertus called out.

The man, without missing a chew, gulped back: "Yep, and glad to get it too."

Minutes later, Albertus watched as a soldier on horseback rode past. The boy could hardly keep from laughing. The rider was shoeless but had spurs strapped to his bare heels.

Diagonally across Baltimore Street, Albertus could see what appeared to be a Confederate general in a second floor room of Dr. O'Neal's house. The general must have made his head-quarters there for officers seemed to be coming and going with regularity.

The man with the moldy bread saw the question in the face of Albertus.

"That's General Ewell, commander of our Second Corps, one of Lee's three lieutenants," he told the boy.

"And speaking of Lee, look there."

Albertus turned to the left just as cheers from soldiers along the street rose to a respectable roar. Along High Street the man rode slowly, nodding to the troops.

Albertus thought him to be a grand-looking old man, white hair and beard giving him a kindly grandfather look. The boy found himself standing in awe as the general passed.

Very much the soldier, the boy thought. Erect in his saddle. Short-cropped beard. Neat gray uniform.

He could see some officers riding with Lee cautioning him to stop before wandering out into the range of the sharpshooters on Baltimore Street.

Lee and his officers dismounted and, from the cover of the McCreary home, took quick glances with their field glasses toward the enemy on Cemetery Hill just four blocks away.

Albertus never stirred until Lee had ridden off, back out along High Street to the west.

As he watched the general leave, Albertus glanced at the barn at the far end of the property. He wondered how his pet rabbits were faring. He couldn't cross the yard to feed them, his mother said.

"That fence protects those soldiers along High Street, but you'd be inside the fence to get to the barn and them sharpshooters of ours can't tell you apart from a Rebel at this distance," his mother had told him that morning.

Albertus passed his tale of woe along to the man munching on the moldy bread.

"Shucks, boy, don't worry. I got me some rabbits at home, I'll feed yours," the soldier said.

Albertus counted four bullets kicking up dirt around that Reb's heels as he ran through the yard to the barn. Ten minutes later, and another four shots, he was back, unscratched and grinning.

"Cute bunnies, boy. Sure hope no one cooks 'em for dinner."

Albertus wondered if he had done the right thing telling a hungry man where rabbits could be found. That night he crept out to the barn and dragged the rabbit cage to the house and down to the cellar.

Four-year-old Rosa was the most tired of the Snyder children who had arrived at Aunt Susie Benner's house just the day before. She had been exhausted by the walk from home. On Thursday, when she learned she'd have to walk some more, little Rosa cried.

"Rosa, we can't help it. The soldiers say we may not be safe here. They want us to move farther away from town," said 18-year-old Mary, her guardian as well as sister.

Aunt Susie packed some food and Mary got her brood on the road again. She carried tiny Erz, just a year younger than Rosa. Lob, at five, felt big enough to drag Rosa along by the hand.

Mary tried every farmhouse along the road. Each house was filled with Union troops. At one, an officer picked up little Rosa and kissed her.

"Oh, poor children," he cried, hugging the tiny girl to his

chest. Then he saw to it that each had a cool drink of water
from the well.

As the officer helped Rosa drink, he noticed one of her shoes
was missing.

"Where is your other shoe?"

Rosa glanced up at Mary and then at the officer. Her head
bowed as she whispered: "It fell off while we were walking and
if I stopped to find it I wouda lost Mary too."

Mary knelt to brush the gathering tears from her little sister's
face.

"Don't cry, Rosa. You wouldn't have lost me, and don't
worry about your shoe. But I don't want you to hurt your foot
walking like that."

The officer, meanwhile, was tearing the end from a blanket.
Then he tore thin strips from the same blanket.

"Here, we'll fix you up like a soldier who has no boots," he
said, wrapping the blanket end around her foot and tying it with
the strips around her ankle. "Now, you can walk on it like a
real trooper."

Rosa wiped her eyes and examined her new boot. Then she
glanced into the officer's eyes as he kneeled in front of her and
flung her arms around his neck.

"I wish you were my daddy," Rosa whispered to the man.

"I wish I were too," he whispered back.

As they started out again down the road, Mary could see
quite a number of those rough hewn, dirt-caked soldiers wiping
their eyes and dropping their heads.

Mary and the children had walked several miles before they
found a farmhouse without soldiers and a family who felt they
would be safe.

They were there only a few hours when their brother, John,
who had been working at a farm outside town, joined them.

"My farmer and his family took off," John explained to
Mary. "He told me to stay and watch over his house. When the
shootin' got too close, I skedaddled too. What was I gonna do
if a bunch of Rebs wanted to take over the place?

"Well, anyway, I figured east was the best way to go. Each
place I stopped, I heard about three little kids and a young lady

walkin' this way. Dawned on me after awhile that they was talkin' about you. So I just kept walkin' after you."

It was a grand reunion and took hours to explain everything which had happened on both sides, including how Rosa was wearing one shoe and one blanket.

Attorney William McClean awoke Thursday to find both his wife and mother ill.

"I'll go get Doctor Henry," he told them. "No sense in taking chances."

McClean walked swiftly up East Middle Street, took a Confederate soldier's advice and ran with all the speed he could muster across Baltimore Street to avoid sharpshooter fire. He finally turned up Washington Street to the doctor's home on Chambersburg Street.

The illness proved of little consequence.

"Just upset stomachs, both of them. Maybe something they both ate last night," Doctor Henry told McClean.

"I'll leave you some tonic. Just keep them both quiet today."

Both his mother and wife asked McClean how things looked around town.

"Oh, not too bad," he shrugged off the question, not wanting to tell them about the pools of dried blood on the streets, the dead horses, the cries of wounded men in makeshift hospitals.

Never, he thought to himself, have I seen Gettysburg look so ragged and forbidding.

When the women felt well enough to move downstairs, McClean insisted that they go to the cellar for greater safety. During the day the crackle of rifle fire had increased.

Hours of doing nothing but sitting in the cellar and drifting off to sleep finally wore out the patience of McClean, normally an active man.

"Think I'll take a peek upstairs to see what's going on," he told his wife.

He went to the second floor, opened the outside shutter of a window and glanced up toward the Union lines on Cemetery Hill. But McClean felt a danger present. He closed the shutter and moved away from the window.

Before he could cross the room, a bullet came crashing through the shutter and window and hit the footboard of the bed where his wife had been lying earlier.

McClean hit the floor and didn't move for minutes. No other bullets followed that one so he crawled over to examine the bed and found that the bullet had passed through the footboard and entered the mattress. He couldn't find any exit hole.

Then he imagined himself standing in front of that window. The hole was chest high.

"Damn sharpshooters must be watching every house for movement," he whispered to himself. "Wish they'd figure civilians are still living here, not Rebs."

McClean didn't tell the women what had happened but he did allow them to come up to the kitchen for supper.

That night, from a downstairs side window, they watched the gun flashes and heard the noise of battle coming from Culp's Hill, just a few hundred yards southeast of their home.

The firing went on until ten o'clock.

"How can soldiers see each other in the dark?" the younger Mrs. McClean asked. No one had an answer.

Within minutes they could see Confederate troops streaming back through the streets from the battle. One stopped and knocked at the front door.

He was coughing badly but proudly showing off a sword too.

"You folks got some honey or anything for this cough? Dang near got shot a couple of times tonight giving my position away with a good, deep cough."

Mrs. McClean gave him a dose of Ayer's Wild Cherry Pectoral from the bottle she kept in the kitchen.

"Try that. Might help the cough and fix that horrible accent too. Where are you from?" she asked.

"Louisiana, mam. I thank you for the cough syrup. See the Union sword I picked up on that hill tonight? Beauty, ain't it?"

"Yes, it is," McClean said, interrupting his wife.

"You must stay inside, dear," he said to his wife.

"Goodnight, soldier," McClean said briskly.

"Ah, night, sir. Thank you again, mam."

Elizabeth and Jacob Gilbert spent Thursday two doors away, in the cellar of Uncle Dave Troxell, along with three other families.

It was ten o'clock before things quieted down enough for everyone to go home to bed.

Liberty Hollinger's father slipped out early on Thursday morning to check on his warehouse.

When he got back, he sighed to his oldest daughter: "Oh, Lib, it's enough to make you sick!

"Those Rebs broke in, like they said they would, took what they wanted and ruined everything else.

"They opened the spigots of the molasses barrels and let molasses run all over the floor. Then it looks like they threw salt and sugar and everything else they could find on top of the molasses.

"I don't see how we'll ever clean up that mess," Hollinger said, sinking into a soft parlor chair.

Liberty put her arms around her father's head, brushed his hair and said nothing.

It wasn't long before the smattering of bullets against the brick walls of the exposed house sent the entire family to the cellar.

There was a large wheat field south of the Hollinger house on the Culp farm, ripe and ready for harvest, but now it seemed to be full of Union sharpshooters.

Whenever Liberty got a chance to peek out a side window, she could see blue uniforms pop up from the wheat, raise a rifle, fire and disappear again. And beyond the field, Liberty could see riflemen in the trees.

She noticed they'd be particularly active, first firing from trees and then jumping up in the field, whenever Confederate officers rode past the Hollinger house.

Each time that Mr. Hollinger went outside to feed the chickens and milk the cow, bullets from the sharpshooters would kick up around him and he'd have to retreat.

By late morning, Mr. Hollinger told Liberty:

"Enough is enough. Why in blazes are they shooting at me?"

And with that, he took a large white towel from a kitchen drawer, tied it to the broom in the closet and stepped outside, waving that homemade flag slowly to the south. No one shot at him. Hollinger walked slowly off the porch and started across the Hanover Pike and into the fields.

Before he got to the wheatfield, a voice with a definite Yankee ring yelled out strongly:

"Halt right there, mister. What's going on?"

Hollinger could see a raised musket and part of a blue uniform behind a tree less than fifty yards away.

"I live in that house back there and everytime I go out to feed my chickens or milk the cow, you people start firing at me."

"Hell, it's easy to see why. Take off that damn gray suit. From out here it looks like you got on a Johnny Reb uniform. You got another suit?"

"Black one."

"Well, either wear the black one or come out in your drawers!"

"Alright," Hollinger stammered, half embarrassed that he hadn't noticed the color of his suit. "And thank you."

The chickens and the cow were both glad to see Hollinger.

That afternoon, as fighting raged to the south, Confederate wounded trickled back through the Hollinger yard. The less lucky were on stretchers and Liberty flinched when she saw blood dripping down through the stretchers from men—indeed, many seemed like mere boys—with faces as pale as death.

One boy hobbled into the yard on one foot. Blood had soaked through the shoe on his wounded foot.

"You'd best have someone cut that shoe off before your foot swells much more," Mrs. Hollinger yelled after him as the boy kept hobbling.

Towards evening, a group of Confederates, who weren't wounded, sauntered into the Hollinger yard, knocked on the front door and asked to be fed.

"I'm afraid we don't have enough food to do that," Hollinger told them firmly.

The soldiers scowled and Hollinger wondered what he

would say next. He didn't have to say anything because Julia, his lovely young daughter, came up to his side at the door. The soldiers gazed at the child's beauty and began to smile.

"Well, sir, that's alright. We understand," one of the soldiers told Hollinger. "But it would just be great if your daughter here and the other girl we've seen here would sing for us."

"We can't sing to please Confederates," Julia told them. "But possibly our boys in blue would hear us and we'd cheer them."

So the girls sang a Union war song. And the soldiers responded with a Southern song. Then the girls had another and the soldiers responded again.

Finally, the soldiers asked if they could come into the house to continue the singing if the family had a piano.

"We have a piano, but I'm afraid it wouldn't be right to have you do that. We have to say goodnight now," Mr. Hollinger said to the soldiers. And with that he nudged the girls inside and closed the door.


H. S. Huidekoper, despite the amputation of his arm, felt he should have been able to get a good night's sleep on the second floor gallery of the Catholic Church.

"But the moans, groans, shrieks and yells from everyone else in here gave me a horrible night," he told an orderly Thursday who was changing the bandage on the stump.

"Well, colonel, there's a lot of suffering here. Some of the men who kept you awake won't ever keep anyone else awake with noise; quite a few died during the night," the orderly informed Huidekoper.

"You're Confederate, aren't you?"

"Yes, sir, colonel. But it don't make no mind that you're a Union officer. You're hurtin' and someone's got to take care of you."

Huidekoper tried to sit up. His arm ached.

"Best lay still, colonel. You had a shock losing that arm. Although when I first seen you I thought you'd be walkin' out of here. Fact is, you almost did."

Huidekoper looked puzzled.

"Eh, how's that?"

"Well, you was just gettin' up on the operating table when we overran this church. Some of our boys watched the operation.

"Well, sir, after your arm was . . . I mean after it was all over, you got down off the table and was told to go lay down near the pulpit. And you said to the doctor:

" 'Not until I have gone into the street to see what the rascally Rebels are doing.'

"Well, you went to the door, looked out into the street and then came up here. I was just comin' in. I seen you, sir."

"You know, in a way you're lucky, colonel."

"Oh, sure," Huidekoper replied.

"Meanin' no disrespect, sir, but our boys are takin' those who ain't severely wounded out to the sidewalk, linin' 'em up, makin' 'em give up their shoes and then marchin' 'em to the rear as prisoners."

The orderly stopped talking with the sound of voices and the clump of boots on the narrow stairway to the gallery.

"Land sakes," the orderly exclaimed. "It's officers from General Ewell's staff."

Huidekoper turned toward the stairway just in time to see a baldheaded general with one leg being assisted up the last few steps.

Ewell himself, Huidekoper assumed.

Two of the officers then climbed a ladder from the gallery which led to a cupola, but Ewell sat on a bench not three feet from Huidekoper.

"Morning, colonel," Ewell said coldly.

"Good morning, general," Huidekoper answered.

"Your General Sickles has pulled his corps out of the line. He's smacking it out on the open, down through an orchard and a wheatfield with some of our Texans and other boys from old Longstreet's command," Ewell said.

"And who's winning?" Huidekoper asked.

"Who's winning, the man wants to know?" Ewell yelled to his officers in the cupola.

"Things are going spendidly; we are driving them back and gaining everywhere," one of them answered.

Huidekoper felt uneasy. Ewell did not seem to be a pleasant

man and if what he said was true Sickles could be in desperate straits.

The colonel tried to take his mind off the subject. He stared at Ewell and admired the gorgeous gold lace which adorned the sleeves, collar and front of his gray coat.

Then he was angry at Ewell, for it was his troops, or at least Rebels who caused him to lose an arm.

"How in hell do I go through life with only one arm?" he blurted out, then added quickly: "Oh, I apologize, general; I didn't mean to shout out like that."

"Oh, not at all, colonel, and I have an answer. You just do what you have to do. I've been fighting a war since losing this on the Peninsula last year," he said, patting the empty pant leg.

Huidekoper felt somewhat foolish.

Later that day Huidekoper got a second visitor.

"Hello, I'm Salome Myers. Do you need anything?" said the attractive young woman who knelt down beside him.

The colonel threw back his blanket and struggled to sit up.

"Well, the orderly is trying to take care of this mess," he answered, pointing to the bandaged stump of his arm. "But I am awfully hungry. Haven't had a bite since daylight yesterday."

Salome arose and said pleasantly: "I'll run home for some things and be right back."

In ten minutes she was at his side again. From under her shawl, she produced a small bottle, filled with wine, and one cracker.

"Things are scarce," she apologized. "I had to hide these lest some hungry Rebel snatched them away."

Huidekoper nibbled at the cracker, relishing each small bite. And he sipped the wine slowly, until both were gone.

"If you were staying in our home, we could feed you better," Salome suggested. "My parents approve of that."

Huidekoper got to his feet and, with Salome's aid, walked slowly down the narrow, winding staircase.

"Doctor," he addressed a man near the door in a blood-smeared white frock. "This kind lady has offered me a roof during my recuperation. I beg your leave to take advantage of her offer."

The surgeon looked at both closely.

"Write your name, rank, unit, the young lady's name and the address of the house you're going to on this paper," the doctor said as he produced a pencil and a ragtail list which indicated that other patients had been released to private homes.

"Orderly, help the colonel to the lady's house," the doctor shouted to a private nearby.

The orderly walked behind as Salome and Huidekoper moved slowly away from the church to the Myers home, a mere hundred feet.

Huidekoper thought to himself: The orderly is not here to assist, only to make sure I go where I told the doctor I would go.

John Rupp, the tanner, wished at times Thursday night that he had gone with his wife, Caroline, and their children to his father's house at the corner of York and Stratton Streets.

"No," he had told Caroline, "you and the young 'uns go with Pa. I'll stay here to make sure those blasted Rebs don't bust up the workshop."

By that night, the tannery workshop, out back of the house at the southern end of Baltimore Street, was in Confederate hands. So was the back porch.

But federal troops held the front porch. No-man's land was inside the two-story frame home and John Rupp was in the cellar.

Through the windows in the front of the cellar, John was able to tell the federal troops that he was inside. But the Rebs didn't know he was there.

"Can't crawl through these damn little windows but I could go upstairs and escape," he told a Yankee sergeant.

"And go where? We can't move from where we're at cause of snipers. No, mister, you stay in there," the sergeant advised.

John could hear the Confederate troops loading their weapons and firing, but he couldn't hear much conversation through the stone wall at the rear of his cellar.

SALOME MYERS STEWART, care of a wounded soldier led to marriage. *(Adams County Historical Society)*

HENRY E. JACOBS, eighteen years old during the battle, this photograph shows him years later as a college professor. *(Photo No. 79-T-2632, National Archives)*

MOTHER ANN SIMEON NORRIS *(Daughters of Charity Archives)*

**SISTER MARY LOUISE
CAULFIELD**
*(Daughters of Charity Archives)*

**SISTER CAMILLA O'KEEFE**
*(Daughters of Charity Archives)*

**THE VERY REV. FRANCIS
BURLANDO**
*(Daughters of Charity Archives)*

CARRIE SHEADS, who turned a school into a hospital.
*(Ross Ramer, Gettysburg)*

DR. JOHN W. C. O'NEAL, physician caught behind Confederate Lines.
*(Adams County Historical Society)*

JOHN BURNS, a portrait of Gettysburg's old citizen-soldier.
*(Photo No. 79-T-2094, National Archives)*

WILLIAM McCLEAN,
Gettysburg attorney who aided
wounded.
*(Adams County Historical
Society)*

CARRIE SHEADS'
HOUSE: Two views — in
1863 with dark brick and
light woodwork; today
with white brick and dark
wood.
*(Ross Ramer, Gettysburg)*

THE WEIKERT FARM, as it now appears. Tillie Pierce helped care for the wounded here.
*(Photo by Bill Schwartz, Gettysburg)*

JENNIE WADE and the house in which she died. The house still stands and a statue in the town cemetery marks her grave.
*(Photo No. 79-T-2084, National Archives)*

**CONFEDERATE SOLDIERS** lie in shallow grave as Army burial teams move about the field.
*(U.S. Army Military History Institute, Carlisle Barracks)*

**THE SEMINARY, as it now** appears. Sallie Broadhead nursed wounded soldiers in this building.
*(Photo by Bill Schwartz, Gettysburg)*

**JOHN BURNS AT HOME,** seated on his porch recovering from battle wounds. The long, dark object behind his right shoulder is the barrel of his musket. Behind his left shoulder is a crutch. Man at bottom of steps is not identified.
*(U.S. Army Military History Institute, Carlisle Barracks)*

U.S. SANITARY COMMISSION sets up office and unloads supplies at the Fahnestock Store on Baltimore Street. Building, below, stands today.
*(U.S. Army Military History Institute, Carlisle Barracks)*

*(Photo by Rose M. Prouser, Prouser Photographic)*

STRATTON STREET, looking south from Middle Street, a few days after the battle. The church (round steeple) in center background still stands, as shown in photo below.
*(Photo No. 79-T-2027, National Archives)*

*(Photo by Fred S. Prouser, Prouser Photographic)*

# CHAPTER
# 8

# The Third Day

It was early Friday afternoon when Confederates found the three horses the Bayly family had concealed in a dark corner of the barn.

"We'll have to take those colts in the field too," a captain told Joseph. "They look about full grown."

"But they're unbroken and unshod," Joseph protested. "They'd slow you down."

"Tell you what," the captain shot back. "If your wife cooks a good meal today for my colonel and his staff I'll see to it that the colts stay here."

"Agreed," said Joseph. "But one of those horses that was in the barn is named Nellie. It was the pet of our only daughter, Jane, who just died recently. She was only eleven years old. My wife will be heartbroken if you take Nellie!"

"I'm sorry, Mr. Bayly. Best I can do is leave the colts. We need horses desperately."

Harried cooked the required meal. But late that afternoon, when she saw them leading Nellie from the barn, she cried and ran into the yard, grabbing at the man who held the horse's reins. She beat on his back but the soldier hung on.

Finally, the captain ran over, grabbed the reins and thrust them into Harriet's hands.

"Here, Madam, and if you have a parlor lock her up in it, for you will lose her if you don't."

Harriet grabbed the horse by the neck and hugged with all her might.

The captain, noticeably angry, mustered his men and marched them off down the road.

Harriet was smiling and telling Billy to go fetch the horse an apple and a bucket of water when she heard hoofbeats. She turned. It was the captain coming back.

He snapped up the reins and yanked the horse away from Harriet's clinging arms.

"Madam, I was sent for this horse and I must take her. I despise this whole business and would leave her if I could."

Then he galloped off, leading Nellie on the run behind him.

Harriet sat on the ground and just watched. There were no tears, just a vacant stare. Joseph pulled her up from the ground and buried her head in his chest.

Billy stood watching his parents, wondering what horror could visit them next. He thought that the temper of the Confederate troops had changed considerably in the past three days.

Shortly after the noon meal which his mother had prepared for the colonel's staff they heard a tremendous booming of cannons from the south. And they could see white smoke drifting skyward.

"Looks to be in town or maybe slightly to the south," Joseph said to one of the lieutenants who had been at the meal.

"It's between the two ridges just south of town, on the open plain. And it's safe to tell you now that it's the start of Longstreet's assault on the Union center. Our illustrious General Pickett will be out there leading the charge," the lieutenant bragged, obviously feeling important because he knew so much of the important battle plan.

The noise went on like a continuous and nearby clap of thunder for almost two hours. Billy figured that every cannon hauled into Adams County by both armies must be involved.

And after that stopped, they could hear sporadic cannon fire, then muskets. Within twenty minutes that noise died down too.

By late afternoon, there were no Confederate troops near the Bayly home. Billy's Uncle William Hamilton and his son, John, had arrived at the farm to check on conditions there. Their place, nearby, seemed safe now too, they told the Baylys.

"Let's take a look-see what's going on," Joseph suggested to his brother-in-law.

So the two men and their sons, plus the Confederate deserter who had been hiding in the house, walked up to the crest of a hill on the farm where they could see westward, beyond Gettysburg.

They could still hear shots from muskets and some cannon fire, but it appeared that the Confederate army was moving back, toward the mountains, away from them.

"It's a good sign. They're retreating; I'm sure," said William Hamilton. "Maybe now I'll get word of my sons."

(In addition to John at home, William Hamilton had two sons serving with the Army of the Potomac.)

" I know the boys must have been here. I just hope they're both alright," he said nervously.

"Don't worry, Bill. They've come through scrapes before," Joseph Bayly tried to assure him.

A half hour after the Hamiltons left for home the Baylys and their deserter were still standing on the hill, watching as wagon trains, perhaps carrying wounded, moved slowly to the rear.

They hardly heard the two horses come up behind them.

"Hey, which way to Hagerstown, nearest route?" a voice called out.

The three turned quickly and the deserter, forgetting that he was now dressed in civilian clothes, flinched.

The voice belonged to a Confederate cavalryman.

"You have to go west, down there, see, where some of your wagons are moving. You have to get on that road," Joseph told them willingly.

"You'd better be right, farmer, or we'll come back here and slice your ugly head off," the other cavalryman shouted.

It was more than Billy could take.

"You cheap excuse for a soldier!" he started shouting as the two riders galloped off. "You get down off that horse and I'll teach you to talk to my father like that! You—"

The deserter clapped his hand over Billy's mouth.

"Are you crazy?" he whispered in Billy's ear.

Mr. Bayly stood dumbfounded, trying to calculate what he would do next.

He didn't have to do anything. The two riders stopped momentarily, exchanged vile glances with young Billy, then whipped their horses away.

"See? They're scared," Billy shouted.

"Yes, but maybe more of being captured than the tongue of a dumb, but brave, boy," his father smiled.

On Friday morning, a Confederate officer stopped Joseph Broadhead outside his house.

"You'd better vacate this end of town. It may get shelled today," the officer told Joseph.

He glanced up Chambersburg Street toward the Diamond and then west toward the seminary. Some people were moving away from the west end of town.

"I'll not go anywhere while one brick remains upon another. This is my home and I won't be driven away from it!" Joseph answered defiantly.

"Suit yourself," the officer said, "but don't say you weren't warned."

Sallie was at the door looking for her husband as he walked away from the officer.

"What did he want?"

"Ah, love, well, there might be a bit of heavy bombardment. Best we stay in the cellar for a bit."

When Joseph was worried, his English accent thickened into a brogue. It was a dead giveaway.

"Oh, Joseph, perhaps we should go somewhere else!"

"No, no, girl, we won't be turned out into the street. We've been okay through two days of this. We'll remain in the cellar."

And with that he scooped up little Mary who was standing in front of her mother in the doorway.

"Come, little pumpkin, down to the dungeon we go."

They sat for hours, once leaving to get some bread and bits of salted pork from the kitchen for their lunch.

It was early afternoon when the loudest sound they had ever heard began. One cannon shot. A second shot. Then, all hell broke loose!

Mary screamed. Sallie pulled her child into her lap to shield her ears. She held her own too but it did little good. The sound penetrated to the center of her skull and radiated back out until the surface of her skin tingled.

Damn! This doesn't sound too pleasant, Joseph thought to himself. Should have bloody well taken that officer's advice. Well, too late now.

No one spoke. When Joseph tried, Sallie just shook her head indicating she couldn't hear him. So he just sat holding his wife tightly against him with one hand. He placed his other hand on Mary's head to calm her fears.

Sallie tried to picture what was going on. It was impossible. But she knew the sound was more terrible than anything that had ever greeted human ears.

She knew that with every explosion and the scream of each shell human beings were being hurried through excruciating pain into another world, and that many more were being torn and mangled and lying in a torment worse than death. And no one is able to extend them relief.

The thought did not sicken her, though she knew it was repulsive. Rather, it saddened her greatly.

If it is God's will, I would rather be taken away now than to remain and see the misery that must surely follow, she told herself.

Her mind went blank with that inner suggestion. Then, she couldn't tell how much later, she wondered aloud: "God, will this day never come to a close?"

Joseph, she knew, didn't hear that.

Who is victorious? Or with whom does the advantage rest? She thought.

Before three o'clock the roaring guns had quit. Then came the pop of one gun here, and one there. Some muskets joined in. Men shouted. Horses winnied. More and more guns joined in. But the combined noises were a lullaby compared to the two-hour cannonade just ended.

Another hour passed before Joseph felt it was safe to go upstairs. Troops were moving down the street, westward.

Were they defeated? Joseph saw, from the looks on the faces of those dusty Rebel veterans, that this would be a bad time to ask them who won the fight.

"It may be over, love," he told Sallie. "But I venture to say we won't know for awhile. Perhaps tomorrow we'll really have something to celebrate."

Sallie looked puzzled: "Tomorrow? What celebration?"

"Ah, you native-born Americans. Forget your biggest holiday? Fourth of July, pet, freedom day!"

Mary McAllister and her sister had heard the officer's warning that morning too. Like the Broadheads two blocks away, they decided to stay.

Martha had baked a pie that morning and the drifting aroma of that delicacy had attracted two Confederates from the street.

"We'd sure hanker for a piece of that," said one man as he stuck his head in the open parlor window.

"Smells like a berry pie," said the other.

"In, in!" said Martha impatiently. "One small piece for each of you and that's all. We have wounded to feed."

She set the pie on a small table, along with a knife as the men came into the hallway.

"Here, cut it the best way you can," Martha said.

One of the soldiers cut the pie into small wedges.

"Now you eat a piece," he said to Martha.

"You think it's poisoned? Women here don't poison people!" she said angrily.

"Then you eat a bite," the soldier insisted.

"Not me," said Martha.

"I don't trust her," said the soldier to his companion. "I ain't gonna die over a slice of lousy pie. Let's get out of here."

After they slammed the door behind them, Mary dug a fork into one of the wedges.

"Delicious, Martha," she said, smacking her lips after the light crust and crushed berries melted in her mouth.

"The pie or the way we handled those bad-mannered Rebels?" Martha asked.

"Both, sister, both."

It was mid morning when Mary decided to get some molasses from her store stockroom. She skipped across the street quickly.

The door to the store was open. So was the door to the storeroom and Mary could hear voices.

She stepped into the darkened backroom. A candle had been lit and soldiers were dipping crocks and buckets into a barrel of molasses.

"That's my barrel," she cried out. "The least you can do is let me get some to take back home."

They're a mean-looking lot, she thought. Toughest bunch I've seen yet.

"You damn old bitch, get out of here!" shouted one particularly nasty-faced young Rebel.

No one moved against her, so Mary dipped a pitcher full of the thin molasses and marched back out of the store.

The nasty lot followed her out and back to the house. Mary walked around to the back door, where she knew a Confederate officer had posted a guard for their protection.

The nasty-faced young Rebel confronted the guard with his rifle raised.

"Hey, what are you doing here?" he threatened the guard. "Looks like you were sneaking around. Guess we'll have to shoot you."

Mary heard the click of a gun being cocked, and a voice above her.

"You shoot him and you're dead too," said the voice.

Mary looked up. A rifle was trained from the back bedroom window and the face was that of a wounded man she'd been caring for.

"Now, back off, scum!" the wounded man demanded.

The nasty-faced young Rebel lowered his gun and stammered. "Oh, we're just joshin'. No need to take offense."

He lowered his gun and began backing away.

The wounded man watched carefully. Then he warned: "Better keep backin' up til you get home, son, cause I'm gonna tell my captain what you done. If he sees your ugly hide, you'll be wishin' you were up on the firing line."

The young Rebel and his friends backed out of the yard and turned and ran down the alley.

"Bunch of tramps. Sorry about them kind, Miss Mary," the wounded man apologized as he slowly released the hammer and drew his rifle back inside the room.

Feeling safe once again, Mary told her sister that she was going out for milk.

"Where?" Martha inquired.

"Just down the corner. Cobeans' house at the corner of Washington Street. They got cows out in the stable and the whole family took off two days ago. Those cows must be bursting with milk by now."

Mary found that others must have had the same idea. All of the cows but one had already been milked. A pitcher full was all she could get.

Just outside Cobeans' side gate was a dead soldier and twenty feet away were three wounded Confederates, who seemed to be on their own with no help.

"Oh, mam, could we have a drop of that milk, please?" called out one. "They put us out here hours ago to await an ambulance to the rear and we've had nothing to drink."

All three seemed to have leg wounds, Mary thought from their blood-stained trousers. And none appeared able, or willing, to get up.

Each took several large gulps from the pitcher, slopping milk down over their chins and shirts.

"Careful, don't waste it," Mary scolded.

"Thank you kindly," said one of the soldiers.

"Yes, yes," the other two chimed in.

"You're all welcome," she said, hurrying up the street.

"Did you get any milk?" Martha asked as her sister rushed into the kitchen.

"Started out with a gallon and now have a pint," Mary said and then explained what had happened.

They shared the milk remaining with their wounded and for themselves drank tea and ate water crackers.

The afternoon bombardment kept Mary, Martha and her ill husband, John Scott, indoors. But they tended to their patients.

By evening, things had quieted down nicely.

Across the street, Mrs. King was bringing fresh biscuits to the Confederate soldiers who had camped on her front porch to protect her, her children and her mother from that rough element which seemed to infect every army.

"Here boys, fresh from the oven," Mrs. King said.

"No, thank you, Mrs. King. We had a decent supper tonight. Save those for the children," one of the guards told her.

"No, no. I have plenty. Here, if you can't eat them now then stuff them in your knapsacks. You can eat them on the retreat."

The guard laughed. "Oh, we're not retreating. They're just regrouping back there."

Mrs. King insisted: "McClellan will be here before morning with another big army. Oh, yes, I hear from good authority that you're retreating."

The guard's smile disappeared. He took the biscuits and distributed them to his comrades. They stuffed them into their knapsacks.

Inside the house, Mary asked Mrs. King if it was true about the retreat.

"Oh, shaw, I don't know. But I did hear the Rebs got whupped good today. I just like to keep them boys guessin', that's all."

As Mary crossed the street to home, she could hear wagons moving. The noise was coming from the west, out where the guard said the Confederates were regrouping.

"Oh, if it were only true," Martha responded when Mary told her what Mrs. King had said. "I wish they were retreating. I am hardly able to go it anymore."

It had just turned dark when Mary heard shouts in the street.

She opened the front door cautiously just as a Confederate soldier was shaking the guards at the King house from a deep sleep.

"Up, up, men. Get up, damn you! We're retreating. Move!" he shouted as they lumbered to their feet.

"Oh, Martha, it is true! They are leaving," Mary said with tears beginning to stream down her cheeks.

"I feel like saying goodbye to them, but I guess that would seem like mockery," she said. Then she closed the door slowly and quietly.

Anna and most of her family were in the cellar on Friday morning but her mother was up in the kitchen when she heard the front door open. Mrs. Garlach rushed into the hall just as a Confederate soldier hit the first step.

She grabbed him by the coat: "Where are you going?"

The soldier, startled, wheeled around and shouted back: "Second floor, lady! Gonna do a little sharpshootin'."

"Not from this house, you're not! You can't go up there. You'll draw fire on this house full of defenseless women and children."

"Lady, I gotta use this house. It's in the right spot."

And with that, little Mrs. Garlach shoved the gray-clad soldier and his long-barrelled rifle toward the front door.

"Lady, if I go out there now it'll mean instant death!"

Mrs. Garlach stopped pushing.

"Alright, you can stay in the house, but you can't fire a shot from in here."

The soldier stared in disbelief and thought this little woman sounded like his own mother when she scolded him as a boy.

"Well, can't do any good here arguin' with you," he said. And with that, he pushed open the front door, fired his gun in the air and in the smoke darted out to the safety of Winebrenner's Alley across Baltimore Street.

Mrs. Garlach could see, from the protected area near her back door, that sharpshooters had taken over John Blocher's house just up the street.

"Looks like they knocked out some brick on the second floor. You can see their rifles sticking out," she told Anna later, "and because those Rebs are in Blocher's, we're catching it too. Upstairs, you can hear the bullets—I guess they're coming back from our men up at the cemetery—you can hear the bullets hitting the front of our house. Those bricks out there must be an awful sight."

"Wow!" shouted Will. "When this fight is over, ma, we can dig them bullets out for souvenirs. Can I go up to the garret to see what's going on?"

"Land sakes, no!" Mrs. Garlach shot back. "No eleven-year-old boy can be taking chances like that. You're so foolhardy you'd get shot."

Anna chuckled: "Oh, ma, don't be so down on poor Will. How about if I take him up to the garret for a quick peek?"

"And have two foolhardy kids up there? No, thank you. I'll go. Guess it won't do any harm. Come on, Will."

The small window looking south was covered by a board which Mr. Garlach had attached with a handle so it could be fitted in to keep out the weather and pulled out easily.

"Now, just a quick look. There are snipers, you know, Will," his mother warned as she pulled the board away.

Will glanced through the opening, which was just slightly larger than his head. He could see troops in blue at the cemetery just a few hundred yards away. And he could see cannons lined up along the ridge which swept from the cemetery. And he could see flags—hundreds, he thought.

"Enough," his mother said, slamming the board back in place.

"That couldn't have been more than five seconds," Will complained.

"Plenty of time for a quick look," she responded as they started down the steps to the second floor.

"BAM . . . BAM BAM!"

"My God!" Mrs. Garlach shouted. "Quick, Will, to the cellar!"

They ran down the three flights of stairs.

"What happened?" Anna shouted as her mother and brother came pounding down the cellar steps.

"Snipers—I guess," a breathless Mrs. Garlach whispered.

"Sounded like two or three bullets came through the garret window board just after we'd closed it.

"Enough of that, Will. Now you see what I mean."

"Ma, those bullets must have come from our troops. Why would they fire at us?"

"How do they know who's in the window? Rebel snipers firing at them from Blocher's house probably make them edgy. I guess they've got their field glasses trained this way and when they saw a face in our garret window they just assumed it was more Rebs."

It was the last time for hours that the Garlachs came upstairs. The afternoon thundering of cannons, followed by a continuous roar of muskets, the yells of the victors and the screams of the dying struck them with a deepseated fear of what was transpiring.

By late afternoon, they felt safe enough to creep cautiously up to the kitchen for a bite to eat.

It was just before dark when Anna heard a light tapping at the back door. Her mother was at her heels as she opened the door to several soldiers.

"Beg pardon, miss, but we noticed your shop out back with lots of lumber. Wondered if we might go in to make a coffin. Our General Barksdale has been killed."

The request came from a young sergeant whose unshaven face and dirty clothes gave Anna a momentary scare.

"A coffin?" she stammered.

"Yes, miss, for our general," the sergeant answered with his cap in his hands and a plea in his voice.

Mrs. Garlach spoke up abruptly: "If you go in that shop and light a lantern you'll make yourselves and us targets for sharpshooters again. Look around you, there's enough wood laying around the yard to build a coffin. You can help yourself to as much of it as you want.

"But please don't tear down the stack of wood near the shed which my husband spent so much time on," she asked softly.

Anna looked at her mother and then out at the stack of wood she had mentioned. Then she remembered about the Union general. What was his name? A German one, Schimmel something, oh, never mind. She wondered if he was still hiding under the wood. My gosh, he's been under there since Wednesday, she thought. Oh, maybe he escaped last night.

The soldiers had begun picking up scraps of lumber for the coffin as the sergeant thanked Mrs. Garlach.

"That's quite alright," she told him. "Now, then, I suggest you take that wood up to Daniel Culp's shop; that's just near the courthouse. You can have a light there which won't be seen from the cemetery."

As soon as the soldiers had gone and the women were back inside, Anna asked about the general.

"Schimmelfenning? As far as I know he's still out there. But I was afraid someone would spot me out there and capture him so I've taken him no water or bread since yesterday."

Tillie Pierce awoke late on Friday. With her exhaustion worn off, she fairly ran down the steps of the Weikert farm house to visit with the soldier she'd left the night before.

The soldier still lay there, his faithful attendant at his side.

The soldier was awfully still, Tillie thought. His eyes were closed. But the eyes of his companion were wet, as if he had been crying.

"He's dead," the companion told Tillie without emotion. "I'm afraid he's dead."

Tillie stood gazing in sadness at the prostrate form. It was a rude awakening for a 15-year-old.

Finally, the companion spoke again: "Did you know who this is?"

"No, sir."

"This is the body of General Weed, a New York man."

Tillie looked into the peaceful, sleeping face one last time and then she turned away. She didn't want the companion to see her crying.

She sat under an apple tree in the yard and gazed at the house. Then she turned to look toward the barn and saw a book lying nearby.

It was small, a black notebook or a Bible. Tillie picked it up and leafed through the pages. It was a diary. In her excitement she didn't look at the title page but flipped instead, almost

without thinking, to July. The first entry was July 2. That was
just yesterday, Tillie thought.

"Battle of Gettysburg, Pa.—five miles distant in the morning," the scribbled entry read.

"Reveille at 3 a.m. Orders to go forward rapidly so do not
get coffee for most of the men. After going a little distance we
cross a field and take up a position near or at the extreme right
of our line of battle. 12th Corps here. Pray. Get cup of coffee
at about 10 a.m. After pushing forward skirmishers, finally
recross the Baltimore Turnpike. The corps comes out in solid
columns, side by side, considerably.

"Adolphus says he is entirely willing to trust in God in any
event. May the Lord give me trust in Him."

Tillie was fascinated.

"In the afternoon very heavy artillery to the west. We march
to near the road to Taneytown and up on the top of a rocky hill
lie till cannonading commences heavily at 3 p.m. Orders to
move. Do right in front. Having gone wrong reverse line. Our
position on the hill is near the Baltimore Pike, some 1½ miles
back of cemetery.

"March down through the field and toward the wood where
we hear musketry firing, which is near.

"Along road to Taneytown column files off to the front. Dr.
Wagner near here informs me where the Division Hospital is to
be. The hospital is at the stone house at the left of the line, and
near the Knobb."

Must be talking about Round Top, Tillie thought.

"The house is the Weikert house."

"He's writing about right here," Tillie said softly to herself.

"At about 5 p.m. the regiment goes into action. Soon the
wounded begin to pour in upon us and now all are very busy.
I had early ransacked the house and secured operating tables,
cloths for dressing, etc. The men had brought down a strange
supply of these, among other things a neatly worked lady's
chemise. One young lady discovered it. I would not permit it
to be removed till something should take the place of it as some
of my instruments were already upon it. She gladly supplied its
place. Is nearly midnight before retiring when with Dr.

Whittingham I go and lie under an apple tree. Get a little sleep."

Tillie realized the diary belonged to a doctor, possibly one still on the farm.

She turned to the first page. There, in bold letters, the name of the owner stood out: The Daily Register of Dr. Cyrus Bacon, Jr., Michigan.

A bitter fight early that afternoon, preceded by hours of constant cannon fire, prevented Tillie from seeking out Dr. Bacon. But that night, before dark, when the din of battle had ceased, she found him near the barn.

"I believe this is yours, Doctor," she said after an orderly had pointed Bacon out to her.

The doctor took his diary and, as if checking for missing pages, hurriedly leafed through it.

"Oh, child, thank you so much. I thought that all the notes I'd been keeping of this war had been lost forever."

"I'm afraid, sir, that I read your entry for yesterday. I meant no disrespect," Tillie said, her head downward.

Bacon smiled and put his hand on her head: "No harm done. In fact, if you'd like we can sit on the porch while I put in today's entry."

"But what of the wounded?" Tillie protested.

"Child, I am only mortal. At least once every 24 hours I must sit down or else I shall fall down. I have been ordered to sit for ten minutes, long enough to write down some thoughts."

So Tillie watched as Bacon scribbled in his little black book.

"July 3. Up early. Coffee. Fix my table. Operations, amputations, etc. Orders to remove hospital as there is danger at this point from the enemy's shells. They are shelling a battery a few hundred yards to the front of us."

Bacon stopped writing to explain: "We moved the hospital back a few hundred yards."

Then he went on writing.

"We get shelled frequently during the day. It is amusing to see how all the loose men around have disappeared from the hospital. During one of the shellings Ramsey and I go out and gather the men under shelter from house.

"Shells explode near. Horses killed around by the shell or shot. I am engaged in carrying on the operation I began before the shells were falling and now, of course, the men must be taken care of. By evening the hospital is cleared. Looks like a storm coming up tonight."

And with that Bacon got up and went back to work. Tillie went into the house and to bed.

Daniel Skelly, who had slept in Fahnestock's store Thursday night, had to wait for sporadic firing to slacken before he felt safe running down Middle Street to his house.

It was about 11 a.m. Friday when dozens of Confederates lumbered into the Skelly's backyard, went straight to the well and began drawing bucket after bucket of water.

They all took drinks, to be sure, but it seemed to Dan that they were more interested in washing off the dirt and black smoke of battle.

"Damned hill!" Dan heard one of them shout out. "What the hell do they call it?"

"Culp's Hill," another soldier answered.

"What in tarnation were we buttin' up against? Damn Yankees musta been in the thousands, locked arm to arm with a full year's supply of ammunition!"

Dan sat near the back door, where the soldiers could barely see him, and listened to them banter about the fight. Then he went inside to help his mother. He peeled potatoes, chopped wood, carried water and, when he could, listened to the soldiers talk.

He was loafing at the door when the cannonade began shortly after one o'clock. The ear-splitting roar sent the whole family to the cellar. The noise was too loud to permit any talking, so Dan thought. And the thing that went through his mind most often was a poem he had recently read.

Ah, Charge of, oh, ah, what was the name of the poem? he pondered.

But some of the lines didn't escape him. How could they, with that boiling cauldron of noise pouring through his ear drums?

"Cannon to the right of us,
Cannon to the left of us,
Cannon in front of us,
Volleyed and thundered."

The rest of the words didn't come. Dan thought the poet must have witnessed a battle much like the one which he could hear all around him now.

When the noise died down hours later, Dan crept cautiously up to Fahnestock's corner. He peeked around the corner to see barricades all along Baltimore Street, ready, he imagined, to repulse any attack from the cemetery.

Dan could hear cheers springing up south of town, perhaps near the cemetery where, he understood, the Union army had anchored its line on the first day of battle.

But, for the first time since Wednesday, he could hear none of that bone-chilling Rebel yell. Even the Confederate troops in the street seemed unusually quiet.

Dan went to bed that night restless, unable to sleep. He had been unable to find out what had happened. Whose cannon had been firing for two hours? Why? The Skellys heard only that there had been a Confederate attack. Was it successful?

"I doubt it," Dan had told his mother that night. "These Reb soldiers didn't appear too happy this afternoon."

Dan figured it must have been about midnight when he heard a commotion outside. He went to the window and looked down onto Middle Street.

"Quietly now, fall back! West one block, then north one block, then west again. Move quickly! No noise."

An officer on horseback was talking. Dan could see him plainly in the glow of the moon and campfires along the south side of the street, out of view of the Yankee sharpshooters.

The officer was passing among the soldiers bivouacked on the sidewalk and in the street. He kept repeating his instructions and directions and pleading for quiet. But soldiers moving about with canteens and muskets banging and tempers flaring were not prone to silence.

"Son of a bitch!" Dan could hear a man just below his window mutter after the officer had passed down the street out of earshot. "Just getting to sleep. Now he says to move out. Son of a bitch! Where's my hat? Charlie, you steal my damn hat? Just like the damn army. Fight all day; march all night. Son of a bitch! Charlie! Charlie?"

Dan was afraid to call to the man and ask what was going on. He felt certain that that soldier, in particular, would just as soon shoot him as talk to him right now.

So Dan crawled back into bed wondering what was going on. It was a restless night.

Like most everyone else in town that Friday, the Jacobs family took to the cellar during the cannon battle. Professor Jacobs glanced at his watch when it began.

"It is seven minutes past one o'clock and I suggest that we all go below," the professor said quite calmly.

Henry thought he could hear distinct sounds amid the thundering chaos. First, he thought, is the deep-toned growl of the gun, then the shriek of the flying shell and finally the sharp crack of its explosion.

Then, suddenly as it had begun, the noise stopped.

Henry's father, motioning for him to follow, ran up the stairs to the garret. In his hand was a small but powerful telescope. He trained southward and began describing the scene to his son.

"There's a great amount of smoke hanging over the fields just south of town but I can see Confederates, thousands of them, marching in formation out of the woods down off the ridge. Flags flying."

Father and son shared the telescope but could see a great deal even without it.

"You may never see anything like this as long as you live," Professor Jacobs said excitedly.

"They are charging. Slowly, to be sure, but they are charging our position on Cemetery Ridge. Through those open fields. It must be close to a mile across there.

"Look, look, they're still coming out of the woods. I know they're the enemy, son, but it's magnificent, heroic!"

They stared as the Confederates moved through the fields, sometimes hundreds of them disappearing in small hollows and then reemerging, still in formation, wave after wave, walking steadily onward, as if on a grand parade before an admiring line of spectators.

Henry watched as the Confederates reached the Emmitsburg Road and then began to pile up behind the high fences. They seemed to be having trouble tearing down the heavy logs and no one appeared ready to climb over after the first few soldiers who tried where shot off the top railings.

About that time the Union infantry opened fire and the sudden noise made Henry jump.

The infantry fire was overwhelming, blasting, withering.

Now those glorious lines with flags flying had gaping holes. Henry could see that they were trying desperately to close ranks. Some had gotten beyond the road and the fence and were moving up the slope right into the beckoning mouths of quiet cannon and the stone wall-protected Union troops along the ridge.

"Oh, God, those poor souls," Professor Jacobs lamented as they watched soldiers falling by the score on that battlefield a half mile away.

The smoke of the fight hid from their views the man-to-man clash at the wall, but they could plainly see that thousands of those brave Confederates were already streaming back across the bloody fields, dragging themselves, their weapons and their comrades to the safety of the woods.

Not even the heavy thunderstorm which followed shortly after could eliminate those vivid scenes from Henry's mind.

It took hours for him to calm down. By midnight, when his father told him it was time to rest, Henry had resigned himself to the fact that he could do absolutely nothing about the slaughter he had seen that day. And it was then that he noticed the movement that had begun outside.

Through the front window, he could see Confederate troops moving down Middle Street and turning the corner at his house to go up Washington.

A man on horseback seemed to be giving orders: "Move quickly! No noise. Fall back quietly."

He wanted to go outside and ask what was going on.

"I don't think that would be a good idea. They seem very sullen after that loss this afternoon. No, stay in. Go to bed, Henry," his father advised.

On Friday evening, Salome Myers and her family were caring for Colonel Huidekoper, Major Thomas Chamberlin, also of the 150th Pennsylvania, Sergeant Stewart and eight other severely wounded men.

It was not quite dark when she heard a knock on the front door.

"Evening, mam," said a Union officer as Salome opened the door. "I'm Captain Henry Eaton, 16th Vermont Volunteers. I got my brother, Sergeant Eugene Eaton, same regiment. He's hurting badly."

Salome looked at the horse behind the captain. Slumped in the saddle was the sergeant, his eyes barely open.

"Ah, well, bring him in, bring him in," she said without waiting for permission from her parents.

The sergeant was barely able to walk but with his arm around his brother's shoulder, he struggled into the house.

"Eugene was hit in the back by a piece of shell," the captain explained.

"They looked at him this afternoon at a field hospital but then ordered all of the walking wounded to go back to the regimental hospital so that they could concentrate on amputations and the cases that couldn't be moved.

"Didn't trust sending anyone to bring my brother in so I did it myself. Couldn't find the regimental hospital and first thing I knew we were riding into town.

"Well, man on the street told me a lot of folks were taking in wounded and he mentioned this house. Sure hope you have room here for Eugene. I've got to get back to my company."

Salome smiled, all the while wondering how they could feed or care for another man.

"There are no doctors available, you know. They're all busy in the churches with operations," she told the captain.

"Well, they didn't even dress his wound at the field hospital.

I know how it should be dressed, if you'd be so kind as to help," the captain said.

Salome thought back to just the day before, when the sight of men bleeding and suffering was too much for her to take. What a change, she thought, as she patiently washed the sergeant's back and applied the dressing over shattered bone and torn skin.

She thought, with limited knowledge, that Eaton would survive and possibly carry no more than a scar from his wound. He probably won't go through life bearing the crippling wounds of others—like Huidekoper or Captain Bruce Blair of the 149th Pennsylvania, who also lost an arm, his left, at the shoulder joint and who was, or rather had been, left-handed.

And there was a young boy upstairs—oh, she could never remember that name—but anyway, he had lost a leg and was having a time of it staving off infection and delirium.

Though he hadn't lost a limb, there was also Captain James Ashworth of Philadelphia; 121st Pennsylvania, she believed. Poor Ashworth, he couldn't move without hitting a wound. Shot seven times, none of which hit critical areas or broke bones or severed arteries. Just seven severe, painful wounds.

Yes, she thought, Eaton will be okay. Her warmth and optimism even flowed into Captain Eaton.

"I know my brother is in good hands. Thank you," he whispered as he backed out the door to his waiting horse.


On Friday, Fannie Buehler decided she had to get some yeast to bake bread.

She had only flour, lard and water so biscuits became the substitute.

"But look, I'm blistering my hands making so many biscuits. I need some yeast," she told the German fellow who had been helping out.

"I vill find you somesing vith vhich to raise der bread," he told her. And off he went, sneaking through back yards.

An hour later he was back with baker's yeast.

"Where did you find it?" Fannie asked.

"You don't ask, please, jost bake," he answered.

And, except during the heavy firing that afternoon, Fannie baked and baked long into the night.

Albertus J. McCreary puttered around the house Friday morning, unable to convince his mother to let him leave the property. But when the cannonade ended that afternoon he and one of his brothers convinced her that they'd be safe upstairs since it didn't seem like any shells were coming that way.

They went to the garret, stood on a ladder and opened the trap-door in the roof. They could plainly see Cemetery Hill and the fields near the Emmitsburg Road.

White smoke drifted like low clouds across those fields and partially enveloped the heights a mile apart on either side. But through gaps in that cottony whiteness Albertus began to see troops moving, going across the fields, as if on parade.

"My gawd, look at that, will you!" Albertus cried out excitedly. "Looky that long line of Rebels coming across there."

They watched spellbound while thousands of troops crossed the shallow valley of wheat and rye and corn, knee-high crops for the most part.

Then the cannon opened up again, but only from the Union lines and soon smoke began to cover the scene. Albertus could see men falling as shells exploded among them and he could hear the yells of men charging, of men fighting, of men dying.

Two doors away, Albertus had noticed a neighbor watching the battle from his roof trap-door too. The man had to peep around his chimney.

At about the same time the Union cannon opened up, Albertus heard a rifle crack nearby. From the corner of his eye, he noticed a piece of brick flying away from the neighbor's chimney. Then he saw the man's head drop, his arm shoot up to grab the trap-door and the door slamming down.

His brother had seen it too and the sight of that man disappearing so fast got them both to laughing so hard they nearly slipped off the ladder.

Then, wham, and wham again. Hardly more than a foot from his head, Albertus saw two chips of shingle fly up in the air. Both dropped as fast as the neighbor.

"Shoot, don't that ruin all! Why they shootin' at us, Al?"

"Probably figure we're Reb sharpshooters up there. Look, see that board there in the corner. Lift that up here to me."

Albertus took the board, slowly pushed it up above his head and slid it out onto the roof to cover most of the opening. Then he motioned his brother up on the ladder again. Together, with their heads touching the bottom of the front edge of the board, they raised themselves very slowly until their eyes were peeking just over the roof.

A block to the south and in a sidestreet, they could see flashes and puffs of smoke pouring from the second floor of a house.

"Place must be full of Reb sharpshooters. Look at our boys dancing around up near the cemetery. Rebs must be sightin' in there," Albertus said.

Both boys heard a cannon firing from that hill and both instinctively ducked. And they heard the shell hit.

"Looky, that house that had all the sharpshooters. There's a hole in the roof. That shell must have gone through . . ."

Before he could finish, they heard another shot coming and froze. It hit the same roof.

Within minutes, a half dozen shells or cannon balls or whatever was being fired—Albertus couldn't figure out what—had struck the roof and walls of the house. The flashes and puffs of smoke from the Rebel sharpshooters had stopped.

The sight and sound was frightening. The McCreary boys retreated from the garret. On the second floor they heard laughter from the street and the breaking of glass.

From an open window overlooking High Street, Albertus looked out and saw a young boy standing in the middle of the street. He was throwing stones at the windows on either side and laughing loudly every time he broke a glass.

The boy moved down High Street and Albertus knew he was not from town.

"Hey," he yelled to a Confederate soldier who had been watching from the corner. "Who is that boy?"

"Oh, him. That little devil followed us up from the South. He just hangs around, scrounging food, and in every town he breaks windows. We've tried to run him off, but he always comes back."

"I think he's touched in the head," Albertus shouted.

"I think you're right, boy," said the soldier.

"Son, you there!" another voice, husky and authoritative, called out. Albertus turned to see a Confederate officer pulling up his horse.

"Would you mind holding my horse while I go in that hospital?" the officer asked as he stopped at McCreary's side gate.

Albertus raced downstairs and out the back door. He loved big horses and this one was really big. The officer must be a doctor, he thought, noticing the black bag he carried as he swung down off the horse.

The doctor was no sooner in the hospital, really the Protestant church next door, when Albertus heard it coming. He had gotten used to the sound of shells and this screamer seemed to be heading his way.

Albertus hung onto the horse's reins as long as he could. He tried to pull him away but the horse wouldn't budge. Finally, Albertus could stand it no longer. He let go of the reins and ran down the street toward the church. He was only two doors away when the shell dropped into the street, not twenty feet from where he had been standing.

The explosion knocked Albertus off his feet and sent the horse into a panic-stricken run up High Street. He could see blood coming from the horse's side, apparently from wounds caused by shrapnel. Albertus examined himself carefully, saw no blood, felt no pain.

But he wondered what pain the doctor might inflict on him when he found his horse gone. Albertus didn't give it a second thought. As fast as he could he ran back to the safety of the garret.

Some of the Confederates involved in the attack Albertus had watched began to straggle back through the streets of Gettysburg late that afternoon.

One came hopping to the rear door, trying to balance on the broken stock of his musket. His left foot was raised and blood had soaked through the heavy boot.

"Could use a drink, lady," the man whispered to Mrs. McCreary. As she fetched the water, Albertus ran to the basement, sawed the handle off a broom, nailed a small bit of wood on as a cross-piece on one end and brought it out to the soldier.

"Might be easier going with this here," the boy said proudly, shoving the makeshift crutch at the man.

"That's right decent of you, lad. I'll be eternally grateful." And with that he turned and hobbled down the street.

A few minutes later, while Mrs. McCreary was still praising her son's compassion, two more wounded soldiers turned the corner to escape sniper fire on Baltimore Street.

One, with what appeared to be a minor arm wound, was leading the other man along. The second man's face was so covered with bandages that Albertus could see only the slits of his eyes.

Mrs. McCreary rushed to get another dipper of water.

"His lower jaw was shot away," the first man explained as he guided his friend down to a bench near the house.

There was a gurgling sound and the bandaged man held out his hand as he saw the dipper of water in Mrs. McCreary's hand.

"Aw, easy, Josh," said the first man, who took the dipper and simply poured the water very slowly over the bandage. It soaked through but most simply ran off.

Then they got up and continued their slow walk.

The first man stopped, reached into his pocket and tossed a coin back to Albertus. It was a blackened, battered quarter.

"Found it after the fire at Fredericksburg," the man shouted.

Next came a soldier holding his wrist, asking for a doctor. Albertus walked him next door to the church and watched as the doctor examined the wrist.

When Albertus got back home, his father was talking to two men carrying a third on a stretcher.

"What happened to him?" Mr. McCreary was asking.

"Looks like his hip is broken," said one of the stretcher bearers. "He caught part of a shell."

"He's in awful pain being carried like that. Bring him inside the house. We still have a bed to spare."

They unloaded their patient—a captain—and left.

A doctor who had been in the house for dinner examined the man and told him bluntly: "Captain, gonna have to take that leg off."

"I'd rather die first!" said the captain.

"Your choice," the doctor said as he left the room.

Through that evening, Albertus was kept on the run helping to care for the wounded.

"There's a number of hospitals just within a block of us," he was telling the captain who refused to lose his leg to the surgeon's saw.

"The Presbyterian Church just across the street, the Catholic Church a few doors above, the United Presbyterian Church back of our lot and the German Reformed Church at the end of High Street, all are being used. Then there are two school-houses, half a block up High Street, and of course many homes.

"We even got a red flag. Did you see it? No, I guess you wouldn't have noticed. Well, they gave us a red flag to hang out front to save us from annoyance, to show that the house was a hospital.

"With you here now all our beds are occupied, so my brother and me are sleeping on the floor. Shucks, we don't mind."

The captain stared as Albertus droned on. Eventually he fell asleep and Albertus, after covering the southern officer with a thin blanket, tiptoed away.


When William McClean ventured out onto the street late Friday afternoon, it looked as though the Confederates were getting ready to contest a Union advance.

The troops he saw were sullen, gloomy, almost ugly, he thought.

"Excuse me, sir," McClean said in his best lawyer tone of voice. "My family and I have a meager supper ready and thought you might want to share with us."

"Captain Smith, North Carolina, suh, and I'd be delighted. It's very gracious of y'all to offer."

McClean introduced the captain to his wife and children as they sat.

"Captain, I must admit that I had an ulterior motive for inviting you in. We're glad to share, of course, but I am also greatly concerned at the prospect of very serious fighting in the streets. I am also fearful that your army, from what I can see, might take out its wrath on this community. I am, sir, concerned for the safety of my family."

Smith smiled, sipped the last of a small cup of tea and told his host:

"Mr. McClean, and y'all too, mam, I will do my utmost to see that your home is not disturbed by my men or any Confederate soldier I see in this area. However, y'all understand, I could be moved out of this area with my men at any time. But, while I'm here, I intend to see that your family and home are protected."

Mrs. McClean dabbed at her eyes with a napkin.

"You're most gracious, captain. My husband and I appreciate it."

"Not at all, mam. I would expect the same from Union troops in my home."

Twenty-year-old Mary Virginia Wade and her mother had moved in with Mrs. Wade's other daughter, Mrs. John McClellan, on Baltimore Street when the battle began.

"We've got to help Georgina take care of the baby," her mother had said as they had moved through the streets two days before to that small house at the end of Baltimore Street, near the cemetery.

It was Friday now, the battle in its third day and Jennie's nephew in his sixth day of life. Despite the Union sharpshooters on the hill behind the house and the Rebel sharpshooters just up the street, Jennie did not feel threatened.

"We have nothing to complain about, mom. Just think of poor John in the Army, wanting to be home here with his wife and new son. No, we're the lucky ones, to be here now," Jennie had said that morning.

She had carried water out through the side door to Union sharpshooters near the house, but she didn't step out the front door once.

Jennie had heard some bullets strike the outside of the house over the past three days, but none had struck windows; none had come through; and now she had gotten used to the noise of zinging bullets outside.

"I think I'll bake bread this morning," Jennie told her mother. "Friday is always baking day for me, you know."

She was in the kitchen in the back of the house, alone, her hands working the dough.

The crash behind her, like the splintering of wood by an axe, came just a split second before the thud in her back pushed her down onto the table.

Jennie tried to push herself up, but her knees were buckling and she was sliding down. She could see the bowl of dough just inches away from her clouded eyes, its whiteness now stained a dark crimson.

"Mom!" she whispered as she labored to catch her breath and stop her fall. "Mom!"

Jennie's head, ringed by the blackness of her upswept hair, struck the floor as she spun around off the table. She saw the ceiling floating away into a fog and then her eyes closed and the pain in her back disappeared.

Mrs. Wade heard the bullet come crashing through the side door. She was sitting in the front room where they had put a bed for Georgina and the baby. She rushed into the kitchen, saw the splintered hole in the outside door and the open door between the two rooms. Behind that second door lay her daughter.

"Jennie!" she screamed as she saw her daughter slumped on the floor.

Then she fell to her daughter's side and cried violently.

"Jennie, my God, they've killed Jennie!"

That night, Union troops crawled into the house through a hole in a wall on the second floor. They took Jennie's body out through the same hole and, sobbing for the girl who had risked all to bring them water, they carried her to the basement.

"First civilian killed, sergeant?" a veteran major asked almost bluntly.

"Only one I know of. If there had to be one, the wrong one, sir. Damn war."

"We'll bury her out back tomorrow," the major said.

# CHAPTER
# 9

# The Fourth of July

At six a.m. Saturday, Sallie Broadhead was awakened by loud noises on Chambersburg Street. She peeked around the curtain on her bedroom window.

A Rebel officer on horseback was in the street waving frantically to troops running past him.

"Hurry up, hurry! You'll all be captured if you don't get the hell out of here!" he screamed.

Some of the soldiers were turning around, facing east, and firing back towards the Diamond. Sallie knew at once that Union troops were back in town.

By now, Joseph was up too and at the front door, cautiously peeking up the street.

"Ah, what a glorious sight, love, blue uniforms on the Diamond!" he said, smiling.

"Hey, what's this? White flag? Surrender?" Joseph whispered to himself as he saw a Confederate lieutenant waving the banner.

The lieutenant, who had just stepped in front of the house, overheard him.

"No surrender. Just a truce," the officer told him.

"Truce for what?" Joseph inquired. But the officer ignored him.

Over the back fence, Sallie heard a neighbor shouting to anyone listening.

"Oh, God help us! They're raising a truce flag and telling our soldiers to clear all of the civilians from town. They're going to shell our homes!"

Sallie ran to the front door and repeated to Joseph what she had heard.

"Doesn't make much sense, pet. Why would they waste ammunition to shell a town when they're obviously beaten and pulling back? No, doesn't make much sense. Anyway, we'll stay put until we're ordered out."

Sallie knew that Joseph was right. He made sense; he always did.

By midmorning, the west end of Gettysburg was still subjected to constant sniping, by Union troops advancing slowly down Chambersburg Street toward the Broadhead house and by the retreating Confederates who were moving inch by inch up the long gradual slope of the seminary hill.

By evening, the tide had turned. Union troops were now past Sallie's house and the firing was becoming more distant by the minute.

"Joseph, the Fourth of July, almost over, and we didn't celebrate," Sallie said.

"Celebrate? Greatest Fourth I've ever had, love. Three days of fireworks and the greatest sense of freedom I've ever had!"

"Yes, you're right, Joseph. It was just that."

For the first time in a week, Sallie laid her head down that night with a feeling of security.

After Union troops turned the corner at the Diamond and advanced down Chambersburg Street, Mary McAllister heard music.

"It's a band," she told her sister. "Listen, it's an army band and it's ours."

Across the street, Mrs. Horner was out front with a bucket, trying to clean blood and mud off her pavement.

"You'd best get back inside. Rebs are still down the street," a soldier yelled to Mrs. Horner. That warning changed Mary's mind about going out front too. But she wanted to know what was going on, so she slipped out through the back and stole over to old Mrs. Weikert's house when she heard the woman wailing.

"What's the problem, Mrs. Weikert?" Mary asked as she neared the back porch.

"Oh, it's one of my boys. He's been shot."

Mrs. Weikert took in student boarders and Mary recognized the young man lying near the door as Amos Moser Whetstone, a student at the seminary.

"Take care, or you'll get shot too," Amos yelled as he saw Mary coming through the yard.

Mary ducked her head but kept moving. When she got to Amos she could see he'd been shot in the leg. She tore away the pant leg and examined the wound. The bullet had gone clean through the fleshy part of his leg.

Mary bandaged it. Then she got Amos some bread and butter. Finally, she helped him stumble into the safety of the house.

The shooting continued most of the day as Union forces kept pushing the Rebel invaders away from town. As they fled, the Confederates took some of the wounded from the churches.

By evening, doctors and orderlies began taking the wounded from some of the houses into the churches and other public buildings. They took all of the wounded being cared for by Mary and Martha.

And before darkness fell, farmers from out east of town began arriving with vegetables, chickens, turkeys, bread, milk and apples to feed the starving thousands.

"Thank goodness," Mary exclaimed as she helped unload a wagon load of supplies. And then she wept.

• • •

Gates Fahnestock wanted to be on the street Saturday, and he was a good bit of the time, except during the severe thunderstorm which raked the area in the afternoon.

"Keep off the streets that run east and west, son," a Union officer warned him. "Rebel sharpshooters can sight in along those streets."

So Gates stayed on Baltimore Street and avoided crossing the open intersections on either end of his block.

His mother had given him a bucket of water, some strong soap and a brush to clean the pavement out front. It really wasn't what he wanted to do that day.

Late that afternoon, a lieutenant stopped at the Fahnestock house.

"Mam, beg pardon. We're looking for all the help we can get to set up hospitals and bring in the dead and wounded. Your boy here looks big enough. You mind if he helps? We'll feed him and see that he gets home before dark."

Mrs. Fahnestock didn't like the idea but didn't see how she could refuse, not after seeing a half dozen other neighborhood boys riding the wagon following the lieutenant.

Gates climbed aboard, smiling at the thought of really doing a very necessary war job.

The wagon bounced along over rutted roads and through fields to Cemetery Hill. For the first time, Gates saw closeup the destruction of the day before.

"Reb general named Pickett tried to bring 13,000 Johnnies through here," explained a sergeant puffing on a corncob pipe as he directed a detail of gravediggers. "This is what's left of 'em."

The weather had turned sticky hot and Gates threw up once when the odor of rotting flesh reached his nostrils. The sergeant brought over a dipper of water.

"Here, take a piece of this rag and dip it in here. That's it. Now tie it around your face like a bandit. That's right. Help you to breathe better, boy."

The sergeant directed the boys to cut wood and help set up tents for the wounded. They fetched drinking water and firewood.

The sergeant kept them away from the bodies and even from the wounded and especially from guns laying about.

But Gates watched what was going on around him. He noticed particularly how careful the soldiers were in trying to identify the dead before they buried them in shallow graves. Even the Rebel dead were searched carefully.

"Here, Sarge, this Reb got a billfold," a ditchdigger said. "Two dollars in good money and three in Secesh. Picture of a woman, might be his wife, and a little boy. And here's a letter; got an address to a Virginia regiment. Must be his name here. I'll make a marker for him."

Gates saw the sergeant put the man's billfold into a large envelope. He wrote something on the outside and then put the envelope into a large leather pouch.

"Okay, boys, that's enough for that hole," the sergeant ordered. "Let's say some Christian words over this group of Johnnies and cover the poor bastards over."

It seemed so strange to Gates that these Union soldiers, who the day before perhaps had shot and killed the very men they were burying, were so gentle and humane in this ungodly chore.

Each body had been lifted and laid down again gently. Each face was covered with a hat or a coat or a piece of cloth. Arms were folded on top of chests. Legs were laid straight. And when it came time to "say some Christian words" each gravedigger removed his hat and stood at attention for a respectful moment.

Gates was awed by the sight, and puzzled.

It was just daylight Saturday when Mrs. Garlach rushed out to the back yard. There were Union troops out front and she wanted to tell General Schimmelfennig he was safe.

The general knew it too for he had already crawled out of the woodpile. As he stretched to relieve the stiffness and cramps brought on by three days of only slight movement he told his benefactor about himself.

"I vas born in Lithauen, Prussia, in '24 and vas an engineer officer in the Prussian army during the Schleswig-Holstein var.

"In '53 I came to this country, to Philadelphia and vorked as an engineer and draftsman. Ven the var broke out, I vas vorking for the Var Department in Vashington."

Then he told her how his brigade, on Wednesday, had been forced to retreat through the streets to avoid almost certain capture.

From the description he gave, Mrs. Garlach knew the general must have ridden his horse down Washington Street and then turned into the alley which stopped at the Garlach barn but connected with another alley running north to Breckenridge Street.

"I knew I vas trapped. There vere Confederates running after me down the alley. Ven I got to your barn and saw the udder alley going north I knew I had no place else to go.

"Ven I stopped, they shot my horse. So I climbed over your fence. I vas going to run past your house into the next street but I could hear southern voices out there too. There vas no place left to go."

"But how were you able to get under that woodpile without causing a great deal of commotion?" Mrs. Garlach asked.

"Oh I didn't hide in the voodpile until after dark. I crawled under the vooden culvert there," he said, pointing to the covering over a ditch which carried rain water from the yard around the house and into the street.

Anna saw her mother talking to the general and thought about going out to meet him, but by the time she made up her mind he was already walking stiffly but quickly through the next property.

Anna could see blue uniforms popping up along a fence in front of the general. Then she heard the cheers and saw soldiers climbing over the fence and crowding around the general.

Strange, Anna thought, for mere soldiers to be patting a general on the back. And him smiling and taking it. Strange.

Minutes later, after Schimmelfennig had disappeared, one of the soldiers came into the Garlach yard. So Anna asked him about all that patting and smiling.

"Well, yes, miss, that's unusual. But, you see, he's our general and we thought he'd been killed. Well, I guess we just got carried away with seeing him.

"Lot of us were with him at Manassas and Chancellorsville. He's a good officer!"

Dr. Cyrus Bacon was having coffee at midday Saturday when he pulled out his diary to make a notation:

"Independence Day. We celebrate by the retiring of Lee's Army. They have gone. Gen. Meade follows them early."

Bacon thought about what the folks back home in Michigan were doing on this Independence Day.

No doubt, at least, they're not knee deep in dead and dying soldiers. He had been operating since sunup.

By afternoon, under a heavy downpour, he was still at his makeshift operating room outside the Weikert barn. Two orderlies held a shelter tent over him and his patients as he worked.

"Can't you find some poles to hold that up while you men help out elsewhere?" Bacon asked the orderlies.

"Can you stop operating long enough for us to scare up some poles, sir?"

"No. And I see your point. But if and when this blasted rain stops see what you can do about getting us a regular tent."

Bacon looked around him. Wounded men were lying everywhere in the open, soaked by the rain and dirtied by the mud under them. Some, unconscious or too weak to move, had to be dragged out of low spots to prevent them from drowning in the little pools which surrounded them.

When night came, Bacon was relieved for a few hours of rest.

"Will you be needing this door I've been using as my operating table?" he asked the surgeon in charge.

"No, doctor."

"Fine," Bacon said as he crawled up on the door to sleep.

Later, when the rains came again, Bacon found a space large enough in the back of an ambulance wagon for him to sit if he kept his feet bent underneath his body. And there, exhausted, he fell asleep again, oblivious to the torrent of water that poured down all night.

• • •

It was still dark when the commotion from outside woke Dan Skelly. A half block away he heard the courthouse clock chime the hour of four.

From the open side window in his bedroom, Dan could see to the courthouse corner.

"Ye, gods!" he whispered as he detected the twang of New England accents mixed with some Pennsylvania Dutch. And, in the moonlight, there was no mistaking those dark uniforms. "Must be blue, too dark for gray or that, what do they call it, ah, oh yeah, butternut."

From time to time, Dan could see gray-clad troops moving south on Baltimore Street, in files of two. But they were without weapons. Must be prisoners. Oh, yes, there's a guard now.

Dan got dressed but he didn't venture out mainly because he didn't want to be mistaken for a Reb in the dark.

Soon after dawn, however, he was on the street with dozens of other Gettysburg residents, comparing notes of the past few days.

"Danger ain't over, folks," warned a tobacco-chewing Union captain as he approached Dan and several others who had congregated at the courthouse corner. "Gotta stay off these east-west streets. Reb sharpshooters outside of town can draw a bead down some of these streets.

"Rebs have thrown up breastworks to cover their retreat, so they're shootin' at anything that moves in here. We've seen some rifle flashes from off on that hill."

Dan looked to where the captain had pointed.

"Oh, that's Haupt's Hill," Dan informed the captain. "Named after Herman Haupt. He went to West Point. Ran a school for girls up on that hill years ago. He's a high-ranking officer in the army now."

The captain frowned.

"Wonderful. Now get off the street," he threatened, backing that up with a spit of tobacco juice in Dan's direction.

Dan couldn't see the point of taking all that precaution so he sauntered on home and sat on the front stoop. Just a few minutes had passed when several officers came riding slowly down Middle Street.

Dan heard the bullet whistling and he heard one of the mounted men yell. Out of the corner of his eye, he saw the man fall. In a flash the others were off their horses. They grabbed the wounded man under the arms and dragged him to safety.

"Damn! Go through three days of the worst fighting I've ever seen and then get nicked during their retreat," the wounded man was shouting.

From across the street, Dan could see the officer had been shot in the right arm.

Dan looked at the huddled officers and then glanced out toward Haupt's Hill.

My gawd, he thought to himself, that's some fancy shooting.

Dan stayed off the street the rest of Saturday.

A half block west of the Skelly home, young Henry Jacobs had the same problem. He couldn't venture out his front door because of the Confederate sharpshooters. He wondered how many of those men out there on the hill shooting into town were men who had bivouacked in front of his house.

Henry's 16-year-old sister, Julia, felt penned in too, with nothing to occupy the time.

"Well, with our troops in town you'd think it would be safe to go out," she argued with her mother.

She was watching when several cavalrymen came riding up Washington Street and crossed Middle Street. Shots rang out and horses leaped into quick runs. No one was hit but it gave Julia an idea.

She went to the front door and stood in the entrance, out of sight of the sharpshooters several hundred yards down the street and up the hill.

Each time she saw Union troops, afoot or mounted, coming up Washington she'd shout a warning.

"Look out crossing the intersection. Pickets back there. They'll fire on you. Make a run for it."

Julia became a living danger signal, and a most effective

one. The men, as they caught her words, halted and planned their dashes.

No one got shot while she was there.

But the Confederate sharpshooters at the intersection of the Hagertown Road, less than four blocks away, knew someone was warning the passing Yankees. They couldn't hear a voice but at times they could see a thin, white arm waving from a doorway.

"Must be a girl or a woman," said one of the sharpshooters.

"Don't make no difference," roared his sergeant. "Throw some lead into that doorway. Maybe we can scare her away."

After a few bullets hit brick near the doorway Julia retreated three steps into the hall, but she left the door open and continued to shout her warnings.

Finally, Union sharpshooters moved into Middle Street and got behind the stone wall which the Confederates had built several days before near the Jacobs house. They waved Julia back into the house and gave her a cheer for her bravery.

At noon, as the popping back and forth between the sharpshooters continued, the rains began. It poured, thoroughly soaking the Union sharpshooters lying in the street, but the shooting went on.

It was almost dark, Henry noticed, when the banging back and forth finally stopped.

It was then, given a chance to speak to Union troops, that Henry and his family learned what a momentous battle had been going on around them.


Salome Myers had talked her younger sisters into singing church hymns to the wounded men in their house.

One young soldier, she noticed, became very fond of the singing and frequently asked them to sing his favorite Sunday School song, "There Is No Name So Sweet on Earth."

The singing, she felt, seemed to take the soldier's mind off the fact that he had lost a leg.

The Myers home was filled with men who had lost an arm or a leg, and on this Fourth of July, another arrived from one of the church-hospitals.

"His name is Andrew Crooks, mam," said the sergeant in

charge of a detail who carried the stretcher into the house. "He was wounded trying to carry Sergeant Stewart, who I understand you also have here . . . well, he was wounded carrying Stewart off the field. Strange they both lost legs.

"You know, they're even from the same neighborhood back home."

Salome found room for Crooks in the same room as Stewart. Then she passed the word around that the Confederates had retreated.

Despite the work of caring for the wounded, Salome felt so relieved by the retreat that she bellowed to her mother: "I never spent a happier Fourth! It seems so bright now that those dirty Rebels are gone."

By evening the sergeant and his detail were back again.

"Can you take another one, Miss Myers? This here is another Andrew. Andy Wintanrole. He's from Wyoming, Pennsylvania; that's up north, near Scranton. Arm and stomach wounds."

Salome found another spot on the floor upstairs.

"Sergeant, don't know that we can handle anymore right now. Aside from caring for what we have, you know we're also cooking almost all of the food for the wounded in the Catholic and Presbyterian churches. We'd need some help if we get any more men here."

"I'll pass that on to my captain, mam."

"I thought your superior would be a lieutenant."

"We ain't got no more lieutenants in my outfit, mam. They're either lying out on the field dead or they're in one of these houses dying."

It was almost midnight when a neighbor who had been keeping watch over some of the wounded in the Myers house called out for help.

"Get a doctor; quick, get a doctor!" she blurted in a hushed but excited voice.

Salome ran to her side. The young soldier who had lost a leg and enjoyed hearing the hymns was thrashing about and the stump of his leg was bleeding profusely.

Salome tried to stem the flow while the neighbor scurried down to the church for a surgeon.

By the time they got back, Salome had managed to slow down the draining. But the loss of blood, on top of what he had already lost and the shock of amputation, proved too much. By dawn, the young solider was dead.

In his pocket, Salome found a letter from the soldier's wife, announcing the glad news that their first baby had just been born.


Fannie Buehler felt relived Saturday morning. She had seen no reason to even recognize this day as a national holiday of patriotic pride until late morning when the wagons began to roll in from the east.

Farmers brought jars and crocks of apple butter, jellies, preserves, pickles, bread and meat.

And the Christian Commission and the federal government's Sanitary Commission were right behind them with wagons of bread and smoked hams.

They unloaded at stores and distribution began.

"If you got wounded at your house, give us an order for how much you need and we'll try to fill it. If you can pay for it, fine. If not? Well, we won't worry about it now," Fannie was told by a man who appeared to be a government official of some kind.

"How could you get here so quickly?" an amazed Fannie asked.

"Ain't the first battle fought in this war, you know. Soon as we got the word in Washington Wednesday about the fighting here we got up here, rented wagons, bought foods and hit the road for Gettysburg."

Fannie noticed that the farmers from outside town had donated their supplies, at least the first wagonloads.

"We're collecting money where we can so we can go right out and buy more, rather than wait for the government okay on all of these purchases," the government man told Fannie.

"But I happen to know that people from New Jersey, Philadelphia and Baltimore are right now collecting stuff. Call went out soon as the telegraph news came through that a big battle was shaping up here and that there might be quite a few casualties, maybe in the hundreds."

"Probably more like the thousands, from what I see and hear," Fannie chimed in.

"Right. Well, anyway, government in those places was supposed to get the word out yesterday or today to start shipping in things like wine, pickles, oranges, lemons, sugar, tea, coffee, beef tea . . . anything that sick folks crave or that could give them strength."

"What about bandages and medicine and blankets and clothes and. . . . ?"

"Oh, those things too," the government man said.

For the first time in three days, Fannie took a long walk. The battlefield was all around her.

The wounded, the dead, the dying, all heaped together, it seemed.

Horses that had fallen beneath their riders, with limbs shattered and torn; broken down artillery wagons; guns and knapsacks, cartridge boxes, capes, coats and shoes, indeed all the belongings of a soldier, and the solider himself, all lining the streets, as far as she could see.

Fannie was appalled, now fully realizing that the war had indeed been brought to her very door.

Our men, she thought, have driven the enemy back from our homes. Now, it remains for us to do our part just as well.

She hurried home. The German soldier who had been helping her was flitting around excitedly.

"Mr. Frey, what is wrong?"

"Oh, Mrs. Buehler, nothing is vong. No, no, just the opposite. You remember I told you that I thought the captain of my company had been vounded on Vednesday and carried on a board to this neighborhood.

"Vell, I go looking this morning and in an empty house just down the street, I find Captain Myers. He vas still lying vhere they left him. Rebs gave him vater but othervise let him be.

"He vas lying for three days in his blood. He cannot speak. I just come back here now to get help. Vith your permission ve bring him here, ya?"

"Yes, Mr. Frey, you bring him here. We still have one empty cot."

Fannie thought the captain dead when they carried him to the back porch. She directed Frey to force the captain's mouth open. His tongue, she could see, was swollen and stiff. His body was rigid. There was barely any movement, but his eyes moved.

Fannie got a bottle of blackberry wine. She poured a drop on Myers' tongue. Nothing happened. Another drop. Still nothing.

Drop after drop. Myers was trying to move his jaw.

Fifteen minutes passed before the moisture of the wine took effect. His tongue moved and a drop of wine slid to his throat.

Fannie kept repeating the procedure and, at the same time, directed Frey to cut away the captain's filthy clothing. Then they bathed him and searched for his wound.

Frey found it. A small hole under the right breast, made almost impossible to find by the hair on Myers' chest. Blood had run all over his body but the wound had closed itself. They moved him enough to examine his back.

"My god, Mrs. Buehler, look. The bullet made a clean cut. It came out here, under his left shoulder blade. Too close to the heart for comfort."

"The bleeding must have cleaned the wound," Fannie said softly. "It doesn't look too bad. I think we can wash around it and put a bandage on until we find a doctor to examine him. I think his main problem is weakness from loss of blood and lack of food and water."

That afternoon, three more wounded men—all captains— were brought to the Buehlers. One, from Illinois, had been shot through the throat and Fannie expected that he would not last through the night.

"At least," she told Frey, "it seems like there will be no more killing or maiming in Gettysburg."

Albertus McCreary began Saturday by carrying food from his kitchen to the Presbyterian Church just across Baltimore Street. His mother was using food delivered that morning by the Sanitary Commission to feed the wounded in her house and some of those in the church.

Albertus couldn't help but look around after his first delivery. The pews in the church were covered with long boards. Straw and blankets had been spread on them to make beds.

Near the back door, where he had delivered a basket full of fresh bread, he noticed two men picking up a stretcher. The body had been covered by a white sheet. As they stepped down from the church to the yard, the sheet slid off and revealed a small, pale young man. HIs body had been washed clean and there was only one mark, a small black hole in his chest.

The stretcher bearers asked Albertus to replace the sheet and then moved on.

They headed for a trench out back. Albertus followed.

In that long hole were dozens of bodies, some covered by sheets, some only by the clothes they had been wearing.

The trench is not very deep, Albertus thought.

As he watched them put the body into the shallow trench, Albertus noticed something moving in a field behind the church. It was a woman, a black woman, running from tree to tree.

"Old Liz," Albertus called to her. It was the only name he knew her by. She did wash for the McCrearys and other families in town.

Albertus hadn't seen her since Wednesday, when a group of coloreds who lived in town were marched out the Chambersburg Pike under Confederate guard.

He recalled the tears in the old woman's eyes as she was marched past the McCreary house and could still hear her wailing: "Oh, Lawdy, goodbye, goodbye. We is gun back a slave. Oh, Lawdy, Lawdy."

When she heard the boy call out, Old Liz dashed across the field as fast as her short, fat legs could carry her.

"Oh, massah Al, thank God. I's alive yet."

"I'm glad for that, but how did you escape, Old Liz?"

Gasping to catch her breath, the white-haired woman explained that as they were being marched away, they ran into a crowd of soldiers and wagons near the Lutheran Church.

"Dey was so much 'fusion, I slips off in de church an I hides in de top. I done stay all de days an I'se so in want a watah and eats."

In an instant, Albertus had slipped into the church, ripped a chunk of bread from the loaves he had brought and dipped a cup into a bucket of water.

He had to coax Old Liz to chew the bread and sip the water. Then he assured her that it was safe for her to be on the street and suggested that she would be needed in the hospitals.

"Yassah," she shouted and hurried into the church.

Albertus wondered about the other blacks who had been marched away. If they were all as sly as Old Liz, Rebs would be guarding nothing by now.

When he got home for another load of supplies, a Union soldier was seated in the kitchen eating and drinking.

Albertus began to tell his mother about Old Liz hiding in the church belfry.

"Belfry?" his mother exclaimed. "The belfries in town must have been crowded. This poor man got caught up in that retreat on Wednesday and hid in the belfry of the school house up the street."

"Had a little hardtack and a few drops of water in my canteen when I got there, but didn't dare come out. Didn't want to be captured. Dang near thought I was gonna starve or die of thirst," the soldier explained between gulps of water.

That afternoon, Albertus bumped into a friend on the street whose family had moved out of their house during the fighting.

"Oh, Al, come see what those Rebs did to our place," the boy urged.

Albetus was amazed. Almost everything in the boy's house had been destroyed. Pieces of furniture were burned and broken; a desk had been shattered; bookcases were knocked down; books were torn.

Upstairs was a barrel, half full of a mixture of flour and water. Feathers from the beds had been dipped into the thin paste and then thrown on the walls, on the furniture and down the stairs.

"And for what?" the boy's father was yelling. "Rebs near the house where we was staying were gentlemen, or close to it. But what animals came in here?"

Albertus stayed for a bit to help clean up, but he knew he was expected home to carry supplies and help take care of the wounded.

He got home just as his father was coming out of the house.

"Albertus, come on boy. Let's walk out to the pasture to see if our old cow is still there."

The pasture, near the edge of town, was one used by several town residents who kept cows for milk.

"Don't expect our cow is still alive, son, but don't do no harm to check on her. I suspect the Rebs ate 'er."

The pasture had seen its share of the battle, the McCrearys were soon to learn. The odor of rotting flesh was the first clue. The pasture was overrun with bodies of cows, of horses, of men. Nothing was left standing in that field, not even the fences which had kept the cows in.

Mr. McCreary decided the field was not a good place for his son to be. Too much of the sights of war would fill a young boy's head with terror.

Albetus had been looking carefully, not saying a word.

In one corner of the field he counted up to forty dead horses, their bodies swollen and their stiffened legs pointed skyward. There were wheels, and parts of wagons and the barrels of large guns.

"Must have been gun crews here," Mr. McCreary said softly when he noticed his son's attention to the corner.

It was almost suppertime when they got back and the first thing they noticed was their old cow, tied to a tree behind the house.

"What the . . . ! Look at that!" Mr. McCreary exclaimed.

His wife stepped out of the house and waved to them. Then she pointed at the cow and explained:

"Just after you left, a farmer name of Smith out near the Hanover Pike brought the cow in. Said she and several others had wandered into his barn Wednesday or Thursday. He knew by the markings who they belonged to so he kept them in pasture until he heard it was safe to come to town."

Mr. McCreary and Albetus examined the animal.

"Goodness, pa, look here, bullet holes!" Albetus shouted.

The cow had been shot in the neck and in the side, but neither wound seemed to bother her.

"Take a bigger bullet than those minie balls to bring a cow down, unless you hit a vital spot," Mr. McCreary said.

"Looks like she'll be okay."

After supper, Albertus took a walk down Baltimore Street to the homes at the southern end of town which had been caught in the crossfire between the armies.

At a small house across from Snider's wagon hotel on the Emmitsburg Road, he noticed the bodies of two Confederate soldiers lying against the side of the building.

Albertus went around back and peered into the kitchen window. There were two more bodies inside.

The boy stepped through the open back door and called out: "Anyone home?"

No answer.

It was obvious to Albertus that one of the two inside was dead, judging from the ghastly wound in his stomach. But the other soldier, a very young man, was lying on his back and staring at the ceiling. There was no visible wound, no blood.

Slowly and cautiously, as if he felt the dead man's ghost would seize him at any moment, Albertus walked around the bloody body until he stood over the young man, looking down into those frozen eyes.

He noticed the soldier had a medal pinned to his coat, but he didn't know its significance.

What a souvenir, the boy thought, as he moved his hand to tear away the medal. Something stopped him as sure as a ghostly hand had clutched his wrist.

Don't take it! It may be the key thing to identifying this soldier and notifying his family, a voice told Albertus.

The boy drew his hand away, backed out of the kitchen and ran home.

As the last rays of Saturday's sun threw long shadows over the yard, Albertus sat on the fence and watched through the side window of the church out back as surgeons continued their grisly task.

Every few minutes, Albertus would see an orderly walk to the window and drop a blood-smeared arm or leg onto a growing pile on the ground below the window.

Mrs. McCreary had given every member of her family a small bottle of either pennyroyal or peppermint oil.

"Since we all must be out working among the dead, a whiff

of this will, for a time, take away that horrible stench," she told them.

But Albertus left his bottle in his pocket as he sat on the fence watching that pile of limbs grow ever higher. He became transfixed, forgetting the horror of the sight, the odor it raised in the night air, even the screaming of those whose limbs were being hacked away.

Jacob Gilbert's tour of duty with the 87th Pennyslvania Band had ended with him never suffering a scratch, a fact his wife, Elizabeth, reminded him of Saturday morning when he announced he would scout around town.

"Jacob, them Reb snipers are still around. You best be careful," she said as he skipped out the door and ran up York Street.

It was just a few minutes later, while he was walking down Middle Street, when Jacob got hit.

"Must have been a sniper. Got me here in the fleshy part," Jacob said as he raised his left arm to Dr. Horner. He had sneaked through some alleys to the doctor's house after the bullet nicked him.

"Liz will raise hell about this," Jacob said as he left the doctor's office with a bandage around his arm.

Elizabeth hardly noticed. She was too busy fussing over a wounded Confederate soldier.

"Oh, dear, Jacob," she said as he came in, "this poor man came through the back yard. You can see he's got a wounded leg. Wants us to put him up. Gave us his horse. I asked Mr. Broadhead to take the saddle off and put the horse in Sterner's barn."

Elizabeth jabbered on as she tended to the soldier's wound. Finally, she noticed the bandage on Jacob's arm.

"Goodness, Jacob, what happened?"

The explanation was brief and Elizabeth was in a sweat.

"Wounded? I warned you about going out! I can't take care of everyone, Jacob. Why didn't. . . ."

"Liz, I'm okay. It was just a scratch. I'm going to look at the horse, and I won't go on the street," Jacob said, ducking out the back door before his wife could say any more.

In five minutes, he was back, on the run.

"Was your horse black with a gray mane?" he shouted breathlessly to the wounded Confederate.

"Yassuh, he most certainly was."

"Damn! You give us a horse and then one of your friends steals him. Just as I got to Sterner's, one of your soldiers comes riding that horse out of the barn, bareback. Dang near ran me down!"

"I'm truly sorry about that, suh. I honestly meant for you folks to have her."

"That's alright. We'll still take care of you," Elizabeth said. "Won't we, Jacob?"

"What? Oh, yes, don't worry about it. Just got under my skin to see her being stolen. We'll take care of you. Gettin' shot and then having a horse stolen. Well, that's a little much for one day," Jacob smiled.

Liberty Hollinger and her mother had come out of their house early on Saturday afternoon on their way down to one of the churches to offer assistance. It was quiet on this end of town now although they could hear the crack of rifles coming from the west end of Gettysburg.

"Those guns make it seem like a Fourth of July celebration going on," Liberty was saying as they stepped onto the porch.

They both noticed the tall Confederate officer coming up the walk. He carried no weapons and they felt no fear.

"I beg your pardon, ladies. I don't mean to intrude, but I was wondering if I might sit on your porch for a spell," he said, lifting his hat and bowing slightly.

"I'm a surgeon and I've been operating in that carpenter shop down the street. I've stayed behind to help care for your wounded and ours. Your Union colonel told me to rest awhile."

The doctor seemed a perfect gentleman, both in appearance and manners, Liberty thought.

"Of course, sir, sit. Liberty, get some fresh water for him to drink," Mrs. Hollinger said.

"You're too kind, madam," said the surgeon as he stood on the porch and leaned against a pillar.

When Liberty returned with a pitcher of water and a glass, she was trailed by little Annie.

"This is my sister, Annie," Liberty said by way of introduction.

"My, aren't you lovely! How old are you?" the surgeon asked.

"I'm nine," said Annie.

"You remind me very much of my sister's girl," the surgeon said, taking her hand in his. "Madam, do you mind if Annie sits on my knee for a few minutes? She reminds me so much of my home and my family. I miss them dearly."

Mrs. Hollinger smiled her approval and Annie climbed on the surgeon's knee. He gazed at her softly and told her about his home and his niece, like her.

"Would you stay for supper with us tonight?" Mrs. Hollinger said quickly, as though she had not even given it a thought.

The surgeon moved to rise and Annie climbed off his knee.

"No, thank you very much, madam. I can't possibly eat anything. I'm too weary and heartsick of amputating limbs all day."

As he arose, Liberty noticed his boots were bloodstained below where a surgeon's working frock usually hung.

"You've been extremely hospitable. I am grateful," the surgeon said. "I must get back to my duty now."

He saluted after putting his hat back on and marched down the path to York Street again.

"He never mentioned his name, did he?" Liberty said to her mother.

"No, but I'm sure his mind was filled with many other matters," she answered.

Nursing wounded troops was nothing new for Mrs. Mary Cadwell Fisher. She had been doing it at home in York, Pennsylvania, since the war began. Since it was close to the Maryland border and was a sizeable community, York often got wounded troops directly from battles in Maryland.

Mary had volunteered to prepare supplies for the Sanitary Commission and work in the army hospital.

On Saturday morning, July 4, word was received in York of the battle at Gettysburg, thirty miles to the west.

The word whipped through the old colonial town: Supplies will be gathered in the square and wagons will leave for the battle area this afternoon.

By noon the square was filling rapidly with wagons and the supplies they would carry. Mary got two other women to go along and talked her oldest son into driving a wagon.

By three o'clock, they were rolling, two horses pulling the huge wagon filled with provisions, clothing, blankets and hospital supplies, and, oh yes, several dozen bottles of the finest whiskey they could scare up.

Rather than follow the main road, which was reported dangerous because of bands of deserters, the Fisher wagon headed southwest to Hanover over 18 miles of rutted dirt road.

It was dark when they got to Hanover and a pouring rain was making travel difficult.

"We'd best stop here for a while, to rest the horses and wait for this rain to let up," Mary suggested. It wasn't the rain that bothered her, but rather the danger of washed-out roads.

By midnight, the rain had stopped and a clear moon gave good light so they started out again.

# CHAPTER
# 10

# Sunday—Sabbath of Suffering

Sister Camilla O'Keefe was one of the first to see the gray-clad soldiers straggle into St. Joseph. There were only a few but most of them had no weapons, no packs, not even shoes. They were dirty, unshaven, lean and frightened.

"Please, just a little food!" one begged as he reached a nun outside the church.

The nuns hurriedly heated the oatmeal and boiled fresh coffee. There was bacon and bread and butter.

"Where are we?" asked one soldier as he gobbled down the meal.

"This is St. Joseph's and the town you just came through back there is Emmitsburg, Maryland," a nun replied.

"What has happened? We've heard cannon fire every day from Wednesday until midday Saturday," said Sister Camilla.

"Yanks whup us at Gettysburg. Awful mess. We got out best

way we could. But we ain't got any idea where our outfits got to. We're just headin' south."

Father Francis Burlando and Mother Ann Simeon Norris had been listening too.

"Are there very many wounded back there?" the Mother Superior asked.

"Well, I can't rightly give you numbers, but I ain't never seen so many dead and wounded in one place. The fields around that town is crawlin' with 'em. And some of our boys who fought in the town said the houses and the churches and practically every other buildin' is full of the dyin'."

"Sisters, we must pack a wagon and send nursing help to Gettysburg at once," Father Burlando shouted out.

Within an hour, the entourage was assembled.

"God bless you. I wish we could help but we'd only be taken prisoner if we went back," said the Confederate who had told them of the wounded.

He and the other soldiers started walking, south.

On the road, heading north to the Pennsylvania border, a mile away, and Gettysburg, six miles beyond that, was a carriage carrying Father Burlando and two nuns. Behind them moved a cumbersome freight wagon with supplies, food and fourteen more nuns.

Two miles from Gettysburg, they were stopped by trees which had been cut across the road. Behind the trees were armed troops who raised their muskets and pointed them toward the wagons.

Father Burlando took out his white handkerchief and tied it to his cane. Then he climbed down and walked up to the soldiers.

"We're from St. Joseph's, down the road, and we're taking supplies and nurses to Gettysburg," he explained to a sergeant.

"Sorry, Father, but from the distance we couldn't tell who you was. There's Reb deserters all over the place. You go. But be mighty careful. Most of Lee's army seems to have moved west, but be careful anyhows."

The soldiers moved a small tree limb which allowed room for a wagon to pass through. They were on their way, passing

Union troops who raised their caps in respect and shouted words of praise for the sisters.

There was a peach orchard to the right as they neared Gettysburg. Or, rather, what was left of an orchard. From a distance they could see the severed branches lying about and the bare trunks of the small trees. It wasn't until they got closer that the enormity of the battle became a reality.

"Oh, gracious, there are bodies on the road," exclaimed Sister Camilla, who was riding in the carriage.

Father Burlando pulled the horse up. He looked back. The other nuns had seen the dead too.

"Sisters," he shouted back to them. "I am afraid the sights from here on will be gruesome. I know you would like to give these men a decent Christian burial, but that must come later. Our task now is to help those still alive."

And with that, the aging priest urged the horses on carefully, pulling them from side to side to avoid running over the swollen, disfigured forms on the road.

"There must be hundreds here, just along this road. And, look, in that peach orchard. Oh, what a terrible fight took place here. Such a mass of human beings slaughtered down by their fellowmen in a cruel civil war is awful."

A hundred yards up the road, they could see the rooftops of Gettysburg just a mile away. Over that whole distance men were digging pits and putting bodies in by the dozens.

Father Burlando stopped once again, as the burial party of Union troops cleared the road ahead of him. To the left was a long pit, scarcely more than two feet deep. Sister Camilla counted 50 bodies in the pit, all Confederates by looks of their uniforms.

And across the road, under a tree, lay the body of an older man, with a star upon his collar, a general waiting like his troops for the burial party.

The two wagons crept along at a snail's pace that last mile.

A federal officer on horseback greeted them as they moved up Baltimore Street.

"Hey, you're from St. Joseph's, aren't you? I remember you from there last week. We need you here very badly. Up the

street you'll find McClellan's Hotel. There's room there for
you to set up your quarters."

It was one o'clock. The town, which Father Burlando
recalled as a sleepy village on Sundays, was an inferno of
movement. People rushing between buildings; soldiers rushing
about on horses; wagons carrying in the wounded and carrying
out the dead.

An artillery crew, which no longer had a gun to fire, helped
them unpack the freight wagon. Then Father Burlando, guided
by several Union officers, divided the nuns into groups.

Some went to the courthouse, some to the churches, some to
schoolhouses.

They bandaged wounds; they cooked; they fed; they encour-
aged; they prayed.

Before nightfall, Father Burlando decided to drive back to
Emmitsburg for another load of supplies. Two nuns went with
him to help. Late that Sunday night, Sister Camilla and the
others who stayed laid on the bare floor of McClellan's Hotel
and slept.


When Sallie Broadhead awoke on Sunday morning, her first
sight was that of bright sunlight flooding in the side window of
her bedroom.

"What a beautiful morning," she said softly and sadly.

"What?" said Joseph, who was already up and pulling on his
boots.

"I mean it seems as though nature is smiling down on the
thousands suffering here. One might think, if they saw only the
sky, and earth, and trees, that everyone must be happy.

"But, oh, just look around and see the misery made in so
short a time by men."

She laid back down on her pillow and sobbed.

Joseph held her tightly.

"I see what you mean, love. Yes, it is a beautiful morning
for us, compared to what those men all around us are going
through."

Sallie had made plans to leave little Mary with Mrs. Gilbert
this day so that she could go help at the seminary, which had

been a Union hospital, then a Confederate hospital and now was a little of both.

As she crossed the Chambersburg Pike and started up the long, grassy slope to the seminary, she noticed that most of the dead had been removed from the road. But she had to close her mind to the sight on the slope of dead horses and the bodies of men.

Inside the seminary, it was worse. These men were still alive, moaning and screaming; some staring blankly into space; some with closed eyes whose lives were ebbing away.

Many had already undergone the surgeon's knife, a bloody bandage the only evidence of where a leg or an arm had been. One, inside the first room she entered, was lying on his back with both hands behind his head squeezing with all his might on the legs of a heavy chair. Sallie could plainly see that both of his legs were gone, not neatly amputated, but apparently blown away by some tremendous explosive force.

She had carried a large sack from home filled with bread and some jars of molasses. Before she had moved through one-half of one floor in the four-story seminary, her sack was empty.

In a room filled with the furniture from other rooms in the building, which had served as dormitory and classrooms, Sallie was thanked by two surgeons who were resting from a full night at the operating table.

"What can we do?" Sallie said. "What little I've brought is gone. It's heart-sickening to think of these noble men sacrificing everything for us, and saving us, and it's out of our power to give them assistance of any consequence."

One of the doctors tried to console her: "Don't fret. Like us, you do what you can, madam."

Sallie walked slowly out of the room and down the hall, her empty sack dragging on the wooden floor behind her. A guard swung open the massive front door, which faced west, and Sallie moved slowly down the large, rounded steps to the road.

She walked around the side of the brick building and started down the slope for home. And she cried, not loudly, not in gushes, but softly, slowly, sadly.

I'll gather up more food. I'll get soft material to place under their wounded limbs. I'll make them more comfortable.

Halfway down the slope Sallie was shaken from her melancholy by the baying of horses and shouts of men. On the road below her, heading west on the Chambersburg Pike were hundreds of Union cavalrymen.

She was watching the last of the troops disappear over the crest of Seminary Ridge as she got home. Joseph was waiting with an explanation.

"Cavalry is going to chase the Rebs," he said. "But there's even a bigger surprise. My brother is here. He came through the battle without a scratch but he's hungrier than a hibernating bear."

Sallie's spirits lifted as her brother-in-law popped out from behind Joseph and swept her into the air.

"Ah, Sal, you're a sight for my weary eyes and empty belly."

Sallie cooked him a full meal of scraps and then began baking. She had plenty of ingredients for bread and plenty of mouths to feed, but she never expected the requests she got.

It began that afternoon: Confederate prisoners being marched back by Union guards were stopping at houses along the way, begging for food. Word spread of the woman baking bread and the hungry kept coming.

Sallie never did get back to the seminary that day. But she remembered the words of the surgeon at the seminary. She was doing what she could.

Mary McAllister answered a knock at her door Sunday morning to find Judge David Wills and another familiar man in uniform smiling at her.

"Miss Mary," the judge said, "this gentleman tells me he left something here a few days ago."

Mary peered at the face for a moment and then grinned widely.

"Colonel Morrow? But the Rebels took Colonel Morrow."

"Well, I'm Morrow, alright, and I've come back for my diary. I am going on to join the army. They're going toward Frederick and I want to catch them."

Mary couldn't contain her curiosity: "But how did you escape from the Rebels?"

"Well, they took me from here to the college where they took away my sword and ordered me to help with the wounded. They left me alone while I worked. Several hours passed and no one came to get me. That evening, as it got dark, I put on a surgeon's frock. And when it was good and dark I just walked out a back door. In the dark, the guards just saw that white frock and paid no attention to or couldn't see these blue trousers."

Judge Wills broke in to explain how Morrow had tried to find his way back to Mary's house but got lost and sought refuge in the Wills' house on the Diamond.

"Now I have no coat and no sword, but at least I have my diary," Morrow said.

"Yes, and I'll get it," Mary said as she darted back to the kitchen.

She came back with the book and from behind her back presented Morrow with a sword.

"This sword belonged to General Archer, one of the Confederate officers," she explained. "It was taken from Archer by Dennis Dailey of the Second Wisconsin, but I'm afraid he was probably captured too because he never came back for it.

"But you must promise me that if you ever meet Dailey you will return the sword."

"On the honor of a soldier and a gentleman, I promise to give it to him," Morrow said as he buckled the sword around his waist.

"And thank you, mam," Morrow said almost in a whisper, bowing gracefully and tipping his hat.

Mary blushed but said nothing. She closed the door as Morrow mounted a horse, turned and rode slowly down Chambersburg Street.

By Sunday, Michigan surgeon Cyrus Bacon had at least seen all of the casualities from the Second Infantry and dutifully noted in his log:

'Officers of 2nd Inf: killed—Lieut. Frank Goodrich; wounded—Major Lee, heel and leg; Lt. McLaughlin, left thigh, bad wound of foot; Lieut. Lacey, in back, slight.'

But by nightfall, he allowed the three wounded officers to

leave his hospital and move back to a major recuperation area east of Gettysburg. It had been a good day; Bacon got some oats for his half-starved horse and fell heir to McLaughlin's shelter tent.

A tent over his head felt secure, Bacon thought as he settled into it for a few hours sleep before sunup. By the light of a candle he made his final diary entry:

"I have been so busy today I almost question whether it is Sunday or not."

Dan Skelly was out early on Sunday checking the streets for safety when he met his pal, Gus Bentley.

"Hey, Dan, got any money? I know how we can earn some. But we gotta have some to start with."

Dan's puzzled look brought a quick explanation.

"Well, you know I been workin' down at Hollinger's warehouse. Before the Rebs came, Mr. Hollinger had us hide a whole bunch of tobacco. We hid it and they didn't find it. We can buy it and sell it to the soldiers."

Dan looked skeptical.

"What soldiers? Most of them's gone," he said.

"Gone? Why there must be a couple thousand all around here yet. They left burial details and cooks and doctors. There's guards and some going around picking up equipment and repairing guns and such. There's still lotsa soldiers around.

"I got ten dollars. Can you get ten?"

Dan skampered back into the house and told his mother the plan.

"Well, I guess those soldiers would appreciate getting tobacco, just so you don't cheat them and charge too much," Mrs. Skelly said.

The whole twenty dollars was soon invested, for which the two businessmen got large plugs of Congress tobacco. They cut the plugs into ten-cent pieces, filled two baskets and started out down Baltimore Street for the cemetery, the nearest line of battle.

But at the top of the hill, near the cemetery gate, soldiers manning a battery of artillery stopped them.

"Can't go past here, lads. Orders are to let no one out of town," said a white-haired sergeant.

The boys didn't argue. They walked back up Baltimore to the Presbyterian Church, turned east on High Street and walked a half block to the Adams County Jail. Next to the jail was a not-so-well-marked trail leading to the old Rock Creek swimming hole.

On the first ridge they had to step over the bloated bodies of two Rebel soldiers.

The path then led to a spring and to Culp's Hill where they were amazed by the sights of battle—weapons and equipment strewn here and there as if the men carrying them had suddenly decided collectively to pitch everything they had and walk away—and trees so shot up with cannon shells and bullets that most were denude of branches and many were or soon would be dead trunks.

Surprisingly, they saw no bodies there, though the evidence had pointed to vicious fighting. But halfway up Culp's Hill, as they approached formidable breastworks they could see the burial parties at work.

They had to climb over the breastworks, three feet high, built of tree limbs with dirt from a trench in front thrown on top.

The tobacco went quickly and the soldiers coaxed Dan and Gus to get more.

Several trips to Culp's Hill exhausted the tobacco supply. But Dan was able to give his mother ten dollars back and had as much to keep for himself.

By Sunday, Salome Myers had expanded her duties from caring for the wounded in her own home to making a daily round of the large, makeshift hospitals. She took books for men to read and paper and pencils for them to write. Those who couldn't handle the chore themselves found in her someone to write that first, difficult letter home.

"I missed not having church services today, papa," she said as the family gathered for a sparse noon meal. "None of the churches met today, but I know the Lord doesn't blame us, not with the task we've been given."

Mr. Myers puffed slowly on his pipe and looked at Salome. Then he smiled and replied: "No, daughter, I'm sure He doesn't."

It was midafternoon when a man named Barton appeared at the Myers door. He was, he explained, a brother-in-law of Sergeant Stewart.

"We thought we had lost the sergeant a few hours ago. He seemed to be sinking, but then he rallied again and seems somewhat better," Mr. Myers told Barton as he escorted him to Stewart's room.

"We'd be pleased to have you spend the night here, Mr. Barton, though we can't offer you anything more comfortable than a wooden floor and a thin blanket."

"I'll take that, Mr. Myers, and with great thanks," Barton said.

The cooking of food and caring of the patients went on without another halt the rest of that day. By nightfall, Salome was exhausted. She welcomed sleep.

On Sunday, when she had finally settled into a routine of nursing the wounded in her house, Fannie Buehler began to notice more and more the horrors of the battle.

In the courthouse across the street, the cries and groans went on continuously as the limbs of men wide awake were chopped from their bodies.

At times, Fannie would clap her hands over her ears to block out the noise.

"It's not so much that I can't stomach the agony of those cries. It's more knowing that there is nothing in this world I can do to relieve the pain they're going through," she told Frey, the wounded German.

Several times she noticed carts full of amputated arms and legs pulling away from a side window of the courthouse. The sight sickened her but it also forced her to ask an orderly where the carts were going.

"Outside town, mam. They'll either bury or burn those loads," the orderly explained.

Late Sunday afternoon, Fannie heard a band playing across the street. She looked out to see soldiers, some of whom she recognized as orderlies in the hospitals, playing in front of the courthouse.

"The Star Spangled Banner," "Tramp, Tramp, Tramp, the Boys Are Marching," "Rally Round the Flag, Boys." All the songs she recognized, of course.

"Regimental bands stay behind after a battle," explained the orderly whom she had talked to earlier. "Some of them drive wagons to pick up debris; some are orderlies in hospitals; some cook. But whenever they have a chance, they play tunes the men like to hear. Cheers 'em up, you know."

Fannie smiled. She felt cheered somewhat too.

Albertus McCreary took a walk on Sunday morning down through the fields where the Rebs had made their final charge on Friday. Squads of soldiers were still busy clearing the field of debris.

One squad with a wagonload of rough wooden coffins was digging. Albertus stopped, wondering what they could be doing.

It didn't take long for him to find out.

"They were digging up bodies that probably had been hastily buried Friday or Saturday and putting them in the coffins. It was a horrible sight and the smell was so bad I got sick to my stomach," he told his mother when he got home.

It was that kind of day for Albertus. Later, on an errand down near the railroad station, he watched two men unload coffins from an open car.

Some other boys had opened one of the coffins and were examining the lid. Albertus had to look too.

"See this box built into the lid," one of the boys was explaining, "my dad says they put ice in there. That way they can ship a body a long way without it gettin' rotted."

The conversation reminded Albertus too much of his morning walk through the field. He headed for home again.

Sundays, he thought, will never be the same again.

"Excuse me, captain," he called out to the man standing in front of the courthouse. "My name is William McClean. I live just down Middle Street there and I'm an attorney in town.

"At the moment, my professional training is of little use to the wounded so my wife and I thought perhaps we could carry food. I was told that you could direct me to where there is the greatest need for food."

The captain didn't hesitate.

"You know the McPherson farm, Mr. McClean?"

"Very well, captain, just out the Chambersburg Pike."

"Well, sir, there's a mess of wounded from both sides in McPherson's barn. That's where this fight got started, you know. Some of those fellows got hit right near that barn on Wednesday and are still there."

McClean thanked the captain and hurried back home. His wife had been baking all morning. Biscuits were her specialty.

"And I've used a whole bucket full of gruel. Mother and the children are out back picking raspberries," his wife said.

By late morning, loaded down with as much as he could carry the mile and a half, McClean started out on foot.

"Morning, Joseph," he shouted cheerily as he passed the Broadhead home at the west end of town.

"Oh, morning, Mr. McClean," Joe yelled back.

In the heat and with the load he was carrying, McClean slowed a bit as he moved up the hill past Carrie Sheads' house.

It was there, as the signs of recent battle grew, that he felt a little trepidation in going to what was so recently the front. In the distance, he could hear artillery firing but he knew that Meade's Army was chasing the Rebs back to Virginia, not coming to Gettysburg again.

On both sides of the dirt road he could see work parties burying the dead in the fields where they fell. He walked past a blue-uniformed soldier lying along the road. The body was black and swollen from the heat and rain and disfigured beyond recognition.

At the top of the rise past Seminary Ridge, he turned off the road to the barn.

The scene inside the huge wooden structure was appalling. It was filled on all levels with the wounded of both armies. Some, it appeared, probably had not had a decent piece of food in days. And many, it seemed to him, looked as if they had yet to be treated by a doctor.

When he got home, he didn't want to talk about it. His wife insisted, pleading to know the worst in case she should be called upon to assist at one of the hospitals.

McClean relented.

"There were so many wounded and so closely packed together that I was obliged to tramp on some of them in distributing my supplies.

"You may imagine how pleased and grateful they were for this fresh food in their famished and suffering condition. One of them told me that as he was lying on the field, General Lee had given him a drink out of his canteen. Lee's headquarters were in that locality.

"Many who were there, they tell me, died from gangrene.

"Fortunately, the Christian and Sanitary Commissions are getting established and volunteer surgeons and nurses are appearing.

"The work on burial of the dead goes on, but it's poorly done by details of Rebel prisoners.

"And, of course, there are a great number of dead horses in the fields. Seems to be very difficult to dispose of them. There aren't enough crows or buzzards to dispose of them. Consequently, they rot where they lay and the atmosphere, as you can imagine, is vitiated and corrupted.

"I notice that, even here, with the windows open you can smell those foul odors."

"We'll get used to it, William," his wife interrupted.

McClean knew that she didn't want to hear anymore so, as his courtroom procedure had taught him, he made a closing statement:

"War around the mother and the little ones in the sanctuary of the home has none of the pomp, pride and circumstances which surround it in the pages of history, in the verses of the poet or in the glitter of the parade. Happy will the earth be when war shall be no more."

Liberty Hollinger felt the weather was stifling that Sunday morning.

"Still so humid from all that rain yesterday," her father said as he pulled on his boots.

"Where are you going, Pa?" Liberty asked.

"They tell me there's still wounded out in the fields, particularly south of town, down past the cemetery. I'm going to load the spring wagon up with straw for bedding and bring in those men."

Liberty wanted to help but Mr. Hollinger refused, saying that she would be of more value at home cooking for the hospitals.

That evening, when he returned, Liberty asked how many wounded he brought in.

"Lost track, girl. Picked up three or four each trip with the help of some soldiers. Took them to the churches, the seminary and the college. Must have made five, maybe six trips."

Hollinger burned the straw he pulled from the wagon. Liberty could see that it was stained brown from mud and red from blood. In a way, she was glad her father had not allowed her to go along.

It was the first chance she had to take stock of her property since the fighting had begun five days ago.

So Carrie Sheads walked around her two-story house with the fancy wooden trim and counted the places where shells or bullets had hit. There were sixty definite marks and two holes where shells had passed through the brick walls.

Inside, her students were caring for a housefull of wounded from both Union and Confederate armies. Even the halls were filled.

Mary Cadwell Fisher's wagon rolled into Adams County early on the Sabbath.

The fields on both sides seemed full of small and large tents, pieces of canvas stretched between branches, sometimes just a coat on a stick. And under every piece of cloth was a wounded soldier.

Dozens, mostly Confederates, were lying in the open, without shelter from the sun or rain.

Only a note from the chief burgess of York got the Fisher wagon past Union sentries posted along the road.

"Town, about five miles up ahead, could still be a dangerous place," warned one sentry before examining their pass. "Could be some wild shells from them retreatin' Rebs. And there's a lot of prisoners in the town."

At seven a.m. Mary told her son to pull off the road to what appeared to be a major hospital just east of the village.

"I thought before this that I had learned all the horrors of warfare inside the walls of our crowded hospitals in York and from the continually passing trains of wounded, bleeding men to whom we carried food and stimulants as they went on their way to distant points," Mary told her son.

"But, look at this! This is a new revelation of the brutality of war. No imagination could paint this picture."

A young lieutenant who seemed to be in charge hurried over to direct unloading of the wagon. He and Mary talked as the work went on.

"We got about five hundred here under these trees. No tents. Virtually no food. Most of these men were wounded last Wednesday and hauled out here to remove them from the fighting limits," he said.

"Rain yesterday almost drowned some of them. You can see some of them are lying half in mud. They're wounded, chilled, starving and racked with pain.

"You can't image how much your wagon of supplies will mean to them, though I don't suspect that it will be near enough."

The lieutenant was right. Mary noticed the provisions they had carried were almost gone and yet many were still hungry.

Less than an hour had passed when three more wagons pulled in.

"About thirty wagons stayed in Hanover all night. They'll be along later today," shouted one of the drivers as he guided the lumbering wagon into the patch of woods next to Mary's wagon.

"Where are we, anyways?" the driver asked.

"Fifth Corps," replied the lieutenant, "about four, five miles from Gettysburg."

It was noon when Mary's wagon and the other three pulled out with the meager supplies they had left. They were directed to a barn a mile to the west.

A surgeon, still dressed in a blood-stained frock, came galloping out when he saw the wagons on the road.

"For God's sake, in here! These men can't live without help," he shouted as he reined the horse up sharply. Then he turned to lead the way.

It was worse than the fields back the road, Mary thought. Must be several hundred in here alone.

"These poor devils were dragged out here in wagons after Friday's fighting," the surgeon told them. "Most are desperately wounded. They've received scanty care and no supplies but a little hard bread and coffee in three days."

Mary could hardly believe how the wounded were packed in. In the horse stalls, they had to sit up; there were too many men for any to lay down.

"We got three, maybe four hundred in here," the surgeon said as though someone had posed the question. "Everyone lost either an arm or a leg, sometimes both.

"Look at that poor wretch," he said, pointing to a twitching form. "Both legs and his right arm torn off by a shell. There's another one, still alive, over on the far side who lost both arms and a leg."

Horribly mutilated faces stared up at Mary from the straw-littered floor. Mary had to grit her teeth to control her emotions.

No pillows to rest their bruised and aching heads, she thought. No blankets to cover the shivering limbs.

Then a voice called out, weakly:

"Thank God, there's a woman! She'll help us."

Other heads turned to look at Mary. Some forced a smile.

Mary smiled back.

Supplies were being brought in. For those who couldn't open their mouths for a bit of bread, Mary put a drop of brandy or wine on the lips, then another drop or two, followed by a spoonful of water. Slowly and steadily she fed them like infants.

Even the toughest-looking, grizzled men whimpered as they felt a glimmer of hope through this lady that they might survive.

It was six o'clock when Mary and her wagon left the barn.

Other wagons from the train which had stopped in Hanover overnight were on the road too, one stopping here and there to unload supplies at makeshift hospitals.

Mary followed another wagon still loaded with food and medical equipment to the courthouse.

Armed with a bottle of brandy and a basket of bread she made her rounds.

She felt paused on the threshold of death, wishing that her legs would carry her away. Her nerves felt like they would shatter and her hands, for a moment, seemed paralyzed.

Fatigue, she told herself. I'm just too tired.

The momentary weakness gave way to her natural instinct to help. Through the night she went, from one to another, refreshing the faint with food and drink, cheering the hopeless with words of comfort and, too often, closing the eyes of one who had died without anyone noticing.

Mary knew that the mere sight of women seemed to give the men hope. They were like little boys whose mothers had come to help.

Mary watched the nuns with fascination—she heard some-one call them the Sisters of Charity—as they moved silently about. They seemed able to assist the surgeons in the most delicate tasks; they talked quietly to men who needed conver-sation; they sat tenderly holding the hands of those who were dying.

"Their very presence seems a benediction," Mary told her son.

# CHAPTER
# 11

# Monday—Up From
# the Ashes

The Reverend Joseph Sherfy and his son, Raphael, left early Monday morning from the friend's house where they had gone days before. It was five miles from the house near Two Taverns back to their farm on the Emmitsburg Road, just a mile south of Gettysburg.

"You, Grandma Heagen and the rest of the children will come home in the wagon tomorrow. Raphael and I will get things ready," Mr. Sherfy told his wife.

The father and son rode one horse back over the rolling hills, up the Baltimore Pike and then up the lane which cut between two prominent hills. It was near the hills that they began to notice the odor of rotting flesh.

In the woods on both sides, they could see bodies of soldiers and here and there a horse. Near the jumble of gigantic rocks beyond the hills were more bodies, more signs of the struggle.

Mr. Sherfy urged the horse on through what had been a

wheatfield and then up to the battered remains of his peach orchard.

"At least the house is still standing," Mr. Shefy said softly to Raphael. "But the fighting here must have been fierce."

The small, two-story building was riddled with shot and shell. The fence was down and much of it was gone. The shrubbery and trees were nearly all destroyed.

Where his barn had stood was just a lower wall of stone. The rest was in ashes. Mr. Sherfy glanced over the wall and tried to prevent Raphael from looking too.

"Oh . . . oh, Pa, look . . . they're burned!" Raphael cried out, his eyes frozen on the gruesome sight.

Inside what had been the barn were the charred bodies of fourteen people—men, Mr. Shefy assumed, and most probably soldiers, although all traces of uniform had been burned away.

A Union burial party working nearby came over when they saw the Sherfys ride in.

"Hard way to die," said a corporal who noticed the Sherfys staring at the corpses in the barn.

"We checked 'em over. Every one had been shot. 'Peers they was all wounded and were either carried or drug themselves into the barn. Artillery fire on Friday set the damn barn afire. Never had a chance.

"Hey, boys, let's bury these Rebs here in the barn. Folks would like to get back on their property.

"Assume this is your place, mister?"

"Ah, yes, it is, or was. Doesn't look like we have much left."

"Gonna move out?"

"No, corporal, gonna build from the ashes."

Mary Snyder started out first thing Monday morning for home. It had been five days since her mother told her to take the three youngest children to Aunt Susie Benner for safety.

"Mother will be worried. She really doesn't know that we even got here," Mary told Aunt Susie after arriving back there.

"Are you sure, child? I hate to see an 18-year-old girl alone on the road with three little ones," Aunt Susie protested.

Mary won out and the Snyders began the trek home. She

knew it would take most of the day, even though it was just a few miles.

Erzmanthus, the three-year-old and the youngest, needed constant prodding to keep moving. When he dawdled too long Mary simply picked him up and carried him along.

Rosa, though only four, moved along as quickly as her little legs would permit. So did Lobranson, a year older.

It was late afternoon when they walked down Baltimore Street to their home and their mother's outstretched arms and tear-stained eyes.

"I didn't know if you were dead or alive," she whispered to Mary. Then they sat for hours to exchange stories.

Rosa was amazed by the splintered hole in the front room floor.

"A shell came through the outside wall below, came up through the floor there, broke a table and chair, went through the partition into the closet in the next room and then broke the stove.

"We were in the cellar when it struck, but we got out of the house fast after that," Mrs. Snyder said.

"It was frightening, Mary! So terrible! Virginia Wade, you know, was staying with her sister next door. Poor Virginia was shot and killed inside the house."

"Oh, mother, how awful! Was anyone else killed?"

"Not that I'm aware of, at least not civilians. But the dead soldiers, and the wounded, no telling how many thousands on both sides."

It was just early evening and still light outside when Mrs. Snyder put her exhausted younger children to bed.

"Momma, why you close the window?" asked Rosa from her bed as she heard her mother slide down the creaky window.

"Well, a soldier fell by our garden fence last Friday and they're just burying him there now. The odor isn't very pleasant, dearest. You'll probably sleep better without that to put up with."

On Monday, Father Burlando sent another wagon full of nuns from Baltimore via Emmitsburg to Gettysburg.

"It's quite difficult for him to spare anyone," one of the newly-arrived sisters told Mother Ann Simeon.

"Sister Euphemia was sent south to one of the Confederate hospitals. I believe she was your assistant at St. Joseph's. Some went to the West Philadelphia Hospital; others went to Washington. There are very few left at St. Joseph's."

Mother Ann Simeon nodded, appreciating the demand on the order to provide nurses.

"Yes, and we could use so many more here," she said. "Sister Camilla O'Keefe can give you details on what is happening here."

"Well, it's a scene of terror," Sister Camilla began. "Three miles of space outside town was converted into a hospital of tents and farm houses. Ambulances have been provided for us by the Army to take clothing and supplies out to those men.

"Hundreds of them are lying on the ground on their blankets. Some straw has been obtained from nearby barns; the poor fellows were glad to get that rather than lie on the bare ground.

"You'll notice as you're going through the woods on the side roads little red flags on a board and a marking which may say something like: '1700 wounded down this way.'

"You'll find that, in addition to food and bandages and other common supplies, the men are asking for combs to get the vermin out of their hair and beards. And you'll also find those vermin getting into your clothes too.

"You'll see sights which will turn your stomach. Yesterday, while making our rounds, we gave a drink to a man lying on the ground who was waiting to have a leg amputated. And—I still shudder to think of it—maggots were crawling from the wound.

"Some of you may find it easier to stay out at one of the field hospitals rather than try to get back into town every night. Sleeping here in the hotel, although on the floor, can be a luxury but the traveling in and out every day is tiring.

"You'll also find that many soldiers—both Confederate and Union—will ask to be baptized. That's due in part to a U.S. officer, Doctor Stonedale, who was baptized himself by a Jesuit father down at Point Lookout.

"The man is amazing! After performing the duties of his profession, he often sets to work as a carpenter. From a farmhouse he got a saw and an axe, some boards and nails, In a short time, he can have men who were on the ground up on a kind of frame.

"Some of the first men he did that for were prisoners from Georgia and Alabama and they knew no more of religion than a Turk. They had not been baptized and some of them did not even believe in Heaven or Hell. Their religion was 'live as long as you could and enjoy life while it lasted.'

"But God in His mercy raised up this new convert to instruct them. He talked and reasoned with them, recounting his own experiences and his present happiness, which he would not exchange for all the riches of the earth. Kindness to them in their sufferings had its effects.

"By the mercy of God, sixty of those prisoners embraced the Faith."

With hardly a pause she returned to more practical matters.

"You can pick up supplies from the Army commissaries in town. Provisions began arriving yesterday."

Sister Camilla chuckled as she continued.

"I was at the commissary first thing this morning and the sergeant said to me: 'Sister, I suppose you want these supplies for the Catholic Church Hospital.' And I replied: 'No, I want them for the Methodist Church Hospital.'

"I guess he thought it strange that Catholics would be working in other churches. But you'll notice that no one thinks of these buildings as churches right now. And few think of any difference between the wounded of either army.

"One of our sisters asked the commissary sergeant for clothing for prisoners in the Lutheran Seminary Hospital, and he answered: 'Sister, you shall have what you want for the prisoners. You ladies come with honest faces and you shall have what you want for suffering men, whether Rebs or our own.'"

Mother Ann Simeon broke in:

"You'll not appreciate the working conditions in these hospitals, sisters, but think of the poor men who are lying in these sanctuaries and schools and homes, not knowing whether they can survive another day.

"They're so uncomfortable, some having just been brought in from the field in the last day or two. To lessen some of their sufferings seems to call for our first attention.

"In the churches, they're lying on the pew seats, under the pews, in every aisle. There's scarcely room to pass among them.

"Their own blood, the water used for bathing their wounds and all kinds of filth and stench add to their misery. Gangrenous wounds infect the air. Many are dying from lockjaw alone.

"But through all that you'll marvel at these men. Just yesterday, in St. Francis Church, there was a tall Scotsman lying under a pew. Only his head was visible. He had lockjaw and not long to live. A sister spoke gently to him of death and told him about baptism.

"He said he'd never been baptized, but desired it earnestly. He couldn't be moved because of his condition and the crowding of other men around him on the floor. But he stuck his head out as far as possible so that the baptismal water could be poured on his forehead. Then he smiled and, soon after, he died.

By Monday, nothing had slowed down, it seemed, for Doctor Cyrus Bacon.

"Foks back home in the hospital will never believe this," he told an orderly across the operating table.

"Amputating limbs all day and half the night . . . on an operating table that used to be somebody's front door . . . outside.

"You from Pennsylvania, corporal?" Bacon asked the orderly.

"No sir, Michigan, like you, sir."

"Ah, yes, of course. Well now, you know," Bacon paused to see if anyone else was listening, "it is my deliberate opinion that this part of Pennsylvania is not in the Union for no other Union place will fraternize it."

"Beg pardon, I don't follow you, sir."

"Well, what I mean is that for the last few days I have not seen one act of charity from the people. The people seem to consider us lawful prizes, and are not only extortionate but give us little real sympathy. One dollar for a loaf of bread; that's what one of them charged. Makes one indignant for the honor of his country."

"Begging the doctor's pardon, but I've seen a lot of folks here being very charitable."

"Oh, I don't mean the town folk. The people of the city of Gettysburg in some measure redeem this character of the country residents. They take the wounded into their houses and care for them, and all that.

"No, I mean the people who could be coming to our aid from outside Gettysburg."

"Maybe they are, sir. I hear tell wagons been pulling in since yesterday. Maybe it's just that we ain't seen any of 'em yet down on this end of the field."

"Maybe you're right, corporal. Sure hope so.

"Oh, damn, starting to rain again. Get that canvas up over us again."

When Daniel Skelly learned Monday morning that the Union line had its southern end at the Round Tops, he decided to walk the two-mile route.

At the end of Baltimore Street, Dan ran up the hill into Ziegler's Grove, the old picnic area near the cemetery. He was amazed at how shells had apparently splintered and broken large trees.

He walked down along what had been the center of the Union line. To his left, down over the backside of Cemetery Ridge, Dan noticed a cottage which he knew had been occupied by a widow and her children.

A soldier nearby, loading a wagon with salvageable equipment, told him that the cottage had been used as General Meade's headquarters.

"Trouble was," the soldier explained, "the cannonade last Friday brought Reb shells over the crest of the hill and down to this farm. Meade had to find another headquarters."

Dan saw the effect of the cannon shells. Around the house

and yard were at least a dozen dead horses shot, he imagined, while aides and orderlies were delivering messages to head-quarters.

Just south of the cottage was a stone fence dividing two fields and straddling the fence was a horse which evidently had been killed just as it was jumping over. In the road, a short distance away, was another dead horse, still fastened to the ambulance it had been pulling.

Dan peeked in through the open front door. There was a bed in the tiny main room. And there was blood on the covers.

"General Butterfield, Meade's chief of staff, was wounded. They laid him there," said a voice behind Dan.

The boy jumped. He hadn't heard the soldier walk up behind him.

"Then later they took Butterfield to a hospital."

Dan smiled, gave a quick "thanks" and started back up the hill to the line of battle. He looked back and saw the soldier standing with his hands on his hips, watching Dan moving up the slope.

Something about him I don't trust, Dan thought.

In moments the soldier was out of sight and out of mind. Dan crossed a field which led to the Codori farm on the Emmitsburg Road.

There didn't seem to be anyone there, Dan felt as he circled the house. But on the south side he was greeted by a sight which had him off and running through the fields once again. There, lying on their backs, were several dead Confederates, their faces burned black from days of exposure to the hot sun.

Signs of the severity of the struggle lay all about Dan's route through the fields. There were guns and parts of wagons and dead horses. And hundreds, it seemed, of shallow graves. In places, he could see bits of bodies and clothing protruding through the freshly turned dirt.

He came down over a rise to the Trostle farm where, it looked, the fighting must have been more intense. It too was still deserted but there were no bodies in the yard, at least not above ground.

Dan walked up on the porch in back, knocked gently on the door and waited. There was no answer. He peeked through the window into the kitchen. The table was still set and fragments of half-eaten food, now rotting, were still there.

It was as if the Trostles had gotten up from their table for a moment and would be right back to finish their meal.

It was, Dan felt, ghostly. But he was determined to go to the end of the line.

At the foot of the Round Tops, near the jumble of huge rocks called Devil's Den, the boy wandered onto the strangest sight of his travels.

There, in a clearing, were twenty-six Confederate officers, ranging from a colonel to lieutenants, laid side by side in a row for burial. At the head of each man was a board with the man's name, rank and the command to which he belonged.

A short distance away was another group of thirteen, arranged and marked in the same way.

Dan wondered why a burial party would bother to line them up and then leave without digging the graves.

"I wonder," he whispered to himself, "if Rebs lined 'em up like this and left those headboards before they pulled back. Who else would know their names and all that?"

Dan no longer felt afraid of the ghosts which he had imagined were around him in the quiet of the day. Instead, as he turned for home, he felt a sadness for the officers lined up for burial in Devil's Den and admiration for the men who had taken time to make sure their names would be known.


Sergeant Stewart began coughing about 9 o'clock Monday night. Salome knew that his damaged lungs could not take much more. He had been spitting blood off and on all day.

"The doctors say there's nothing we can do for him now," Mrs. Myers told her daughter.

"I can stay with him," Salome said softly as she sat on the edge of Stewart's bed. His eyes opened and he seemed to smile as she lifted his limp head into her lap and stroked his hair.

The coughing went on, getting worse. By ten o'clock Salome wondered how his body could stand the constant pounding of each cough that exploded from him. Another hour had passed. The hall clock downstairs was chiming eleven when Stewart's chest swelled up with a mighty heave and then fell.

Like that, it was over. No crying out. No dramatic clutching. Just one last great breath.

Salome knew he was gone, but she went on cradling his head. It was almost midnight before she told anyone.

Mary Fisher wished at times that she were back home in York, resting in bed. Now she was beyond fatigue, if there is such a dimension.

Through Monday she helped attend the suffering in the churches of Gettysburg. She found it difficult to believe that three days after the fighting had ended there was still such suffering.

By nightfall, she was near collapse and was ordered by a surgeon to a nearby house for a good night's sleep.

Too tired to fall asleep, she laid on the sitting room floor and told the woman of the house:

"I must pay a most deserved tribute to the inhabitants of this devoted town. Nothing can exceed your generous hospitality.

"You come out of a battle fought in your very midst with hands ready for every needed work and hearts overflowing with sympathy for the unfortunate. With unflinching nerve, you carry the wounded in as they are shot down at your very doors.

"Friends and foe alike are ministered to with untiring effort. Not one complaint of loss, privation or trouble."

The women blushed, and then said:

"But you've come all this distance to help. You sacrificed too."

Mary sighed, thinking of the home she probably would not see for days, perhaps a week or more. Then without giving it much thought, she fell asleep.

# CHAPTER
# 12

# Tuesday—Food,
# Bandages and Prayers

Sallie Broadhead scraped together what food she could find, bundled it up with some old quilts and two pillows and started out for the seminary hospital at the top of the hill.

It was a pleasant enough morning. Each morning became better than the last with more of the ravages of war being swept away. What still bothered her though was that awful stench.

And of course she still felt a deep pain for the suffering she saw each day. But at least things were becoming more orderly.

When she reached the tall, brick building, Sallie found soldiers unloading a small wagon load of bread and, a private told her, fifty pounds of butter.

"Farmers sent it in from the country," the private said, "along with a goodly supply of hard tack.

"Looks like at least everyone in this building will get a bite but probably not enough to fill their bellies. Hear tell some government meat is promised for tomorrow, along with a full supply of provisions."

Sallie dashed up the steps to the front door and disappeared into the building.

Her job today, a doctor advised, would be to get a basin of water and bathe and dress wounds.

In one room (which had probably housed two seminary students in happier times) Sallie found eight men, all with gunshot wounds.

"Can I change someone's bandage?" Sallie asked shyly.

"That fella on the floor can't help himself. Better tend to him first," said one those fortunate to be lying on a cot.

"Where's your wound?" Sallie asked as she kneeled at the young soldier's side.

He threw back a worn blanket to reveal a black and red opening in his leg. Sallie cringed and a shiver ripped through her body. The opening was covered with small crawling worms.

Sallie jumped to her feet and ran into the hallway. Two doors away, she spied a doctor talking to an orderly.

"Sir," she called out, but not too loudly, "sir!"

The doctor turned around.

"Can you please come here? I must see you!"

Sallie ushered him into the room and pointed to the repulsive wound.

"How could a man ever come to be in such a condition?" she demanded.

"Madam, I understand your concern. First, enough men had not been detailed to care for the wounded. Second, that man was wounded last Wednesday in the first day's fighting and held by the Rebels until Sunday. Third, we have not had time to attend to all the wounded. Fourth, there are not enough surgeons. And fifth, what few surgeons there are in this building can do little because the Rebels stole their instruments.

"Besides," he whispered in her ear, "many of these men are beyond any help and will die from sheer lack of timely attendance. This man is one of them."

The doctor turned to leave and then turned back to face her again.

"I am truly sorry, madam. War leaves us so few opportunities to do even that which is considered humane."

Sallie kneeled again and began to dab a wet cloth around the wound. Then she covered it with a clean cloth, bunched up one of the pillows she had brought and put it under his head.

"What else can I do for you?"

The soldier glanced up and replied: "If I give you my address will you send for my wife?"

"Yes," said Sallie.

It had been two days since Mary McAllister had given the captured confederate sword to Colonel Morrow. And with the constant attention she had to give to the wounded in her brother-in-law's house, she had completely forgotten about it.

A knock came to the front door that Tuesday morning. Martha answered.

"Mary, someone here to see you," her sister yelled out.

The man seemed to be a stranger and the slouch hat he wore did much to conceal his features in the shadow of the doorway.

"You don't recognize me. I'm Dennis Dailey, Second Wisconsin. I left General Archer's sword here for you to hide for me. Don't you remember?" the soldier said.

"You were taken prisoner! How did you get back here?" the flabbergasted woman asked.

"I escaped and came back for the sword."

"I thought you'd be in Libby Prison by now. I'm sorry. I gave the sword to Colonel Morrow."

Dailey removed his hat. Mary could see the disappointment in his eyes.

"I'm really sorry, I didn't think you'd be back and I thought the sword might be of some use to another soldier.

"Look, why don't you come in and we'll give you something to eat."

"Oh, that would be nice," Daily smiled. "I haven't had any real food since the piece of bread you gave me last week."

Mary got him seated, poured him a cup of hot coffee and

buttered some fresh bread. As he ate, she begged him to tell her how he got away.

"Well, they walked me and some other prisoners west to the mountains. The Rebs were all tired out so they gave each of the prisoners a little flour. I don't know what they thought we could do with that, so I took out that piece of bread you gave me and chewed on it awhile.

"They set us off in a field, away from the road, with only one guard. I watched him as we laid there. After a while he sat down and leaned up against a tree. Then his gun sank down and he went to sleep.

"Well, mam, I rolled over once to see how it would work. I swear I never heard so many little sticks crack in all my born days. But the guard didn't move. So I rolled over again and then again and I just kept going like that, over briars and rocks until I rolled up against a big log. Well, I just commenced to scrape leaves up over me.

"Would have given anything for a slug of water, but I didn't dare move. Couldn't see nothing for the leaves and, of course, it was getting dark.

"Next think I know it's morning. Here I'd slept all night. Didn't hear nothing, but I still didn't dare move for fear them Rebs had missed me and was looking. Laid there all day. That night, I got up. Swore every bone in my body had been fastened without a joint to the next one. But I loosened up and began to move. Let's see, that must have been Thursday night.

"I could hear firing all around, it seemed. Took a mighty wide swing around the whole Reb army and got way out in the country. Been trying ever since to get back here to town.

"Finally found a stream on Friday. Water sure tasted good. Hid in a wheat field all that day.

"On Saturday, when it seemed things had simmered down, I started moving south again. Guess it must have been Sunday morning when I ran into a farmer who told me our boys was chasing Lee back to the Potomac. Then I knew it was safe to get back.

"But I've been so famished that I've had to move slow and still carefully, since I wasn't sure all the Rebs had pulled out."

As he talked, he munched on the bread and motioned for a

second cup of coffee. By then, Mary had found a piece of smoked ham and some molasses.

Dailey devoured everything she set in front of him.

"What else did you give me to keep?" Mary asked suddenly, recalling Dailey turning something else over to her.

"My pocketbook," he answered.

"While you're eating, I'll hunt for it," she said.

Mary searched until she could think of nowhere else to look.

"What in heaven's name are you looking for?" Martha asked impatiently.

"Mr. Dailey's pocketbook."

"Land sakes, Mary, it's right here," said Martha as she pulled a table away from the wall. The pocketbook dropped to the floor.

Dailey stuffed the pocketbook into an inside pocket of his coat, pulled the slouch hat over his matted hair and stood up.

"Now where are you going?" Mary inquired.

"Found me this old musket along the road into town. It still shoots. Me and it'll catch up with our army."

Dailey grabbed the gun he had left standing in the hallway and was out the door in short order.

"Thank you for your kindnesses, mam," he said as he turned to look at Mary. "Be seein' ya now."

And off he strutted out Chambersburg Street; a lone, half-starved, filthy, proud soldier looking for an army.

Sister Camilla O'Keefe was working in the Methodist Church on Tuesday when a young, seriously wounded soldier asked why baptism was so great.

"Sister, it's very strange that nobody else says baptism is so necessary but you sisters," he argued.

A tall man dressed in black standing nearby overheard the remark.

"Yes, young man, I say baptism is necessary too and I'm a minister. If you desire it, I will baptize you," the tall man said.

The soldier looked up at both of them thoughtfully.

"Well, I'm a Protestant, so I guess you should do it, but only if you do it as the sister would," the soldier said to the minister. Then he looked at Sister Camilla and added:

"Sister, I want you to stay right here and see that he does it right."

"Well, here is how I do it," the minister said and then explained his ceremony.

"Sister, is that alright?" asked the soldier.

She smiled and nodded, "yes."

After the brief ceremony, the soldier asked again? "Sister, did he do it right?"

"Yes," she answered. "It was done properly."

Sister Camilla hardly knew whether to laugh or cry. Instead, she knelt and prayed. The solider began praying with her. And the minister joined them.

The young soldier's voice rose and cracked as he tried to breathe.

At the end he shouted out: "O Lord, bless all the Sisters of Charity."

With that, his chest fell and his hand went limp.

"At least he got baptized," said the minister.

"Yes," said Sister Camilla, "at least that."


By Tuesday, Dan Skelly had formed an opinion: war was too horrible to even think about.

"Town is filling up with people coming from all over— fathers, mothers, sister, brothers—all hunting their wounded or dead," he told his mother that morning.

"All of these undertakers who have come in are preparing bodies for shipment right on the streets near the hospitals.

"And you wouldn't believe the sights outside town.

"Wherever there was a bit of woods which had been in direct line of artillery fire of both sides, good-sized trees were knocked off, splintered and branches thrown in every direction.

"There are emergency hospitals in the fields. Surgeons are still at work, still performing amputations among the severely wounded men.

"I wonder if we will ever return to normal?"

"Well, Daniel, you need to keep busy until Fahnestock's store reopens. Mrs. Fahnestock stopped here earlier while you were out. She'd like you to help her."

"Help her with what?" Dan asked.

"Well, it seems that the store is taking inquiries from relatives looking for their men. She'd like you to pick up the names each day and then check around among all the wounded until you locate them."

"I'll go check with her right away," Dan said as he headed for the door.

# CHAPTER
# 13

# Wednesday—More Surprises

Carrie Sheads, still running from basement to first floor to second tending her soldiers, had begun to gather some semblance of order. She had gotten no new casualties since the day before, the first time that had happened in the week since the battle began.

She was on the first floor, in the front room, when she heard the rap on the door.

Carrie immediately recognized the soldier before her, despite his unshaven appearance and torn and dirty uniform.

"Colonel Wheelock! How . . .? What . . .?"

"My dear Miss Sheads, how good to see you!" the New Yorker said, sweeping his hat in a wide arc.

"Charles Wheelock! And it's nice to see you too. Won't you come in?"

The colonel hesitated, then stepped through the doorway.

"I don't have much time, Miss Sheads. I want to catch up with the army, but I do owe you an explanation.

"I, along with several others from my regiment, escaped from the Rebels in the confusion Sunday while crossing South Mountain.

"They were trying to push their hospital wagons through before being overrun by Union cavalry and they lost a few of us in the shuffle.

"But, it has taken us all of this time to filter back through their rear guard. I had to come here for my sword."

Carrie put her hand to her mouth.

"Oh, oh my, I had almost forgotten! Yes, of course, I'll get it."

In a minute she was back with sword, scabbard and belt.

Wheelock buckled it on, saluted and whispered:

"Miss Sheads, I'll not forget your bravery in hiding this for me nor your kindness."

And with that he was out the door, tipping his hat once more as he climbed into the saddle and trotted off across the seminary field, southward.


Mary Cadwell Fisher was almost ready to go to her friend's house Wednesday evening after a full day of caring for the wounded. She was leaving the College building when an orderly called to her.

"S'cuse me, mam, but there is a little chap out here who heard there was a woman here from his hometown, York, and he wants to see you," the orderly said. "He's in the last room at the end of this hallway, right side."

Mary, exhausted, walked to the room. A doctor in the hall stopped her to say: "Those boys in there are all hopeless cases. Careful what you say."

Mary nodded, understanding.

Two candles threw eerie shadows in that room of death but she had no trouble picking out the "little chap."

The others were all grown men and, despite their wounds, were trying to cheer the boy.

And boy he was. Mary thought he couldn't have been more than about fourteen. She knew she couldn't ask. She couldn't make him feel like a child, not around his soldier companions.

"Eh, lad, here's the lady from your home. Ain't it grand that she came to visit?" said a pale, thin sergeant who was lying closest to the boy.

Mary sat beside the boy on the floor.

"So you're from York too?" she said pleasantly.

"Well, no mam. Just said that so's you'd come by. I run away from home in Providence, Rhode Island, to join the drum corps."

"Brave lad and a dandy drummer," said the pale sergeant, forcing a smile from beneath a bandage that obscured his jaw. "We served together."

"Mam, you remind me of my mother. Wish I hadn't run away from her. Wish she was here now. I'd like to see her face one more time and hear her sweet voice."

Mary could see no wounds on the boy, although he looked quite frail.

"Where do you hurt, son?" Mary asked.

"Oh, I ain't hurt, just tired," he whispered.

"Lad did his duty," the sergeant spoke up. "Constant marches, not enough food, sleepless nights . . . too much for anyone. His strength wasn't enough to ward off a fever. Don't worry, lad, me and the boys here won't leave ya. We'll take care of ya."

But Mary could see there was nothing those men, in their condition, could do to help.

She felt his forehead. He was burning up with fever. Mary wanted to go for help, but she felt the boy didn't want her to leave.

"Can I do anything for you?" she asked.

The boy's eyes, glassy and half shut, looked at her strangely and, feebly, his voice called out:

"Oh, mother!"

Mary took the frail boy in her arms, cradling his head and shoulders and rocking back and forth on the hard floor.

The boy looked up at her again and whispered:

"I am so tired."

Then he rolled his head toward her bosom and closed his eyes. She could barely hear him breathing.

The room was silent, save for a moan now and then from one of the other men. Mary could see their contorted faces in the flickering candle light.

She took his hand in hers and was astounded by its smallness, almost like that of a young child. Perhaps he wasn't even fourteen. Maybe twelve?

His hand tightened in hers as though he was holding on to the last thing in the world that was truly his.

A half hour passed with Mary rocking back and forth, watching the pale face snuggled in sleep against her.

Then, suddenly, the boy's hand went limp and his head turned. His eyes shot open, widely, searching, frightened.

He looked long and earnestly into Mary's tear-streaked face.

"Kiss me before I die," the boy pleaded.

Mary hugged him tighter, pressing her lips against his forehead like she had done so many times when her own son was a small boy.

The drummer boy smiled, but just for a few seconds.

Then his eyes closed and his body relaxed. And Mary kept rocking him, forcing herself to believe that she was rocking him to sleep but knowing that somewhere in Providence, Rhode Island, there was a woman who would never hold her little boy again.

Sallie Broadhead felt somewhat relieved when she got to the seminary hospital Wednesday morning. Several doctors and nurses had arrived the night before from Washington.

Things are beginning to look better, Sallie thought.

Despite the fact that limbs were still being amputated and that bullets, some in their victims a full week now, were still being extracted, Sallie at last saw a ray of hope that the ordeal of her town would, sometime, be over.

An effort had been made to start regular cooking.

New volunteers were coming in every day.

The army was replacing exhausted surgeons and wounded orderlies with fresh men from Washington, Baltimore, Harrisburg and Philadelphia.

Yes, Sallie thought, the worst is over.

The morning hours went by quickly and Sallie had been

asked to search the building for plates, cups and spoons. She couldn't remember seeing any on the three floors where she had worked.

"Perhaps in the cellar," someone suggested.

"Oh, I don't think so," Sallie answered. "I've never been down there but I've been told that it's only partially dug out and still has a dirt floor. I doubt that they would have kept kitchen utensils down there.

"Worth a look," someone else said.

"Yes, guess it is," Sallie said, giving in to the suggestions as she lit a candle.

The stairway at the end of the hall was dark, even with the door behind her open. But she immediately knew the cellar wasn't empty.

There was the odor of unwashed human beings; the sounds, mostly moans and coughs; and the scattered light of small candles.

There was also water, at least several inches. So much rain had fallen in the past few days that the ground was holding rather than absorbing it.

When her eyes became accustomed to the darkness, Sallie tried to muffle her cry of despair.

"Oh, for heaven's sake!"

There, in the dim light, she could see several soldiers, too badly wounded to lift themselves out of the water. Some, semiconscious, were within inches of having water cover their face.

Pillars of dirt and brick which supported the building hid most of the cellar from her view, but Sallie didn't bother to investigate further.

She dashed back up the stairs and ran down the hall to the desk in the center corridor where one of the new nurses from Washington had set up a command post.

"Please, come with me! There are wounded men in the cellar! In all the confusion, they've apparently been ignored," Sallie pleaded.

The nurse ran back with her.

"My God, they must be gotten out of this or they'll drown!" she said as quietly as she could to Sallie.

Sallie stayed while the nurse ran back upstairs to get orderlies with stretchers. She peeked around some of the pillars and waded through water halfway across the cellar.

She was astounded. There were dozens of men, most of them halfsubmerged; a few perhaps already dead. Some were in almost total darkness, their candles long wasted away to a clump of wax.

One who could talk rationally told Sallie that he had lost all track of time. Periodically, he said, someone had come through the cellar with water and bits of bread.

"But, each time it was someone else. And each time they'd say, 'don't worry, boys, we'll get you out of here soon as there's room upstairs,' " the soldier said.

"Guess everyone who came down assumed the doctors or whoever's in charge knew we was down here."

It took hours to clear the cellar. Sallie counted almost one-hundred men carried out and taken to rooms upstairs and into the hallways. Most were in horrible condition, although none seemed to have the types of wounds which could have meant certain death or amputation.

But now, after a week in that hell hole, many would have to lose limbs to gangrene, Sallie overhead a surgeon say. Some, he added, probably would not survive, whether they had surgery or not.

"The ones you hear coughing real bad are too weak to take much more. I don't know how many of them we'll lose," the doctor said.

Sallie was amazed when she found the man she had talked to in the cellar and learned that they had all been down there since the first day's battle, a full week ago.

The man was a Union soldier but many of those in the cellar were Confederates.

"Rebs put us and their own wounded down there after they'd overrun this hill. We was laying on the ground near this building so they brought us down here thinking it would be the safest spot.

"Then they planted cannon just outside. We could hear some of those shells going through the walls upstairs.

"Guess in all the confusion, they forgot about us down here.

Didn't do no good to yell, even if you had the strength for it.
With those thick walls and no windows they couldn't of heard
us outside.

"We didn't see no one come in til a couple of days later.
Some of our boys came in; said they were chasing the Rebs;
said it was Sunday.

"Ceptin' for bein' hungry and thirsty wasn't too bad in here.
All that rain day or so before pretty well soaked in but it mustta
soaked the ground, cause every drop since is just been layin' on
top.

"Well, them boys that came through left us some food and
water and said someone would be along directly to help. And
till you come along, everybody else through here gave us the
same story."

Sallie listened patiently and wondered how many other
wounded men were lying somewhere with no attention being
given them.

She spent the rest of her day caring for these "new"
patients—feeding, washing, soothing.

It was almost time to go home; others would come and work
through the evening.

"Mrs. Broadhead, could you feed one more man before you
leave? He can just have some broth but he can't feed himself,"
the head nurse asked.

"Certainly," Sallie responded.

She was escorted to the first floor, to a room next to where
the surgeons operated.

"This young man was operated on this morning. He was one
of those in the cellar. He's awake now and needs nourish-
ment," the nurse said.

Sallie looked at the pitiful form lying on a blood-soaked
canvas cot. Both legs and his right arm had been amputated.

Sallie tried not to show any reaction but the spoon trembled
as she dipped it into the cup of broth. Then, she was ashamed.

What was left of what had been a handsome man in his early
twenties was smiling at her. Sallie smiled back; her hand
stopped trembling.

"Let's try some of this, okay?" she said, moving a broth-
laden spoon toward the soldier's mouth. His lips parted and he
swallowed the juice slowly. Then he smiled again.

From what she had seen of war wounds in the past few days, Sallie did not think the young soldier could live more than a few hours, a day or two at best.

But she went on feeding him very carefully as if it were the first meal of a long and healthy life.

The first light of Wednesday had barely hit the street when Mary McAllister stepped outside for a breath of morning air before starting a breakfast of coffee and mush for her patients.

Across the street, leaning against a tree, was a woman. She was sobbing. Mary rushed over and the woman looked up. She was no one Mary knew.

"What's the matter?" Mary asked hurriedly.

The woman wiped her eyes with a soiled handkerchief.

"I got this here dispatch Saturday," she said, waving a piece of paper. "Said my husband was wounded here. Got here last night on the train. Every place was shut up, but the hospitals. I searched them but couldn't find him! Couldn't find no place to sleep! Just waiting here for morning so I can look some more."

After she blurted that out the woman began sobbing again.

"You come over to our house and have some breakfast. Then we'll help you find your husband."

While the woman sat at the kitchen table Mary asked one of the soldiers who was able to get about despite an arm wound to see what he could find out about the woman's husband.

Armed with the missing man's name, rank and regiment, the soldier checked the lists being assembled by the Sanitary Commission on all casualties. It took only minutes to find his name.

"Yes, here it is," said a commission worker, "Says he was wounded; dispatch sent to his wife; he died the next day. That would have been last Thursday. Buried in a trench with dozens of others.

"We can't take time to dig up that whole trench now. Man's from here in Pennsylvania and the governor has promised the state will pay full transportation to all Pennsylvanians to take their dead away. But we don't have time to dig him up right now."

The soldier called Mary aside when he returned and gave her the details.

Mary broke the news of the man's death to his wife as gently as she knew how. For some reason, she got the feeling that the woman expected that news all along.

"I'd like to take him back and bury him in our church cemetery," the woman said.

"That won't be possible right away," Mary said, without explaining why. "You go home. The Sanitary Commission will make arrangements."

"But I can't get on that train unless I'm accompanying a coffin," the woman sobbed. "Took all the money I had for the train to get here."

"We'll see about that," Mary said.

At the station, Mary learned that the woman was right. Without a coffin she could not ride free, the stationmaster explained.

But word got around the station and before long the railroad workers coming off the night crews and those starting the day runs took up a collection.

It was Joe Broadhead who brought the money to Mary and the woman.

"We took up a collection. Here's enough for her ticket and a few meals til she gets home," Joe said, handing Mary a small bag full of change and dollar bills.

Mary smiled. The woman cried and bowed her head humbly toward Joe and the other railroad men who had gathered around.

Within the hour, she was on an eastbound train to Hanover Junction and from there on home.

Home? Mary had forgotten to ask the woman where home was. But it really didn't matter, she reasoned as she walked back home from the station. She was sure that dozens, maybe hundreds, of other wives from many towns would be coming to Gettysburg on similar missions.

There would be no time to get involved with each one.

• • •

"What a day!"

Salome Myers was resting late Wednesday night and speaking to herself as she jotted in her diary.

"Busy all day." she wrote. "Lieutenant Ruth (who came with Captain James Ashworth, both of the Pennyslvania Volunteers, to the Myers home on Tuesday) left today but the captain is still with us. He cannot be moved.

"Very busy all day going to the hospital and back.

"Get very tired as I do not get enough time to sleep.

"Captain Blair, who had his right arm amputated, came to stay with us for some time. His servant, Cato, came along.

"Frank Decker . . . came also from the hospital."

Salome glanced back over the entry.

Names, just names. She hadn't had time to ask where they were from, or who was waiting for them back home, or anything else. Just names, and yes, faces to go with the names.

But there was no time for any other chattering.

Names, just names, Salome thought as the pencil slipped from her fingers and her eyes closed.

# CHAPTER
# 14

# Thursday—On the Move

Sallie Broadhead said a quiet prayer Thursday morning for the
men she had helped move from the flooded cellar of the
seminary building the day before. The rain was pouring down
when she arose.

"Thank God we got them out of there, before they took in all
this water too," she told Joseph as he climbed into his work
clothes. Since the railroad had to keep rolling Joseph was one
of the few men in Gettysburg still working his normal job.

The mud in the road and on the hill kept Sallie from getting
to the seminary so she gathered some supplies of clean
bandages and bread and headed up Chambersburg Street to the
church hospitals.

"The men here seem to be in better condition than those up
at the seminary," she remarked to a doctor.

"Well, mam, that's because the men here in town got some
care from the townfolk during the fighting but those poor devils

at the seminary were in an isolated building so they mostly had to wait for the shooting to end."

Makes sense, Sallie thought.

It also seems, she thought, that the men in the town hospitals had plenty to eat, although very few had beds to lie in.

At the seminary food was not as plentiful but, because much of the building had been a dormitory, there were more beds or, rather, cots.

At noon, Sallie was back home, preparing for another round of visits. Little Mary had come home from Mrs. Gilbert's house next door to be with her mother for a short while.

"You go back?" Mary asked.

"Yes, my sweet, mother has to go back to the hospitals after lunch," Sallie answered softly. She didn't like to leave the child so often but she felt an obligation to help.

It was almost time for her to leave when she answered a knock at the front door.

"Afternoon," said a white-haired sergeant. Sallie saw an ambulance wagon behind him in the street.

"Yes, what can I do for you?"

"Well, mam, we've had a field hospital just outside town in a meadow. No proper shelter there for our wounded, just some old torn pieces of tent. Rain s'morning almost finished some of 'em. Chilled 'em, you know.

"We're trying to get 'em inside but all the big buildings are jam packed. We was wondering if you might take three into your home?"

Sallie stared at the ambulance. She couldn't see who was inside and her first reaction was one of uncertainty.

Into my home? What would Joseph say? The questions raced through her mind. But there was only one answer.

"Why, yes, sergeant, bring your men in. We can arrange to put them in the parlor."

Sallie ran to get pillows and blankets.

By the time the first stretcher was carried in Sallie had pushed back the two chairs and small sofa, the round table near the window and the square table.

The orderlies brought in blankets for the men to lay on.

Sallie, smiling and greeting each patient, slipped a fresh pillow under his head as the orderlies laid each down.

"You go now, momma. I be nurse," Mary said after the orderlies had left.

"No, Mary," Sallie laughed. "Momma doesn't have to go now. I can stay home and help."

Twenty minutes later the sergeant was back with a large white sack.

"Food, mam, for the men. You can draw more from the Sanitary Commission. Here's an authorization slip with your patients' names. You just sign it and show it when you need supplies."

Sallie prepared some lunch and then chatted with her new boarders. All were in pain, but all had received medical attention and were in no immediate danger, the sergeant had told her.

"Just feed 'em and watch over 'em. Right now they ain't got no one else," the sergeant said as he left.

Eight days had passed since Colonel Henry Huidekoper lost his arm to a Rebel bullet and a surgeon's knife.

On July 9 orders came, instructing him to report to the railroad station at noon where a train would take him to Baltimore for further recuperation.

Huidekoper thanked the Myers family and Salome walked with him to the train station. They looked in vain for a passenger coach.

"Colonel, colonel, over here," a voice called out.

Huidekoper turned to face a young lieutenant who was directing wounded men to freight cars.

"Sorry, sir, best the Army could do. Cars are bringing in supplies and taking out wounded," the lieutenant said apologetically.

Huidekoper climbed some boxes to get into the car. The floor was sopping wet.

"They had ice in there, sir, trying to keep food from spoiling," the lieutenant explained.

Huidekoper was followed in by Major Chamberlin of his regiment.

Together they gathered some straw to lay on, not wanting to take a chance of falling while the train weaved its way east and then south to Baltimore. Huidekoper knew it would be at least a twelve-hour ride.

He was surprised to see only one other man get aboard that car. It was General Joshua Owens, who was suffering from rheumatism so bad that he had to turn command of his Philadelphia Brigade over to General Webb.

"Can't sit in all that wet," the general said as he rolled an empty barrel into a corner of the car and proceeded to prop himself atop it.

Oh, lord, thought Huidekoper, this is going to be some ride! But Baltimore . . . a city . . . with cool water and a soft bed. Something to look forward to.

The train inched forward. Huidekoper rolled on his side and watched as the buildings of Gettysburg slipped by. It was so quiet, so peaceful, such loving people.

Outside town, the train bumped past one tent hospital after another.

"The suffering goes on," Huidekoper said to his companions. Then, for the first time, he really noticed the empty sleeve pinned to his jacket.

# CHAPTER
# 15

# Friday—A Week
# of Peace

A full week had passed since the battle ended and each day brought more visitors to town. Many were just sightseers or souvenir hunters; others were relatives of the dead and wounded; and some were considered high-ranking officials.

For Gates Fahnestock, Friday brought guests to his father's house and a thrill to the boy.

A delegation from Ohio, led by Governor David Tod, arrived on the 10th of July. So did Bishop McSwaine of the Protestant Episcopal Church.

Gates eventually lost track of names of relatives and delegations who came to care for their people and, where possible, move them home or to wherever the best care could be obtained.

Sallie Broadhead asked Mrs. Gilbert to watch after her little Mary and the three wounded men on Friday morning.

"I'm just going to take some homemade jellies up to the seminary," Sallie said when Mrs. Gilbert arrived.

She walked quickly up the street and then cut through the field below the seminary. An anxious feeling swept over her as she recalled her last visit two days before and finding men lying in water in the cellar.

But this time, as soon as she stepped inside, she rejoiced. That sense of urgency was gone. Someone had scrubbed the floor. She peeked in the rooms and saw that nearly each man now had a cot and clean clothing.

She also noticed some familiar faces missing and new ones in their place.

"Quite a few have died since Wednesday," the head nurse told Sallie, "including the one whose wife you wrote to. Oh, by the way, one of the ladies stayed with him until he died and then cut off a lock of his hair. She thought perhaps you could save it for his wife when she comes."

The wisp of hair—dark brown and curly—had been placed in an envelope. Sallie felt strange about slipping it into her apron pocket.

She stayed only long enough to smile and wave to each roomful of men; then she hurried home to her own mini-hospital.

Her three men looked better then they had the day before too. At least they all had clean shirts and were eating well.

"Was glad to get rid of that old shirt last night, Mrs. Broadhead," said one. "Had it on since before this fight started. Couldn't stand to get downwind of myself."

Everyone chuckled. Sallie smiled, feeling good that she helped.

Salome Myers couldn't get over the amount of liquor that was being accumulated in her father's house. Everyone who came felt obligated to bring a bottle "to keep our boys' spirits up."

Salome wondered whose spirits needed to be kept up. By now, she felt, the wounded had resigned themselves to either quick cures or long convalescence.

Captain Ashworth's brother had come the night before to

help care for him. Then on Friday, Captain Blair's brother arrived.

With all the extra help at home, Salome resumed her trips to the church hospitals. She particularly checked on those she knew by name.

"Wilson Race is doing well, Miss Salome, but I don't think he's quite up to being moved to your house. Perhaps in a few days. It's kind of you and your folks to offer however."

Salome knew there was no sense arguing. The doctor was adamant that Wilson Race would stay there.

"Who about Will Sheriff of Pittsburgh?"

"Miss Salome, the wounds in Sheriff's legs are somewhat better but he can't be moved either. Soon enough you're going to be wanting to get rid of these men."

"Alright, doctor, if you have someone you'd like to move to our house, we have an empty cot."

And with that, Salome continued on to the next church.

# CHAPTER
# 16

# July 11–12—The Living
# and the Dying

The army, the people of Gettysburg, the Sanitary and Christian commissions, new volunteers, relatives—all were working to save lives.

Mary Caldwell Fisher felt it was safe to leave now.

Her son had harnessed the team early Saturday morning but Mary hesitated.

"Let's wait until after breakfast," she told him and the women who had come with them. "I can't leave until I've said goodbye to some of these boys.

"Each day has brought some new experience and revealed new phases of character. We could fill volumes with the touching incidents that presented themselves in the short space of a week."

So Mary said goodbye to her "boys."

She felt that many of them had become very dear to her

through their long suffering and patience. But she didn't tell them that.

"Got to move on and give someone else a chance to wait on you," she joked with many.

Others, too far gone to remember her or even realize she was there, got a kiss on the forehead, a hand squeezed and a tear falling onto their cheeks.

Then Mary and her troop went home.

Salome was more overwhelmed by visitors—really helpers—on Saturday than by the task of caring for her patients.

"This is unbelievable, mother. So far today there've been those four men who came in from New York to . . . how did they put it? . . . oh, yes, to render any assistance in their power."

"Goodness knows, we need the help," said Mrs. Myers. "But I'm a mite suspicious yet of strangers."

"Well, at least we don't have to worry about the others. Wasn't Captain Ashworth thrilled to see his mother, particularly when she said she could stay to nurse him?

"Course I hate to see Will Sheriff going but he'll be better off traveling back home with his parents. They seem to be nice people.

"Oh, did I show you this? Will gave me a photograph of himself in uniform. See!"

Mrs. Myers looked over the top of her glasses and then through them studying the photograph. Then she smiled politely and handed it back to Salome.

Sunday was not as happy a day for Salome.

Sergeant Stewart's father came to arrange the transfer of his son's body back home.

Salome thought he looked like such a poor, weak old man who was much distressed with his son's death.

And to complicate the sadness he was accompanied by a Mr. Baldwin, who had also lost a son in the battle.

"Poor Mr. Stewart. How I pity him and Mr. Baldwin," Salome whispered to her mother.

It had become such a dismal day, with the two old men looking for their sons' bodies on such a rainy Sunday.

"And on top of everything else, the doctors still won't let Wilson Race be moved to our house! They say the weather is too poor to have him transferred. I guess they're right but it's very frustrating to see the treatment those men get in the hospitals compared to what we can do for them here."

"Patience, Salome, patience," Mrs. Myers told her daughter calmly.

The Hollingers had been too busy taking care of visitors for Liberty or her sisters to take a walk over areas where heavy fighting had taken place.

But on Sunday, Liberty and Annie walked down around the base of Culp's Hill and up the steep slope on the east side of the cemetery.

"Liberty, look at that trench! They must have buried soldiers there. Look, there's a hand sticking out!" Annie whispered, as though she might disturb someone's slumber by speaking loudly.

Liberty saw the hand and, further along, another hand and a foot.

She shivered and rushed her sister along. In a clearing between Culp's Hill and Cemetery Hill they saw other people from town out walking too.

She particularly noticed two young boys on their knees, examining something with great interest.

Liberty and Annie rushed over and peered down at the boys. There on the ground was a severed hand, dried almost to parchment so that it looked as though it were covered with a kid glove.

Annie picked it up and Liberty jumped back.

The boys were amazed that a girl would touch it.

But the more they stared at it the less repulsive it became.

Finally, it became a fascinating relic; although no one else touched it.

"Look at how small the fingers are," Liberty finally said. "He must have been a very young soldier or someone who never worked with his hands."

Annie laid the hand back down. She and Liberty continued up to the cemetery. The boys got back down on their knees and examined the hand some more.

Albertus McCreary thought he had been hardened, after a week and a half, to all the hardships of war. He had seen more of its effects than most boys his age.

But he became extremely depressed on Sunday—normally such a happy day—by watching people who came to town seeking wounded relatives.

It seemed to Albertus that most of these visitors had had a son, or husband, or father, or brother wounded at this place. But, when they arrived, the person they were seeking was dead.

The night before, a young lady had come in on the late train seeking her brother. Mrs. McCreary brought her home to spend the night with the idea that they would search the hospitals for him Sunday morning.

Albertus' older brother escorted the young lady around on Sunday morning and they found that her brother had been in one of the church hospitals. At the hospital they learned that he had died—late Saturday night.

Despite the lack of formal services, the Sisters of Charity tried to make this Sunday a more meaningful day. They paid a great deal of attention to prayers and stressed religious feelings with the men.

Sister Camilla O'Keefe had maintained that composure as she ministered to the needs of the body and the spirit—until about noon. That's when a surgeon at the Methodist Church hospital, where she was working, asked her to stop by the Sanitary Commission store on her way back from her noon meal to pick up bandages.

The counterman at the store took the order and said:

"There's too much here for you to carry. I'll have a wagon deliver these bandages this afternoon. You belong to the Catholic Church, right?"

Sister Camilla, without a smile, replied:

"Why, no sir, I'm at the Methodist Church."

The counterman, who had been hunched over a makeshift desk, straightened up quickly.

"But the Methodist Church doesn't have nuns," he protested.

"It does today," chuckled Sister Camilla as she turned to leave the store.

When she got back to the church, Sister Camilla found one of the other nuns in a highly excited state. A doctor was trying to calm down Sister Serena Klimkiewicz.

"Sister," the doctor said to Camilla, "we're getting a wagon and a driver. Would you please accompany Sister Serena out to one of the field hospitals? She was copying casualty lists and found that her brother, Thaddeus, was wounded here and is in one of the field hospitals.

"She hasn't seen him in nine years and didn't even know he had been fighting here.

"We've told her she can bring him in here and help take care of him.

"He was wounded in the ankle and the chest, but the record indicates that it's safe to move him."

Later, Sister Camilla smiled gently at the tearful reunion.

How strange, she thought. A hardened man of war and a woman of peace—brother and sister—needing each other at a critical time after so many years apart.

The Lord works in mysterious ways, she thought.

Sallie Broadhead had forgotten all about the woman she had written to the previous Tuesday, telling her that her husband had been wounded and saying that he wanted his wife to come and help.

The soldier had died a few days later and on this Sunday his wife arrived at the Broadhead house.

"I never pitied anyone as I did when I told her he was dead," Sallie told her husband later.

"I hope I may never again be called upon to witness such a heart-rending scene. The only comfort she had was in recovering his body.

"Oh, Joseph, it was simply so pathetic. The only satisfaction

I had was that I marked the grave. If I hadn't she might not have recovered his body."

Sallie's spirits were down all that day, partly from her experience with the widow and partly from other visitors who were going door-to-door in search of lodgings and being turned away.

The Broadhead home was full of wounded men and some visitors. Sallie wanted to take more in, but there was no room.

"Every house in town is full. Last night, I slept on a chair tilted back on the front porch of the hotel," said one old man who had come to search for the body of his son.

"I really wish we could do more, Joseph," Sallie said, crying softly on her husband's chest.

"Here it is, another Sunday, and really, since the battle we have had no Sunday with all the churches converted into hospitals.

"Trains running and this hustle and bustle in the streets. If it weren't for the calendar you made, we'd never know this was to be a day of rest."

Joseph knew he had to get her mind busy again, too busy for these melancholy states.

"How are your patients, love?"

"One is getting worse. I'm afraid he's sinking," Sallie replied, still depressed.

"It's difficult to get proper medical attention. These surgeons don't like to quit their hospitals and run from house to house. And our own physicians are overwhelmed with business."

"Ah, but at least we can feed them, right? There now, love, let's get some supper on for these men."

Sallie wiped her eyes.

"My yes, here I'm feeling sorry for myself and forgetting about them. Will you help me, Joseph?"

He smiled, took Sallie by the hand and led the way to the kitchen.

# CHAPTER
# 17

# July 13–19—Some
# Go Home

On Monday morning, Salome Myers got a doctor's permission to take Amos Sweet from the Catholic Church to her home.

Amos protested: "Gawd, lady, man without his right leg is gonna be a burden."

"Nonsense," Salome shot back. "Taking care of one more is no burden.

"Put him on that cot," she instructed the stretcher bearers as they brought Sweet into the Myers' sitting room.

While Salome was gone, Wilson Race's father had arrived to visit his gravely-wounded son.

"I told him that his boy had been shot through the lung and couldn't talk for long periods," Mrs. Myers told Salome. "But I didn't say how bad he was; that he might not live."

Salome went to meet Mr. Race and found him to be a very pleasant man in his son's presence. But later, away from his wounded son, Mr. Race couldn't talk about him without crying.

"He's in bad shape, ain't he, miss? Don't see how he can live through this," the old man lamented.

By evening, Mr. Race did what the Myers told him was best: to go home. He couldn't help his son and, in his depression, he could do more harm.

"This day has passed much as yesterday and the day before," Sallie Broadhead told Joseph as they rested on a bench near the back door.

"The town is as full as ever of strangers, and the old story of the inability of a village of twenty-five-hundred inhabitants, overrun and eaten out by large armies, to accommodate from ten to twelve thousand visitors, is repeated almost hourly."

Sallie watched the sun slowly sinking behind the mountains. Then she sighed.

"What's wrong, love?" Joseph asked.

"Wrong? Oh, nothing's wrong. We've got twenty people in our house, filling every bed and covering the floor. And just before I came out here, one of the nurses who stopped by said that one of our patients is dying."

Sallie took Joseph's hand and looked at him tenderly.

"I'm sorry I'm so grumpy. I guess I'm just tired. I want to help and I feel so helpless.

"What our soldiers are in the army I can't say, but when they are wounded, they all seem perfect gentlemen. So gentle, patient, kind and so thankful for any kindness shown them.

"I've seen a lot of them, and I have yet to meet the first who showed ill breeding. And everyone I talk to says the same thing.

" 'Come and see our men; they are the nicest in the army,' someone will say. And the reply generally follows: 'They cannot be better than ours.'

"You see, Joseph, these men have sacrificed so much and complain so little. What do I have to complain about?"

"Aw, you're not complaining, love, just tired, that's all. Look at all the good you're doing. Off to bed with you; a good night's sleep will help."

• • •

On Tuesday, Mr. and Mrs. Sheriff left for home with their son, Will. Salome hated to see him go but she knew that he was anxious to be home again.

Two men from New York state were leaving too, vowing to help each other on the long train trip up through Pennsylvania.

Salome thought about poor Mr. Race, wondering if he had gotten home yet and doubting that he would ever see his son alive again.

The Myers took in another patient from one of the church hospitals, Corporal George Bates of Philadelphia.

"Rebs got me twice, in the arm and in the leg," Salome overheard Bates telling her father as he helped the soldier settle into a cot. "Damn ball is still in the arm. Doc didn't want to go cutting around. Says I lost too much blood when they cut the one out of my leg. Son-of-a-bitching arm hurts."

"Yes, it does look painful, Mr. Bates. We'll try to take real good care of you," Mr. Myers said.

"And I sure appreciate you and your family for that, sir," Bates answered.

On Tuesday night, Sallie Broadhead sat quietly by herself at the kitchen table, another day of cooking and nursing behind her—the last day, in fact. For on this day, the army had removed all of her patients to a new general hospital in tents outside town. From the top shelf of a cabinet she took down a small black diary and made an entry:

"July 14—It is now one month since I began this journal, and little did I think when I sat down to while away the time, that I would have to record such terrible scenes as I have done.

"Had anyone suggested any such sights as within the bound of possibility, I would have thought it madness. No small disturbance was occasioned by the removal of our wounded to the hospital. We had but short notice of the intention, and though we pleaded hard to have them remain, it was of no use.

"So many have been removed by death, and recovery, that there was room; and the surgeon having general care over all, ordered the patients from many private homes to the General Hospital. A weight of care, which we took upon us for duty's sake, and which we had learned to like and would have gladly borne, until relieved by the complete recovery of our men was lifted off our shoulders, and again we have our home to ourselves."

She wrote no more, although she knew her home had been cleared of wounded because she also had a young daughter to care for. Other families, with older children, continued to keep patients.

Sallie, for a moment, envied them.

But that's not fair to little Mary, she thought, nor to Joseph.

She got up, put the diary away and gathered Mary up off the floor, where she had been playing with a doll.

"Off to bed, little one," Sallie said, clutching the child to her bosom.

"More soldiers coming to get better?"

"No, Mary, all the men are better now."

"I miss them, momma."

"Yes, we all do, Mary."

It was just about noon, two days after Amos Sweet had been brought to the Myers home from the hospital, when he died.

Salome tried to keep busy. But she kept remembering back to Monday when they had carried Amos in and him protesting how much of a burden he'd be. And then she'd cry.

A surgeon at the hospital who stopped by to check on Captain Ashworth tried to console Salome.

"Sweet was not in good shape. Bringing him here from the hospital didn't kill him. In fact, the loving care you folks gave him was the best thing that could have happened to him. Just too many complications," the surgeon explained.

On Thursday, Salome said goodbye to Captain Blair, who left for home with his brother, his wife and his son. As she stood at the front door waving them off, a wagon carrying a wooden coffin pulled up and Mr. Stewart looked down.

"Taking my boy home now, Miss Myers," the old man said, turning halfway around to gaze at the coffin. "Just wanted to thank you again for all your kindness."

It took Salome a few moments to recognize the man seated

next to Mr. Stewart because a slouched hat covered part of his face.

"Mr. Baldwin here found his son in a hospital but the boy's doctor said he can't be moved. So Mr. Baldwin is gonna ride back part way with me."

"Take care of yourselves," Salome said softly. She didn't know what else to say to the two men and after she said that she thought it was dumb.

The wagon pulled away. The men doffed their hats. Salome waved weakly, stared at the coffin and then disappeared into the house.

On Friday, July 18, the Myers took in another soldier. He hadn't been wounded, just sickly. His name was James Goodrich of Company K, 14th Vermont.

"Oh, we have other Vermont men here, upstairs in fact, Sergeant Eugene Eaton of the 16th Vermont Volunteers. His brother, Captain Henry Eaton, is here too, helping to take care of him."

Having never met anyone from Vermont before, Salome thought it strange to now have three Vermont men in the house. On Sunday, it became even stranger when Henry Frazer of Company C, 14th Vermont, fell ill and joined them.

On Saturday, the 19th, John Rupp, the tanner, took time to write to his sister, Anne, in Baltimore.

"I am very thankful to Almighty God for his merciful goodness in protecting and bringing us all safely through this terrible slaughter of human life. We have all escaped bodily injury. My property sustained very slight injury indeed, considering the heavy cannonading of both armies. Our house was under fire of both armies."

John described the day-to-day activities of the battle, particularly the day when he was inside the house with Union troops out front and Rebs out back.

And he told her about Virginia Wade being killed.

"Several others were hit on the shins with spent balls, where, if they had stayed in their houses, would not have happened to them."

And he gave his sister his assessment.

"I think we have given the Rebs a sample of Pennsylvania life, in which they will remember Gettysburg forever. Our beautiful cemetery has suffered very much, but I would go through all again, the same fire again, if we had them back again to repeat the same woes to them again.

"But I think the fall of Vicksburg and all our recent victories will bring things to a focus. Grant is doing things up. We call our baby John Grant, fine little fellow he is, too."

# CHAPTER
# 18

# July 20–31—An End to Nursing

On Monday, July 20, Salome Myers greeted Mr. Eaton, from Illinois, who had come to see his two sons, and she moved Wilson Race to a place near a window where he could get fresh air.

"It'll do you good, Mr. Race," she said soothingly.

Wilson smiled weakly but said nothing.

By Tuesday, Salome was feeling sick herself. She felt warm and her head ached. The day was made worse by the departure of four patients, including the Eaton brothers who left for New York by train.

With the cool of evening, Salome felt somewhat better. She wrote a letter to Mrs. Race, telling her that "your husband seems some better."

And in the mail that day was a letter from Will Sheriff with photographs of his mother and sisters. Salome smiled; she felt she knew them.

More visitors came Wednesday, but one in particular saddened Salome immensely. It was Mrs. Sweet, who didn't know her husband was dead.

"You didn't get our letters?" Salome asked.

"No," the tearful Mrs. Sweet replied, "only a letter from a man at the hospital who said Amos seemed to be coming along."

Salome talked the woman into spending the night but first thing Thursday morning she was on her way back to the train station.

That evening, Wilson Race took a turn for the worse.

Salome was up early on Friday, tending to Wilson. She could see he was failing and a doctor confirmed that fear.

It was almost eight o'clock when Wilson whispered to her: "Tell mother I died loving Jesus and trusting Him for salvation."

Then the soldier smiled at her and closed his eyes.

So peaceful, so happy, thought Salome as she cradled his head in her arms one last time.

That afternoon the army did what Salome feared was coming. They began moving all wounded men from the churches and private homes to a tent hospital east of town. Those who needed further hospital care but could be safely moved by train were taken up to Harrisburg.

That night was the first in three weeks in which the Myers home was not a haven for wounded soldiers.

Salome went to bed early and slept soundly until 4:30 Saturday morning. Then she arose, ate breakfast and ironed clothes until eight.

In the afternoon she went shopping and bought paper and ink for Andrew Crooks, who had been moved to the tent hospital. It was raining when she left home after supper to deliver the supplies to Andrew. A neighbor passing by in a buggy gave her a ride out and said he would pick her up later.

Salome visited with Andrew and then went outside to await her ride. The man never showed and Salome didn't feel like walking two miles in the rain.

"Is there someplace I can stay?" she asked a nurse.

"Yes, there's a women's tent for us and visitors," the nurse answered.

All of the beds were taken but Salome found a pile of blankets. She laid a gum blanket on the ground in a space between two cots, put two blankets on top of that, laid down and pulled two more blankets over her. The rain on the tent was soothing, although Salome thought as she drifted off to sleep that she'd rather be home. At least she was glad she had told a soldier walking into town to tell her parents she was staying the night.

It was barely five a.m. Sunday when Salome got up quickly and quietly. Wagons and horsemen were already on the road but she didn't ask for a ride because she didn't recognize anyone. By six, she was home fixing breakfast for the whole family.

At eight o'clock Sunday night, she got another ride out to the hospital with a neighbor, visited the patients who had stayed at her house and then rode back into town.

On Monday, July 27, Wilson Race's father came back to Gettysburg to claim his son's body.

"Poor Mr. Race. I gave him all the consolation I could," Salome told her mother later. "He mourns very much for his son's early death.

"I took one last look at Wilson and put some flowers on the coffin."

That night, Salome began a long letter to Mrs. Race. By 11 o'clock she was too sleepy to finish. But it was her first priority Tuesday morning. And when she finished it she began a letter to Wilson's brother, who had written to express his appreciation for her caring for his brother.

As patients were released from the hospitals, surgeons and orderlies were moved too. Dr. Willing, who had gotten sick and stayed a night with the Myers, got orders to rejoin his regiment Wednesday. And Joe Lewis, a hospital steward who had been boarding there, left with Dr. Gates and Mr. Spencer for their regiments.

The highlight of Salome's day, however, came with the mail on the afternoon train. It was a letter from Henry Stewart, a brother of the late sergeant.

"What a splendid letter coming from a grateful heart," Salome said in a whisper to herself as she read the letter over and over.

On Thursday she received a letter from Sergeant J. B. Wilson, who had been moved from the Catholic Church to a hospital in Harrisburg.

"I'm writing to inquire about my fast friend, Wilson Race. We were in the same company," J. B. Wilson's letter began.

How do you tell a wounded man that his friend is dead? Salome's response told how Race had suffered and how death was his escape and how he had talked about his friend, J. B. Wilson.

"He always kidded about your names, telling me often about you saying that the army had mixed his name up, making Wilson the Christian instead of the family name," Salome wrote.

On Friday, July 31, Salome couldn't find a ride to the General Hospital and it was so hot. She decided instead to go to the seminary hospital to help out.

But it wasn't the same. She knew no one there.

It was Monday, the 20th of July, before Albertus McCreary and his friends discovered that all the lead which had been fired over and around them more than two weeks ago was worth its weight in gold.

"Well, almost," Albertus told his friends. "Army's payin' thirteen cents a pound and there's a lotta pounds of them bullets around."

They started on Culp's Hill, which was close by and had been the site of heavy fighting.

With the largest bullets, it only took about eight to make a pound. In some spots, particularly near the breastworks, they found up to ten pounds of bullets within an area a boy could cover by taking one step in each direction.

Within days, they also learned that some large shells which hadn't exploded were full of lead pellets.

An artilleryman who thought he was just telling stories to innocent boys explained how the cap of such shells could be unscrewed with care. Then the shell had to be filled with water before the lead could be extracted.

With that lesson learned, Albertus and his friends scoured the woods for shells and pocketed pound after pound of lead.

The searching and finding and money-making went well all week. By Friday, almost every young boy in town had a can of powder hidden in his house or shed. And in wooded hiding places they cached rifles found on the battlefield.

Each afternoon, they'd load the rifles, leave the ramrods in and shoot up into the sky.

"We never knew where the ramrods went," Albertus wrote in his diary one night. Then, he added:

"Another trick was to go to the woods, place five or six large Wentworth shells among dry leaves and sticks, set fire to the pile, and run to a safe distance and wait for the explosion. It made a racket that put the Fourth of July in the shade."

It was Saturday when the boys were hunting for lead on Cemetery Hill.

A school chum of Albertus had found an unexploded Wentworth shell and unscrewed the cap.

"Got any water to pour in this shell?" the boy yelled to others scouting for their own shells.

"Nope," they yelled back, almost in unison.

Albertus was watching as his impatient friend picked up the shell, held it upside down and tried to shake the lead out—but with little success. Then he banged it on a rock.

Albertus saw the spark, then the flash and then the explosion.

When the boys reached their friend they didn't know him. His face was a mass of blood and torn flesh. His hands had been torn away. His shirt and the top of his trousers were stuffed like rags into the hole which had been his stomach.

Two smaller boys screamed and ran from the hill.

Several older ones stared and vomited, yelling even as their throats welled up with everything that had been inside them.

Albertus and three other boys who had witnessed a good many amputations in the military hospitals gathered up their friend and ran, as best they could, toward town.

Two soldiers on horseback on the Baltimore Pike near the cemetery gate stopped the race and made them lay the injured boy on the ground. Then, one of the men galloped up the street to get one of the doctors still left in the Catholic Church.

Within minutes, three surgeons came rushing back in a small wagon. They lifted the limp body into the back of the wagon and went to work.

Almost an hour passed before Albertus saw the doctors shaking their heads and, one by one, climbing down from the wagon.

"He never regained consciousness, but he held on all this time," said one.

Each of the boys turned away in a different direction and each, to himself and almost silently, cried.

By noon, notices were posted and the word went out: the Army would buy no more lead from anyone in town under the age of eighteen.

Three days had passed since the accident and Albertus had busied himself with chores at home. And so had his friends.

On Tuesday, July 28, Albertus was running an errand for his mother on High Street when he heard an explosion much like the one of the previous Saturday. As he spun around he saw a schoolmate lying on his back a half block away.

Albertus ran to the boy. They stared at each other for a second before the boy closed his eyes in death. Albertus cringed when he saw the boy's bowels had been blown away.

Lying against a house a few feet away was a man whose hands were hanging in shreds.

Within seconds he was being cared for by a white-frocked surgeon who seemed to appear out of thin air.

It took another day before Albertus got the full story. A woman on High Street told him that the man was a stranger who had come to see the battlefield. He had found a shell and had been told how boys made money by removing the lead pellets. He was trying to get the pellets out by banging the shell on sidewalk brick.

"Well, he was banging that shell time and again when the boy came down the street," the woman told Albertus.

"I could hear the boy yelling that hitting that shell was a very dangerous thing to do. And just as he said that, down came the shell on the brick again and blew up."

Days later, Albertus learned, the man was still alive and expected to survive, although he had lost both hands and a leg.

That night, Friday, he told his mother he was glad July was coming to an end.

"I never want to see a month like this again."


Jacob Gilbert was thrilled when the Iron Brigade Band stayed in town after the battle. Its men performed hospital orderly duties, served as cooks and messengers and helped out wherever help was needed.

But, most importantly, Jacob thought, the band played. In the evenings, they would march from hospital to hospital, playing the patriotic tunes men loved to hear.

Jacob was thrilled too. When he happened to mention to a bandsman that he had been a musician with the 87th Pennsylvania Regiment he was immediately asked if he'd like to play.

"We're shorthanded. What do you play?" the bandsman asked.

"Cornet," answered Jacob.

"I'll tell the captain. I'm sure he'd be glad to have you play with us as long as we're in town."

So from July 6 to July 29 Jacob's evenings were spent trooping about his hometown with the Iron Brigade Band.

And on the 29th he told his wife that he had made a decision.

"There's still a place for me in the army, Elizabeth. You've seen what good work these musicians do, both in the hospitals and as bandsmen.

"They're leaving today for Washington and I'm going along. I'll be sworn in when we get to Washington and when this war is over, I'll be back."

Elizabeth knew there was no sense in protesting. She had seen the pride in Jacob's face these past few weeks.

She packed his bag with a change of clothes and his shaving kit.

When he had gone, she cried. She had seen what war—violent war—could do physically to a human being. And she knew that being a musician in the army was not always the safest job in the heat of battle.

# CHAPTER
# 19

# August and September—
# Lingering Effects

By the beginning of August Fannie Buehler was totally exhausted. Her doctor told her she must get more rest.

It was near the end of the first week of the month when Fannie answered a knock at the door.

A small, thin man, dressed in Union blue with sergeant stripes merely pinned to a ragged jacket, stood before her.

"Morning, mam. I'm orderly to Colonel John C. Callis, who was severely wounded here almost five weeks ago. My colonel has been up at the college hospital but they want to move him out to the tent hospital east of town.

"I'm afraid the confusion there would do him poorly. I'd like to get him into a private home where he could have a room. I'll continue to take care of him."

Fannie felt weak.

"Oh, no, I just can't. I'm too weak now. Doctor ordered me to rest," she protested. "Can't you find another place?"

"Mam, colonel's mortally wounded. He may not live long. I just want to make him comfortable."

Fannie felt that surge of pity she had on the first day she had taken in wounded men.

"Sergeant, I'll talk to my husband and my doctor. If you will, please come back about six tonight and I'll give you an answer."

David told her it was her decision, but that he would help where possible. Her doctor said it was alright since the colonel's orderly would be there to care for him.

"Okay, sergeant, you may bring your colonel tomorrow morning. Our third floor is empty and he may have the front room," Fannie told the orderly that evening.

"Thank you, Mrs. Buehler, but, ah, there's more. We got a telegram today that the colonel's wife is on her way."

"No problem," Fannie answered quickly, "as I said, the third floor is empty except for some things we've stored up there. There are three rooms, one for each of you."

"The colonel will pay for the rooms," the sergeant said.

"No need," Fannie told him. "Doesn't cost us anything to have you here. And we can certainly share our food with you."

The sergeant saluted, smiled and thanked her again.

"We'll be here in the morning."

The next day was Saturday, August 8th. It had seemed such a long time since the battle had ended.

But when four soldiers carried Colonel Callis in, Fannie felt as though the fighting had just ended the day before.

The man was pale and thin beyond belief.

He smiled weakly at Fannie and she thought he whispered "thanks" but she wasn't sure.

After making sure his colonel was comfortable, the sergeant came downstairs for a pan of water and a cloth.

"The moving made him a little feverish. A wet cloth on his brow might be good," he explained.

As Fannie was tearing up some clean cloths and getting a pan for the water, she asked questions about her new house-guests.

"Oh, we're from Lancaster, Wisconsin. Colonel Callis was a merchant there. When the war broke out, he closed the store;

I was clerking there. We both joined the army and went into the same regiment.

"He got hit in the left breast, near the heart, but the bullet went in on an angle. Doctors seem to think the bullet is in his right lung. He's had frequent hemorrhages. They don't give him much chance to live. They're surprised he's held on this long.

"Since he is a colonel, they said he was entitled to an orderly, so he wanted me to stay with him. Week ago, the doctors told me to notify his wife cause they didn't think he'd last too much longer. She's due in by train tomorrow."

Fannie gave Mrs. Callis the run of her house throughout the whole month of August.

Three weeks had passed and although the colonel seemed somewhat stronger, Fannie was amazed that he was still alive. There had been bad days and nights when everyone in the house was convinced that a coughing spell would kill the man. But he clung to life fiercely.

Three more weeks passed when Mrs. Callis got a telegram. It was from relatives back in Wisconsin who were caring for her children.

"Children ill. Measles. Can you come?" the message said.

Fannie walked up the two flights of stairs with Mrs. Callis as she went to tell her husband.

"I best go today," she told him. "But you're in good hands here and I'll be back as soon as the children are well."

"I'll go too," he murmured.

Mrs. Callis, Fannie and the sergeant were shocked.

They argued with him, but to no avail.

An army doctor was asked to talk to him.

"Colonel, I'll be very blunt. I forbid your going. The slightest movement could cause the bullet to move. You could bleed to death from a massive hemorrhage."

"Can you say that I'll survive if I stay here?" the colonel asked.

"No, I can't guarantee that either," the doctor admitted.

"Then, by damn, dead or alive, I'm going home. I have to make that effort to see my children one last time. I'm no good to the army here."

On the following day, September 1, a special bed was constructed that could be placed between two seats on a train and moved from car to car like a stretcher.

The Buehlers kept trying to talk the colonel out of the trip, even after they had seen him lain on the special bed in a car headed for Harrisburg by way of Hanover and Hanover Junction.

Fannie packed a lunch that would last the first day's journey.

Amid tears of gratitude mingled with pain and anxiety, Colonel Callis, his wife and orderly left Gettysburg.

By early evening, as they sat at home talking about the colonel, a boy from the telegraph office pounded on their door.

The cable was from Mrs. Callis.

"At Hanover Junction. Motion has dislodged bullet. John dying. Will take his body home."

Fannie wept for hours.

By the following day, she was so raked of all emotion that she paid scant attention to little Allie's coughing.

It was only when the boy complained his chest hurt did Fannie muster up the strength to wipe all other problems from her mind and concentrate on her son.

That evening, the doctor came and ordered the boy put to bed.

"I'm not sure what it is, but he's feverish," the doctor told her. "A four-year-old like Allie, who's been sickly off and on, has been through a lot these past weeks. We adults may not have noticed. No telling what kinds of disease he's been exposed to."

The fever didn't let up.

On September 4, little Allie died and on September 6, like mothers who had lost their soldier sons at Gettysburg, Fannie Buehler buried her dear boy.

"I remember so clearly how little Allie clapped his tiny hands when the shells went whizzing over the house. He thought they were birdies passing over," she told David as they walked home slowly from the cemetery. She smiled at the thought. Then tears welled in her eyes and she walked on in a daze.

But her head was rushing through the maddening last two

months and to forget her own sorrow, she thought about Mrs. Callis at the Junction just five days ago.

She thought about the long, lonely ride of Mrs. Callis, accompanying the body of her husband, the father of her children, and of the sadness of her long journey.

On Sunday, August 2, Salome Myers walked up to the seminary hospital.

Andrew Crooks looks well, she thought. So did some others she recognized.

In fact, Crooks felt well enough to introduce her to a Rebel colonel, several captains and some lieutenants.

The hot days of August passed that way—visits to the hospitals; conversations with old and new friends; letters to and from those she had helped nurse and words of thanks from the families of men she helped care for.

And there were still the death letters. On August 5 she wrote to William T. Strouse of Stroudsburg, Pennsylvania, informing him of the death of his son.

And she wrote an account for a newspaper of the death of Sergeant Stewart, plus a letter to the sergeant's brother, Henry.

On August 12, Salome cleaned and straightened her own bedroom. It was the first time she had slept in there since June 30th.

# CHAPTER
# 20

# November 19—"Four Score and Seven . . ."

The stench and the sights of battle were gone, save for the mangled trees and bullet-torn buildings. The weather was crisp, as usual the week before Thanksgiving.

School had dismissed on Tuesday, the 17th, so that students could spend Wednesday at home helping to spruce up the village. Brick walks had to be swept and fallen leaves gathered and, oh yes, the bunting and flags were to be hung.

The President was coming!

Edward Everett, the renowned orator, would speak.

The new National Cemetery, next to the town's Evergreen Cemetery, would be dedicated.

On the morning of Thursday, November 19th, Dan Skelly and his friend, J.C. Felty, stood in the Diamond in front of the McClellan House. They wanted a glimpse of Abraham Lincoln.

Dan overheard conversations about how the four hotels were filled to capacity.

"Lot of private homes took in guests too. Yes sir, must be a thousand visitors in town," Dan heard one man say to a companion.

"Where'd the President stay?" the companion asked.

"Why, right over there, in Judge Wills' house," the man said, pointing to the large home on the southeast corner.

"Heard tell some folks just walked the streets all night. Couldn't find no place to stay," the man added.

Units for the procession, mostly soldiers, had formed on all four streets leading into the Diamond, itself occupied by Colonel Ward Lamon's bodyguard for Lincoln.

Dan saw the President come out of the Wills' house and mount a horse which seemed a trifle short for Lincoln's long frame. When Lincoln got to the middle of the oblong body-guard formation, the procession started slowly for the cemetery along Baltimore Street.

Dan ran along the edge of the street, keeping close to Lincoln's side.

It got more crowded when the procession swung southwest along the Emmitsburg Road and when it turned east into the rear of the new cemetery Dan lost his favored position.

But, like other boys, he sidestepped his way through the crowd to the wooden platform which had been constructed for the dignitaries.

When Mr. Everett arose to begin his oration Dan climbed up unnoticed on the side of the platform, his feet resting on the wooden floor and his left arm wrapped around the bottom railing.

Everett went on and on. Dan figured the speech had lasted perhaps an hour and a half, maybe more, but he listened attentively, awed by the grandeur of the man's words. He found it historical and classical and Everett's tale of the battle as near fascinating as the event itself.

Finally, Everett finished and a band played some music.

Dan watched silently as Lincoln lifted his gaunt frame from a chair, placed his tall black hat on the seat and took several steps forward.

Isn't as dramatic as Everett, Dan thought. But he seems earnest and forceful.

And while he was still comparing the two men, he found that Lincoln had finished, half smiled at some polite applause and returned to his chair.

Dan watched as the President greeted people after the ceremony.

Lincoln's face was lined and looked sad and worried. But the expression, Dan felt, was one of kindness and strength.

Albertus McCreary was at the Diamond too that morning. In fact, he was close enough to the Wills' house to see the President walking around inside.

"He seemed very tall and gaunt to me," Albertus would tell his mother later. "But his face was wonderful to look upon. It was such a sad face and so full of kindly feeling that one felt at home with him at once."

Someone had left the door open at the Wills' house and Albertus kept inching closer until he was standing next to the door. Inside was Lincoln pacing up and down the hall. Albertus assumed that all speakers do that before they make a speech.

Later, at the cemetery, Albertus squeezed his way through to within ten feet of the platform. He listened patiently but didn't try to comprehend Mr. Everett's speech. He wanted only to hear the President.

Albertus was impressed by Lincoln's brief address but got no closer than those ten feet to this man of greatness.

"Maybe you can see him tonight," his mother said after Albertus arrived home. "There's a service in the Presbyterian Church and the President is to be there."

The church was so crowded that guards were turning people away at the door. During one confrontation between church-goers and a guard, Albertus eased past into the sanctuary. He got halfway down the aisle and then became hopelessly mired in a sea of human legs and arms. From where he stood, he could see only those packed in against him. He wondered if Lincoln were there at all.

As the service ended, the aisle began to clear but Albertus

stood and looked to the front. Then, disappointed, he turned to leave but bumped into a man coming out from a pew behind him.

Albertus looked up to apologize. That sad face was smiling down on him.

"Mr. Lincoln, will you shake hands with me?" Albertus stammered.

"Certainly," the President replied. The grasp was strong and sincere.

Just as quickly as he had appeared, Lincoln was gone. But Albertus stayed, feeling the warmth in the grip yet. Then he made his way home, smiling and proud.

Despite the chill, which was closing the huge tent hospital east of town and forcing the army to transport the remaining wounded to York and other nearby cities, Albertus felt that the community had gained a sense of warmth, a touch of hope from Lincoln's visit.

His town, Gettysburg, had come alive again.

# EPILOGUE

Some of the Gettysburg residents who kept diaries or wrote of their experiences in years to come can be traced into later life. But the future lives of others are seemingly lost, at least for the moment, perhaps to reappear when a dusty, forgotten trunk in an old attic is opened for the first time in decades.

Here are brief notes on some of *The Gettysburg Civilians*:

## Sarah M. Broadhead

Sallie Broadhead's brother-in-law, Paul Broadhead, the soldier who stopped at their house for food, died in the battle of Fair Oaks, Virginia. After the war, Sallie and Joseph had a son, Benjamin. Sallie is buried in her hometown of Pleasantville, New Jersey.

## Fannie J. Buehler

Colonel John C. Callis, the wounded officer brought to the Buehler home a month after the battle, survived his wound. The Buehlers had seen Colonel Callis and his wife off on the train for their home in Wisconsin. The colonel wasn't expected to survive and late in the same day the Buehlers got a telegram saying that he was dying from a hemorrhage. No further word was received and the Buehlers assumed the colonel had died. Near the end of that year, they learned that Callis was still alive. In fact, years later, he visited Gettysburg after a business engagement in Washington. Near the turn of the century, he was still alive, despite the bullet in his lung.

Fannie Buehler wrote of her experiences while living with a married daughter in Winchester, Virginia, in 1896. She was then 70 years old. In a foreword to those recollections, Fannie said, in part:

"We all have the experiences of our lifetime. I had mine before, during and after the great battle which was fought on the 1st, 2nd and 3rd of July, 1863, and of these I am now going to write.

"I do not do this for self gratification, but to please my children, my grandchildren, possibly my great-grandchildren, and many friends whom I dearly love. We all know, as the years go by, the story of this great battle, so often told in our days, will grow in interest, to those who may come after us, and that my experience may not die with me, I will endeavor to tell what I know, what I saw, and of the little help I was enabled to give to the wounded and dying in the momentous struggle."

## Elizabeth Gilbert

She recounted her experiences in an interview with *The Gettysburg Compiler*, a weekly newspaper, in September 1905. Her husband, Jacob, who joined the Iron Brigade band after the battle, served with the brigade until the end of the war.

## Liberty Hollinger

She wrote her reminiscences in 1925, three years before her death at the age of 81. Years after the battle, she married Jacob A. Clutz, a graduate of the Lutheran Theological Seminary at Gettysburg. He served as pastor of a number of churches, was president of Midland College in Atchison, Kansas, and later became a professor at the seminary. Dr. Clutz was struck and killed by a car while attending a religious meeting in Sweden. Liberty lived out the rest of her life in Gettysburg, happy with her garden, her friends and her books.

In writing her account of the battle, she said:

"The time I have spent in recalling to mind and writing out these memories of the Battle of Gettysburg has been of mingled pleasure and pain. Living over the days when our family was an unbroken circle has brought back the joy of childhood and youth; but I cannot help feeling again some of the mental and physical strain under which we passed our days and nights. This very tenseness served to fix impressions in my young mind so indelibly that now when I have grown old, I find them clear and undimmed."

## Henry E. Jacobs

An 18-year-old student during the battle, he was the Reverend Dr. Henry E. Jacobs, dean of the Lutheran Theological Seminary, when he recited his adventures for a Philadelphia newspaper, *The North American*, in 1913.

## William McClean

This attorney and his family were saddened three months after the battle when diphtheria took the life of his youngest daughter, Fannie. Four years later his wife, also named Fannie, died. Recalling those losses at the end of a newspaper article he wrote for *The Gettysburg Compiler* in 1908, McClean said:

"War around the mother and the little ones in the sanctuary of the home has none of the pomp, pride and circumstances which surround it in the pages of history, in the verses of the poet or in the glitter of the parade."

McClean served as president judge of Adams County from 1874 to 1894. He died in 1915.

## Elizabeth "Salome" Myers

A year after the battle, Salome Myers was visited by the widow and brother of Sergeant Alexander Stewart, the wounded soldier who died in her arms. In 1867, she married the brother, Henry F. Stewart. A year later, he died of injuries he had suffered during the war. But the marriage produced a son, whom Salome took back to Gettysburg to raise.

In 1897, she put down her "recollections of the Battle of Gettysburg. Written for my son, Harry." The narrative was based on a diary she had kept. Her story also appeared in the *San Francisco Sunday Call* on August 16, 1903. And in 1944, her grandson, Henry Stewart, used various sources to put together her complete story.

## Carrie Sheads

The Sheads family story was tragic. Four sons were in the Union army. David, the oldest, contracted turberculosis, was discharged and came home to die. Elias had both feet shot off at the battle of Monocacy Junction and died in an ambulance wagon. Robert was seriously wounded in the neck, was discharged and lived as a physical wreck for several years. The youngest son, Jacob, couldn't get his father's permission to enlist. He ran away, joined the army and died in camp of mumps.

Their mother and a daughter, Louise, were worn out by hard work in caring for the wounded. That, coupled with anxiety and sorrow, shortened their lives. Carrie and her sister, Elizabeth, were later given jobs in Washington. Carrie worked as a clerk in the Treasury Department and Elizabeth as a clerk in the Post Office.

A descendant, Colonel Jacob M. Sheads, still lives in Gettysburg where he is honored as a historian.

## Daniel A. Skelly

Johnston Hastings Skelly, Daniel's older brother, was engaged to Jennie Wade; they were to be married in September, 1863. Johnston was serving with the 87th Pennsylvania Volunteer Infantry and was wounded at Winchester, Virginia, on June 15, 1863, more than two weeks before the Battle of Gettysburg. He died there of his wounds on July 12, not knowing that Jennie had been killed.

Daniel, a teenager during the war, penned his experiences in 1932. At the end, he said:

"A kind Providence has prolonged my life far beyond the

Psalmist's 'three score years and ten,' giving me health and strength and walking capacity beyond my age. For many years it has been my habit, in company with my lifelong friend, Herman H. Mertz, every Sunday afternoon, summer and winter, weather permitting, to stroll over this historic field recalling incidents of the battle and studying the movements of the troops as gathered from military accounts of the conflict here . . ."

## Rosa Snyder

As 85-year-old Mrs. Rosa Gettle in 1944, she told her story in an interview published near Memorial Day in the Wymore, Nebraska, Arbor State newspaper, where she was then living.

In that interview one of the things she recalled as a four-year-old was Lincoln's visit. She was standing at the garden gate when Lincoln came riding past on his way to the cemetery. She waved a handkerchief and Lincoln nodded.

"His pictures look just like him," she recalled.

## Jennie Wade

There are indications that Virginia Wade's nickname was spelled differently. Her school friends reportedly called her Gin or Ginnie. A newspaper reporter, writing a story about her death, mistakenly used the spelling commonly used today.

Jennie's body was kept in the house from her death at 8:30 a.m., Friday, July 3, until 5 p.m. Saturday. She was then buried in the back yard. In January, 1864, the body was moved to a church cemetery and in November, 1865, to the town's Evergreen Cemetery. A large statue marks her grave there today.

(Also see Daniel Skelly)

# LIST OF HOSPITAL SITES

In addition to tent hospitals established by military authorities at Gettysburg, many buildings were pressed into service as places for the treatment and recuperation of both Confederate and Union troops. There is no known complete list of all such buildings but the following is felt to be fairly complete. Credit for compiling most of this list goes to Kathleen R. Georg, historian, National Park Service, Gettysburg. Some additions were made by the author.

## PRIVATE HOMES:

1. Joseph Broadhead, Chambersburg Street (Pike)
2. David Buehler, Baltimore Street
3. Isaac M. Diehl, location unknown
4. S. A. Felix, Black Horse Tavern Road
5. Henry Garlach, Baltimore Street
6. McCreary, West High and Baltimore Streets
7. Salome Myers, West High Street
8. John Scott, Chambersburg Street
9. Elias Sheads, Chambersburg Pike
10. Catherine Snyder, Baltimore Pike
11. Henry Stahle, Baltimore Street
12. John Tenant, Black Horse Road at Willoughby Run

# FARMS:

13. Joseph Benner, Harrisburg Road at Rock Creek
14. Leonard Bricker, Taneytown Road at Wheatfield Road
15. George Bushman, Hospital Road
16. Lewis Bushman, Taneytown Road
17. Adam Butt, Black Horse Tavern Road
18. Christian Byers, near Knoxlyn
19. Samuel Cobean, Carlisle Road
20. Peter Conover, Baltimore Pike
21. John Crawford, Plank Road at Marsh Creek
22. Michael Crist, Herr Ridge Road
23. George Culp, Willoughby Run Road
24. Henry Culp, off Middle Street
25. John Cunningham, near Marsh Creek in Freedom Township
26. Michael Fissel (Fiscel), off Hospital Road
27. John S. Forney, Buford Avenue at Mummasburg Road
28. Michael Frey, Taneytown Road
29. Peter Frey, Taneytown Road
30. Catherine Guinn, off Taneytown Road near cemetery
31. J. Hankey, Mummasburg Road
32. Jacob Hummelbaugh, Taneytown Road
33. Jacob Keim, Table Rock Road
34. E. Keller, off Knoxlyn Road
35. Daniel Lady, Hanover Road
36. Isaac Lightner, off Baltimore Pike
37. Nathaniel Lightner, Baltimore Pike
38. Samuel Lohr, Chambersburg Pike
39. W. H. Monfort, Hunterstown Road
40. Sarah Patterson, off Taneytown Road
41. William Patterson, Taneytown Road
42. H. A. Picking, Hunterstown Road
43. E. Plank, Willoughby Run Road
44. Jacob Plank, off Hagerstown Road
45. William Ross, Carlisle Road
46. M. Schwartz, off Hospital Road
47. Daniel Shaffer, Baltimore Pike at White Run

48. M. Shealer, Shealer Road off Hunterstown Road
49. D. Shriver, Mummasburg Road
50. Henry Spangler, Baltimore Pike
51. Jacob Swisher, Hospital Road
52. J. or M. Trostle, off Hospital Road
53. Jacob Weikert, Taneytown Road
54. Widow Wible, Shealer Road off Hunterstown Road
55. J. Worley, off Baltimore Pike

## CHURCHES:

56. Christ Lutheran, Chambersburg Street
57. German Reformed, Stratton Street
58. Presbyterian
59. St. Francis Xavier, High Street
60. St. James Lutheran, Stratton Street
61. United Presbyterian

## PUBLIC BUILDINGS:

62. Adams County Courthouse, Baltimore Street
63. Adams County Poor House (Farm), Harrisburg Road

## COLLEGES:

64. Lutheran Theological Seminary, Seminary Ridge
65. Pennsylvania College (Old Dorm), Gettysburg College Campus

## SCHOOLS:

66. Granite Schoolhouse, Granite Schoolhouse Lane
67. Pitzer Schoolhouse, Black Horse Tavern Road
68. Public School, High Street
69. Schoolhouse, Hagerstown Road

# COMMERCIAL BUILDINGS:

70. Black Horse Tavern (Francis Bream), Hagerstown Road
71. Bream's Mill (John Currens), off Plank Road at Marsh Creek
72. McCurdy Warehouse, near railroad
73. Mill (John Socks), off Route 327 at Marsh Creek

# BIBLIOGRAPHY

BACON, Dr. Cyrus, *The Daily Register of Dr. Cyrus Bacon, Jr.*, Walter M. Whitehouse and Frank Whitehouse, Jr., The University of Michigan, Ann Arbor, Michigan

BAYLY, Mrs. Joseph (Harriet), *Mrs. Joseph Bayly's Story of the Battle*, Gettysburg National Military Park Library

BAYLY, William Hamilton, *Stories of the Battle, Gettysburg Compiler*, 1903

BROADHEAD, Sarah M., Gettysburg National Military Park Library, 1863

BUEHLER, Fannie J., *Recollections of the Rebel Invasion and One Woman's Experience During the Battle of Gettysburg*, 1896

BURNS, John, Gettysburg National Military Park Library

FAHNESTOCK, Gates D., Adams County Historical Society, 1933

FISHER, Mary Cadwell, *Annals of the War* (unknown newspaper)

GARLACH, Anna, *The Story of Mrs. Jacob Kitzmiller*, Mrs. Jacob (Garlach) Kitzmiller, U.S. Army Military History Research Center, Carlisle, PA

GILBERT, Elizabeth, *The Gettysburg Compiler*, September 6, 1905

HOLLINGER, Liberty, *The Battle of Gettysburg*, Mrs. Jacob A. (Hollinger) Clutz, 1925

HUIDEKOPER, Col. Henry S., Letter to Gettysburg Battlefield Memorial Commission, November 23, 1916

JACOBS, Henry E., *The North American*, Philadelphia, June 29, 1913

McALLISTER, Mary, *Philadelphia Inquirer*, June 26–29, 1938

McCLEAN, William, *Gettysburg Compiler*, June 1, 1908

McCREARY, Albertus, *Gettysburg: A Boy's Experience of the Battle, McClure's Magazine*, Volume 33 (July, 1909), No. 3

MYERS, Elizabeth Salome, *Mrs. Henry (Myers) Stewart, San Francisco Sunday Call*, August 16, 1903

O'KEEFE, Sister Camilla, Notes, Archives of St. Joseph's, Emmitsburg, Maryland, 1863

O'NEAL, Dr. John W. C., *Gettysburg Compiler*, July 5, 1905

PIERCE, Tillie, *At Gettysburg*, or *What a Girl Saw and Heard of the Battle: A True Narrative*, Mrs. Tillie (Pierce) Alleman

RUPP, John, Adams County Historical Society, July 19, 1863

SHEADS, Carrie, *Women of the War*, Frank Moore, S.S. Scranton, Hartford, Conn., 1866

SHERFY, Joseph, *The Sherfy Family in the United States 1751–1948*, William E. Sherfy, Greensburg, Indiana, U.S. Army M.H.R.C., Carlisle, PA

SKELLY, Daniel A., *A Boy's Experiences During the Battle of Gettysburg*, 1932

SNYDER, Rosa, Mrs. Rose (Snyder) Gettle, Wymore (Nebraska) Arbor State, May 30, 1944

WADE, Mary Virginia, Philadelphia Public Ledger and Daily Transcript, September 16, 1901

# Index

306